P9-DMJ-518

Berkley Sensation titles by Linda Winstead Jones

THE SUN WITCH
THE MOON WITCH
THE STAR WITCH

The Star Witch

LINDA WINSTEAD JONES

BERKLEY SENSATION, NEW YORK

THE BERKLEY PUBLISHING GROUP
Published by the Penguin Group
Penguin Group (USA) Inc.
375 Hudson Street, New York, New York 10014, USA
Penguin Group (Canada), 90 Eglinton Avenue East, Suite 700, Toronto, Ontario M4P 2Y3, Canada
(a division of Pearson Penguin Canada Inc.)
Penguin Books Ltd., 80 Strand, London WC2R 0RL, England
Penguin Group Ireland, 25 St. Stephen's Green, Dublin 2, Ireland (a division of Penguin Books Ltd.)
Penguin Group (Australia), 250 Camberwell Road, Camberwell, Victoria 3124, Australia
(a division of Pearson Australia Group Pty. Ltd.)
Penguin Books India Pvt. Ltd., 11 Community Centre, Panchsheel Park, New Delhi—110 017, India
Penguin Group (NZ), Cnr. Airborne and Rosedale Roads, Albany, Auckland 1310, New Zealand
(a division of Pearson New Zealand Ltd.)
Penguin Books (South Africa) (Pty.) Ltd., 24 Sturdee Avenue, Rosebank, Johannesburg 2196, South
Africa

Penguin Books Ltd., Registered Offices: 80 Strand, London WC2R 0RL, England

THE STAR WITCH

A Berkley Sensation Book / published by arrangement with the author

PRINTING HISTORY
Berkley Sensation edition / January 2006

Copyright © 2006 by Linda Winstead Jones.
Cover art by Bruce Emmett.
Cover design by Lesley Worrell.
Interior text design by Stacy Irwin.

ISBN: 0-425-20128-7

BERKLEY ® SENSATION
Berkley Sensation Books are published by The Berkley Publishing Group,
a division of Penguin Group (USA) Inc.,
375 Hudson Street, New York, New York 10014.
BERKLEY SENSATION and the "B" design are trademarks belonging to Penguin Group (USA) Inc.

PRINTED IN THE UNITED STATES OF AMERICA

10 9 8 7 6 5 4 3 2 1

The Fyne Curse

In a land where magic is accepted, if sometimes feared, and prophesies are made and fulfilled with regularity, and the impossible is always possible, it is both wondrous and dangerous to be a witch. With power comes responsibility, and envy, and even heartache.

For three hundred years, a wizard's curse robbed the Fyne witches of a chance at true love, taking their husbands and lovers before their thirtieth birthdays if they were young men, and causing the older men to see something in the women they had once loved so that they were driven away in horror.

But three strong and loving sisters were born, and they dared to defy the curse. Isadora, the eldest, married, and was forced to bury her beloved Willym when they'd been married a mere two years. Punished for dismissing the curse as insignificant, she became determined that neither she nor her sisters would fall into the trap of love again. The Fyne bloodline would die with them.

But as is often the way with life, such plans did not hold fast and true. Sophie, the youngest, fell in love with the rebel Kane Varden, gave him a daughter, married him, and became pregnant once again. Kane has not yet turned thirty, and while Sophie continues to attempt to end the curse, she has not been successful. She has come to realize that she needs her sisters with her if there is to be any chance of bringing the family curse to an end.

Juliet found love with an Anwyn shape-shifter and discovered during their journey to The City high in the mountains that she herself is Anwyn. Not only that, she is a rare Anwyn female, and is therefore Queen. A gifted psychic, she knows the curse will one day be ended, and she believes that it will not take her husband from her. But there are still many questions to be answered, and as always what is to come is fluid. Undecided. As long as the curse survives, she cannot rest easy.

In Arthes, the capital city of Columbyana, the emperor and his empress anticipate the birth of the long-awaited heir, as they watch for the rebels who wish to take the palace and the throne from them. Isadora, through circumstances over which she has no control, finds herself on Level One, caring for the empress and her unborn children while the powers that have been weakened grow strong once again.

She has loved and lost once before and cannot imagine suffering that pain again. The curse will not affect her. It cannot touch her because she has locked love out of her heart.

But love is coming for Isadora, whether she wants it or not.

Prologue

LUCAN TRIED NOT TO TREMBLE, BUT ZEBULYN, THE grand wizard of the Circle of Bacwyr, was an imposing man. The old man had long white hair and a craggy face and wrinkled hands with long fingers that looked like bones with a bit of skin stretched across them. His purple robe, a sign of his high station, hung on a thin but somehow strong frame.

The meeting, which had come as a surprise to Lucan, was held in the deepest reaches of the cavern that was an important wing of the home of the Circle. Many buildings had been constructed in the hills beyond, but the wizards lived and worked their magic here, deep in the hillside. Firelight flickered off the cold walls, and an unnatural light tinged with purple filled the stone-walled room. Wizard's light. Lucan had been in the cavern before, but never this deep . . . and never alone. No one else was present for this meeting but for him and the wizard. No one! Not a warrior or a minor wizard or another student.

Lucan himself had not yet celebrated his tenth birthday, so as the wizard spoke he kept his eyes downcast.

"The Circle of Bacwyr was broken by betrayal from within," the wizard said, the tremble in his voice one of anger, not fright. "Today we build anew, with young men like you. Tomorrow we will be stronger than ever before. We will be smarter, this time."

The betrayal Zebulyn spoke of had happened so long ago, Lucan could not understand why the wizard's anger remained so strong. The fall had taken place long before Lucan had been born, even before his father had been born. Perhaps his grandfather, who was almost as ancient as the wizard, remembered when the Circle had been powerful, but then again . . . perhaps not.

There had been a time when the Circle of Bacwyr had ruled Tryfyn from border to border. Circle warriors had served the King; Circle wizards had counseled the King and the warriors. No man had dared to stand up against such strength. But it had been a very long time since the Circle knew such power, and the Kings of Tryfyn were no more than a memory. For as long as Lucan could remember, for as long as his parents and grandparents could remember, Tryfyn had been a country of warring clans without a King to unite them.

The Circle had gone underground after the betrayal and the battle that had seen the slaughter of so many warriors and wizards, but it had never entirely disappeared. Those few who had survived met and trained in secret, and they rebuilt their ranks with the most extraordinary young men they could recruit, waiting for the day when they were powerful enough to once again rule. Boys of every clan were taken from their homes at a young age and raised to be warriors or wizards, depending on their strengths. They grew stronger with every passing year but did not even approach their former glory.

Lucan had been living amidst the Circle for three years now, learning the ways of the warrior. He did not have the blood of the wizard, which was required of those who mastered the magical ways, but he was strong and fast and cunning—or so his instructors told him.

"It was a woman of the Circle who caused our downfall," Zebulyn said in a lowered and trembling voice.

Out of the corner of his eye, Lucan peeked up at the old man. "There were once women here?" The only females he had seen in the Circle ranks in the past three years had been those the age of his grandmother, and older. They cooked and cleaned and mended, and they served the warriors and students. They were not a part of the fellowship. He had heard that younger, prettier women sometimes came at night to visit the warriors, but when he'd asked why, the older boys had laughed at Lucan and told him that such women would be wasted on a child such as he.

"Witches," Zebulyn said, spitting the word as if it had gone sour in his mouth. "It was a mistake to allow them access to our ranks, but we saw through their witchery too late."

Lucan closed his eyes tightly and called upon all his strength. Warriors of the Circle of Bacwyr did not tremble at the mere mention of the things that frightened them, but . . . witches! True, the wizards of the Circle used magic, but they were honorable men who served only good. Witches were spiteful creatures who would cast a spell on a boy simply for looking at them in the wrong way. That is what he had heard. He was very glad they were no longer allowed in the Circle.

"Now is not the time to teach you aspects of the past. You must look to the future," Zebulyn said, his voice growing stronger. "It is time to look to tomorrow. You are destined to be Prince of Swords, boy," the wizard said. He was no longer angry, but he did not sound pleased at the prospect, either.

Lucan lifted his head slowly. "Prince of Swords?" His heart skipped a beat as his eyes met those of the aging wizard. When the Circle had been in power, the Prince of Swords had commanded not only the warriors of the Circle but the clans of Tryfyn, as well. Second only to the King in power, it was the Prince who wielded true control over the armies of this country. There had not been a Prince of Swords since the fall of the Circle.

"Prince." Zebulyn said the word as if it were bitter. "In my meditations I have seen that you will travel to the emperor's palace in Columbyana, and there you will find and collect the Star of Bacwyr. It is destined to be yours, and without it, you cannot command."

"What is the Star of Bacwyr?"

The old man scoffed. "You will know the Star when you see it, if you are truly meant to be Prince of Swords."

"But you said I was—"

"No one aspect of the future is so set in stone it cannot be changed. If you succeed you will become Prince of Swords, and you will be the man to lead this country into a time of strength. If you succeed, the true King will come to us, and with you at his side all will be as it once was. However, if you *fail* in the task that has been set for you, Tryfyn will remain a country of strife and disharmony." He scowled. "There will be danger in the palace. I have already seen with great clarity that you must beware the witch."

Lucan rose slowly. The wizard was never wrong in his prophesies. If he was truly meant to be Prince, he should not kneel and cower before an old man. He could not be afraid of any witch. Forcing his knees to stop shaking, Lucan lifted his chin and stared at the wizard.

"When do I leave for Columbyana?"

For a moment it seemed that the old man was going to smile, but perhaps that was an illusion. "In twenty-seven years."

"Twenty-seven years!" Lucan took a small step forward. "You said tomorrow."

The old man sighed and waved a dismissive hand. "I meant tomorrow in the larger sense. You must learn not to take each word so literally."

"In twenty-seven years I'll be an old man. I'll be as old as you!"

"Hardly," the wizard said beneath his breath.

Lucan's shoulders slumped. Twenty-seven years was a lifetime. "How old are you?" he asked bravely. The Prince of Swords, after all, could not be afraid of a wizard. Not even this one.

"I am older than the dirt beneath the hut where you were born," Zebulyn said in a gruff and rumbling voice. "Older than the star on which you made a wish last night, when you were carrying in the firewood."

Again, Lucan was afraid. How did this man know so much about him? He understood swordplay and stamina and taking orders and making decisions. He did not understand the magic that the wizards practiced, while young, would-be soldiers trained and served their masters.

"What am I to do while I wait?" Lucan asked.

This time there was no mistake. The wizard smiled. His lips were thin, his teeth were yellowed. He pointed with one of his bony fingers. "You will learn."

"What am I to learn?" Lucan asked.

The wizard leaned forward, until it seemed he would

place his long, hooked nose directly on Lucan's. It took all the courage of a young man to stand his ground and not step back or drop down.

"Everything," the old man answered. "You will continue to learn the ways of the warrior, and you will also be instructed in the ways of the wizard, so that when the time comes no one can stop you from taking the Star that will make you Prince."

Lucan did not trust what he had seen of the wizards, because he did not understand their magic. He preferred the blade, which was real and true and reliable. "I was not born to magic."

"No, but there are some things that can be learned."

Lucan's first thought was that his days had just become longer. This would require more lessons, on top of the ones he was already taking.

"Why is the Star so important?" he asked. Why couldn't he be Prince of Swords *now*? The older boys would not order him around or laugh at him, if he were Prince. He would not be made to shine his instructors' boots or fetch firewood, if he were Prince.

"Power, that is why the Star is so important," Zebulyn said with only a trace of amusement in his old eyes. "Until you understand power, you cannot hope to wield it."

"Who will teach me such things?"

The old man sighed tiredly and muttered a word Lucan did not know. He did not know the word, but he definitely understood that it was a curse of some kind. He had heard the older instructors curse, and the expression and tone of voice was much the same. "I will be your teacher, Lucan Hern."

Even without the addition of the curse word, Zebulyn didn't sound happy about the idea. Maybe the wizard thought he was being saddled with a child who would be reluctant to learn all he had to teach. Maybe he thought the boy who stood before him was not worthy of the time it would take to teach such important matters.

With the dignity of a future Prince and the arrogance of a nine-year-old boy who had just that day bested an older and taller boy with a dull wooden practice sword as his weapon, Lucan straightened his spine and lifted his chin. His knees no longer trembled.

"I am ready to begin."

I

Twenty-seven years later

LIVING HIGH IN THE IMPERIAL PALACE, ISADORA HAD
barely felt the passing of winter. Thick walls, well-fed fire-
places, and luxurious clothing and blankets kept the residents of Level One quite comfortable—even the witch
whose duty it was to care for the Empress Liane and her unborn child.

Unborn *children,* to be precise. Twin boys, though no
one knew that but Isadora and the empress herself. The
Emperor Sebestyen would be furious when he found out
that his wife was carrying two sons, rather than one. It
would muddy the imperial bloodline to have two heirs born
at almost the precise same moment.

Spring was coming. On occasion Isadora would open
the window of her small room and breathe in the warming

air as if it fed her soul. She was tired of this damned palace. Tired of the people and the chores and even the luxury.

But until she was strong again and could find her sisters, this was her place. Liane needed her. She had pledged to protect the empress and her children, but once the babies arrived, there would be no reason to stay.

The strength of her magic had begun to return slowly but with a certainty she felt to the depths of her soul. The destruction of the past several months had depleted her powers; it was only through protection that the magic grew strong again. On his final visit to her, the spirit of her late husband had told her that she must choose. Dark or light. Goodness or evil. For a long time she had danced on the edge of both, but one could not live forever in that gray domain.

There were times when she believed that destruction came to her more naturally than protection, but in order for that power to grow she would need to embrace it fully. Over the years her sisters—and her beloved Will, before and after his death—had kept the protective side of Isadora's nature alive and thriving. They were not here, now.

She could not believe that Juliet was dead, as Bors had reported before his death at the emperor's hand. Sophie might be safe in the company of her husband, but still, she would need her sisters again. Juliet had said as much on the night the soldiers had kidnapped them and burned the cabin that had stood for more than three hundred years, and where her sisters were concerned, Juliet was rarely wrong. Rarely, not *never*.

Isadora knew she could not remain in this place. With the coming of spring, the return of her magical strengths, and the birth of Emperor Sebestyen's heirs would also come the time for Isadora Fyne to leave this dreadful place.

Standing at the window of her quarters on Level One, Isadora closed her eyes and took in a deep breath of the air. It was the first truly warm day of spring, and she longed to be out of this palace, away from the crowded city of Arthes, away from all these people who were not her own.

She longed to be on Fyne Mountain, surrounded by the land she loved and close to her sisters. They would rebuild the cabin Emperor Sebestyen's soldiers had burned to the ground, and things would be as they had once been. Sophie would cook and sing and smile and embrace the world around her. Juliet would tend the gardens and treat those women who were brave enough to seek out a healer who was also a witch. And Isadora would protect her sisters with every ounce of power she possessed.

On Fyne Mountain she could care for her sisters, and live in isolation, and mourn the husband who had been gone so long.

Will's spirit had not visited her in months. She expected him to be true to his promise and never visit her again, which meant he was finally truly *gone*. In the past few months, Isadora had been thrown into a new type of mourning. She'd buried Will's body years ago; now she had to bury his spirit just as deeply.

It was harder than she had imagined anything could ever be.

"Isadora." The breathless voice came with the opening of the door to the tiny room she now called home.

Recognizing the voice, Isadora turned slowly and glared at the intruder. Mahri's eyes widened. She backed into the hallway, closed the door solidly, and knocked.

"Come in," Isadora said.

Again, the door swung open. "I'm sorry," the young girl said. "I forgot. The Empress Liane wishes to speak with you. Now."

Isadora sighed as she headed for the doorway. She was quite sure Liane had never been gifted with patience, but becoming empress had only exacerbated the failing. Pregnancy had not softened the empress. Instead, she grew more strident and demanding with every passing day. Liane expected her orders to be obeyed immediately, and she was quite comfortable with issuing orders. If she wasn't family—Liane's brother Kane had married the youngest Fyne sister, Sophie—Isadora would not feel compelled to stay here one minute longer.

The twins Liane carried would be Sophie's nephews. The Emperor Sebestyen was blissfully ignorant of his wife's relation to the rebel Kane Varden, which was a blessing. Sebestyen in a foul mood was a frightening sight, indeed. Learning that his beloved wife was the sister of one of the rebels who was trying to overthrow him would definitely put a nasty turn on his disposition.

Liane had been confined to bed for several weeks in order that her children might have time to grow before they were delivered into this world. She had not taken to her ordered bed rest very well. The empress was irritable, demanding, and potentially dangerous, so it was odd that in a twisted sort of way she and the witch who tended to her had become friends. It was possible neither of them had ever had a true friend until this moment in time.

Isadora entered the imperial bedchamber just as Liane grabbed a pretty vase of greenery and rare flowers—courtesy of her husband—and threw them at the man who was trying to deliver her an early supper. The servant ducked at an appropriate moment, and the vase flew past his shoulder and shattered against the wall.

"How dare you deliver such a pathetic excuse for a meal!" Liane shouted at the terrified servant.

Isadora studied the remains of that meal, which were

scattered across the floor. Roasted meat of some sort, an assortment of vegetables, freshly baked bread. There was nothing pathetic about it.

"What would you like for supper?" Isadora asked in a calm voice. "Whatever you wish, it can be arranged, as you well know."

Liane glared at Isadora with steely green eyes. "I wish to have this man's head on a silver platter."

The servant edged toward the door. Isadora glanced at the poor man. His face had gone red, and his knees wobbled visibly. "He doesn't look at all tasty to me." She gave him permission to leave the room with a gentle wave of her hand, and when he was gone, Liane relaxed against her mountain of pillows. She did not continue to yell, but she did pout. She pouted in the same way she did everything else: to extreme.

"What's the real problem?" Isadora asked.

"The roast was overdone, and I do not care for that sort of bread, and—"

"No," Isadora interrupted. "What's the *real* problem." It was likely no one had spoken so plainly with the empress for a very long time. It was certain that no one else in the palace, with the exception of her husband, would dare to interrupt her.

The empress and her emperor were well matched, when it came to bad tempers.

The pout did not fade. "Sebestyen is entertaining a very important guest for supper tonight, and I'm stuck here, confined to bed like an invalid or an ancient old biddy, or a . . . a . . ."

"A mother-to-be who wishes only the best for her children," Isadora supplied.

"I'm doing very well, you said so yourself. Could I not leave my bed for just this one evening? I promise not to overexert myself or indulge in any excitement. I won't even speak, if you tell me that silence is best."

"Just who is this guest who has you so anxious to leave your bed?"

Liane smiled, as if she'd already won. "Have you met Esmun Hern?"

Isadora curled her lip. "Briefly." Esmun Hern was handsome enough, that's true, but he was also a blatant rogue who apparently thought himself charming. He had impregnated one of the concubines, Elya, on that day when Sophie had wielded her magic in a way that had left so many of the women in this palace with child—including the empress. Since that time Esmun Hern had left the palace for his native Tryfyn, returned to see Elya, and made a general nuisance of himself by all but laying claim to one of the emperor's concubines. Sebestyen was wary of annoying the man, since he represented one of the larger clans. Their help would be needed, if Sebestyen was to defeat the rebels once and for all. It was the only reason Hern lived.

"Esmun has decided he wants to marry Elya."

"Surely she is not foolish enough to agree," Isadora said. After all, the man was an outrageous flirt, and if he had been faithful to Elya in his time here, it would be a miracle.

"She did agree, and now Esmun must have his elder brother's permission."

"A fully grown man asks his brother's permission to marry?"

Liane shrugged her shoulders. "It is the way in Tryfyn, or in their clan. In any case, Esmun's brother arrived last night."

"And you wish to see him," Isadora said. "Is it worth risking an early delivery?"

Liane sighed in that annoyed way she had. "I have heard

that he is quite extraordinary. Sebestyen said he's a member of the Circle of Bacwyr."

"The Circle of Bacwyr is a myth," Isadora said. "And if the Circle is not a myth, then its time is so far past it might as well be."

Liane sat up, as much as she could. "It is said that only the finest of men are admitted to the Circle. It is said that no ten men can defeat one Bacwyr warrior in battle."

"You have never before struck me as being gullible, Liane."

She did not take offense. "No, but I have always been curious, as you well know."

Isadora ignored the empress and began to pick up the dishes from the floor. Some pieces were broken, others were not. Food had been scattered everywhere.

"You could come with me," Liane said in a lilting, singsong voice.

"I'm sure the Emperor Sebestyen wouldn't approve of your midwife standing behind your chair while he entertains this important man."

"Well, no. We could dress you in one of my old gowns and tell everyone that you're my cousin, come to stay with me until the baby is born." She sounded quite proud of herself for coming up with the plan.

"That's very devious of you," Isadora said.

"And while we're dining with a warrior from the Circle of Bacwyr, someone else can clean up this mess. The empress's cousin should certainly not be assigned such a demeaning chore."

Isadora lifted her head; Liane was grinning. "It will be such fun," the empress said softly. "It will be an adventure. When was the last time you allowed yourself to have an adventure?"

In truth, Isadora had had enough adventure to last a

lifetime, mostly in the past six months. None of it had been of the pleasant sort. None of it had been fun.

"We will play dress-up, Isadora," Liane said in a coaxing voice. "When was the last time you donned a luxurious gown and had your hair fixed and wore imperial jewels?"

"Never," Isadora answered plainly.

Liane cast her a smile of victory. "Oh, dear. In that case, it is time."

LUCAN TUGGED ON THE PURPLE ROBE HE'D DONNED FOR supper with the emperor. He was more comfortable in loose trousers and a vest, which is what he wore for training and for fighting. Purple was the color of the Circle, and as he was First Captain and this was a formal occasion, it was only fitting that he wear the uniform that was worn only by the leaders of the Circle.

Zebulyn had been right, all those years ago. Too bad the old man hadn't lived to see his prediction come true. All of the prophesy had not yet come to pass, of course, but after twenty-seven years he was here, in the palace of the Emperor of Columbyana. All he had to do was find the Star.

And beware the witch.

The task would be much simpler if he knew exactly what he was looking for, but Zebulyn had never given a precise description of the object Lucan needed to retrieve. Neither had any of the other wizards who made up an integral segment of the Circle. Lucan had finally accepted that if he was meant to be Prince, he would know the Star when it was presented to him.

The three attendants who escorted Lucan to Level One and the emperor's dining hall were heavily armed, and they would be more aptly called guards. They thought they had the upper hand, but they did not.

Concealed against Lucan's body were three knives of varying lengths. Outwardly, he appeared to be unarmed, and the casual inspection he had been given had not revealed any of the hidden blades. The knives he wore, and the leather scabbards that housed them, had been made to fit against his body so precisely the skim of a hand would not detect them. If he needed the weapons, he could retrieve them in a matter of seconds.

He doubted he would need the weapons tonight. Emperor Sebestyen was anxious to impress. Not on account of the outward reason for this visit. Esmun was unimportant; the woman he wished to wed was less than unimportant, she was insignificant. No, that was not the reason for this fine treatment. The ruler of Columbyana wished to persuade Lucan to sway not only his clan but the Circle itself to his side in the brewing war.

He'd likely only need to battle boredom over the emperor's table tonight, but who knew what tomorrow might bring?

Lucan was escorted into a finely furnished dining room. A fire burned in the stone fireplace, and those odd lights set in the walls burned with yellow light. He had been told those lights were not magic, but they looked like magic to him. Witch's magic, most likely, since it was rumored that there was an entire Level of this palace devoted to women of that sort and their work. He was no longer afraid of witches, as he had been as a child, but neither did he trust them. If the emperor relied upon the counsel of witches, it could very well sway Lucan's sympathies to the rebels.

A wide window looked out over a clear, crisp black sky, but panes of glass kept the evening chill at bay. The long table was set for six, each place setting far from the others. A priest and a minister, both of them clad in plain crimson, claimed two seats on one side of the table. They lifted their heads as Lucan walked into the room, and they smiled insincerely. Both men stood and introduced themselves, and Lucan did the same.

"Captain Hern," the priest said with a thin smile. "It's a pleasure to meet you. I'm very well acquainted with your brother, Esmun. Fine man, very fine man."

Apparently they had been instructed to appease tonight's guest. "My brother is a fool who can't keep his cock in his pants," Lucan said coolly. "I believe that's why I'm here."

The priest blushed, but the minister stifled a smile and turned his head so the older man at his side wouldn't see his reaction.

Lucan accepted that he was destined to be in Emperor Sebestyen's palace, here and now. His presence here was fated, and what happened in the days—or even weeks—to come would affect every man and woman in Tryfyn. And so he waited patiently and carried on unimportant conversation with the two insufferable men who did their best to be entertaining.

At last he heard commotion in the corridor and turned to face the entryway. The emperor struck him as an unpredictable and possibly dangerous man who was willing to do anything to get what he wanted. How long would it be safe to remain here while staying uncommitted to either side? Not long, he imagined. Long enough to find the Star of Bacwyr? Perhaps. Perhaps not. Zebulyn had never assured his student that he would succeed in his quest. That, he had always said, was left to Lucan.

It sounded as if twenty men were tromping down the hallway, and as the group grew close, Lucan heard a woman's voice.

If the emperor thought he could sway the First Captain of the Circle of Bacwyr with the charms of his harem, he was mistaken. Unlike his brother, Lucan was discriminating about the women who shared his passions.

Four men carried in a litter that was piled high with pillows and a very pregnant and very beautiful woman. The empress, he assumed, since he had heard that she, like Esmun's Elya, was with child. The Emperor Sebestyen, a man Lucan had met with briefly just that morning, followed the woman. He looked a tad perturbed, which did not bode well for the evening to come. Armed, green-clad sentinels surrounded the imperial couple. They were the best of the soldiers who filled this palace, dedicated and ready to die for those they had been commanded to protect.

Behind the emperor trailed another woman. The guards paid her little mind, which meant she was unimportant. The unimportant woman was finely dressed, not in crimson like the empress, but in a silver gray gown touched with a few accents of midnight blue. Dark hair, not black like his own but almost that dark, was styled simply atop her head, and she wore a few jewels that matched the blue accents in her gown. A simple necklace; a bracelet; a ring, which adorned the middle finger of her right hand. As the men who had carried the empress into the room stopped, the woman in gray was there to assist them in very gently helping the empress to her chair, which was at the emperor's right.

All of the lady in gray's attention was focused on the empress as the pregnant woman was settled into her chair. After a moment, the imperial bride slapped at the other woman's hand with impatience. "I'm fine, Isadora. Really, I am. I do not need to be coddled."

Since the priest and the minister had both claimed their seats, and Isadora sat beside the empress, that left Lucan with the seat at the foot of the table. The table was too large for six, and the diners were sitting too far apart for intimate conversation. Still, sitting at the foot of the table, he had a clear view of all the diners. Including Isadora, a dinner guest who claimed his attention more than she should.

Once she was settled in her seat, Isadora lifted her head and looked at him. Her dark eyes were curious and unafraid, and there was a sternness about her that spoke of hardships and determination. She was not pretty, but she was elegant and striking. The sharply angled face and wide mouth were most definitely memorable. The body, which was too well concealed beneath the gray gown, was slender, and he wondered if there was softness beneath that elegant fabric or if the angles that made her face so striking extended below the high neckline.

Sebestyen introduced her, in an offhanded way and with a wave of his hand. "This is Isadora, my wife's cousin come to assist until the baby is born." For some reason, he rolled his eyes as he finished the statement. "Please forgive her intrusion this evening, but my wife is determined to be here, and she's just as determined that Isadora be here as well. Apparently one never knows when a maternal emergency might arise."

"Don't apologize. It's always a pleasure to have not one but two beautiful ladies at the evening meal," Lucan said, calling upon his most charming voice and smile.

Isadora's head snapped up, and she looked at him as if she expected to find him laughing or winking at the other men. She thought it was a joke that he'd called her beautiful.

But it was no joke. She was not pretty, but she was beautiful in the way only a strong woman can be. Too bad he had no time for distractions of the female sort. He was here to find the Star of Bacwyr, to take it, and to return to Tryfyn and become Prince of Swords.

Isadora reached out to take the goblet of wine in her

hand, and as she did so, candlelight sparkled on the ring she wore. For a moment, just one heart-stopping moment, the stone there sparkled very much like a star.

HER YOUNGER SISTER, SOPHIE, HAD PLAYED DRESS-UP AS a girl, donning clothes and a persona that were not her own for entertainment purposes, but Isadora had not. Even as a child, she had firmly embraced the reality of who and what she was. She did not pretend.

And now here she was, past thirty and old enough to know better, dressed in a gown that had once belonged to one of the emperor's sisters and adorned with imperial jewels that were not the empress's favorites. Empress Liane did not care for wearing blue, not after all those years as a concubine whose primary wardrobe was the blue of Level Three.

Lucan Hern didn't say much during the course of the meal, but he had intelligent eyes that studied everything carefully and with great interest. Isadora was amongst those things he studied with perhaps too much interest. It had been a long time since a man's eyes had lingered on her this way, and his constant perusal made her nervous.

He did look somewhat like his younger brother, but there were significant differences. Where Esmun's dark hair was brown and worn in a long braid, Lucan's was black as a raven's wing and worn much shorter, though not as short as Liane's favorite sentinel, Ferghus, who stood against the wall throughout the meal unsmiling and vigilant. Lucan's thick hair curled slightly, and the ends almost touched his shoulders.

She was too far away to see his eyes well. They were not dark, as they should've been, given the blackness of his hair. Blue or green, she guessed, or perhaps both. Lucan

Hern was taller than his younger brother and wider in the shoulders. His hands were large but were also unusually graceful. Even in eating a meal, he moved with an unexpected masculine grace. There was not a wasted movement nor a single misstep.

The conversation remained casual. Any talk of alliance and war would happen when the emperor and Lucan were alone.

After an endless meal, Isadora poked at her dessert, studying the fine sweet frosting on the slice of white cake and contemplating what might happen if the Circle of Bacwyr joined forces with Emperor Sebestyen. If the warriors were like this man, they could very well swing all coming battles in Sebestyen's favor. Sophie's husband Kane was a rebel and a fine soldier, but if he went up against a man like this one, what chance would he have?

Not much of a chance at all, she suspected.

The priest who sat across from Liane directed his attention to their guest. "We have all heard tales of the Circle of Bacwyr, Captain Hern. Are they true?"

Isadora lifted her head to watch the man at the foot of the table, as he responded. "I cannot know what tales you have heard."

"Tell us of the fall of the Circle," Liane said brightly.

Lucan looked at Liane, and then he turned his gaze to Isadora. "I was not there, of course. The fall happened long before I was born. But I can tell you what little I know, if you wish."

"Please do," Liane said almost sweetly.

Lucan had eaten only a bite of his dessert, and as he began to speak he pushed the remains away. "As often happens in such circumstances, the warriors and wizards of the Circle had become overly confident. No one could challenge their strength, not physically and not magically.

The King was a mere puppet who answered to the commands of the Prince of Swords."

"The Prince of Swords?" the priest repeated in an interested tone of voice.

"Leader of the Circle of Bacwyr," Lucan said.

"Why was the King not the ultimate ruler?" Sebestyen asked.

Lucan smiled slightly. "The King was chosen by blood, the Prince by strength and destiny. No man can defeat the rightful Prince in battle, not with swords or fists or weapons of any kind."

"Who is the current Prince?" Liane asked. "I have never heard of such a position, or of a man who cannot be defeated."

"There has not been a Prince of Swords since the fall of the Circle. It was the defeat of the Prince that started the downfall of the Circle and ultimately all of Tryfyn."

Isadora pushed her own dessert away. She had been silent throughout the meal, but something about this man got under her skin, and she felt compelled to respond when a moment of silence fell. "So, despite your talk of invincibility, even your Prince could be defeated."

"Yes," he answered simply.

"What sort of man could defeat the strongest amongst you?"

"No man can defeat the Prince of Swords."

"You just said—"

"The Prince was killed by a woman," Lucan said before she had a chance to finish her sentence. "A witch who seduced, influenced, and finally betrayed the man she claimed to love. She poisoned him, and he died in agony."

The bitterness in his voice as he said the word *witch* was potent and filled with hate. Everyone at the table looked at their dessert and hemmed and hawed. No one informed

Lucan Hern that he was dining with a witch this evening, and of course as they planned to woo the man to their way of thinking, they would not.

His gaze locked to hers, and when that happened her stomach fluttered and clenched. No, she admitted reluctantly, that was not her *stomach* reacting so strongly to the power of those eyes. Her reaction to Lucan Hern was strictly that of a woman to a man. She tingled. Her toes curled in the fine, borrowed slippers. It seemed that her breath came differently, harder, more shallow, as if the man stole her very ability to breathe.

Isadora briskly yanked her eyes away and pulled the dessert back to her. She had not responded this way to any man but Will in her entire lifetime, and she would not allow it to happen now. Even if she were ready to consider a physical association with the opposite sex again, she refused to fall victim to the charms of a man who likely left a multitude of moaning, naked women and broken hearts in his wake. A man who looked as if he had never heard the word *no*. A man who was much too confident for his own good.

A man who made it very clear that he detested witches.

2

"YOU LIKE HIM; I CAN TELL," LIANE SAID AS ISADORA ADjusted the bedcovers over the empress's ever-expanding belly.

"I don't like anyone," Isadora answered in a calm voice.

Liane had changed into her nightgown, but Isadora remained dressed in the borrowed gown and jewels. She couldn't wait to get out of the binding clothes that were not her own, brush out her hair, and return the jewels that did not belong to her.

"Don't lie to me, Isadora," Liane said as she snuggled down into the soft bed. "The only thing in this world I know better than my husband is sex. Lucan Hern wants you, and you want him."

"I don't want anyone," Isadora insisted.

Liane's smile faded. "Now, I know that's a lie."

Isadora reached around to work the clasp and remove the necklace she'd worn in her role as Liane's "cousin."

Liane waved her hand dismissively. "Keep it, and all the rest. The blue suits you in a way it doesn't suit me."

"I can't possibly—" Isadora began.

"It's a gift," Liane snapped. "Has no one ever given you a gift?"

Isadora's hands fell, and the necklace remained in place around her throat. "Not in a very long time," she admitted. She knew that these jewels were not Liane's favorites, and in comparison to the other imperial jewels they were insignificant. But they were much finer than anything she'd ever owned. Will had never been able to afford jewelry.

"Now, back to Lucan Hern," Liane said with a growing smile, as she rested her hands on her rounded belly. "I will expect a full accounting of his attributes and his skill as a lover."

Isadora laughed. "Don't be absurd."

"You won't share your exploits with a poor woman who has been confined to bed and ordered not to partake of such pleasures?"

"I have no plans to take a lover, and if I did, it would not be that insufferably overconfident Captain Hern."

"He has large hands," Liane mused.

"That means nothing," Isadora replied. "Besides, he has an obvious distaste for witches."

"Then don't tell him you're a witch. I believe he has already noticed that you are a woman, and when it comes to sex, that's all that matters."

Isadora had closed herself off from her emotions for a long time, and she didn't intend to allow them to rule her now. Maybe the day would come when she'd want to take a lover. Not a husband to take Will's place, not a man to love and lose thanks to the Fyne Curse, but a sexual partner.

Until tonight she had not even considered doing such a

thing, and she refused to admit that Lucan Hern's presence had anything to do with the sudden consideration.

"Did you notice the way he moved?" Liane asked. "The man doesn't have a clumsy bone in his body. I suspect he's quite good in bed."

"That doesn't concern me," Isadora insisted, and yet again there was an unwanted response deep inside her body, a response that until this time only Will had elicited.

"I wish only to live vicariously through you." Liane pouted, but her eyes grew hard. "All you have to do is lie with Lucan Hern and share with me the details of the encounter. Will you not do me this one, small favor?"

"You want me to sleep with a stranger for your entertainment?"

"It isn't as if you don't need a man in your life, Isadora," Liane said impatiently. "I have never known a woman who needed to have an orgasm more than you do."

The fun immediately went out of the conversation. "You go too far, Liane." Not that the empress had ever cared about going too far in any respect.

"I only want what's best for you, Isadora. I would not wish for you the life I led when I first came to this palace, where any powerful man who desired me could have me at the snap of his fingers, but neither do I wish for you a life of celibacy. Sex, done properly, is one of the true and simple pleasures of life, for women as well as for men."

The conversation would continue all night if Isadora told the empress that she could not sleep with another man while she still felt bound to her departed husband. They'd had that discussion before and never came anywhere near an agreement.

"I'll think about it," Isadora said as she repositioned the covers once more and smiled down at the pregnant woman on the bed. The emperor would join his wife soon, when his meeting with Captain Hern was over. The two men had adjourned alone to a private chamber near the ballroom after the evening meal was done.

Well, Lucan Hern was alone. Emperor Sebestyen was surrounded by armed guards, as always. These days, Columbyana was not a safe haven for anyone, not even the emperor. Especially not the emperor.

It was testament to how much Sebestyen needed Hern that the captain was not dead. Not yet, anyway.

IF HE DID NOT NEED THIS MAN, HE'D HAVE HIM KILLED here and now. Lucan Hern was trouble. What kept the Tryfynian alive was the fact that if they joined forces, he and the rest of his kind would be trouble for Arik and his rebels.

Sebestyen sat back in his chair and studied First Captain Hern. Hern was big and austere and had the build and facial expression of a true warrior. He was the sort of man Sebestyen usually went to great lengths to avoid. Still, every man had a weakness. All he had to do was find Hern's and use it.

Their discussion of war was brief and unsatisfactory. Hern refused to commit himself one way or another, though he did at least listen to Sebestyen's reasoning with proper interest. There had been a time when such a lack of commitment would've led the man to Level Thirteen, but not today. Today, Sebestyen needed the Tryfynian too much. It galled him to need anyone this way.

"During your stay, anything you need or desire is yours," Sebestyen said, calling upon his most cordial voice. "If your quarters are not to your liking, we will find something more suitable."

"My assigned rooms on Level Four are sufficient," Hern answered without emotion.

Sebestyen took a deep, calming breath. Hern's rooms on Level Four were more than sufficient, comprising the finest and most elaborate visitor's chamber in the palace. In long years past, Kings and Queens had resided in that very room, and yet for Hern it was merely *sufficient*.

"If you give your approval for your brother to marry, we will of course be happy to assist with the details of the wedding."

"My brother wishes to marry one of your whores," Hern said without anger or derision. "I hardly think an elaborate wedding will be necessary, if I decide to give my approval."

A knot of anger formed in Sebestyen's stomach. Heaven above, he wanted to see this man dead. No offer was good enough, his hospitality was taken for granted, and the man did not fear the emperor before him, as he should. A lift of his hand, a silent signal, and Hern would be dead. Pity he needed the man alive.

"You've traveled a long way," Sebestyen said. "I'm sure female companionship would be welcomed, after such a journey. Do you prefer fair-haired women, as your brother does?"

"Unlike my brother, I do not choose my women based on an attribute so superficial as the color of their hair."

Of course, the blasted Tryfynian had to make things as difficult as possible. "I'll arrange for you to have a tour of Level Three. Any of the women there will be happy to spend the night in your bed, and you are welcome to as many of them as you require."

"No, but thank you for the offer. I'm sure it's well-intentioned."

No? What man turned down the opportunity to browse the emperor's fabled Level Three and choose whomever struck his fancy? Perhaps Lucan Hern, for all his size and apparent manliness, didn't care for women at all.

A spark of something new flashed in Hern's usually impassive eyes, an unmistakable light of interest that caught Sebestyen's attention. "I'm sure the women on Level Three are fine, beautiful, enjoyable females, but unlike my brother, I am rather discriminating when it comes to the women with whom I share my bed."

Sebestyen lifted his eyebrows slightly. Hern's refusal of the offer of Level Three and the odd reaction that followed was meaningful in some way. The man was not a eunuch, and it was obvious that something—or someone—had caught his attention. The captain's face was not quite so apathetic as it had been all evening.

"If you have special needs, I promise you that nothing you require is out of the realm of possibility." With any luck, Lucan Hern's special needs would be so perverted they'd make for fine blackmail.

"Your wife's cousin, Isadora," Hern said. "Is she married?"

When Liane had first proposed her little outing and the deception involved, Sebestyen had said no. But of course, Liane had gotten her way in the end. She was enormous, unable to engage in sexual relations, overly emotional, demanding, petulant, and given to tears for no good reason. And he could not deny her anything.

"Isadora is a widow, I believe," Sebestyen answered in a calm voice.

"Newly widowed?"

Sebestyen shook his head. He did not know the details, but he had heard Liane and the witch talking, on occasion. They chattered, as women were wont to do, when they did not know he was nearby. "No. Her husband has been gone for several years."

Hern relaxed. "There is no other man in her life at the present time?"

Should he tell Hern that Isadora was a witch? That she was not a cousin, but a servant? A slave, if he were to be completely honest. She'd been captured and brought here against her will, and she did as he commanded. "No," he answered simply. "There is no man in her life."

"Good." Hern placed his hands on his thighs and straightened his already-straight spine. "I want her."

Of all the possibilities . . . "Surely you would prefer a woman more experienced and genial than my wife's irritable cousin."

"Only Isadora has caught my eye."

"But you have not yet seen the other pleasures this palace has to offer," Sebestyen argued.

Hern leaned slightly forward. "If it meets with your approval, my lord, I would like to make a proposal. We both know that the Circle of Bacwyr would be a great asset to you in your war against the rebels. In fact, it could put an end to the conflict quite quickly. While others among the Circle have been speaking to Arik and his representative, I am First Captain, and I will be the one to make the final decision on with whom we will fight. The Circle will not be divided."

Sebestyen needed this man to make the right decision; his rule, his very life depended on it. "And if I'm hearing you correctly, Isadora in your bed will make the decision for you?"

"A willing Isadora, within the next three days." With that, Hern stood, ending the meeting.

It was Sebestyen's place to call an end to this session. It was his right and his privilege. But instead of bristling at Hern's arrogance, he smiled as he slowly rose to his feet. The Tryfynian could have Isadora, if it meant the support and the swords of the Circle of Bacwyr. But when the war was over and his reign was without opposition, the insufferable man would die.

* * *

EACH NIGHT BEFORE BED, LUCAN DID THE EXERCISES THAT honed his body and his mind. He shed all his clothes in order to remove any obstacles that might come between his body and his spirit and the powers of the universe and performed the *hroryk elde,* a deep meditation combined with slow, controlled poses of strength and grace. Usually his mind was blessedly clear as he performed the ritual, but tonight Isadora crept into his thoughts.

The ring she wore was certainly the Star of Bacwyr. Zebulyn had told him he would know the power when he saw it, and he had. The Star fed the magic that encircled Isadora. It was the reason his eyes had been drawn to her all evening, the reason she remained strongly and clearly in his mind, even now.

Lucan did not have inborn magic, but the wizards had taught him what they could. He had not been a good student when it came to languages, though they had tried. Spells and incantations disturbed him, and he had never embraced that craft.

But he had learned to see, as the wizards had instructed him. It was more than a warrior's instincts, his ability to discern what was true and what was not. It was a hard-won gift, one that took concentration, meditation, and strength to accomplish. Tonight he had been prepared when he'd walked into the emperor's dining hall, and he had seen an incredible power enveloping the empress's cousin. The Star was power; she possessed the Star; he must possess her.

Esmun was a fool for spreading his seed and his sexual energies with abandon, but then the youngest Hern son had always been a fool. As a child, as a man . . . Esmun meant well, and he did have his own strengths, but where women were concerned he was without control. There was power in sex when it was properly practiced. Power given and power taken. Energy of a commanding sort was exchanged to strengthen both participants, if the choice was properly made. Esmun followed his cock when it came to choosing his bed partners; Lucan followed his spirit.

It wasn't as if Isadora didn't want him. She might deny it in a foolishly feminine way that was likely meant to make him want her all the more, but she did find him attractive. She wanted to be in his bed as much as he wanted her there.

When the exercises were done, Lucan crawled into the bed in question. He remained naked, as he had been as he'd practiced the *hroryk elde,* but his weapons were within reach. His door was bolted, and he had experienced no trouble since coming here, but one could not be too careful. In any case, he always slept with his knives close at hand.

His blades would not help him in his current quest. The Star he had come here to collect could not be stolen; Zebulyn had reminded him of that fact many times. It must be freely given in order for the magic to survive and to thrive. In order for Lucan to become the next Prince of Swords, as he was destined to be, Isadora would have to give him the ring off her finger.

He had to be very careful until then. Over the years he had been prepared for this moment in many ways. There was much deception here—and he needed no magic to see that truth for himself.

Beware the witch.

The words echoed through his mind as he fell toward sleep. The woman who had enchanted and killed the last Prince of Swords, so long ago, had been a witch, and he would not forget that fact. Filthy, untrustworthy creatures, witches.

Lucan blew out the candle at his bedside and smiled in the dark. Charming the Star of Bacwyr out of Isadora would be pleasurable enough.

ISADORA QUICKLY REMOVED THE GRAY AND BLUE GOWN and stored it in the wardrobe in her chamber. Next the jewelry was removed. The necklace first. It was beautiful, but just heavy enough to become cumbersome after several hours around her throat. The bracelet was next. Like the necklace, it chafed her skin, and she was glad to remove the piece and place it in the box the jewels had been stored in for so many years.

When she tried to remove the ring she wore on the middle finger of her right hand, it refused to budge. It didn't seem too tight; it wasn't at all uncomfortable or binding. But try as she might, the ring wouldn't slide off her finger. Maybe something in the meal she'd eaten tonight had made her fingers swell a little bit. Tomorrow would be soon enough to remove the last remaining piece of the set.

She studied the stone, sparkling blue against her pale hand even by faint candlelight. She had never longed for pretty things that were not meant for her, but she did find herself admiring the sight of that ring on her hand. It was . . . pretty.

But that wasn't the reason she'd accepted Liane's gift. When she got out of the palace, the proceeds from the sale of this jewelry would finance her search for her sisters and maybe even the rebuilding of the cabin on Fyne Mountain.

Isadora stripped down to nothing, donned her night shift, and then brushed her hair and braided it. Nighttime preparations done, she climbed into bed. Spring was coming, but the nights were still cold. She drew the warm coverlet to her chin. She was so tired, sleep should come quickly. But it did not. Instead, she found herself replaying the conversation over dinner, imagining the way Lucan Hern had looked at her, and experiencing once again that dance deep in her belly. Liane said she needed to feel pleasure once again, that she needed a man. Isadora was insistent that she needed no one and nothing, but in the bed alone on a cold night she couldn't help but wonder if maybe Liane was right.

Maybe the wizard who had cursed the Fyne witches had unknowingly done them all a favor. Love alone could be a curse. Loving Will had certainly changed and weakened Isadora. Even now, long after her husband's death, her love for him made her vulnerable in a way nothing else ever could.

She was so lost in thought her heart almost burst through her chest when the door to her chamber flew open. *Mahri, again,* was her first thought when her heart resumed beating. The girl refused to knock! Her second thought was that Liane must need her. It was too early for the babies to come. Even another two weeks would make all the difference in their health and chance for survival.

But it wasn't Mahri at all, she saw as the intruder moved toward the bed, and the candle that was carried by the soldier at his side lit one half of his face.

Isadora clenched her fists tight beneath the covers. What was Emperor Sebestyen doing here?

He carelessly drew the covers off her body, commanded her to sit, took the candle from his sentinel, and ordered the armed man from the room. Again, Isadora's heart beat too fast and hard. As far as she knew, the emperor had been unfailingly faithful to his wife, in the past couple of months, at least. If he had changed his mind about his fidelity, there was an entire Level of willing women for him to choose from. Like Lucan Hern, he did not care for witches and witchcraft. Why was he here, looking up and down her body as if judging her in a purely male and sexual way?

"You're pretty enough, I guess," he said when they were alone and the door had been closed behind the sentinel.

Isadora stood so she'd be in a better position to fight if she had to. "Pretty enough for what, my lord?" She didn't care who this man was, she wasn't going to allow him to touch her.

But he didn't touch her. He stared insolently, but he did not touch.

"My wife cares for you," he said almost distantly, as if he didn't know what it felt like to care for a friend. "I'm not sure why, but she does. However, the needs of a country outweigh the reluctance of one woman."

"What sort of reluctance?" Isadora asked in a soft voice.

Emperor Sebestyen looked her in the eye, and she saw in him the violence and depravity and arrogance she had heard so much about. But she also saw something unexpected: love. He did love his wife.

"Captain Hern wants you in his bed, and what Hern wants he will have."

She blinked fast, and her knees weakened. "You can't be serious."

"If you think I would come to your room in the middle of the night to play a joke on you, you're mistaken," he said coldly. "The outcome of the war is at stake. Please Hern, do as he asks, and he will join my imperial forces and the war will soon be over. Think of the lives you'll save, simply by bringing the war to a speedy end."

Isadora tried to force her knees to be strong and steady, but they wanted to wobble. She hated that indication of weakness; there was no time for weakness in this place.

"That's a nice argument, but somehow I don't imagine bringing the Circle of Bacwyr into Columbyana will *save* lives."

The emperor smiled. "Perhaps not, but it might save your life."

"Are you threatening me, my lord?"

"Not yet. If threats becomes necessary, I will gladly use them."

The emperor stared at her breasts, which were barely covered by the thin fabric of her worn nightgown. In defense, Isadora crossed her arms over her chest. "What if I refuse?"

The emperor sighed. "If you say no to Hern's attentions, then the Circle will join the rebels, and they will likely win this war. The rebel forces are growing; that is what I hear. Some of my soldiers have deserted to join them. Common men who should care nothing for who rules have joined them. Arik's forces are stronger than they have ever been before, but they are not quite strong enough. An allegiance with the Circle of Bacwyr will elevate them to the strength they need to defeat me. They'll storm the castle and kill me, and my wife, and my son."

"The rebels would not kill a child!"

"He is to be heir to the throne, and therefore he is a threat to Arik's supposed right to rule. They will most certainly kill him. And you, I imagine. All the sentinels you have come to know, Mahri, Gadhra. I imagine they might let the concubines live, since they will be of some use, but everyone else in the palace will surely die. Is the sanctity of your celibate body more precious than all those lives?"

"It isn't that—"

"Would you allow my wife and child to die in order to maintain your virtue?"

"Offer him another woman," she said hotly.

"I offered him any woman in the palace. He wants *you*!"

For a moment, Isadora stared into the emperor's eyes, unable to believe what he was telling her.

"Say yes," he said softly, "and when this war is over I will give you anything you want. Freedom, treasures, luxuries beyond your imagination."

"I want my sisters and the cabin your soldiers burned to the ground."

"You shall have it all. I have the power to make it happen, Isadora. All you have to do is lie with one man, for the duration of his visit. Who knows? You might even enjoy yourself." The emperor moved in closer and lowered his voice, even though there was no one about to hear his words. "You can save us all, Isadora Fyne. To be honest, I care little for my own life. I am trapped in this damned palace and will always be trapped here. But I will not give up my rightful place without a fight, and I will not allow the rebels to harm my wife and child. Liane deserves more happiness than I have had a chance to give her, and my son deserves to have a long life. I want to see Liane happy, and I want to watch my son grow to a man. Nothing else matters."

Did he really care for his family so much? In truth, the emperor did not seem to be a man who cared about anything or anyone but himself.

Love weakened even him.

"I can't do as you ask," Isadora whispered.

He laid one strong hand on her shoulder, and a thumb stroked against her throat. "I have tried to be gently persuasive. I have tried to do this nicely. Damn it all, I am sick of those who defy me at every turn. I am emperor, and no one, least of all a witch who lives by my grace, answers my requests with *no*. Here's your position, Isadora Fyne. You're to offer yourself body and soul to Lucan Hern. Give him whatever he wants of you, and no matter how depraved and immoral his desires might be, you're to make him believe you enjoy them. Fake your delight in his touch, even if he does not please you well. Make him need you in the way that a man can come to need the woman who takes his fancy." The stroke of that thumb became so hard it was painful, and when Isadora tried to back away, Sebestyen pulled her back and grasped her throat. "I want to know every word Hern utters about the Circle of Bacwyr and their plans. How many warriors are they, have they regained their full strength, how many are leaning toward joining Arik. If he's planning to betray me, I need to know it before he leaves the palace."

"You want me to sleep with Hern and spy on him," Isadora said, her voice raspy.

"Yes," Sebestyen said almost happily. "And if you don't, I'll personally kill you. Liane likes you, and she'll be sorely disappointed, but a man can only abide so much, even for his wife's sake." He leaned so close she could feel his breath on her neck. "Don't play the shy innocent with me, witch. I know you killed Father Nelyk."

Isadora's heart skipped a beat. "I did no such—"

"I don't know how you did it, but I know. I won't punish you for that murder, though I certainly could do so. In a way, I understand. You're not a midwife, you're a warrior, just as Liane was once a warrior. You are not a passive woman satisfied to sit back and take what comes to you. There is a soldier within you, Isadora Fyne. Hern is the enemy, and if the first weapon you use against him is your body, then use it well." He dropped his hand and backed away. "He expects you in his bed within three days. I will give you two." He held up two long, slender fingers. "Don't disappoint me, Isadora. Those who disappoint me have a habit of disappearing."

The door closed behind him, and Isadora dropped onto the bed, her knees going weak once again. She pulled her knees to her chest and huddled as she hid beneath the covers. Two days. Two days! Damn Lucan Hern. He had come into the palace and with one request ruined all her plans.

"Willym." She whispered her husband's name. "Tell me what to do. Help me." Of course, Will didn't answer. He had not answered her call for a very long time. He was well and truly gone, and she was on her own. If she had never needed him, she wouldn't feel betrayed and hurt now. He was not here to help her. No one was here to help.

Would the rebels truly kill Liane and her babies if they stormed the palace? Would they murder the sweet, innocent, and annoying Mahri? Kane would not commit such atrocities, at least she didn't believe he would, but there were other rebels, and not all of them would be so noble as the man who was surely Sophie's husband by now.

It was Isadora's calling to protect the innocent around her, but she couldn't believe the only way to do that was by becoming Lucan Hern's strumpet.

She'd suspected that Liane was right and the visitor from Tryfyn had a sexual interest in her, but she'd never imagined that he'd be bold enough to order her to his bed, particularly when he believed her to be a royal relation. Liane's suppositions about Isadora's own desires were wrong. Well, not entirely wrong, but rather incomplete. There was an animal magnetism about the man that elicited a physical response that many women might mistake for desire or even for love. Isadora was not so frivolous.

Maybe Lucan Hern did awaken something inside her, but Isadora preferred for that part of herself to remain asleep, as it had since Willym had died. She was stronger than the baser longings of her body, and if she did one day decide to take a man into her bed again, it would be after she had left this palace and regained some semblance of control over her own life.

She had two days to find a way around the emperor's edict.

3

LACK OF SLEEP MADE ISADORA CRANKY, AS SHE ADMINIS-
tered the empress's medicines and examined the pregnant
woman. Twins always came early. Often nothing could be
done to save them, if they came into the world too soon,
but if Liane could keep those babies inside her for another
two weeks, perhaps a month, then all would be well.

All would be well until Liane's husband discovered that
she was carrying twins, not one large and difficult child,
and that she and Isadora had known all along that there
were two sons, not one. The line of ascension could not be
muddied.

"What's wrong?" Liane asked as Isadora helped her to
sit up, her back resting against a mountain of pillows.

"I did not sleep well," Isadora said sharply.

Liane just smiled. "You were dreaming of Lucan Hern,
I imagine. I told you, Isadora, you want—"

"I was not dreaming of Captain Hern," Isadora insisted. "Your husband paid me a visit last night."

Liane's smile disappeared, and her pretty face paled. "He didn't," she whispered.

"You misunderstand," Isadora said sharply. "Your husband expects me to . . . to give myself to Hern, as if I were one of the Level Three concubines to be given away on request."

"Oh." Color returned swiftly to Liane's face. "Is that all?"

"Is that all?" Isadora leaned in close. "No," she whispered, "that's not all. The emperor said he knows I killed Father Nelyk."

Since Liane was not at all surprised to hear the news, Isadora realized how the emperor had come by his information. "At first I thought he'd be upset if he knew you and I had a hand in Nelyk's death," the empress said, "but it became clear to me that he was not at all disturbed so I told him—"

"I didn't kill Father Nelyk."

Liane's eyes widened in obvious anger and horror. "What do you mean? Nelyk attacked Ryona, and there were others, too. He threw a pregnant girl into Level Thirteen and left her there to deliver her child, *his* child, in filth. He was—*is,* apparently—a lecherous, depraved, power-hungry—"

"Calm down before you hurt the babies and yourself," Isadora ordered. "Nelyk won't be harming anyone else, I promise you. He might be dead, but I didn't kill him."

Liane lay against her pillows and pouted. She was becoming quite the expert at sulking. "What did you do?"

Isadora remembered the night too well. She'd been forced to choose in an instant. Death or life? Dark or light? She still wasn't certain she'd made the right choice. "I cast a spell that made him decide. I asked him, 'Where does a man like you belong? What would the God you claim to serve consider proper punishment for the crimes you have committed?' Nelyk rose from his bed and donned a crimson gown, and together we walked down the stairs to Level Thirteen. At his order the guards on duty opened the hatch in the floor, and he jumped down." By that time, of course, the priest had been bordering on insane. "I cast a spell to make the prison guards forget what they had seen, and I walked away."

Liane seemed appeased. "A quick death would have been easier. It might've taken Nelyk weeks to die down there."

"He chose," Isadora said in a lowered voice.

"In any case," Liane dismissed Father Nelyk with a wave of her hand, "I told Sebestyen that if we ever needed an assassin no one would suspect, you'd be perfect. If he asked you to sleep with Hern, then he must have that possibility in the back of his mind. Too bad. It would be a waste of a perfectly good man."

"Hern asked for me," Isadora said. "In fact, he demanded me."

"That's very romantic," Liane said sweetly.

"It is not!"

"Fine. It's not romantic at all. It's erotic. It's thrilling. It's flattering, Isadora. Do you not see that? A man like Lucan Hern can have any woman he desires. He can have his pick of the women on Level Three, and even those who are not concubines would surely be happy to oblige him in all ways."

"He needs to choose anew," Isadora said sharply. "I don't want him or any other man."

Liane reached out and took Isadora's hand. Maybe, just maybe, she wouldn't feel the deep, telling tremble.

"I have said all along that you need a lover to help you get over your husband's death. Will is gone, but you live. You *live,* Isadora. You don't love Hern the way you loved your husband. I understand that, truly I do. But sex isn't always about love. Let Hern adore you for a while. Let him pleasure you and find pleasure in you. If you must close your eyes and pretend—"

"Not that," Isadora said quickly. "I can't . . . I can't pretend."

"Then look Lucan squarely in the eye while he makes love to you. Understand fully that life goes on, and that there's much enjoyment to be had."

Liane actually believed her convoluted reasoning. Maybe she'd had to believe, in order to survive so long in this place. "Your husband says he will kill me if I don't lie with Lucan Hern."

"He probably will," Liane replied without emotion. "I would stop him if I could, but my influence only goes so far." The empress leaned slightly forward and whispered, "I still need you, Isadora. My babies need you. Don't choose death over meaningless sex just to spite Sebestyen and Hern. Turn this situation to your advantage. They think you are weak, but you're not. They think they are in control, but we have a strength they will never understand. They believe they can scare you with their threats and demands, but you are stronger than they will ever know. Take control of the predicament and make it your own. That's what I'd do in your position."

"How?" Isadora whispered. "How do I take control when none of the choices made are my own?"

"Do not be afraid," Liane said with the confidence of a woman who had learned to deny her own fears. "When the time comes, walk into Hern's bedchamber with your head held high. Look him in the eye, smile, order him to do as *you* please. Don't ever let him see that you're afraid or uncertain."

"That's not who I am."

"Perhaps not," Liane said lightly. "Perhaps the witch Isadora Fyne is too noble and virtuous to behave in such a way." The smile that crossed her face was positively wicked. "My cousin Isadora, on the other hand, is an entirely different type of woman."

EMPEROR SEBESTYEN PROVIDED SENTINELS TO SPAR WITH Lucan in the courtyard, as he had requested. He beat them all, in swordplay and in spear work, wounding a few in an insignificant fashion but being very careful to kill no one. He did not call on his gifts as he sparred with one inadequate partner after another; he did not prepare mentally as he would if he were going into battle. Such an advantage was unnecessary.

The sentinels were no match for him, so the exercises were all but wasted.

Lucan thought of Isadora while he fought with the inadequate opponents. The woman had invaded his dreams last night, unexpectedly and quite strongly. In his dreams she wore the ring he sought . . . and nothing else. As he had suspected, her body was angular and fetching, perfectly proportioned and welcoming. In the dreams she had laughed. How odd that he remembered so clearly something as insignificant as a woman's laughter, almost as clearly as he remembered the swell of her breasts and the curve of her hip.

He called an end to the exercise and walked to a basin of water that had been provided for bathing in this courtyard. Splashing the water over his face, he dismissed all thoughts of the empress's cousin beyond the necessary.

How childish to carry the memories of a dream with him through the day!

There was nothing childish about what he would accomplish here. He would take Isadora into his bed, they would share power as only a man and woman intimately joined can, and she would give him the ring he had come here to collect. And then he would leave this place.

Honor dictated that if he got what he had come here for, with the emperor's help, he should provide that which the emperor himself sought: Circle warriors. Sebestyen was the rightful heir, the only legitimate son of the previous emperor, so siding with him seemed the right decision in any case. It didn't matter that the emperor was an obnoxious tyrant.

Inside the palace, Lucan chose to run up the stairs from the ground-floor Level Ten to Level Four, rather than taking the lift that could very easily carry him to his destination. Even though the emperor had explained the machines on Level Eleven, which powered the lift and the lights that were set into the walls, as well as fans that ran during warmer times of the year, Lucan didn't trust the contraption. It wasn't natural.

Besides, running up the stairs was good exercise. He certainly wasn't getting a sufficient workout sparring with the inadequately trained sentinels.

His warriors could take this palace in a matter of hours, if not sooner. Luckily for Emperor Sebestyen, Lucan wasn't interested in gaining control of the palace. He just wanted the Star of Bacwyr and the position of Prince of Swords, so he could bring peace to his own country.

Inside the quarters that had been assigned to him, Lucan stripped off his clothes and tossed them aside. Franco would be along soon to pick up the soiled clothing and see that the palace laundresses cleaned them well; someone had already readied his bath. The tub was situated in the small sitting room attached to the bedchamber, and the water steamed enticingly. He grabbed the soap and stepped inside, sitting in the warm water and leaning back against the tub, splashing a few drops of water onto the floor.

It was a large tub, a luxury he had not expected to find here. Of course, Sebestyen was anxious to impress, so Lucan felt certain he saw only the best of the palace and its luxuries. The food and wine, his assigned rooms, the abundant candles and artificial lighting, the constant attention of ministers and servants alike—he felt as if he were being ardently wooed by a wealthy suitor. If his reason for being here were not so momentous, he might take a moment to enjoy what the emperor offered. He had no time for luxuries, and never had.

Dipping down to wet his hair, Lucan closed his eyes and remained submerged for a long moment. While he was underwater, the knowledge came to him in a flash. He was not alone.

He sat up quickly and drew a long knife from the sheath that was strapped to his calf. And found himself face-to-face with the woman he had dreamed about last night. In his reality, she was fully dressed. Pity.

ISADORA STOOD OVER THE TUB. SHE DID NOT EVEN FLINCH when Captain Hern drew his blade in a threatening manner. "You bathe with a knife?" she asked, her voice calm.

The hand that grasped the knife's thin handle dipped into the water once again. The motion was smoothly made, so that there was barely a ripple on the water's surface.

"Yes." When the weapon had been returned to its proper place, Captain Hern leaned back and relaxed. "I did not expect you so soon. Forgive me for being unprepared. Make yourself comfortable in the bed, and I'll be along shortly."

His arrogance was so absurd, Isadora found herself smiling. "I am not here to entertain you. I came to talk."

The disappointment was as evident as the arrogance. "I feel quite sure that you and I have nothing of interest to talk about."

"Then perhaps you should simply listen." She refused to be intimidated by Hern's state of undress or the fact that the portion of the body that was revealed above the water was extraordinary. Lucan Hern was large and hard, all sculpted muscle and masculine grace. There was nothing soft or ordinary about this man. Still, no man or woman should make her feel this way, atwitter and uncertain and nervous.

Wearing one of the emperor's sisters' castoffs, a rose colored gown with an absurdly full skirt, Isadora took Liane's advice—in her own way. She became someone else for a while.

She pulled a padded stool to the side of the tub and sat demurely. The ring Liane had given her last night still would not come off her finger. You'd think something that fit so tightly it was stuck would be uncomfortable, but that was not the case. She found herself fiddling with the ring, and Hern's eyes were drawn there. She ceased the fidgeting that revealed her nervousness and looked him in the eye.

Last night she had judged from a distance that those eyes were blue or green. Today, so close, she could see that they were both, as if the colors had melded into a stunning shade of dark aqua. She had always believed that you could tell a lot about a person by looking into their eyes. There was nothing magical about that, just common sense. Did the person look at you when they spoke or listened? Did

their attention wander? Was there life in the eyes or darkness? Or worse . . . nothing at all? Hern's eyes were lively
and bright, and never wavered. They were the eyes of a
strong and confident man.

She could be no less confident. "The emperor has commanded that I give myself to you no later than tomorrow
night. I don't understand why you would request me when
Level Three is filled with women who are trained in the
ways of sexual relations and would be more than happy to
oblige you."

His eyebrows lifted in obvious surprise. "You have
come to ask to be released?"

"Yes."

"Where I come from, the women I invite to my bed are
honored. They are pleased to be chosen. In fact, they often
vie for my attentions and do their best to catch my eye."

Isadora leaned slightly forward. "In case you have not
noticed," she said sharply, "you did not come from here."

He took a moment to digest that reply. "I repulse you."

Isadora sighed deeply. She could lie and say yes, but in
truth she did not find the man at all repulsive. Besides, she
suspected he would know if she lied. "No, but I am not a
concubine who will be ordered to a man's bed because he
commands it." She cocked her head and studied his face.
"If you expect any woman you desire to come not only
willingly but anxiously to your bed, why did you give the
emperor a deadline of three days?"

"The emperor was annoyingly protective of you when I
first mentioned the possibility of our alliance. Even though
I insisted that I want only you, he tried to persuade me to
choose another." He leaned forward. "I always get what I
want, Isadora."

Not this time. "Emperor Sebestyen is not at all protective, as you can see. In fact, he shortened the timeline so

you would not have to wait so long. He has given me until tomorrow night to become your harlot."

"We need not wait until tomorrow, when you are here now."

Isadora closed her eyes in frustration. Why had she thought she could reason with this maddening man? "I will not be ordered into your bed, or any other."

His smile was brilliant. "You wish to be courted," he said with confidence, as if he had discovered all the secrets of the universe.

"No."

The smile faded quickly, and Isadora realized that it was possible no one had ever told this man *no* before.

"If you refuse to lie with me, then why are you here?"

"The emperor threatened to kill me if I didn't do as he, and you, commanded. I have come here to ask you to tell Sebestyen that you changed your mind, or else lie and tell him you bedded me and are satisfied."

Those blue green eyes darkened and hardened. "He threatened to *kill* you?"

"Yes."

"That was never my intention, Isadora."

"I'm glad to hear it. Will you do as I ask?"

He looked her in the eye again without smiling, without the arrogance she had come to expect from him. "I will give the matter some thought."

"I am placing my life in your hands," Isadora said. "If you tell the emperor that I came here and asked that you lie to him, he will kill me."

"We can't have that, now, can we?"

He seemed quite unconcerned about her or her reservations, so she threw another obstacle at him. "The concubines on Level Three take medicines that render them unable to conceive. I have taken no such medication, and there is not enough time for anything I take now to be fully effective. Would you leave me here to give birth to your child? Do you scatter your bastards wherever you go?"

"The Circle wizards have divined that my first son will be born when I am thirty-eight years of age. I am presently thirty-six, so you are in no danger of finding yourself carrying my child."

She scoffed.

"You do not believe in magic?"

"No, I most definitely believe in magic."

"You are afraid of magic, then."

"No. I simply refuse to take a risk of this sort because a wizard, who may or may not be powerful enough to be accurate at all times, predicted the birth of your first son." She leaned slightly closer. "What of your first *daughter*?"

"You're quibbling over words." Moving smoothly and without warning, Captain Hern stood.

Isadora backed away and closed her eyes tightly, but not before she'd seen the man from head to toe, naked and magnificent and aroused. Most definitely aroused.

A drop of water fell onto her gown, and then another, and then another. "Open your eyes," Hern commanded in a soft, deep voice that was very close. "You're a widow, so I suspect I possess nothing you have not seen before."

Isadora did as he asked, slowly obeying his command to find his face inches from hers. Naked, smiling, and dripping wet, he had bent down so that he could meet her eye. Even wet, his black hair curled a little, hanging damply to his shoulders. This close she could see the individual hairs of the stubble on his jaw, though he had shaved that morning. She could see the small lines around his eyes, and the little wrinkle on his brow, and the shape and hardness of his high cheekbones.

"If I do as you request, what will you do for me in return?" he asked.

Isadora kept her eyes on his face. The cheekbone was a safe enough place to look upon. "Must you receive something in exchange for nobility?"

This time his smile was softer, and new lines appeared on his face. "No, but I feel I should receive something in return for willingly giving up the woman I dreamed about last night."

Her heart skipped a beat. "You did not dream of me."

"Ah, but I did."

She was not the kind of woman men dreamed about, and she knew it well. "There are prettier women in the palace, many of them," Isadora said in frustration. "The women on Level Three are trained to offer pleasure in ways you can only imagine, and you could have your rooms filled with these women each and every night."

"Why do you insist on all but throwing these concubines at me?"

Her frustration won out over all else. "Because your request makes no sense! It is not at all logical! Why me? Are you only attracted to women who do not want you?"

For a moment she thought she had gone too far. The smile was gone, the face was harder, less amiable. "Why you, indeed?" Hern finally said. "Who can explain why a man is drawn to a particular woman?" One finger brushed against her cheek. "I am drawn to you, Isadora. I want you, and I am a man who always gets what he wants. Always."

"No man can have everything he wants," she said, trying to sound as if she was completely unaffected by that finger on her face. She had not been touched gently by any man since Will's death, and the caress stirred something that would be best left unstirred. "It isn't the natural way of the world, not even for a man like you."

She expected an argument. What she got was a kiss.

Captain Lucan Hern, naked and aroused and completely insufferable, laid his mouth on hers and moved his lips very gently. He did not touch her anywhere else, and when she pulled away, he did not draw her back.

Even after he backed away and grabbed a towel to dry himself, she felt those lips on hers. No only that, she felt a response deep inside that told her she'd been too long without a man. She spoke to Lucan Hern about what was not natural. Surely it was not natural to need and want something this deeply and not take it.

But instead of taking anything, she stood quickly and stepped toward the door between the sitting room and his bedchamber, keeping her back to the naked man. "Will you do as I ask?"

"I will consider your proposition."

Before she exited the sitting room, Isadora glanced back. Lucan was busy drying himself with the towel. The knife he had drawn from beneath the water was still strapped to his muscular calf. Was he never without a blade on his person? No, she decided, he was not. He was a warrior, a man who embraced death and destruction—the destruction she was trying so hard to distance herself from in order to regain her power.

He had no scars. Not one that she could see. A man who lived by the sword should have scars. Was he so talented with the blade that none other had ever touched him?

She walked briskly toward the door that would lead into the hallway, anxious to escape, but Hern's voice stopped her. "Enough consideration," he called. "I will expect you here tomorrow night, as the emperor commanded. Wear something blue. The pink doesn't suit you at all."

As Isadora stepped into the corridor of Level Four, she slammed the door forcefully. She had the distinct feeling she'd just made matters worse.

SEBESTYEN STOOD BACK, QUIET AND ATTENTIVE, AS HIS wife and the witch conversed in low, hushed tones. They did not yet know that he had arrived.

Liane was his, and he did not wish to share her, not even with a witch she called friend. Watching them smile, listening to them speak, he felt an outsider in a place that should be his. They spoke of womanly things that would likely not be of interest to him, and yet he experienced a rush of what could only be called jealousy.

His wife had slept with a number of men before he'd claimed her as his own, and yet he never felt jealousy over what had passed during that time. She had never cared for any of the men she'd serviced. She had, in fact, killed a few of them without a qualm, when it became necessary. But this friendship . . . it bothered him deeply. Liane shared a part of herself with Isadora Fyne that he himself had never touched.

Marriage had been so much easier when he had not loved his wives.

Even pregnant and irritable and moody, Liane was beautiful. He looked at her, and the world shifted a little. He touched her, and all the problems of the country seemed insignificant. The problems that plagued Columbyana weren't at all insignificant, but when he concentrated on Liane he could forget war and betrayal and his ambitious bastard half brother. For a while.

Sebestyen missed the physical alliance he and Liane had always shared, before love and after, but oddly enough he was not at all tempted to take his own gratification elsewhere, though as emperor he was entitled to do just that. He'd tried to find a substitute for Liane, once upon a time, and it hadn't worked out as he'd expected it would.

After the baby arrived and they sent the heir to Level Two to be fed by a wet nurse and educated by the priests, his previous relationship with Liane would resume. If the priests had the next emperor in their control, they would care little for the woman who shared the current emperor's bed. It would be best, however, if they never knew that she also shared his heart.

Sebestyen didn't understand what Lucan Hern saw in Isadora, not when there were so many other women in the palace to choose from. True, many of the women were as pregnant as Liane, thanks to the interference of that witch Sophie, but he had replaced them with others. Why her?

He wasn't blind to Isadora's finer physical attributes, but she had a harshness about her that did not appeal to him. She rarely smiled, and when she did, it didn't seem at all real. She was not agreeable, not in the way a bedmate should be. She was not soft and compliant, as any man would surely want his woman to be.

With any luck, she'd annoy Lucan Hern, and Sebestyen would have an excuse to be rid of the witch once and for all.

And if that luck was *very* good, Hern would become so annoyed he'd do the deed himself. Perhaps if word reached the warrior that he was sharing his bed with a witch, Isadora Fyne would disappear.

When she was gone, and the baby was housed on Level Two, all here would be as it had once been. He and Liane would make love every night, and they would discuss matters of state and nonsensical things in their bed.

And he would share her with no one.

4

ISADORA KEPT HER HEAD HIGH, BUT HER CHIN TREMBLED slightly. She should've known the emperor wouldn't trust her to make her own way to Hern's quarters. Two of his most disagreeable sentinels bracketed her, escorting her from the doorway of her own small room, to the lift that was reserved for those of a high station, to the corridor of Level Four.

She could fight them both, if necessary. She could bring them to their knees, wound them, even kill them. Her magic had grown strong enough, of late, to accomplish just that.

But she could not afford to call upon her powers of destruction. What if this time the use of those dark powers completely destroyed her magic? It was a chance she couldn't take.

Not unless the time came that she had to choose destruction and put protection aside, once and for all.

Even though she could not kill, she was not entirely un-prepared for the evening. In the pocket of the elaborate pink gown she had chosen purposely to annoy Captain Hern, there rested a vial of a harmless potion. Well, the potion was almost harmless. With any luck Hern would try to ply her with wine before he attempted to seduce her. One taste, and in short order he would fall into a nice, deep, and very *suggestable* sleep. While he slept she'd whisper in his ear, and he'd wake in the morning believing he'd gotten what he wanted. Perhaps she'd even suggest that they were not well suited, physically, and he'd look elsewhere for female companionship during the remainder of his visit.

Isadora shouldn't have access to the ingredients necessary for such a powerful potion. The emperor was cautious, and his wife's witch was not allowed free run of the palace. She was especially not allowed access to Level Seven, where the witch Gadhra and her apprentices worked. But since Gadhra was often consulted about the empress's pregnancy, Isadora had come to know the old woman well. Gadhra could be persuaded, on occasion, to slip a few nonlethal herbs to a fellow practitioner.

Empress Liane continued to tell Isadora that it was time for her to take a lover, and goodness knows Lucan Hern was handsome and intriguing enough to stir something inside her. But she would not be ordered to any man's bed. If and when she decided the time had come to take a lover, she would make the choice for herself.

After Will's death, she had been determined to live alone for the rest of her days. Lately, she had begun to doubt the wisdom of that decision. Seeing Sophie and her Kane, hearing the girls from Level Three laugh and smile when their favorite caller appeared, even watching Liane when she spoke about her husband, made Isadora question her resolve. Alone was, well, lonely.

Love remained impossible, but companionship, and even pleasure, could one day be hers for the taking.

But not today.

The ugliest and most boorish of the two sentinels knocked on Captain Hern's door, and it opened immediately, as if the man who had demanded her presence had been waiting on the opposite side of the door. The captain looked her up and down, smiling as he took in the pink gown she wore. He himself wore a lush purple robe that draped from the full-collared neck to the floor. How many weapons did he wear beneath that robe? she wondered. Would he use one or all of them if he caught her slipping the potion into his drink?

Hern offered his hand. When Isadora did not immediately take that hand, he lifted his eyebrows ever so slightly. It was tantamount to an order. She slapped her palm against his, and he drew her inside. She had no idea if the sentinels would wait outside the door, in case she tried to escape, or if they would now return to Level One.

Not that it mattered.

"You didn't wear blue as I requested," Hern said as he led her across the main room.

"No, I did not. Your requests mean nothing to me." The coverlet on his large bed, which was positioned against the far wall, had been turned down, and candles of many shapes and sizes burned on the tables that were scattered about in the spacious room. Through the sitting room doorway to the right she spotted the now-empty tub and a padded chair, as well as one end of a table. Hern had been assigned very nice rooms, almost equal to the empress's quarters on Level Five.

"I don't suppose it matters, since you will not be wearing the gown for very long."

Her heart skipped a beat, and then she spotted the small table where a silver tray, a decanter of wine, and two fine, crystal glasses sat.

"As a matter of fact, you may take it off now," Hern said in an insistent voice.

"Now?" Isadora yanked her hand from his in annoyance. "Do you want nothing more than a warm, unwilling body beneath yours? I suppose I should be grateful. If this deed is done quickly, I'll be able to see to my mending tonight before I go to sleep."

Her annoyance amused him. "You won't have the time nor the inclination for mending tonight, Isadora, I promise you that."

She answered with a small, indignant huffing noise and turned to see that he held out to her a purple robe similar to the one he wore, only the one he offered her was much smaller than his. "You travel with nightclothes for any paramours you might find along the way?"

"No. I ordered the robe made especially for you. The emperor's seamstress has worked long hours to have this finished for tonight. You should be honored. Among the Circle, this color is reserved for those of great importance, rather like the emperor's crimson."

"I would rather be naked," Isadora responded, her teeth clenched.

"As you wish," Hern answered.

Isadora took the robe, yanking it from Captain Hern's grasp. It was made of a fine fabric, perfect for a cold night but not too heavy. She edged toward the table where the wine sat. "Will you turn your back while I change?"

"If you wish. Of course, if you need assistance with buttons or ties or the like, I'll be glad to—"

"I'm sure you would be more than happy to assist." She

shooed at him with her hand, and while he did not go away, he did turn, presenting a wide and finely shaped purple-clad back to her.

Glancing at Hern to make sure he wasn't peeking, Isadora grabbed the vial from her pocket, uncapped it, and poured the contents into the bottle of wine. That was her only choice, since both glasses were empty. She would simply decline his offer of drink, citing nervousness or a dislike for wine. When that was done, quickly and silently, she dropped the vial into her pocket and began to unfasten the buttons of the gown. Removing it without assistance would be difficult but not impossible. She had chosen this gown not only for the color Lucan did not like but for the fact that she could slip in and out of it without help. How else could she be expected to sneak out while he slept the sleep of the drugged?

"You're certain you don't need any help?" he asked again.

"I'm fine, Captain Hern. Please be patient," Isadora said as she shimmied the gown over her hips.

"I have never claimed patience as a trait."

"How sad for you," she said as she kicked the gown aside and pulled on the robe, leaving her foundation garment in place. She'd never worn such a thing until coming here. Her own simple dresses did not require such a contraption, but many of the finer gowns did not fit correctly without one of the blasted things beneath. "I understand a patient lover is a man to be much admired." When the purple robe was fastened as far as it would go—which was not far enough up or down to suit her—she turned and steeled her spine. "You may turn around now."

Hern turned slowly, looking her over with an all too easy to read expression in his eyes. She did not understand why, but he truly did want her.

Maybe in the morning, he'd think he'd actually *had* her.

* * *

LUCAN HAD PREPARED FOR THIS EVENING WITH MEDITA-
tion and an abbreviated session of the *hroryk elde*. He
could see all that which he was meant to see. The Star
Isadora wore on her finger infused her with magic and energy, and the woman positively glowed. No one who had
not been trained for years to recognize the power would see
the light and feel the pull of energy, but he did.

Unfortunately, he also saw deception.

Her robe's buttons began midbreast, but she had clasped
together the collar high on her chest so he could not see
much flesh. Those buttons ended not far below the apex of
her thighs, so no matter how demurely she tried to stand,
her legs could not be completely concealed. They were fine
legs, strong and shapely, and he could not wait until they
were wrapped around his hips.

Lucan suspected that would not happen tonight, not unless he was willing to lie with a woman who truly did not
want him. He was not. Most men, women, too, were ignorant of the knowledge that in sharing and linking bodies
there was more than pleasure. There was also a sharing of
power, a mingling of sacred energy. Sex, properly practiced, fed one's vitality and enhanced one's spirit.

The darker side of sex was just as powerful. If a body
was taken rather than shared, or abused in any way, the re-
sults were not the same. Instead of feeding one's power,
such dark bonds sapped much-needed energy and made
the soul turn dark.

He would not force himself on Isadora, but that didn't
mean he was going to allow her to walk away untouched.
Seducing her was going to take more than one night. Was
she worth the time and effort necessary? Was any woman?
Even if she were not, the Star was worth any sacrifice—

including seducing an unwilling woman until she was more than willing.

He walked to her, and she stiffened. Instead of touching her intimately, he removed the pins that bound her hair and watched the thick strands fall around her shoulders. He ran his fingers through the unbound locks and watched the whirl of her dark hair as it flowed through his fingers.

"I wish for you to admit that I would never hurt you," he said.

"How can I admit to such a thing when I don't know you well enough to believe that to be true?"

He would be insulted, but it was true enough that Isadora did not know him. She didn't know that he was destined to be Prince of Swords, that the Circle of Bacwyr was an honorable institution, that it was his legacy to protect, not to harm. And so he forgave her.

He cupped her breast and frowned at the resistance his palm encountered. "You did not remove your undergarment."

"No. It's rather complicated, with hooks and eyes and ribbons, and since it only covers my top half, it won't get in the way of what you want from me."

"You don't know what I want from you, Isadora. You don't have any idea."

She took a deep breath, and her breast filled his hand. He wanted the softness, the give, the reaction of her nipple against his palm. "Take off the robe."

"I just put it on!" she protested. "Have some wine first," she added quickly, backing out of his embrace and pouring one glass of wine. One only.

So that's where the deception was located. Lucan took a deep breath and once again shifted his mind to the place the wizards had taught him to access. It had taken years, and the method was not yet perfected, but he could see many things when he shifted his mind into this state.

There was no death here, so at least she wasn't trying to kill him. That was rather a relief. Still, the deception itself was in the wine.

"You will join me, won't you?" he asked.

"I don't care for that particular wine," she responded.

Lucan lifted the single filled glass. "All right. While I drink, you rid yourself of that damned undergarment. Do we have a deal?"

"Deal," she said reluctantly, turning her back to him and unfastening the robe.

Lucan did not swallow the wine. In fact, the liquid barely touched his lips. He watched Isadora's back as she dropped the robe and began to unfasten the undergarment that bound her breasts. He quietly poured a small portion of the wine onto the rug at the foot of the bed, aiming for a wide dark blue stripe that would not show the spilled wine. She was smart enough to look at his glass and realize that he had not consumed whatever drug she'd intended for him, if he didn't dispose of more than a few drops.

Isadora's body was elegant, well-shaped and strong, with fine, flawless skin and gentle flowing lines and curves, much as it had been in his dreams. Why did she not see why he would prefer her over a trained concubine? He did not want sex simply for release. It was the sharing of energy that called to him, the shared pleasure that fed his spirit. Even if Isadora was not in possession of the ring he desired, he would be drawn to her.

Undergarment discarded, she lifted the robe and slipped her arms into the sleeves. Before she had a chance to fasten the buttons once again, he placed his wineglass on the table and walked up behind her. His arms circled around her, and his hands slipped into the parted robe and found warm, silky skin.

"I will not allow you to be sorry I asked for you."

* * *

HE WAS A BIG MAN, AND OF COURSE THE POTION WOULD
not take effect right away. Isadora closed her eyes as
Hern's wide palms settled over her bare flesh. She should
not enjoy the feel of those hard hands on her skin, not so
much, but she did. Instinctively, she reveled in the touch. It
had been such a long time . . .

"I am already sorry," she whispered, though her body
was anything but sorry. It was sheer neglect that made her
feel this way, she reasoned. She was tired of being alone,
tired of sleeping in a cold bed without touch, without tenderness. Any man's caress, even that of the ugliest and
most unpleasant sentinel in the palace, would likely elicit
the same physical response. That didn't mean she wanted
Lucan Hern's touch.

His hands raked up and cupped her breasts, and his fingers very gently tweaked her nipples. She gasped at the intense response, and when he rubbed his rough palms
against the pebbled peaks, she closed her eyes and allowed
herself to simply experience that which he offered. After
all, he would soon be insensible, so there would be nothing
between them but this touch. There was no reason to fear
something that would not, could not, happen.

She expected him to falter, to grow weary, but the caress
continued. In fact, his touch on her breasts and her stomach
grew bolder and more sure. Her knees began to go weak.
The room grew hot.

The room grew so hot that when Hern drew the robe
down and let it fall to the floor, she didn't protest or try to
cover herself. The cool air against her flesh felt good. His
hands on her breasts and his hard body pressed against her
back felt even better, and between her legs she throbbed.
Heaven above, she wanted him.

"You drugged me," she said, unable to protest too loudly.

"I did not."

She hadn't eaten or drunk anything here in this room. Maybe her simple supper, eaten hours ago, had contained a potion to elicit passion, or else Hern had coated the purple robe she'd worn so briefly with a poisonous compound that made her react this way. The intensity, the unexpected delight, the need . . . it couldn't be real.

"You're very beautiful," he whispered as he moved her hair aside so he could lay his mouth on her shoulder.

The touch of Hern's mouth on her skin made Isadora gasp, and she almost reeled against him. "I'm not beautiful, not like—"

"You are," he interrupted before she could finish her protest.

For a moment, just a moment, she allowed herself to believe that she was truly beautiful. She allowed herself to believe that the man who touched her thought she was beautiful. Hern caressed her as if she were precious and fragile, as if he had a great regard for how she reacted to his touch. Fingers traced skin that had been untouched for such a long time, and she felt each fingertip to the center of her being.

Any moment now Captain Hern was going to pass out, so she did not worry about where this dangerous exploration might end. She just enjoyed the caress of his hands and the illusion of beauty. She felt his arousal pressing into her backside, and yet he did not seem to be in any hurry. Perhaps Hern thought they had all night; it was best that he continue to believe that was true.

He said he did not possess patience, but his hands and his mouth moved with a determined laziness. Isadora found herself leaning against him, falling back while his hands caressed her breasts and he kissed her neck and her shoulder with talented lips that aroused her. She seemed to be caught in a hazy world that consisted of only sensation. Sensation that wafted through her body and befogged her usually clear mind.

When Hern laid his hand low on her stomach, she had a fleeting and horrible and unexpected thought: *Don't pass out before this is done.*

He turned her in his arms, and she did not protest. He lifted her easily and laid her on the bed, and still wearing his long purple robe, he came with her. His hands spread her legs, gently and yet forcefully, and he ran long fingers along the tender skin of her inner thighs. Up and down, not quite touching her where she throbbed for him, he caressed her.

Isadora was not a shy, retiring maiden who was ashamed for a man to look upon her as Hern now did. She would not pull the covers over her body and hide from him, not when he so obviously liked what he saw. Not when she was a fully grown woman who did not shy away from anything or anyone.

The mouth that had kissed her neck and her shoulder so well brushed against her belly, and Hern trailed his tongue there. He kissed his way up her torso, finally finding and capturing one nipple and drawing it deep into his warm mouth. Isadora threaded her fingers through his black curls and arched up into him. The sensations he awakened danced through her entire body, from the top of her head to the toes that curled.

If he stopped now she would die.

Her breath came hard and just short of gasping, and when he laid his hand between her legs, she bucked slightly and moved against his caress. The tip of his finger made small, quick circles against a very sensitive place, while his mouth moved from one breast to the other. She arched up against him, against his mouth and his hand, and he slipped a finger inside her . . . and then another.

The orgasm should not have caught her by surprise, but it did. It came quick and hard, and she cried out while release whipped through her body. Not only where he touched her, but everywhere . . . from her head to the toes that curled, to the center of her femininity where long unused muscles clenched and released. She grabbed a handful of dark, curling hair, as Hern continued to draw her nipple into his mouth. As her movements slowed, so did his. As her senses returned to her, he lifted his head and looked her in the eye.

"By the way, love," he whispered, "I didn't actually drink any of the wine."

ISADORA'S EYES WIDENED, BUT SHE DIDN'T TRY TO ESCAPE. He had expected some response to his touch, but he certainly had not expected that reaction to be so wonderfully extreme. Her sexual release fed him, and apparently fed her, as well. The magic he had always sensed around her glowed brighter than ever before.

He took her right hand in his, studied the Star of Bacwyr she wore upon her middle finger, and then took the tip of her finger into his mouth and sucked gently. If he asked her to give him the ring she would, but he wanted her to offer it to him entirely of her own free will. She trembled as he slowly pulled the finger out of his mouth, sucking gently. When that was done, he guided her hand to his erection.

"As you can well see, I have need of my own gratification."

She licked her lips and said nothing.

"What was in the wine? Something to make me ill? To make me impotent? To make me sleep?" A flash of her dark eyes gave her away. "Sleep it is." He guided her hand up the length of his erection once, before releasing her. "You apparently think very little of me, if you believe I would force myself upon a woman who does not want me."

"You ordered me here, and now you expect me to believe that you care about what I want?" she argued, her voice still softly rasping from the climax. He loved that smoky voice with a surprising intensity.

"I see in you the need and the desire to be here. You simply have not seen it for yourself." He rolled away from her quivering body and left the bed. "Until you do, I have no need of you in my bed."

Isadora scrambled off the mattress and grabbed her clothes. She struggled with the undergarment, and after a moment he assisted her, uninvited. She was so anxious to be dressed and away from him, she did not protest.

"It is that easy?" she asked, still breathless. "You're just going to let me go?"

"Not entirely," Lucan said as he finished with the final hook and eye. "The emperor must believe we are intimately involved. If he thinks you did not please me tonight, he might be angry with you. That will never do."

Isadora grabbed the pink dress from the floor and stepped into it. The hue looked a bit better on her now, while she had the flush of a powerful orgasm coloring her cheeks. "What do you suggest?"

"You will come to my chambers tomorrow night, and the next, and the next, and every night until I return home."

"That could be weeks, if you stay for your brother's wedding!"

"Yes, I know."

Fully dressed, she did her best to restore her dignity. "I

suppose you expect to change my mind about having relations with you."

"Perhaps. Then again, perhaps you will change my mind, and during our evenings together I will be satisfied to enjoy games of cards or scintillating conversations about worldly happenings or philosophy."

"I'm sure," she said dryly as she turned away to leave his quarters.

"Isadora?"

She stopped at the sound of her name and spun around almost angrily. "What?"

Lucan stepped toward her, his pace slow. "I won't force myself upon you, if that's what you're worried about. I will touch you again, I will make you tremble and scream. But I won't join with you until you ask it of me."

"How very noble of you," she said dryly. "I suppose you will send for a girl from Level Three to ease your pain tonight."

"No," he replied honestly. "I don't want any other woman but you, and I will wait until you are ready for me."

He saw the surprise in her eyes, and then the disbelief. He didn't take offense at her disbelief. Eventually, she would understand.

"Good night, Captain Hern."

"Call me Lucan," he said amiably. "If we are to be lovers, it is only fitting."

She made a gruff sound of displeasure as she opened the door. The sentinels who had escorted her to him waited. Lucan laid a possessive hand on Isadora's shoulder and looked the eldest of the sentinels in the eye.

"If the emperor happens to ask . . . she was magnificent."

5

"SHE IS THE ONE WHO WILL LEAD US TO OUR GOAL?"

Lucan nodded and muttered a distant, "Yes," as Franco entered the room. As far as the palace residents were concerned, the amiable young man was a personal manservant who served the visiting Circle warrior. In truth, Franco was a warrior himself, though he was not as highly placed in the order as Lucan. In spite of his young age, he was a talented swordsman and possessed a sharp, logical mind.

"I do not trust her," Franco said.

"Neither do I," Lucan replied. "But she is necessary."

Franco's midlength dark blond hair was pulled back into a neat queue, and his uniform was a serviceable buckskin. The smile and easygoing attitude he assumed for this role was not entirely a false one; when he was not called to fight, Franco was truly a good-natured fellow.

"What do the servants say?"

Franco laughed lightly as he dropped into a chair and

thrust out his long legs. "Very little, I'm afraid. They do not trust me."

"And you have such a trustworthy face." Lucan smiled for the first time since he'd closed the door on Isadora. "I thought you would be able to charm a few secrets out of a chambermaid or two by this time."

"It is early yet," Franco said.

While it was true that Franco was an agreeable sort, the man was as deadly as any warrior in the Circle, and would do whatever was necessary to see the order restored to its glory and power.

"We don't have much time," Lucan reminded the younger man.

"I understand."

After Franco left the room for his own small quarters nearby, Lucan prepared for bed as usual, first with physical exercises to burn the energy that glowed within him, and then with the *hroryk elde,* to still his mind and spirit. Neither was entirely successful in cleansing him of Isadora's influence, but they did calm him to a certain degree.

He wished, as he doused candles, that he would not dream of Isadora tonight. She was a means to an end, a necessity, as he had informed Franco just a short while ago.

He could have finished what he'd started when he'd made her tremble and buck beneath him, naked but for the ring as she had been in his dreams before tonight. She had wanted him then. Her body had been ready and willing to take his. And if he had asked for all she had to give, she would have said yes without hesitation.

And yet, he had known even as she lay trembling on his bed that she was not ready for what he wanted from her.

He wanted Isadora ready for him in all ways, and she would be. Eventually. How long was he willing to wait? They did not have much time here. He needed to accomplish his goals as quickly as possible, so the Circle could reclaim their rightful place and Tryfyn could grow strong again.

The needs of one man, or of one woman, were trivial in comparison.

EVEN THOUGH IT WAS STILL EARLY IN THE MORNING, Isadora was awake when the door to her chamber creaked slowly open. For a moment she held her breath, wondering if Lucan Hern would be so bold.

But of course it was Mahri, who had once again forgotten to knock. Isadora sat up and glared at the skittish maid.

"I thought you might still be asleep," Mahri whispered. The girl was loaded down with clothing. The gowns she carried were elegant, like the ones Isadora had worn in her guise of the empress's cousin. But there were so many of them, and they were constructed of all sorts of fabric and colors. For a woman who had dressed herself in plain black for so many years, those colors were almost frightening.

"I've been awake for a while," Isadora said as Mahri deposited the armload of fine fabrics on the padded chair that sat in the corner of the room.

But not very long, to be honest. When she'd crawled into her own bed after returning from Hern's rooms, she'd expected a sleepless night. Her body trembled with release and anger and surprise long after the man's hands had ceased touching her. How dare he? How dare *she*?

Angry or not, she'd very soon fallen into a deep and dreamless sleep. She hadn't slept so well in years.

Mahri came to Isadora's bed and smiled in that completely innocent and guileless way she had. "I hear Captain Hern was very well pleased."

News did travel fast in this damned place. "Did you?"

"Yes. Apparently he is quite taken with you."

Isadora threw off the coverlet and sat. "Captain Hern is quite taken with the empress's cousin, a woman who does not exist." A homeless witch without a decent dress or a single silver coin to her name would likely not please him near as much.

Mahri sat on the side of the bed and lifted her feet off the floor in a girlish fashion. "An order has been issued that no one is to tell Captain Hern that you are not a part of the royal family. The emperor issued the command himself, and no one wants to displease him." The girl shuddered. "Emperor Sebestyen scares me. I would not wish to be the one to displease him."

"Of course the emperor scares you," Isadora said. Anyone in the palace who cared for their hide was scared of their unpredictable ruler. "What if the captain's own brother, Esmun, tells him that I am not the woman he believes me to be? They don't spend a lot of time in one another's company, but surely they speak."

"This was discussed, and the emperor even suggested that Esmun could . . . disappear, if necessary."

Isadora scoffed. The emperor knew no boundaries!

"But it was finally decided that Esmun Hern does not know enough about you to ruin the story. He only knows that you serve the empress, that you care for her and are her companion. Those are acceptable duties for a cousin. Most of the palace servants don't even know you're a witch. You don't stay on Level Seven, like the other witches, and it isn't as if the empress and emperor discuss such matters with those who serve them. Those few who do know, some of the sentinels and ministers, will be warned not to share the secret. You have no need to worry."

It was odd for Mahri to be so friendly, to sit on the side of the bed beside Isadora and converse. They had come to a truce of sorts, and Mahri was no longer afraid of the witch. But in truth they had very little in common. They were both female, and they both served Empress Liane; beyond that, they were as different as night and day.

"What's it like?" Mahri asked, her gaze flitting shyly to the window that looked out on a chilly, gray day.

"What is what like?"

"To be with a man . . . that way. I have heard that it can be wonderful, but I have also heard that it can be terrible. Which is the truth?"

She should not be surprised that the girl was a virgin. Mahri's life and position here were sheltered, and she did not have an outgoing personality. While her face was pretty enough, it was not extraordinary in any way. She would not draw many admiring glances of the men in the castle.

"Both can be true," Isadora said gently. "It depends upon the man and the situation."

Mahri cast a shy smile Isadora's way. "Which applies to Captain Hern?"

Anything she told the maid would likely find its way through the palace, probably within the hour. Isadora was tempted to tell Mahri that Hern was an inadequate lover with an unusually small male appendage, but she was wise enough to know that tale would come back to bite her. She and her *lover* had reached an agreement, and she suspected Lucan Hern was a man who abided by his word. He would not force himself on her . . . though if he touched her again as he had last night, she would very likely force herself upon *him*.

No, last night her body had responded with intensity because it had been neglected for so long. Tonight, and all the nights to come, would be different. She did not want Lucan Hern, she did not need him or anything he had to offer.

"He was more than adequate," she said in a calm, mysterious voice.

Mahri sighed and clasped her hands in her lap. "Do you love him?"

"Of course not!" Isadora stood quickly.

"I should not have asked," Mahri said as she, too, left the bed. "It just seems very romantic to have a man command you to his bed because he wants you above all others."

Romantic? No. Demanding, insufferable, and egotistical. But never romantic.

"His valet is quite handsome," Mahri said too casually. "Have you met Franco? We ran into one another at the laundry yesterday, and he was very friendly."

"I have not met Franco, but if I am to offer you womanly advice, it would be to beware of handsome and friendly men." Isadora opened her wardrobe and touched the dark blue everyday gown she wore so often. There was a brown and a gray fashioned much like it, simple, ordinary frocks that suited her life in this place. Hern liked her in blue. She reached past the gown she had intended to wear and grabbed the brown.

"No!" Mahri snatched the plain dress from her hand. "I have brought you several new, pretty things to wear. Empress Liane insists that as long as Captain Hern is residing in the palace, you are to *be* her cousin."

DRESSED IN A SPRING GREEN GOWN THAT WAS MUCH TOO fancy for her tastes, Isadora placed her hands over the empress's belly and closed her eyes. Her powers seemed to have grown stronger overnight. She did not have Juliet's gift for divining the future, but this morning she saw many things as she touched Liane and her children.

"They are healthy," Isadora said. "Small, but well-formed and strong."

"*He*," the empress said in a lowered voice. "Not *they*. You don't know who might be listening."

Eventually everyone would know that Liane and Sebestyen had created twin boys, but the empress was determined to keep that news to herself, for now. The emperor would be furious, unless they could convince him that they had not known. That was unlikely.

How angry would the emperor be? Mahri was right to be afraid of the man. If Isadora allowed herself to be afraid of anyone, Emperor Sebestyen would be at the top of her list.

There had been a time when she'd had the power to cast a protection spell strong enough to keep men and danger and war away from Fyne Mountain. That spell had been broken, eventually, but it had held strong for many years. Did she have enough power to cast a protection spell over Liane and her sons now? Was the return of power she felt enough? Not yet, she suspected.

When Isadora stepped away from the bed, Liane asked, "All is truly well?"

"Very much so, yes," Isadora said.

The empress sat, with Isadora's help, and as she settled into her mountain of pillows, she smiled. "Tell me all about Captain Hern."

The heat in her cheeks might be a blush. She never blushed! "That is a private matter, my lady."

"He said you were magnificent."

"Yes, I know."

"And yet you cannot utter even one word of compliment for him?"

"I was offered to Captain Hern with no more consideration than a welcoming gift of wine and fruit, with no regard for my own wishes, and you want me to compliment him?"

"You're much too sensitive about such matters, Isadora. In the past I was offered to many men with no regard for my own wishes, but that doesn't mean I was fool enough not to enjoy myself when I was lucky enough to land in the bed of a real man."

Isadora cocked her head and studied Liane. "You made the best of the situation in which you were thrown. You even embraced your situation, and the outcome was right, for you. You have said many times that you and I are alike, my lady, and in many ways that may be true. But I have never been one to easily accept what fate throws at me, when what comes is not of my choosing."

"You should," Liane responded, not taking offense at anything Isadora said. "There is a time to fight, but there is also a time to accept." She grinned. "You look beautiful in the green gown. Some of the dresses Mahri delivered to your quarters once belonged to Sebestyen's sisters, but a few were once my own."

"I assumed as much." Liane's discarded gowns would be the ones crafted of sheer fabric, or that sported a neckline cut to the navel. It had been very easy to discern which of the frocks had been made for the emperor's concubine, and which had been made for his more proper sisters.

She would go to Hern naked before she'd wear those seductive gowns.

The spring green gown fit relatively well, which was why she'd chosen to wear it today. Many of the others needed to be altered. She was not a talented seamstress like Sophie, but she could take a tuck here and there and lower a hem.

"Perhaps you are too shy to share details about your love life, but I can see that Captain Hern pleased you."

"You cannot see—" Isadora began.

"I can," Liane interrupted. "Your eyes are livelier than

usual this morning, and your cheeks still display the flush of love."

"If my looks are improved this morning, it is because I slept unusually well."

Liane's smile widened. "I imagine you did."

Isadora turned to leave Liane. She had lots of mending and alterations to deal with, a chore that could be accomplished in the privacy of her room.

Before she reached the door, Liane called, "He wishes to see you this afternoon."

"What?" she spun. "I'm to go to his chambers tonight, but—"

"Apparently he wishes to woo you properly. You should be flattered."

"I'll have Mahri send the message that I'm too busy to be wooed," Isadora said sharply.

"You will go," Liane said, her voice sharper, less friendly than before. "Sebestyen wishes for you to befriend Lucan Hern and to listen. In the flush of his infatuation he might say something that we need to know."

"You wish me to spy, I know. Is tonight not soon enough? I have mending and alterations to see to today."

"We have seamstresses to see to the alterations, Isadora. Your job is to keep an eye on Hern." The empress lifted a pale, slender hand. "Seduce him, Isadora, night after night after night. Enjoy. Listen. Remember. Last night you left his room quite early, I hear. Eventually you will want to spend the night in his bed. Some men talk in their sleep, and—"

"I have no desire to sleep at Lucan Hern's side."

Liane's features hardened. Pregnant and all but helpless or not, she could be a fierce and formidable woman. "I told you months ago that I did not know how long I could keep you alive. I did my part. Now it's your turn."

* * *

LUCAN FOLLOWED BEHIND AN INFURIATED ISADORA AS she stalked down the wide corridor of Level Eight. Her pale green gown looked perfectly suited to a cold day—not that she was at all cool—and the skirts of that gown swished with the full force of her swagger. His eyes fell to her backside, which was too well hidden in the folds of fabric. He knew that backside to be firm and shapely, and he wished to see it again. Now.

The palace artists and entertainers lived and worked here on this Level, and several rooms of paintings and sculpture had been put on display for palace residents and guests. When he'd invited Isadora to join him for a tour of this Level, he had not expected such a violent response. Of course, he *should* have.

"It is perfectly reasonable for a man to ask permission to call upon his mistress, even in the middle of the day."

"I feel quite certain you have never asked permission to do anything," she responded hotly. "You demand, you push, and you take."

In two long strides, he had caught up with her. He grabbed her arm and spun her around. There were residents of this Level in the corridor, all of them briskly on their way somewhere else, but they very blatantly ignored the scene.

"I did not *take* last night," he said in a soft but stern voice.

She looked him in the eye, strong and unafraid. He had never before known a woman who was so incredibly unafraid. "Didn't you?" she whispered.

In that instant, he saw something besides Isadora's strength. Something he'd rather not see. Whether it was a touch of the wizards' magic or simple instinct that struck him with the knowledge, he couldn't be sure, but as he looked into her eyes he *knew*.

"You are still in love with your husband."

Isadora was so fearless, he was unprepared for the tears that sprang to her eyes. "You don't have the right to speak of him."

He raked a thumb across her soft cheek. "I understand he's been gone for several years. Is that not correct?"

"I told you, you have no right—"

"It's you who concerns me, Isadora. Not him."

Her lips thinned, and she was trying so very hard not to cry. "He's been gone more than six years."

"And how many lovers have you taken since his death?" He knew the answer before Isadora spoke, and it pained him more deeply than it should.

"None," she whispered. The tears that had threatened were gone, forced away by a strong will and an even stronger heart. "I had planned to live the rest of my life faithful to him, but you had other plans for me, didn't you?"

"If I had known—"

"You didn't ask, so you could not possibly have known," she snapped. "You have no concern for anyone's feelings but your own. *You* want, *you* need, *you* desire . . . Nothing else matters in your world."

He leaned down and kissed her forehead. It was an undemanding and almost friendly kiss. "If you had passed into the land of the dead first, and your husband was fated to live many years without you, would you have wanted him to live the rest of his days without a woman in his life?"

Isadora twitched, startled by the question. "That's not . . . it's different. And I told you, you have no right to talk about Willym."

Willym. A strong, common name, spoken with passion. "Fine. I will say one thing, and then we will not discuss him again." He dipped down and placed his mouth near her ear. "If your Willym loved you, he would not want you to live the rest of your days without touch, without pleasure, without affection."

"Perhaps not," she conceded, her voice as low as his and just as bold. "But I doubt he would want me to partake of those precious things with a man I do not even *like*."

Lucan drew away a little, so he could see her face well to discern if she was teasing or not. She was not. Women *always* liked him. Not that he'd had many dealings with females in his position in the Circle, but there were strong and beautiful women available for sexual relations, and there were cooks and seamstresses and maids. They all *liked* him.

But he had never had anyone like Isadora in his life.

In spite of her strength and her stubbornness and her beauty, she was a woman like all others, and before he left this place she would like him, very well.

He took her right hand and raised it, kissed the knuckles gently, and touched the ring . . . the Star of Bacwyr. "You always wear this stunning ring. Does it have some significance to you? Was it a gift from someone special?" From her husband, perhaps, who might not have been so ordinary after all?

She yanked her hand from his grasp. "The ring was a gift from Empress Liane, and I wear it always because it's *stuck* on my finger."

It was not the answer he had expected from her. He blinked quickly. "Stuck?"

She wiggled her fingers at him. "Stuck. I've tried soap, lotions, and sheer muscle, and the ring refuses to budge."

"It's a very interesting and different piece."

Isadora scoffed at his admiration. "I'm so glad you like it. If you can get the blasted thing off without cutting off my finger, you can have it."

Just like that, so very easily and nonchalantly, the ring was offered to him. The ring and all that came with it. Power. Responsibility. The position of Prince of Swords. He grasped the ring and tugged, and sure enough it was stubbornly wedged on Isadora's slender finger. It did not move, but neither did it fit her finger so tightly it was binding. He would think the circumstance odd if he did not see the magic around the ring and the woman who wore it.

After a moment, he gave up the task. The Star of Bacwyr was not going to slip into his hand here and now, that much was clear. "Tonight, we will try again," he said as he took Isadora's arm and led her toward the room where a number of paintings of the Beckyt family, past and present, were on display.

THEY GREW NEARER THE CAPITAL CITY OF ARTHES AND the battles to come, but they moved too slowly. Sophie was anxious. The answers to her questions about Juliet and Isadora awaited in that city, and yet it seemed that everything and everyone hindered their progress as they made their way there.

The rebels grew more and stronger with every passing day, and she understood that until Arik believed with all his heart that his army could take the palace, they would not move in that direction. She had been trying to convince him that a spring attack would be better than the summer siege he estimated. Her own powers would be much stronger before the new baby's birth. After that . . . she would still possess magic, but it would not be so powerful.

She wanted to have every advantage when Kane went into the palace, as she was certain he would.

Sophie had almost given up on trying to end the curse that would take Kane's life by the end of summer. She'd tried, again and again, but she could not do it on her own; she knew that without a doubt. Juliet and Isadora would be necessary . . . if the curse could be broken at all. Some days, she wondered if she was kidding herself in believing that was possible.

This afternoon, she and Kane sat in Arik's tent, along with several of the leaders of the revolution. They were soldiers all, like her husband, but she did not sense goodness in each and every one of them, as she did in Kane. Some were ambitious, some bitter, some noble.

All of them were anxious to see this revolution done. Sebestyen would be ousted, and Arik would take his place. Then, maybe, she and her family would know peace once again.

Myls, a soldier who had been with Arik from the beginning, had recently rejoined the leader of the revolution— and their next emperor. He spoke in a solemn voice. "A highly placed representative of the Circle of Bacwyr is living in the imperial palace at this very moment. The First Captain," he added solemnly. "Lucan Hern."

"The warriors I met with have all but promised to support my cause," Arik argued.

"But they have not pledged you anything, have they?" Myls argued. "The Circle will not divide its warriors. They will take one side or another—the First Captain will choose—and when that is done, the battle will be decided."

"They might decide not to choose a side at all," Sophie said.

All the men looked at her. Many of them did not like

allowing a woman to have such a high place among them. Others respected who she was and what she could do.

Myls did not like her very much.

"We will know soon enough."

"How?" she asked, when no one else would. "How will we know when the decision is made?"

Myls grinned at her. It was the first time she had ever seen him smile, and he did not do it well. "I have a spy in the palace."

6

ISADORA ALMOST EXPECTED TO FIND HERN NAKED, WAITing impatiently for her in his bed, when she was once again escorted to his room. Not that she would mind seeing him naked again, if she were to be completely honest with herself. No man could be as flawless as she remembered; no man could be built so perfectly. Lucan Hern was most definitely *not* perfect.

Tonight she had not even been served supper before the sentinels arrived at her small room to escort her to Level Four. As if it wasn't difficult enough to face the infuriating man, now she had to do so on an empty stomach. Mahri had been there to help Isadora dress in something more fitting for the evening, though she'd refused the initial offer of one of Liane's castoffs. The simply cut pale gray gown she'd decided upon had a low neckline to which Isadora was not accustomed, but at least it didn't plunge past the valley of her breasts as many of Liane's frocks did. As it was, she kept tugging on the neckline, hoping to make it more suitable. Her efforts did not help matters at all. Isadora did not have Liane's curves, but she didn't care for displaying what little she did have . . . especially where Captain Hern was concerned.

As she made the too-short trip from her room to Hern's, Isadora resolved not to respond to his touch in any way. She would not cry and beg him not to touch her, but neither would she allow herself to enjoy what he offered. No matter what that might be.

Again tonight, he seemed to know she was approaching before the sentinel knocked on his door. It opened almost immediately. In spite of her musings, he was not naked, but once again wore one of his purple robes. He took her hand and drew her into the room, and the guards took up their stations outside the door, where they would remain until Captain Hern was finished with her.

Because she was hungry, she immediately noted the aroma that filled the room. Not incense or scented candles or oils, not tonight. Tonight, she smelled food.

"I thought we might dine together." Hern took her arm and led her to the table for two that had been placed just a few feet from the end of the bed. Matching chairs faced one another, and the small table was laden with an abundance of food. Her stomach growled. So much for not enjoying anything he offered.

Even though he once again wore the purple robe, he did not insist that she change clothes, as he had last night. He held a chair out for her, and she sat. He sat across the table from her and poured them both a glass of wine.

Hungry as she was, Isadora studied the meal with suspicion. "Is it drugged?"

"No."

She looked him squarely in the eye. "Why should I believe you?"

"Because I do not lie."

"A man who does not lie." Isadora grinned. "I did not think such a creature existed."

He did not take offense. "I might not always tell you everything that's in my mind, but I will never lie. Honesty is one of the teachings of the Circle of Bacwyr. It is expected of all warriors." He lifted his own glass of wine. "What of you, Isadora?"

She lifted her own glass. "Deception is sometimes necessary in order to survive."

"Deception is never necessary; it is just often easier than the truth."

"I've never been one for taking the easy way out, but neither do I purposely choose the most difficult path."

His grin was startling, the dimple in his manly cheek oddly appealing. "Most women would've simply agreed with me that honesty is always best."

"And in doing so, they'd be telling you the first of many falsehoods."

"So you *do* tell the truth?"

"When it suits me."

It was unlikely that he would poison her, not when he was so obviously doing his best to impress. She ate, and so did he. She waited for the effects of some sort of potion—something to arouse or befuddle—but she remained clearheaded and determined not to enjoy anything this man had planned for her tonight. Except the fine meal, of course.

His manservant arrived to clear away the remains of the meal. Franco never looked at her, not directly, but if she was not mistaken, he did study her out of the corner of his eye in the brief time he was in the room. Mahri found the young servant handsome and charming, but to Isadora he was just another man. If he toyed with Mahri, she would . . . Isadora glanced away from the servant. She'd do what? Kill him? She couldn't do that, not unless she decided to embrace the dark side of her powers and leave the light behind. All she could do was warn Mahri that love was a curse for every woman, not just the Fyne witches, and she must always proceed with caution where the opposite sex was concerned.

She was quite sure the naive Mahri did not know caution, especially not where matters of the heart—or of the body—were concerned.

After Franco departed, Isadora straightened her spine and waited for Hern's command. She didn't have long to wait.

"Sit," he said, leading her to a short sofa that was placed against one wall. Since it was a harmless command, she did as he asked. Of course, he sat beside her, and one long arm draped over her shoulder. Isadora stiffened, determined not to encourage him in any way. She did not want to enjoy any of this, but she did like the feel of his heavy arm across her shoulder and his warm body next to hers. There was a tightening response low in her belly, and she closed her eyes and did her best to chase it away.

He lifted her right hand, studied the ring on her middle finger, and then without warning slipped the tip of that finger into his mouth. That action did nothing to ease her discomfort, especially when he drew in his breath and tenderly sucked. Her heart lurched and her knees trembled, but she did not yank her hand away, as she could have. Hern eventually extracted her finger from his warm mouth. He kissed his way down the finger, kissed the base where her finger joined palm, and then he very gently tried to slip the ring off. As always, it remained solidly and steadfastly in place.

The failed attempt to remove the ring ended with a kiss on her palm, and Hern released her hand.

"Do you have any family other than the empress?" he asked, his tone conversational.

"What?"

"Family. Brothers, sisters, parents, children . . ."

"I know what family is," she snapped. "I'm just not sure why you asked such a personal question."

"I'm curious," he said.

Conversation was not something she had prepared herself for this evening. "I have two sisters," she said tersely.

"Are you close to them?"

Her heart reacted to the question with a lurch. "I once was. Lately, circumstances have torn us apart."

"Where are they now?"

"I don't know," she whispered.

The hand in her hair was comforting and friendly, nothing more.

"What about you?" she asked, anxious to change the subject. "Do you have family other than your brother Esmun?"

"Parents, both living and healthy, two other brothers, and three sisters, all younger than I. There are a few nieces and nephews, as well."

"Are you close to them?"

"No. I went to the Circle when I was six years old, and—"

"Six?" Isadora leaned forward slightly. "Your parents sent you away when you were *six*? That's not right." If she had given birth to Will's child, she would never have sent her away. Sophie would certainly never allow Ariana to be given to strangers to be raised. It didn't seem at all natural to send one's child away from home at such a young age.

Hern gently pulled her back against the sofa and his arm. "There is no need to be indignant on my behalf."

"I'm not indignant on your behalf," Isadora said harshly.

"My parents did not send me away," he explained. "I was chosen, as all Circle warriors are chosen."

"Chosen how?" She should not be curious, but she was.

"By wizards and warriors and instructors. They visit each of the clans every two years or so and choose those boys who are destined to be Circle warriors and wizards."

"At the age of six, they took you from your family in order to make you a soldier," she said, horrified.

"The Circle became my family," he countered.

"No wonder you and your brother Esmun are not close." She found herself growing comfortable so close to Hern. His arm cradled her, and she could not make herself pull away. "You barely know one another."

"I was allowed to visit my family every year." He sounded as if he believed that sufficient.

"I have been apart from my sisters for a few months, and it feels like a lifetime. I can't imagine only seeing them once a year." She didn't allow herself to think overly often on how desperately she missed her sisters. She did not believe that Juliet was dead, no matter what Bors had told the emperor, and she knew Sophie's Kane would protect her with his life.

But she also knew, deep inside, that nothing would ever be as it had once been, no matter how she wished it to be so. She was facing a life of loneliness, something she had never imagined for herself.

"Why are you wasting your time talking to me?" she asked sharply.

"I don't feel that talking to you is a waste of my time."

"You know what I mean, Captain Hern."

He pulled her slightly closer, so that she was caught up tightly against his side.

"I would like for you to call me Lucan."

"Why?"

"It is my name, Isadora."

She already felt too close to this man. Anything more familiar would not be a good thing. Not for her. "I prefer to call you Captain Hern. It helps to remind me why I'm here."

"Why are you so difficult? I only want you to like me."

"All the conversation in the world won't make that wish come true," she responded.

"Really." He did not sound at all convinced.

"Just because you feed me and talk to me, that doesn't change the fact that I was ordered to be here."

"An insignificant detail," he said.

"Insignificant for you, perhaps, but not for me."

"Last night you did not seem to mind being here."

"This is not last night," she responded in a stern voice.

"Perhaps it will be even better."

"Unlikely."

"You might not believe it to be possible, but what is to be between us can be even more pleasurable than—"

"That's not what I meant." She snapped her head around to glare at Hern, and he took the opportunity to lay his mouth over hers. He kissed her, and after the initial shock faded, she kissed him back.

The kiss melted her. Body and heart and soul, she felt as if she were dissolving in his arms. Their mouths were fused, and their tongues danced, and no matter how staunchly she wanted to feel nothing . . . she felt so much.

For a while they simply kissed. Hern held her close. His large and capable hands cupped her face and held her head, but not too tightly. Not with demand, but with a gentle passion. She reached up, grasped the back of his neck, and pulled him tighter against her mouth as if she couldn't get enough. They shifted their heads and their bodies as they kissed, in order to be closer. Ever, ever closer.

She had forgotten how a kiss alone was enough to spark her deepest longings, her most ardent feminine needs. Mouth to mouth called up such simple and strong pleasures. She liked it, and Hern also seemed to enjoy the kissing well enough. He did not stop for the conversation he said he wanted. He did not even pause in kissing her but claimed her mouth entirely.

He had proclaimed himself to be an honest and honorable man, and she knew that if she told him to stop, he would. If she ordered him to cease kissing her, he would. But she did not want him to stop. The time to pull away would come soon enough . . . but that time was not now.

One large, masculine hand found its way beyond the low neckline of her borrowed gown, and fingers teased the soft flesh there. Isadora's heart raced, and she found herself undulating against Hern's body, pressing her body to his. She could not get near enough, and the dress bound her everywhere and kept her from being truly close to the man who kissed and caressed her.

The kissing continued, growing more intense with every heartbeat that passed. She was fused to the man who had chosen her, linked by mouth and by need. Like it or not, she wanted Hern. Naked, on top of her, inside her . . . she wanted him so badly she ached to the pit of her soul.

No, this wanting was not of the soul, it was entirely of the body. Nothing more. Nothing deeper.

His wandering fingers met resistance. "You are wearing one of those blasted contraptions that binds your breasts," he whispered against her mouth.

"Yes," she said breathlessly.

Out of nowhere he produced a sharp knife. He neatly ripped the bodice of her gown from neckline to waist, and next he neatly shredded the detested undergarment. He folded the fabric back and revealed her bare breasts.

"You have ruined this gown," she said without rancor as he lowered his head to kiss the exposed flesh.

"I will have another gown made to take its place. A better one."

Isadora closed her eyes. She didn't care about the dress, which she had never wanted to wear in the first place. Maybe later she would feel some concern, but now . . . she only cared about the way Hern's mouth moved over her skin and the intense response of her body.

For some things he had no patience, but when he aroused her this way, he seemed to have an abundance. Lips, tongue, teeth . . . they moved with precision over her breasts, her throat, and the flesh above her heart. When he drew a nipple deep into his mouth, her back arched and she almost came off the couch, which she now seemed to be reclining more than sitting upon.

He brought his mouth back to hers and kissed her more deeply than before. She grasped the back of his neck and held him there, while her body undulated against his, her bare flesh rubbing against the soft fabric of his purple robe. "Now do you like me?" he asked in a raspy voice.

"No," she whispered.

"Pity." The knife was in his hand again, and he finished the job he'd started at the bodice, slicing the gown from waist to hem, and letting the ruined garment fall away from her mostly bare body. A portion of the undergarment remained, more off than on.

Hern spread her trembling legs, and Isadora let her head fall back. She closed her eyes and waited for the joining that was to come. By the moon and the stars, she did want him. Her body wanted his, at least. Last night's release had been marvelous, but it hadn't been enough. She had departed this room fulfilled in one way but deeply yearning in another. Tonight she wanted all of him, and she wanted him now.

He lifted one leg and kissed the back of her knee, and the resulting unexpected jolt of pleasure shot through her body and made her quiver to her bones. The next kiss was on her inner thigh, where the flesh was soft and sensitive and untouched. He kissed his way up her leg, and then he placed his mouth on her, and his tongue flickered.

He aroused her that way, with flicks of his tongue and a dance of his lips that had her swaying against him in a demanding rhythm. She wanted to hold Hern; she wanted his weight upon her. But she lay upon the sofa with cool air on her heated skin and Hern's attentions focused upon her very intently and specifically, in a way she had never imagined.

There were so many things she wanted to say to him, but words would not come. *Thoughts* would not come. She couldn't think of anything but the sensations he aroused, until a quick and powerful orgasm made her soar and scream.

As she melted into the couch, sated and boneless, Hern's hands raked up her body once again. He remained fully dressed, though she didn't imagine that state would last much longer. She'd had her pleasure, and now he'd expect his own.

She wanted it, more than she'd ever admit. She wanted the weight of his body atop hers, and the sensation of joining, and the feel of his sweat and desire on her own naked body. It was time to properly finish what had only begun.

Hern slowly kissed his way up her torso and ended the trip with a long and lingering kiss on her throat. Isadora closed her eyes, and one leg rose up to rest on his hip. Close, so close.

"You can wear the purple robe I had made for you back

to your room," he said. "It would not do for you to be seen walking the corridors of the palace in the rag we have made of your gown."

He left her abruptly, and she sat up, moving slowly, since the release had apparently dulled her mind . . . or her hearing. "You're finished with me?" Again?

Hern returned to her with the robe the emperor's seamstress had so hurriedly made for Isadora, and handed the soft garment to her in a gentlemanly and polite manner, as if he hadn't just had his head between her legs. As if he hadn't made her scream. As if he had not stolen her very thoughts.

"As I told you last night, I will wait for you to invite me for more."

"What if I never invite you?"

"Then I will likely die," he teased. "A man cannot live in this state forever."

Isadora slipped her arms into the warm robe and hugged it to her body without fastening the buttons. She wasn't yet ready for the complexity of buttons. "You could ask for another woman," she suggested.

"No. You are the only woman in this palace who was meant for me. I will wait for your invitation. One of the attributes the warriors of the Circle are taught is control."

Isadora stood slowly. "If you're willing to wait for me to come to you, then why . . . last night and tonight . . . why do you . . ."

"Why do I make you climax when I deny myself?"

"Yes," she whispered.

"Because your pleasure is my pleasure. Because to touch and feel and watch you as you scream and tremble is almost enough to satisfy me. Almost," he repeated, again with that trace of humor. "I am learning you, Isadora."

"What do you mean, you're *learning* me?"

"You make a little noise deep in your throat when we kiss, and your strong legs quiver just before you find fulfillment. You react very strongly to some stimuli, and not at all to others." He cocked his head and looked at her as if he were learning her as he spoke. "While I have found some of your most wonderfully sensitive areas, I do not believe I have yet found them all. Some things are worth waiting for, Isadora. To be inside you in all ways, to be *invited*, that is worth waiting for."

She studied his face, searching for the lie, but she only saw the honesty he claimed to possess.

Dammit, she could like him, very easily.

Isadora buttoned the robe and ran her fingers through her hair. When had he taken it down? She did not remember, but then much of their time on the sofa was a blur to her. She remembered sensation and need, and nothing more.

"Do you have plans for tomorrow?" she asked.

"I am to meet my brother to discuss his desire to marry."

"You have not yet decided to give your consent?"

"His chosen bride is a concubine," he said. "She has given herself freely to many men before, and perhaps after Esmun. I do not believe she is worthy."

"I didn't believe Esmun was worthy of *her*." Isadora walked to the door. "But I saw them in the hallway yesterday, and it seems that he loves her very much, and she loves him."

He reached past her to open the door, and the surprised sentinels snapped to attention.

Hern lifted her hand to his lips, and as he lowered and released it he said, "There is no woman such as this one in all of Tryfyn. A country that is home to such rare and passionate beauty is blessed, indeed."

* * *

LUCAN DID TWO HOURS OF EVENING EXERCISE AFTER Isadora left him, rather than the usual one, trying to work off his frustration. The *hroryk elde* had always centered him in times of trouble, but tonight he remained distracted. When that was done, he bathed, polished his knives and swords—all of them—and tried a quiet meditation. The evening rituals he practiced had been a part of his life since the age of six, but tonight his mind would not be still long enough to achieve even a moment's peace. He finally crawled into bed, knowing sleep would not come easily tonight—if at all.

It was the woman, not the ring, that preyed on his mind and made his thoughts spin. The ring was an object, a thing of power, the reason for his presence in this palace, and it was important. It was very important to who he was meant to be, and to his country and the Circle.

But Isadora was an enigma, and that was where his rambling thoughts took him. His thoughts went to *her*. She claimed not to like him or want his attentions, and yet when he touched her, she responded with an intensity he had never before seen in a woman. She was more intelligent than the other females he'd known in his lifetime, hardheaded and difficult and strong to the point of being hard . . . and yet she sometimes held him with an unexpected gentleness, and when she had told him that Esmun and his Elya were in love, there had been a true tenderness in her eyes, as if she understood love too well.

She apparently saved none of her tenderness for him, however. He couldn't even charm her into admitting that she liked him a little bit. Even if she did like him, she would likely not tell him so. She was just stubborn enough to keep that information to herself.

What would it be like to possess such a woman in body and heart and soul? How powerful and difficult would such a connection be? He pitied the man who fell under Isadora's spell. A lifetime with such an incredible woman would not be easy. Then again, nothing worth having came easily.

As he had suspected, sleep did not come to him, as usual. Just as well. He could only imagine where his dreams would take him tonight.

The door to his room was securely locked, and Franco had retired hours ago, and still, Lucan was suddenly sure that he was not alone. He reached for the knife beneath his pillow and turned in the bed so that he could see the room. No candles burned, but a trace of moonlight shone through the window so he could see the figure moving silently toward him.

Lucan relaxed and released his hold on the hilt of the knife, after returning it to its place. He would recognize the sway of those hips anywhere. Even in the dark.

"How did you get into this room?" he asked in a whisper.

"I'm here," she answered in a soft voice. "The why and how can wait."

"Yes, I suppose it can."

Isadora came to the side of his bed. She stood there for a moment and then, without saying another word, she began to unfasten the buttons of her robe.

He lifted the coverlet and invited her in, and she crawled into the bed and rested the length of her body aside his.

"You sleep naked," she said as her hand found and caressed his hip.

"Yes."

She pressed her tender mouth against his throat and kissed him there, and then she rose up to look down at him. Right before she kissed him on the mouth, she whispered, "That's good."

7

Isadora pressed the length of her body to Hern's, closing her eyes as she drank in the sensation of being flesh to flesh beneath the covers on a crisp, cool night.

Last night when she'd left this room and gone to her own she'd slept so very well. Tonight she'd been unable to so much as lie down. She'd paced, she'd talked to herself, she'd even come close to tears.

Like it or not, she needed this; she needed Hern. And she was a fully grown woman unafraid to take what she wanted.

She put one arm around him and raked her hand down his spine. The man had a well-shaped back, a dip at the waist, firm, strong hips, muscular thighs. There was no softness about him, no hint of tenderness on his body. He was all male, with a masculine hardness that called to her. She let her fingers brush against the length of his erection, and her body trembled from head to toe at the thought of that shaft pushing inside her. It was that thought which had kept her from sleep tonight. It was that thought which had called her here.

"You have no scars," she whispered as her hands continued to explore his flesh.

"No."

"A warrior with no scars. How is that possible?"

"When it comes to battle, no man touches me."

While she learned his hard planes, he caressed her soft curves. But as they had been spiraling toward this moment for more than one full day, they did not explore for very long.

She wrapped her leg around Hern's hip, instinctively trying to bring him closer. He rolled her onto her back and spread her legs, and then he guided himself to her, and the thoughts that had kept her awake and brought her to his bed became reality.

Isadora did not think while he made love to her. Instead she let her instincts and her body rule completely. Their hips moved in an easy rhythm, and nothing else mattered. Nothing. She grasped the sheet in tight fists and then reached up to hold him with her arms as well as her legs. He moved faster, and she gasped. He drove deep, and she shattered. She cried out as the force of the orgasm whipped through her body, and then she felt it . . . Hern's release as his body stiffened and the liquid of life pumped into her welcoming body.

He remained cradled inside her for a long moment, while they both regained their breath and heartbeats returned to somewhere near normal. Then he rolled off of her, though he did keep his arms around her.

"I had begun to think you would never come to me," he said breathlessly.

"I hadn't planned to," Isadora began, "and even when I accepted that I wanted this . . ."

"Even then?" Hern prompted when she faltered.

"I did not want to come to this room, to you, in the company of an armed sentinel. I decided that if I were to come of my own free will, then the time and the coming would be truly of my own choosing."

He rose up on one elbow and looked down at her. "How did you get in?"

"Secret passageway," she answered.

His alarm was natural . . . and apparent. "You must show me."

She reached up and touched a black curl that brushed his face. "Later. You needn't worry about anyone else coming into the room that way. Only a small handful of palace residents know of the passageways. To ease your mind, and mine, I wedged a piece of wood into a crack in the stone to hold the door shut."

Even in the dark, she could see him smile. "Very good. So, now do you like me?"

"No," she whispered.

"Why not?"

Hern wanted the truth, and so she gave it to him. This time. "I cannot afford to like you."

He considered her answer for a moment, then dismissed the matter. "You will spend the night here?"

"No." She closed her eyes and snuggled against him. "But I will stay for a while." She wasn't ready to give up this feeling. Sex was only a part of what she craved. The holding, the flesh to flesh, she craved that sensation almost as much as she had craved the feel of Hern's body joined to hers. "I do not like you, and I certainly do not love you."

"I never asked about love, Isadora. That's not what I want from you."

"That's good, because I have none to give." Love was the greatest weakness of all, and she would not fall into that trap again. Not ever. "I will be your mistress for as long as you are living in this palace, or until you grow weary of me." Now that Lucan had gotten what he'd wanted all along, was he already tired of her? She hoped not, since she was not yet tired of him.

"I cannot imagine any man ever growing weary of you in his bed." With that, he gathered her into his arms and pulled her body against his, and within moments he was asleep.

She was not sorry that she'd decided to give Lucan Hern what he wanted, and she did not regret the decision to be his mistress. She was beholden to no one, and only the possibility of a child could stop her. The Circle wizards had told Hern his first son would be born in two years. Since the Fyne women did not bear sons, then some other woman would be in his bed a year from now.

Isadora suspected she could not have a child, not without Sophie's assistance. She and Will had been married two years, and they'd wanted children . . . they'd tried. Sophie's gift of fertility had not yet been discovered, so they had not been able to call upon that magic. She didn't know if it was Will who had been unable to have a child, or if it was her, but . . .

She hated thinking of Will while another man held her in his arms, but she did not cry. The time for crying was past.

The girl who had loved Willym had been gone a very long time. The woman who remained didn't want love and the complications that came with it, but heaven help her— she wanted more of the way this man made her feel.

What she felt and what she wanted wasn't love, and it couldn't ever be. But it was right for the woman she had become. For now.

* * *

He had never slept with a woman before. Those who came to him for sex never stayed after the act was done.

But it was nice to wake and find Isadora's spine pressed against his chest. It was nice to find his arms so comfortably draped around her warm softness. He liked the feel of her skin against his, the even way she breathed in sleep, the gentle rise and fall of her chest.

The sky beyond the window was barely gray. Morning was coming and with it the responsibilities that had brought him here: the Star, Esmun, his pledge to the Circle of Bacwyr.

But right now he did not think of any of those duties.

He shifted Isadora's hair aside and kissed the back of her neck. She squirmed but did not wake. He kissed his way very slowly down her spine, allowing his lips to trail along the soft, silky flesh of her back. When she woke he felt it in the way her breathing shifted and the sway of her backside against him.

"Are you awake?" he whispered.

"No." Her voice was sleepy, satisfied.

"Pity." He continued to kiss his way down her spine until he reached the shapely small of her back—and there he lingered. "If you were awake, there are other things we could do."

"What other things?" she asked, sounding slightly more awake.

He reached around her bare and beautiful body and slipped his fingers between her legs, while he worked his way back up her spine again with feathered kisses. "Do you know I have been hard more often than not since I first saw you?"

"No, I did not know." She laughed airily, and her legs fell slightly apart so he had greater access. While he caressed

Isadora she grew wet, and her body began to rock gently back and forth, as if he were already inside her.

"It is true," he said. "You know I will not lie. When I saw you at the emperor's table that first night, when I opened my eyes and found you standing over my bath, when you told me that you did not like me . . . always."

She reached around, pressed her hand against his stomach, and let her hand fall gently and slowly downward, until she could see for herself that he was telling the truth.

"But you are a man of great control," she said, throwing his own words back at him as her fingers circled his erection.

"Yes, but I am also human, Isadora." At the moment he felt more human than he ever had before, more vulnerable. He needed this woman.

She turned to face him and brought her lips to his for a long, deep kiss. There was a touch of desperation in that kiss. Passion and yielding and even a hint of something he did not quite grasp. Sadness, perhaps, or regret, though he did not feel regret in her body. Still kissing, Isadora continued to roll until Lucan was on his back and she hovered above him, kissing and caressing and taking command. Interesting.

She straddled him, still kissing, and guided him into her body. She moved slowly, deliberately, sinking down an inch at a time until he was buried deep within her. She remained there as they kissed, making only the smallest of movements. It was the kind of motion that could drive a man wild. And did.

Eventually her movements grew faster and greater, until she stopped kissing him and sat up tall so that he was deeper within her than before. There was some morning light, which kept the room from complete darkness, so he could see her much more clearly than he had last night.

Every curve of her face and feminine angle of her body was pronounced in the gray light, and the sway of her soft hair was sensual and free. She had come to him of her own free will, and that made this night more precious than he had thought possible.

She possessed such power, such intense feminine energy.

As she rode him, Isadora kept her eyes on his face. Such dark eyes, so expressive and strong. It was only when she experienced release that she closed those eyes. She trembled around and above him, she moaned and gave a small, sharp cry. While she still pulsed around him, Lucan pushed up and into her and found his own release.

It was all he wanted from her, everything he required. And more.

Isadora drifted down, kissed him again, and whispered, "I must go now."

"Why?"

She smiled at him, though as usual it seemed a sad smile. "I cannot stay in your bed all day."

"Why not?"

"That's not who I am."

It was true enough. Isadora was not a woman to be commanded to a man's bed . . . though that's just what he had done.

"Do you know how to fight?"

She rolled off of him but looked back as she sat on the edge of the bed. "Fight?"

"With a sword."

She shuddered slightly and tried to hide the response. "Of course not."

He sat behind her and wrapped his arms around her waist. She was afraid of the power of deadly weapons, as a proper woman should be. Still, war was coming, and if she was to protect herself she would need to know.

"I will teach you, while I'm here."

It seemed she trembled more deeply than before. "I don't wish to kill anyone."

Of course she didn't. In spite of her evident strength, she was a gentle woman. "I can teach you to defend yourself. That doesn't mean you have to kill."

"Why?" she asked again.

He moved her hair aside and kissed her shoulder. "So that if any man ever dares again to order you to his bed, you can say no with confidence."

"Saying no did me no good with you, Lucan Hern."

Again he kissed her shoulder. It was so well-shaped and pale and fine. "Since the age of nine, I have been given all that I desire without question. I suppose that makes me . . ." He hesitated, uncertain.

"Spoiled," Isadora supplied with a touch of humor in her voice. "Obnoxious. Demanding."

He hauled her back and gently pinned her to the bed. "You find me obnoxious?"

She smiled gently. "Sometimes."

"Do you know what I find you?" Still pinning her down, he bent his head to kiss her throat.

"What?" she asked gently.

"Fascinating." His lips moved lower. "Beautiful. Magnificent." She was all that, and more. When he moved his mouth to a taut nipple, Isadora tangled her fingers in his hair and held on. It wasn't until he felt the metal of her ring pressing against his head that he remembered why he had ordered her to his bed in the first place.

He sat up reluctantly. "I will escort you to your room."

"That isn't necessary. I'll take the hidden stairway."

"All the more reason for me to go with you. I should like to know the way."

"The passageways within the walls are musty and dirty,

and there are spiderwebs everywhere. The way is certainly not fit for a man of your station."

She was teasing him, but he replied honestly, "If the stairway is fit for you, then it is more than suitable for me."

THERE WERE HIDDEN STAIRWAYS AND DOORS WITHIN other hidden stairways, proof that whichever of Emperor Sebestyen's ancestors had overseen the construction of this portion of the palace had been just as mistrustful as the current emperor.

Isadora led Hern up the narrow stairwell, a candle in one hand and the other resting lightly against the cool, curving stone wall.

Liane had gladly given Isadora precise directions to Captain Hern's chambers. Her smile had been wide and true as she'd delivered the careful instructions. This was what she wanted, after all. Isadora had taken a lover, and with that taking Will had been firmly put into the past, where he belonged. It was sad to leave that part of her life behind, but at the same time she felt invigorated. Isadora was no longer a prisoner of the past; she was no longer bound by a love that had done nothing but hurt her.

Yes, Liane had gotten what she wanted. There would be no sharing of details, however. In that respect the empress would have to remain disappointed.

Isadora was very sure the emperor would prefer that their guest remain ignorant of the secret passageways, which could very well lead an assassin to his bedside, but she was not about to hide the way from him. There were so many twists and turns, it would be impossible for him to find his way to any room of importance. Her room was of no importance at all, and there were no hidden doorways between her chamber and his. Just a few twists and turns.

"I do not know why you feel you must return to your own room," Hern said softly. His voice echoed, as hers did when she answered.

"I have duties. The empress needs me."

"The empress can find someone else to tend to her while I am here. I need you more than she does." He sounded puzzled, and she wondered if he had ever in his life needed anyone.

"It is my duty."

Isadora thought of the emperor's words about what might happen to Liane and the babies if the palace was attacked. She could not imagine that anyone would harm innocents. She had defended herself in the past, she had fought for her life, and she had killed. But she was not a soldier, and she did not understand how they thought during combat.

As she reached the door to her chamber, she turned to face Hern. He was her lover. She still felt him inside her, and she still marveled at the pleasure he had offered her. She did not love him, thank goodness, but there was an unexpected tenderness in her heart for this man who had helped her heal in a way she had not expected.

"In battle, do you kill innocent women and children?"

"Of course not." He reached out and touched her face with tenderness. "Is that why you don't like me? You think because I'm a warrior I'm a cruel barbarian."

"No. I just worry about what will happen if war ever reaches Arthes."

"It will, I imagine. All the more reason for me to teach you to use a sword."

"If warriors don't kill innocent women and children, then why do I need a sword?" She knew the answer but needed to hear it from him.

"Not all soldiers are honorable, Isadora."

She nodded her head slightly. She knew too well that many soldiers were not at all honorable. Those who had burned her cabin certainly had no honor. "This afternoon," she said. "You can begin to teach me this afternoon, if you are available."

"Of course I am available, for you."

Her destiny was protection, and she had already learned that it wasn't always so easy as a spell or a health potion. Sometimes, in order to protect, one had to fight.

"And tonight?" she asked. He'd had her in his bed. Did he still want her there, or was his curiosity satisfied?

"Come to me, in whatever way suits you. By this hidden stairway, by armed sentinel, on the arm of the emperor himself. I don't care how you come to me, Isadora. Just come."

He stood on the step beneath her, which brought them almost face-to-face. It was nice to simply lean forward and lay her mouth on his for an all-too-brief moment. "I will, Captain," she said as she drew away.

He grabbed her arm, not too tight, but certainly with a firmness she had not expected. "Surely now you feel free to call me by my given name."

His name teased her tongue. She did enjoy the way he said her name, with just a touch of a Tryfynian accent and as if he enjoyed the taste of her name in his mouth. Still, calling him Lucan would bring them that much closer, and she knew some distance was best.

"You hesitate," he said in a low voice.

"I'm not sure I know you well enough to call you by your given name, Captain," Isadora argued.

He leaned down and kissed her throat. "Mere moments ago I was inside you. Do you still feel me there?"

"Yes," she admitted in a reluctant whisper.

"You slept in my arms, you kissed my mouth again and

again, you rode me like a tigress. And yet you say you do not *know* me?"

His scattering of kisses on her throat made her tingle from head to toe, and she closed her eyes. "I will consider your argument," she conceded.

He drew away from her reluctantly. "You have the stubbornness of a Circle warrior, Isadora." A smile barely touched his lips. "Though I have never seen a soldier near as pretty as you."

"I'll see you this afternoon," Isadora said as she opened the door to her room, handed Hern the candle he would need to find his way down the stairwell, and slipped into her own room. She closed the door, and for a moment after stood there with her hand over the cold stone of the doorway that was built into the wall.

She took a deep breath, turned . . .

And almost ran into the Emperor Sebestyen.

JULIET ROSE FROM HER PALLET AND FACED THE MORNING sun. All around her, Anwyn soldiers slept. They had not made camp until very late, so she could not wake them so early. The trip had been a long one, and they needed their rest.

There was no hurry. She was not needed in Arthes just yet.

Her beloved husband Ryn awoke and reached out to lay his hand on her belly. That roundness was covered by gold silk. As Queen, she was not only allowed to wear the golden gowns that marked her station, she was required to do so. It was not a chore, as the gowns she had brought with her were cut amply, and many were sleeveless and short, as well, to allow her skin to breathe. She had taken to the Anwyn heat quickly and could no longer endure the binding frocks she had worn all her life.

She had grown large of belly more quickly than she'd imagined was possible, but of course when she conceived this child she had not known that the Anwyn Queen's pregnancies did not last nine months, as human pregnancies did.

In less than two months, Juliet would give birth to the daughter who would one day be Queen of the Anwyn, as her mother was now Queen.

"Full moon tonight," Ryn said as he kissed her shoulder.

"Yes, I know." For the next three nights, the Anwyn would change into wolves when the sun set. It would slow down their journey considerably. It would also be the last time the change came upon them, as they were moving too far away from the mountains and The City that fed their Anwyn magic.

"Isadora needs me," she added. "She's so strong, I've never before sensed that need from her. I don't want to fail her."

"You won't."

She was not so sure. As always, where her sisters were concerned, her visions of the future were cloudy.

As they watched the sun come up, Kei—the father Juliet had not met until recently—joined them.

"I don't care if you are a King," Kei said gruffly, "get your hands off of my daughter."

Ryn was wonderfully good tempered and did not take offense. Besides, he was getting accustomed to his father-in-law's brusqueness. "Not just yet," he responded without anger.

Kei just snorted, and then he sat beside them. "This is not our battle we're going into, Daughter," he said with his usual lack of grace. "The Anywn have no quarrel with the emperor or the rebels. I don't care who sits on the throne of Columbyana, and neither should you."

"We're not going into battle for a throne. We're going for my sisters."

"Half sisters," Kei muttered.

"Sisters," Juliet said precisely.

Kei muttered something she could not understand.

"Did you care for my mother at all?" she asked.

Her father's head snapped around, and he glared at her with eyes almost as golden as her own. Kei was a fierce Anwyn male, a rogue who had left The City to live in the mountains. "Of course I did. She was not my mate, but if I had not cared for her, I never would have laid with her. You know that is not the Anwyn way."

Kei had never told Juliet—or anyone else—that on the night when she was conceived, Lucinda Fyne had cast a spell that made herself look and sound like the mate Kei had lost. She had not tricked him; he knew very well that it was not his mate who lay beneath him. But there had been a comfort there that he'd needed at the time. In a way, Lucinda had saved Kei that night. If not for her gift of sight, Juliet would never know the truth of what had happened.

"Yes, I know it is not the Anwyn way," she said gently. "You have the opportunity now to repay Lucinda Fyne for giving you a child, and to prove that you did care for her, by fighting for her daughters. All of them."

He did not like that contention, but he didn't argue. For now, anyway. As Kei rose he looked at Ryn again and scowled. "Can't you keep your hands off of her for the span of a few heartbeats?"

"I'd rather not," Ryn responded truthfully.

Juliet leaned against her husband and rested her hand over his . . . and over their child. "We don't have much time," she said as her father walked away. She had seen in a glorious vision that the curse would be ended, and that it would not take Ryn or Kane from the Fyne women who

loved them. And yet, all things in the future were suscepti-
ble to change. Decisions made, or not made, could alter
what was to be.

"Time enough?" Ryn asked.

A sliver of forewarning sliced through Juliet, and her
body jerked slightly. "I don't know."

8

The witch held her breath for a long, quiet moment.

Sebestyen leaned closer to Isadora. She looked freshly tumbled, and there was a flush to her cheeks that he had not seen on her before. "What do you think you're doing?"

"What you asked . . . what you ordered me to do, my lord."

He felt a potent rise of anger within him. "I told you to make yourself available to our guest in whatever way he chose, not to show him the secret passageways of the palace." She herself should not know of the passageways. Only Liane could've instructed her. More secrets shared between the two women. "To give a visiting dignitary a tour of those secret hallways is considered treason, and is certainly cause for severe punishment." Death. Level Thirteen. Imprisonment.

Isadora's cheeks paled. "My lord, you asked me not

only to lie with Captain Hern, but to earn his trust and to listen. Was I mistaken?"

"No."

"I cannot earn his trust merely by going to his bed as if I were no better than the concubine you have asked me to be."

Isadora had courage, which could be a very dangerous trait here on Level One. And yet, he did admire her bravery—foolish as it was. "What have you learned thus far?"

Again, she took a moment to consider her answer. "The opportunity for making inquiries which might be of use to you has not arisen. I must gain his trust before I am so bold."

"Surely you can offer me some information that makes your continued existence worthwhile." Isadora Fyne was not like other women. She did not wear her emotions on her face, as many females did. She was stoic, and it bothered Sebestyen that he could not read her innermost thoughts simply by looking at her face. Fear, treachery, happiness, truth. He saw none of these telling expressions.

"I can tell you what I know of his character, my lord," Isadora said. "Captain Hern is an unfailingly honest man. He seems unacquainted with intrigue and deception, preferring the brutal truth of a blade to politics. He strikes me as being a man of his word. If he makes a promise to you, he will not break it."

The report she gave was insufficient, but perhaps all she had to offer, for now.

Isadora still smelled faintly of sex, and Sebestyen closed his eyes and took a deep breath. The scent was so arousing, if he were willing to be unfaithful to Liane he'd have Isadora here and now—if he were foolish enough to touch a witch in that way.

He wasn't. And besides, he *was* faithful. It was an unexpected turn of events, to fall so deeply and completely in love with one's wife.

Apparently Isadora was doing as he had commanded, so he didn't have an excuse to kill her just yet. If Hern was besotted, she might even prove to be useful. "Anything you need in order to accomplish your duties, you need only ask, and it is yours."

Isadora lifted her chin. "Captain Hern wishes to teach me swordplay."

Sebestyen smiled. "Good. That means you have awakened his masculine protective instincts. Perhaps he will even wish to take you with him when he leaves."

"And what would you say if he asked for such permission?"

"I would say no, of course. You're mine, Isadora Fyne, and until I am finished with you, you're not going anywhere."

"Well, you needn't worry." Her voice was firm, but there was worry in her eyes. "This affair with Captain Hern is not a love match, as you well know. It's a political arrangement. It's loveless sex in exchange for the information you desire."

Sebestyen leaned in closer and closed his eyes as he inhaled deeply once again. "For all your protests, you liked it, didn't you?"

"That's none of your business," she answered crisply. "My lord," she added belatedly.

Her courage was quickly passing over into impertinent territory. He could not allow this witch, this slave, to speak to him as if she were his equal. "Watch your step, Isadora. If the man finds out what you are, he'll kill you in an instant. You've heard him speak of witches. He cares little for your kind."

"I know," she whispered.

He lifted her right hand and studied the ring there. It was a simple piece, but the stone was large. "You wear this all the time now. Do you like it so much?"

"No," she said sharply. "It's stuck on my finger."

He held her hand and studied the ring. "I believe this belongs with the rest of the imperial jewels."

"Liane gave it to me," the witch protested.

"It was not Liane's to give," Sebestyen said as he rubbed his thumb over the stone. "This ring, and the other pieces that match it, once belonged to the favored concubine of the emperor, Iola. My great-grandfather had the jewels set for her, because the blue matched her eyes. Iola always wore this ring. It didn't come off her finger until she died." Sebestyen leaned closer to the witch and lowered his voice. "The emperor had her killed when he discovered that she had betrayed him. His love for her was so great that he could not bear to do the deed himself, but after she was dead he took this ring from her finger and packed it away, along with the necklace and bracelet, and no one wore them for a very long time. My mother had a liking for blue and did not care about the sordid history of the jewels, so she wore them on occasion." He cocked his head. "What makes you think you could ever deserve the jewels that once adorned the emperor's favorite concubine . . . and my mother?"

"I will return the ring to you before I leave the palace, of course."

He smiled at Isadora. Poor, gullible girl, she still thought she might one day leave this place. "Of course you will," he said as he dropped her hand.

UNTIL SHE'D RUN INTO EMPEROR SEBESTYEN THIS morning, Isadora had been feeling very strong. Stronger than she'd felt in a long time. It was as if the light at her center had grown ten times brighter overnight. Her confrontation with the emperor had sapped that power, but as she sat in the tub of warm water, some of the power began to return. Slowly but certainly, her magic grew.

Isadora soaped her hands well and tried to remove the ring the emperor insisted belonged to him. She had no idea if the tale he'd told her about poor Iola and yet another mad emperor was true or not. She did not sense pain or blood or betrayal in the ring. In fact, it seemed to hold only positive energy. Still, one could never tell. For all she knew, Emperor Sebestyen had spun the sordid story for her benefit, to scare the ring off her finger.

What did Liane see in that terrible man? It was more than power, more than sex. The emperor and empress loved one another, without fail. Love was a strange emotion that didn't always make sense, and it had ruined many a life— including her own.

Even when her hands were wet and soapy, the ring would not budge. It was almost as if . . . she held her hand out and studied her fingers and the ring . . . as if magic of some sort held the ring in place. It was not too tight, it did not bind or squeeze her finger. Since her own magic was growing stronger, she concentrated on the ring until she saw nothing else. She took deep breaths and caught in her mind's eye the light and the brightness of her magic. And then she whispered, "Release."

Nothing happened, so she repeated the word in the ancient tongue of the wizards, a language that was almost lost to the world. *"Avar."*

The single word spoken, she was able to remove the ring with ease. It slipped so easily off her finger, it was hard to imagine that just moments ago it had refused to move.

She placed the ring in the palm of her hand. Now what? The emperor wanted the ring returned to him, and Lucan had expressed an interest in the piece. His interest had been perhaps too strong, now that she thought back on it. The ring wasn't special in any way that she could see. It was pretty, but the stone was not spectacular, and the setting was relatively plain. What did they see in this ring that made them want it?

It was old, that was true, and perhaps there was a history to the piece, but the stone was far from precious. Liane wore more valuable stones each and every day, even when confined to her bed.

The safest place for the ring was likely on her own finger, so she returned it there. Sure enough, it slipped on easily, and then once again refused to slide off.

A year ago she had been living a different life, and she had been a different person. Sophie had given birth to Ariana in the spring a year ago, and the baby's father had been thought gone forever. Juliet had been safe and happy, caring for her sisters and those women who chose to seek her herbal assistance and advice about the future.

And Isadora had lived one day to the next, not at all concerned that those days did not change. She worked on Fyne Mountain, she protected her sisters, she provided common sense when they could not see for themselves what was best. And she'd mourned. Will's spirit had visited her on occasion, then, and on many nights—cold or not— she had walked away from the cabin to seek his ghostly visitation.

Now Will was gone completely and forever, Juliet and Sophie were far away, their fates unknown to her and to one another, and Isadora was offering protection for the empress and her children, and not only sleeping in another man's bed but reveling in the physical attentions he offered her. Just a year ago, she would have thought all those things impossible.

One thing had not changed. She could not, would not,

fall in love with Lucan Hern or anyone else. The Fyne Curse had killed Will before his time. If she were to fall in love with Lucan—which she would not, she insisted to herself, not for the first time—he would not die. He was well past thirty. No, he would not die. Instead he would come to despise her. He would walk away from her and break her heart . . . not that she had much of a heart left for breaking.

Isadora pushed the men in her life, past and present, out of her mind, and sitting in the tub of quickly cooling water, she closed her eyes and found the spark of magic at her center. Yes, it had certainly grown. The spark was now a flame that burned steady and strong. She was spiraling toward her fate—destruction or protection, she still was not sure which called to her. But it did call, and as she sat in the tub she allowed the strength to grow and claim her, as it always had.

Love and the complications that arose from it were for mortals who did not know magic. Never again would she sacrifice who and what she was, who she was meant to become, for a man and the feelings he aroused. She would grow strong; she would embrace her magic once again.

Soon she would be powerful enough to make her way out of this palace, and no one would be able to stop her. No one.

LUCAN IGNORED THE FOUR GUARDS WHO HAD ACCOM-panied Isadora to the courtyard. They were alert, well armed, and vigilant. Was the emperor so concerned that something terrible might happen to his wife's cousin? Why else would Isadora rate four of the emperor's best sentinels?

Franco sat on a stool at the edge of the courtyard, looking bored. His sword was nearby, and if it came to a fight he'd be ready. Franco was always ready for a fight. The sentinels thought him to be a valet and paid him little mind.

Lucan gave Isadora his full attention, smiling at her as she acquainted herself with the sword he had chosen for her. It was short-bladed and light, but sharp, and every bit as deadly as his long sword. She hefted it this way and that and studied the swing of the blade as it cut the air before her.

For the exercise she had dressed plainly, and in blue. He liked her in blue, and he liked her hair in that long, simple braid that made her look like an ordinary woman, not an imperial cousin. She seemed more real this way, more attainable, more *his*, without the trappings of finery that were necessary for someone of her station.

He was a man accustomed to going long periods of time without sex, and yet even after last night and this morning, he wanted Isadora again. She was like a drug that had worked its way into his blood, and he craved her. Maybe Franco could lead the sentinels on a chase, leaving him and Isadora alone in the courtyard so that he could make love to her beneath the sun. He wanted to see her naked in the sunlight, he wanted to watch her face as she shuddered and cried out in fulfillment. Yes, she was like a drug, and he yearned for her. He did not *yearn* for anything, ever, and yet—

"Why are you smiling, Captain?" Isadora asked as she lowered her sword. "Did I do something to amuse you?"

"Am I smiling?"

"Yes," she answered with a wide smile of her own.

"I was just thinking," he said honestly.

"Of swords and lessons?"

"Not exactly."

Her dark eyes flashed. She knew exactly where his mind had taken him. She understood him too well, considering the short amount of time they had known one another.

He showed her how to grasp the grip, how to swing the sword with control, how to protect herself with the blade and the angle of her body. They started casually, but before long he was teaching her in earnest. The idea of Isadora being confronted in such a way that she needed these lessons angered him, and she began to listen to his instructions with sobriety; as if she, too, was wondering what it would be like to be called to fight.

Isadora learned quickly, and before long she was moving with grace and ease. The weight of the sword was not too much for her, and she was not afraid of the power of life and death that she wielded. There was some trepidation. She asked for instructions on how and where to make nonlethal blows that would stop an opponent without taking his life.

Women like Isadora should not have cause to fight, but war was coming to Arthes, and she needed to know. Lucan did not like the idea of Isadora coming face-to-face with a soldier. As the lesson continued and she grew quicker and more graceful, he could not wipe the thought from his mind. If rebels stormed the palace, one woman with one sword—no matter how well wielded—could not stop them. Especially if she refused to kill.

In that instant, he made his decision. The Circle would side with Sebestyen in this war. He and his men would keep rebels out of the palace and away from his woman.

He had never thought of a woman as his before, and the notion stopped him cold. Isadora was not the reason for his presence here, and his alliance with her would not bring peace to Tryfyn. He was simply infatuated with her because she was unlike the other women he had known. If he were not meant to be Prince of Swords he would pursue her with the same determination with which he had always fought and led and learned.

But of course, that was not to be.

"Enough for today," he said. The simple exercises had made Isadora sweat, and her breath came hard. Even though she took to the sword well, she was unaccustomed to hefting such a heavy object in her delicate hands.

She was made for finer things than this.

He sent Franco ahead to prepare his bath, and then he and Isadora walked into the palace. The sentinels followed. Three of them went to the lift. The other remained, guarding the entrance to the courtyard. There was a larger, more well-armed guard at the other entrance to the building, but this sentinel remained at the courtyard door. His eyes flitted to Isadora more than once.

The truth hit Lucan like a thunderbolt. The emperor's sentinels weren't keeping Isadora safe; they were making sure she didn't run away.

"We will take the stairs," he said, grabbing Isadora's hand and heading for the stairwell that wound up the full ten floors. Not one of the sentinels followed, confirming his suspicions. Isadora wasn't under protection, she was under guard.

Lucan walked quickly, and Isadora had to run to keep up. When they reached the landing at Level Seven, she tugged on his hand and breathlessly asked him to stop. He turned to find her leaning against the stone wall, her breath coming hard.

"We could have taken the lift," she said as he moved in to hover over her, their bodies so close he could feel the heat radiating off of her.

"I do not like the lift," he responded.

"Why not?"

"Because I do not fully understand how it operates."

"A large, noisy machine on Level Eleven powers it. Is that not enough of an explanation for you?"

"No."

"Just let me catch my breath." She closed her eyes and inhaled deeply. Her cheeks were pink, her hair mussed, her lips full and wide, and so it made perfect sense to kiss her.

His attraction to her was as puzzling as the emperor's lift. Both were new to him and not easy to define. He didn't like that which he could not fully explain. Sexual need was one matter; needing one specific woman to distraction was another entirely.

Lucan pressed his hand to Isadora's heart and felt the even, quick thud against his palm. The swordplay, the run up the stairs, and the kissing made her heart beat fast. His fingers brushed against her breast, and he felt the hardening of her nipple against his fingers. She did not wear the undergarment he despised today. There was very little between his body and hers. *Very* little.

For a while the kissing was enough, but as was always the case with Isadora, it soon was not. He needed her in a way he had never needed anything but air to breathe and water to drink. She had become quickly and annoyingly necessary.

"Who resides on this Level?" he asked as he slowly lifted her skirt.

"The emperor's witch, Gadhra, and her apprentices," Isadora answered. Her arms were draped around his neck, and she kissed his throat as he lifted her skirt higher. "They do not wander the palace at will, so it is extremely unlikely that any one of them will walk into the stairway and disturb us."

Lucan glanced at the door behind him, a door that would open onto witchcraft. His distaste for witches was both instinctive and learned, and so it went deep and complete within him.

"It is unlikely, in fact, that anyone will come this way at

this time of the day." Isadora took his face in her hands and kissed him again, and he forgot what sort of witchery and deception might be lurking behind that door as he touched her intimately.

She brushed fingers along the length of his arousal as he caressed her and said, "And yet, we should not linger, Lucan."

At last she called him Lucan instead of Captain. He did not make verbal note of the fact, since he did not want Isadora to stop what she was doing to take it back or argue about her slip of the tongue.

Her mouth pressed against the pulse at his throat, and she rose up on her tiptoes to whisper in his ear, "We should not waste time." Her fingers began to fumble with the fastenings of his trousers. "Hurry, Lucan," she whispered. "I need you *now*."

Against the stone wall of the palace stairway, with witches at his back and a woman he did not understand wrapping herself around him, he gave Isadora what she asked for.

ISADORA LEANED OVER A PARTICULARLY IRATE EMPRESS and checked the pregnant woman's temperature. Liane did seem a little warm, but not alarmingly so. A special tea would calm the empress and lower her body temperature to a healthy level.

When she was finished here she'd go to Lucan's room, via the hidden stairway. He would be waiting for her.

"You have changed," Liane said softly.

"I have not." Isadora sent Mahri to the kitchen for the ingredients for the tea that Liane needed, and then set about straightening pillows.

"You have," Liane insisted. "Now and then I catch you

smiling for no reason at all, and you are no longer so pale, and your mind wanders—"

"My mind never wanders."

"In the past few days, it has wandered quite a bit." Liane struggled into a straighter sitting position. "And you will share *nothing* with me. It's so unfair. I should order you to tell me everything that man has done to you."

"And what would you do when I refused?" Isadora asked, unafraid.

Liane relaxed against her pillows. "I'm bored. I grow weary of staying in this bed all day, of not being able to touch my husband, of coddling myself as if I were an old woman. I want to dance, and make love, and go where I please when I please."

"Soon enough," Isadora said, trying to ease the empress's mind.

"How soon?"

Isadora placed her hands over Liane's belly and closed her eyes. Her powers had grown stronger in the days Lucan had been her lover. Was he responsible for the changes in her? Perhaps. It seemed that every time she found pleasure in his embrace, her strength grew. She didn't understand how or why, but she could not deny that it was true.

"A week, give or take a day."

"And the babies will be ready?" Liane asked, her voice hushed.

Isadora smiled. "Yes. They will be ready." She sat on the bed and leaned closer to Liane, so no one could hear. "What are we going to do when they come?"

"I have been giving the matter some thought. No one can be in the room when the babies are born, but you."

"The priests will insist on being here to verify that the baby who is presented to them as the next emperor is truly yours, and not a replacement for a son who died at birth."

"They can insist all they want," Liane interrupted sharply. "No one but you." Her eyes met Isadora's. "We will bar the doors, if we must."

"After the babies are born, how will we explain—"

"We will explain nothing. You will take one of the babies and carry him, by way of the hidden stairs, to Ferghus."

"I don't understand."

"Ferghus will take the baby to a safe place, to a couple who lives in the country. They can't have children of their own, and the baby will be well cared for."

A chill walked up Isadora's spine. "You're going to give the child away."

Liane glared at Isadora. "If Sebestyen knows there are two, he will kill the weaker child."

"He would not—"

"In his mind, he would have no choice. Such an act would save Columbyana from war in twenty, thirty, forty years. We will send the stronger child with Ferghus and keep the weaker here. A stronger child will have a better chance of surviving the trip and the separation from his mother." If her lower lip didn't tremble slightly, Isadora would think the empress completely cold about the decision to send one of her sons away.

"You have already made arrangements with Ferghus?"

"Yes," Liane answered. "He is loyal to me, even above Sebestyen. He will do as I ask."

Ferghus would do as Liane asked because he was in love with her. Isadora had realized that the first time she'd seen the two of them together. Liane seemed to be completely oblivious to the man's infatuation.

"I will tell him to prepare for this event to take place in a week," Lianc said.

Mahri returned with the makings for tea, and Isadora prepared the empress one small, hot cup of the medicinal brew. There was no magic in the tea, just good common sense and useful herbs. The maid left, and once again Isadora and the empress were alone.

As Isadora handed the cup to Liane, the empress once again looked her in the eye. "It is not an easy thing, to send my child away knowing I will never see him again. We all do what we must."

In that instant, Isadora realized that Liane's heart was breaking for the child she would send to live with strangers. The empress did not display her feelings with abandon, so most would not have seen the heartbreak. But Isadora saw.

In true Liane fashion, the empress dismissed the unpleasant subject and turned to other things. "I can't believe you won't tell me anything about your trysts with Lucan Hern. You don't have to share everything, but since I was such a diligent matchmaker, I don't think a juicy tidbit or two is too much to ask for. Really, Isadora, what kind of friend are you?"

She had never been a friend, she had never had a friend. Her sisters did not count, as they shared blood and home and history. In truth, she and Liane were so dissimilar it was amazing that they could stand one another, much less become confidants.

Isadora sat on the side of the bed once more, and again she lowered her voice. "He is *magnificent*."

In a scene she had never imagined possible, she and the empress erupted into peals of girlish laughter.

SEBESTYEN ENJOYED SURPRISING ISADORA FYNE, SO HIS brief visits to her were made at different times of the day. Today he chose to walk into her room as she was preparing for yet another evening with Lucan Hern.

The witch was half dressed. Or rather, half undressed.

Apparently Hern had been giving her lessons in how to fight each and every afternoon, and sweat clung to her skin and the unruly tendrils of dark hair that framed her face and the frock which was more off than on. Women should not know how to fight; it went against their natures. Liane was the exception, of course.

Isadora's bath awaited her, steaming hot and sweetly scented. On Sebestyen's abrupt arrival she'd twisted the bodice of the gown she had half removed, and held it before her, covering her breasts.

"I have seen women naked before," Sebestyen said as he shooed the skittish maid out of the room and closed the door behind her. "There's no reason to be timid."

She did not drop the bodice. "What do you want, my lord?"

"A report," he said succinctly. "Surely in the week that you have been sharing Lucan Hern's bed, he has said something of consequence."

"We do not talk very much, my lord," she answered, blushing.

"No, I don't imagine you do." He had never found Isadora Fyne overly attractive, but since she'd become involved with Hern that had changed. She was prettier, somehow, more a woman . . . as well as a witch. He would do well to remember that fact. Gadhra looked like a proper witch, and he was never tempted to forget what she was when he looked at her.

Isadora, like her sister Sophie, was another matter entirely.

"Will he join me?"

"He is a man of his word, my lord, as I have told you. If he promised to ally with you in exchange for . . ."

"For you in his bed," Sebestyen finished when she faltered.

"Yes," she said softly. "If he promised, he will comply. It is not in his nature to deceive."

"He has yet to sign the accord." Until that was done, he could not be assured of anything.

"He will, my lord," Isadora assured him.

Sebestyen took a step closer to Isadora. "Are the warriors of the Circle as talented as I have heard them to be? Will they strike fear into the hearts of my enemies?"

Her eyes darkened, and with this expression on her face . . . yes, he was reminded that she was a witch and not to be entirely trusted. "If they all fight like Lucan, then they will win this war for you."

"Spoken like a woman who's fallen in love," he teased.

"I am not in love," she responded hotly. "Love is for foolish girls who know no better."

Sebestyen smiled at the woman. In spite of the fact that she was mostly naked and barely covered by the bodice she held before her pale torso, she was fierce. She would make a mighty enemy, if she chose.

"I want a commitment from him. I want the men he promised me. Soon."

"I can't push Lucan, my lord."

"Of course you can."

For once, he could read her expression; she wanted him gone, the sooner the better. "I don't have that kind of power over him. We do not discuss politics or matters of war, and it is too soon for me to broach the subject. Such a change would only make him suspicious of me. It would be best if we wait until *he* mentions the alliance you desire."

"You underestimate yourself. Every man has a weakness, and you are Captain Hern's."

"I am no man's weakness, my lord. I am just a woman."

He took another step toward Isadora, unafraid of her witchcraft. Bors had told him she was dangerous, that she had killed, that she was powerful. But Sebestyen had seen none of that strength for himself. In fact, the witch Bors had delivered was often downright meek. Perhaps she was not a witch at all. Perhaps her sisters had all the power in the family, and Isadora had been gifted with nothing but a fearsome glare she called upon on occasion.

"Just yesterday I once again offered Captain Hern any woman in this palace, sure he would be tired of you by now and would welcome companionship of a different sort. Someone younger, prettier, more adventurous. Again he told me he is interested only in you. That is power of a mighty sort, Isadora. Use it wisely."

9

"THAT IS AN UNUSUAL GOWN," LUCAN SAID AS HE STUD-
ied Isadora. From head to toe, she was astoundingly beautiful. Her dark hair was loose, there was a flush to her
cheeks and a wry smile twisting her lips.

The lavender gown she wore was more revealing than
anything he had seen her wear thus far. It draped over her
flesh like a cloud, barely covering, barely touching. The
sleeves were slit to show naked, strong arms, and the float-
ing neckline plunged well past the valley of her firm
breasts. Isadora was not a busty woman, but oh, that swell
was tempting and feminine. She was such a contrast of angles and curves, he could study her all night in what could
only be called awe.

It was clear there would be no binding undergarment to
deal with tonight.

"Unusual? That's all you have to say?" She placed a
wooden wedge firmly in the crevice of the hidden door she

had used to enter his room, so that no one else would be able to make use of it, and then she walked toward him, displaying that odd combination of strength and grace that he had never seen in any other woman's walk. "I chose this ridiculous frock in order to elicit a response from you, and all you can say is it's unusual."

"I apologize. Apparently that *ridiculous frock* has robbed me of my ability to speak."

"That's nearer to what I had in mind."

"I did not know you possessed such blatant feminine wiles."

Her smile dimmed a little. "Neither did I."

They had been lovers a week, now. Lucan had never been with any one woman for such a length of time. Women were provided for him, and he had enjoyed some more than others. But there had never been one who called to him the way Isadora did. There had never been one who felt so much like his own. He would have expected to be bored with her by now, but he was not.

She was no longer with him simply because she wore the Star of Bacwyr.

They kissed for a while, and as they kissed he gradually removed the lavender dress from Isadora's body. There was no rush, not tonight. He was content to bare a shoulder, and then an arm. One breast, and then the other. Each segment of her body received proper attention as it was bared.

Isadora possessed such wonderfully feminine muscles throughout her body, it was clear that she had not led a life of leisure, as her cousin the empress had. Lucan was accustomed to soft, fleshy women chosen for their abundance of curves and their traditional beauty, women who had been trained to please as he had been trained to fight. He had never considered that the women provided for the warriors of the Circle were very much the same as the emperor's concubines, but he could see now that it was true.

Some of those women he had chosen himself, while others had been chosen for him. None had been fierce and witty and headstrong like Isadora. None had ever touched him as she did, at the very pit of his soul.

He had never known a woman quite like her, and he wondered, as the lavender dress dropped to the floor at last, what she would think of living in Tryfyn. With him.

It was a jarring thought. When he became Prince of Swords, he would be expected to choose the daughter of a clan chieftan as his bride, or perhaps even a relation of the King who would come to them soon after the Star was returned to its rightful place. His bride, the mother of his sons, would be chosen for him, just as the women who warmed his bed had been chosen.

But that did not mean he had to set Isadora aside. He could have both. A bride picked and presented by the wizards; a mistress he selected himself. Would Isadora consent to be mistress to a married man? From what he knew of her it was highly unlikely that she would embrace such a station in life. But then again, she continued to surprise him. He could hope . . .

Naked at last, she began to undress him. She removed his leather vest first, which was easy enough to discard, then the knives he wore at his waist. Had he ever allowed a woman to touch those weapons before? No, he was quite sure he had not. Isadora discarded the knives with proper caution and even respect, and then she unfastened his trousers, easily working the ties and buttons that restrained him.

She had such capable and talented fingers, and if they trembled at all it was not with shyness or trepidation. Passion alone made Isadora quiver.

They fell onto the bed, arms and legs entwining, mouths

mating, hearts beating fast and hard. Lucan rolled Isadora onto her back and spread her legs, and then he teased her with what was to come. She wore nothing but the ring, which infused her with an ever growing magic as if it shared their very passion.

Did Isadora sense the strength within her that grew with every encounter? Did she realize that what they shared each night went beyond physical pleasure? She had not been trained to recognize and harness power, as he had, but surely she felt the force they generated.

"Now do you like me?" he asked, his voice gruff.

Isadora's dark eyes met his. "Perhaps a wee bit," she responded. She did not seem at all happy about the confession.

He watched those eyes closely as he filled her. Whatever uncertainties she had about him vanished quickly, and they were left only with the desire that had brought them together.

Maybe he would not be able to keep her, but for this moment in time Isadora was his, completely.

UNTIL SHE'D WALKED INTO LUCAN'S ROOM ON THAT cold night days ago and offered herself to him, Isadora had not realized how much she'd missed the physical closeness that came with an intimate relationship. Lying in bed caught in Lucan's arms—awake or asleep, it didn't seem to matter—she felt different. Whole again. No longer alone.

Heaven help her, she did like him. Very much, in fact. If only they had met in another time and place, maybe things would be different.

Foolish thought. The curse remained and would always keep her from that *different*. If she had not been ordered to his bed, she never would have allowed herself to get close enough to fall in . . .

Like. Not love. She caught herself just in time, as the words teased her tongue. It was a truly foolish woman who confused the needs of the body with the workings of the heart. She was old enough and wise enough to know better.

"You're going to fight with the emperor against the rebels, aren't you?" she asked as she and Lucan held one another long after the lovemaking was done. Two candles burned, one bowl of oil flickered, so that the room was lit with faint, dancing flames. The light made everything look unreal.

"I said that I would."

Her heart leaped. Liane and Mahri and countless other innocents would be hurt, maybe even killed, if the rebels overtook the palace. And yet Kane was one of those rebels, and she knew his intentions were honorable. She also knew that he and his kind did not have a chance against the Circle warriors, men who had been trained from childhood to do battle.

"For me," she whispered. "You promised yourself and your men to Sebestyen for *me*."

One large, comforting hand raked up and down her back. "Sebestyen's cause is just," he reasoned. "As the only legitimate son of the late Emperor Nechtyn, he is the rightful ruler of this country and has been for nigh onto twenty years."

"So, you would have agreed to take his side in the matter in any case?"

"Not necessarily. I might have walked away without taking any side at all."

She raised up and looked down at Lucan. In candlelight, he looked younger than his thirty-six years, more vulnerable than she knew him to be. It was the curl of his hair and the dimple in his cheek, she imagined, that made him appear helpless. He was not. He was far from helpless.

"You still have not signed the accord," she said gently. She had heard the emperor complaining about that fact, more than once.

"Not yet."

Isadora licked her lips and leaned down so that her nose was close to Lucan's. No one was listening, she knew that, and yet she felt it was necessary to speak as privately as possible. "Don't," she whispered. "Don't fight for him. Walk away, while you still can. Run, as fast as you can, from this terrible place. Go back to Tryfyn and keep your Circle warriors there."

"You side with the rebels who wish to overthrow Sebestyen?" He sounded surprised but intrigued.

"No," she answered in a soft voice. "I just want it to stop. The battles and the waiting and the intrigue. I want it to go away." She wanted her life to be simple again.

"War isn't over until someone wins."

"That's . . . stupid."

"Stupid?"

Isadora sputtered. "Yes, stupid."

Lucan did not seem insulted, which was a good thing. After all, war was his livelihood; killing was his gift.

"I have given my word," he said again. "Emperor Sebestyen kept his part of the bargain in sending you to me, so I must do the same."

She pinned his arms to the mattress—not that he couldn't escape her hold if he wished to do so. "Do you really think that I would be here if I had not decided *for myself* to be your lover?"

He sighed. "No."

"Then Sebestyen has given you nothing. The only bargain that exists is between you and I."

In a move so strong and quick and easy that it took her breath away, Lucan freed himself from her flimsy hold and reversed their positions so that he hovered over her. His weight pressed her into the mattress; his body heat warmed her. She was helpless here, unable to move in anything more than a subtle way.

And yet she liked being here. Lucan had always given her power in this association. He had never used his physical strength against her.

She had never used magic against him, and she could do just that, now that her powers had returned. A softly spoken spell, an influence he would not be able to deny, and he would do as she asked. But Lucan did not know she was a witch, and if she had her way, he would never know. She would not risk exposing her magic in that way, or any other. For once in her life, she wished not to be a witch. She was just a woman, and for now Lucan Hern was her man. Any influence she had over him had to be genuine. Real. There could be no magic in it.

"Emperor Sebestyen is a bad man, Lucan," she whispered. "You don't want to ally yourself with him."

"It is your contention that the bargain I struck concerns only the two of us?"

"Is anyone else in this bed?" she snapped.

He smiled down at her. "No." He kissed her throat, and then her chest, and then the valley between her breasts and the soft swell to one side. "Fine. I accept that argument. I will bargain only with you. What do you ask for in exchange for coming to Tryfyn with me?"

"What?" She tried to sit up as she responded to his question, but Lucan's hold was much more steadfast than hers had been, and she found herself pinned to the mattress while he continued to kiss her.

"You heard me, Isadora. Come home with me. Stay. And in return . . ." He continued to kiss and caress her body until she closed her eyes and wallowed in the sensations his mouth aroused.

It was a ridiculous notion, so why was she actually considering saying yes? Juliet and Sophie still needed her, she was almost certain of that fact. When the curse took Kane's life, Sophie would need her sisters' love and support, and heaven only knew where Juliet might be.

And then there was the matter of Lucan's distaste for witches. If he knew what she was, he would not touch her this way. He would not talk of taking her home with him, or tell her she was beautiful, or teach her how to fight, or laugh with her, or listen . . . all of that would go away, if he knew. She could hide that part of herself from him now, but if they stayed together, eventually he would learn the truth.

"I cannot be a part of so much death," she said. "It drains me in a way I can't explain."

Lucan kissed her flat stomach. "That is why you ask me, in our instructions with the sword, to show you how to stop a man without killing him?"

"Yes."

He was relentless in caressing and kissing her. "Even though death is a part of who I am, and that death repulses you, might you still consider coming home with me? You would never need to see battle. I would protect you from that, always. You would be a part of my home, not my call to war."

Yes, yes, yes . . . "Maybe. After the empress delivers her . . . her child." In the heat of the moment, she had almost said *children*. She could not share that secret, not even with Lucan.

"What do you need from me to make this alliance happen?"

She felt like she was flying, like her body was not her own. A moment more, one more well-placed kiss of those lips, and she'd agree to anything he asked of her. "Walk away from this palace," she said while she could still think. "Keep your warriors in Tryfyn and away from this conflict."

"And if I do as you request, you will come with me?"

"Yes," she answered quickly. "Yes."

And then she stopped thinking, gratefully and completely.

LUCAN WATCHED ISADORA DRESS IN THE LIGHT OF DAWN that broke through his window.

He was about to risk everything for a woman who shared his bed, and he had no second thoughts about the matter. There were many other women in the world, but none as this one. And he wanted her.

His instincts told him Isadora was right about Emperor Sebestyen being a bad man. The way she continued to be under guard when they went to the courtyard for lessons in swordplay told him she was a prisoner here, not a guest.

He would not allow her to be any man's prisoner.

The Star of Bacwyr sparkled on her finger. "You must choose a more suitable gown for travel, when the time comes for us to leave." The time would come soon, of that he had no doubt. "Something sturdy and warm, unlike this lovely gown." She was trying to dress, but he hampered her efforts, and she did not seem to mind.

"I hope you realize that I would not allow any man but you to see me in this frock."

The statement warmed him more than it should. He possessed a part of Isadora no man ever had or ever would. "We will travel light and quickly. You may wear the ring you favor, but you must leave everything else behind."

She glanced down at the ring. "Sometimes I think you like this little piece of jewelry more than you like me."

He should . . . but did not. "It is small and insignificant."

"I am growing rather fond of this silly little ring." Isadora waggled her hand at him, and the Star flashed. "It feels quite at home on my finger."

She had promised to give it to him, days ago. Now, it didn't matter. He would return the Star to the Circle; it would simply be delivered there on Isadora's finger.

"We must plan our escape soon. You and I, Franco and Esmun, we will leave here together."

"And Elya," Isadora said as she pulled the lavender sleeves up and wiggled her hips until the gown was in place. "We can't possibly leave her here. The emperor will take his anger out on her and the baby she carries—your niece or nephew, in case you have forgotten that fact. Trust me, Sebestyen will have no qualms about taking his anger out on an innocent."

Lucan sighed. "And Elya." A cumbersome pregnant woman would slow them down, but he knew Isadora was right. They could not leave her behind. "Must we wait for the empress to deliver?"

"Yes."

"Why?"

Mostly dressed, her hair unbound and falling over her shoulders and down her back, Isadora walked to him and laid her hands on his shoulders. "Because I gave my word that I would stay until it was done."

Lucan was accustomed to having his way. No woman had ever disobeyed or argued with him before. He found it annoying. "So I am to break my word to have you, but you will not do the same for me."

"No more than a few days, Lucan. I promise. Soon. The empress's pregnancy is complicated. She needs me."

He draped his arms around her, and she just stood there. He wanted her, he even needed her, but he had not been totally honest with her, and that would never do.

"I told you I would never lie," he said.

"Yes, I remember."

"That means there will sometimes be unpleasantness between us, when I am forced to tell you a truth you do not want to hear."

"As you are about to do now?" she asked, not sounding at all concerned about what might come next.

"Yes, as I am about to do now." He tipped her face up and looked her squarely in the eye. "I want you more than I have ever wanted anything for myself. But I cannot marry you, Isadora. When the time comes, wizards of importance in the Circle will choose my bride. You will be mine, and no one will be allowed to disrespect you, but we cannot be wed."

Isadora did not flinch, and there was no reaction in her dark eyes. No tears of anger or disappointment sparkled there. "I never said that I cared to marry you, Lucan."

He had been afraid he might hurt her with the truth, and yet he was the one who felt a pang of something that might be called regret. She did not want him?

A knock on his door had him reaching for his sword, but Isadora just patted his arm and walked away. "No need for weapons," she said. "I recognize that knock."

He did not put the sword away until Isadora opened the door and he saw a mousy woman in a brown maid's uniform standing in the hallway, her face pale and her hands clasped tightly.

"What is it, Mahri?" Isadora asked.

"Thank goodness you're here," the maid said in a loud whisper. "The empress sent me to fetch you. It's time. It's time!"

10

"No, this way," Mahri said, as Isadora hurried toward the lift that would carry her to Level One and the empress. Mahri pushed her way into the stairway that wound tightly the entire height of the palace, and there she ran not up but *down*.

Isadora followed. "Where is she?"

"The empress awaits you in her old quarters on Level Five, where she lived in the weeks after she and the emperor married."

Of course. At this hour of the morning the emperor was still abed. Liane had likely decided it was safer to move to another room than to take the chance that she'd be able to kick her husband out of his own room, when the time came.

Isadora had spent many nights in the Level Five quarters herself, before Liane had insisted that she move to Level One so she'd be near at all times.

Two of the empress's sentinels were posted at the entrance to the apartment. One of them was Ferghus, who knew very well that the empress would soon give birth to twin sons. Isadora caught his eye as she entered the room; he already looked guilty.

As the door closed behind her, Mahri ran into the narrow hallway that led to the bedchamber. Liane's shout echoed off the walls.

"What took you so long?"

"I was only gone a few moments, my lady."

"No, you were gone much too long." The empress's sharp eyes fell on Isadora. "While you were off fucking your pretty warrior as if you had no concern in the world but his cock, these damned pains began. I tried to wait until Sebestyen left the bedchamber for the day, but by dawn I knew I couldn't wait any longer."

Isadora did not take offense at the empress's bitter words. Childbirth pains had made even Sophie curse.

"You should not have made your way here on your own," Isadora admonished.

"I did not come alone. Mahri and Ferghus escorted me." The empress flicked her eyes to the trembling maid. "Go fetch Isadora a proper work dress. I don't want childbirth fluids staining one of my favorite frocks." After Mahri had rushed from the room, Liane looked squarely at Isadora. "Ferghus and Tatsl will guard the main door, but there's a secret passageway in this room. Sebestyen knows his way in. You must find the entrance and block it somehow." Liane pointed to one corner of the room, not far from the window that looked out on new morning light. "It's over there somewhere."

"Why did you come here if you knew there was a secret passageway?"

"It was the only place I could think of. The passageways

are everywhere, and Sebestyen knows them all. At least here I know the general location of the door."

Many of the hidden doorways were so well concealed, finding them was next to impossible. Isadora searched the grout between stones for spaces that should not be there, but she found none.

Her efforts were on Liane's behalf, for Liane's protection, so she did not feel that it was inappropriate to call upon her magic. She held out her right hand and whispered, *"Tyrnet."*

The ring she wore began to glow, and Isadora was so startled she almost snapped her hand back to her side. But instead of reacting in that way she allowed the glow from the ring to feed her own powers. It did just that, until her hand was drawn sharply downward and the outline of the doorway was revealed in shades of blue.

"No wonder you could not find it," she said. "It's not a proper doorway at all but a very low opening. Anyone who used this would be forced to crawl to make use of it."

"Are you sure?" Liane sounded truly surprised. "Sebestyen never crawls, not for anyone or anything."

She could find something handy to wedge in the narrow crevice the spell revealed, as she did in Lucan's room each night, but as her powers were returning, that was not necessary. With Lucan she was forced to hide her magic, but with Liane that wasn't the case. Kneeling on the floor. Isadora ran her fingers along the revealed crevice and whispered powerful words her mother had taught her. She ended the incantation with the word *"Sintar,"* and the secret entrance to this room was securely sealed.

Isadora returned to Liane, who lay upon the bed, pale and sweating and terrified. The empress was not one to admit to her own terror, but Isadora saw the fear very clearly.

"You look very fetching in my castoff gown, even though you don't have the proper curves to fill it out."

"Thank you, I think."

"I didn't think you cared to wear any of my more seductive gowns. Lucan Hern seems to have brought to life a new aspect of your nature."

"Yes, I suppose he has." She had not come here to talk about Lucan or aspects of her own nature, but it was likely that during the day she and Liane would have more time to talk than usual. Talk of such unimportant matters might make the hours pass more quickly for the mother-to-be. "I wanted him to think I was pretty." The fact that she cared about such an inconsequential thing was a cause of wonder to her.

Liane smiled weakly. "Captain Hern has always thought you pretty, Isadora, from the first time he laid eyes on you."

"A man who wants a woman in his bed will often see that which he wishes to see. There is no explaining how their minds work."

"I doubt you have ever cared much for Lucan Hern's *mind,*" Liane teased. "And you are very attractive, in an unusual fashion. Have you not seen the way some of the sentinels look at you?"

Surely the empress was suffering from delusions. Talk of her own beauty—or lack of beauty—made Isadora uncomfortable, so she set to straightening the covers over Liane's body. "How long since your last pain?"

"While Mahri was gone to fetch you," Liane said. "It hurt," she added, as if she were surprised. "To the very depths of my bones, it hurt. How long before the babies come?"

"A few hours," Isadora replied. Since there had not been another pain since she'd arrived, delivery was certainly not as near as the empress believed it to be.

"A few *hours*?" Liane shouted, sitting up awkwardly. "This can't possibly go on for hours. You can make it better; you can make them come faster."

"It is best that the babies come in their own time."

Liane accepted this statement, somewhat, and leaned back. "How can we expect to keep Sebestyen out of the room for that length of time? I will probably have to see him at least once, but he cannot be in this room when the babies are born."

There had been a time when Isadora would not have believed that any man might be a danger to his own child, but that had been before she'd met Emperor Sebestyen.

Minutes later, Liane suffered a long and painful contraction. She grasped the sheet and tensed, and made a long, moaning sound. When Isadora took the empress's hand, Liane squeezed so hard bones crackled, and the moan turned into a litany of curses befitting the most battle-hardened sentinel.

When the contraction was over, Liane closed her eyes and relaxed. "Hours," she said weakly.

"The time will pass quickly," Isadora said optimistically.

Liane gave her a glare which revealed very clearly what she thought about that weak promise.

Isadora continued to hold the empress's hand. "You know, it was in this very bed that I saw Willym for the last time."

"If you weep, I will kill you. I cannot bear to listen to you whine about your dead husband while I am in pain."

Isadora smiled. If she did not know Liane, she would take offense. The empress could be harsh at times, and she did not play games of decorum. Perhaps she should be allowed her social failings, given the course of her life. Captured as a girl, made a sexual slave to the emperor and his men, called upon to kill. In spite of all that, Liane had not only survived, she'd flourished. She'd found love with the most unlikely of men, and she cared deeply for those few she deemed worthy: her husband, Mahri, Ferghus, Isadora. And most of all, the children she carried inside her.

"Thoughts of Will no longer make me weep," Isadora said. "I loved him, and he loved me, but our time together is past."

"You love Captain Hern now, is that it?"

"No, I don't love him." She couldn't, no matter how tempted she might be. "But he has made me see that life goes on for the living. A woman should only mourn for so long."

"I told you that a thousand times."

"Yes, I know." Isadora smiled. "But Lucan communicates in a different and much more persuasive way."

"I imagine he does." Liane relaxed against her pillows. "Be careful, or you'll find yourself in my position, pregnant and cursing the man for touching you, ruining a perfectly good body, and bringing you incredible pain."

"I don't have to worry about that for a while," Isadora said lightly. "According to the Circle wizards, Lucan's first son will be born in two years. There hasn't been a boy child born in the Fyne family for so long no one remembers when it might've happened."

Again she thought, *But what of his first daughter?* Perhaps the son the wizards saw were the result of his politically planned marriage. Maybe she would give him daughters . . . and then again, maybe she could not. Or simply would not.

"Wizards are sometimes wrong, you know. Emperor Nechtyn's wizard, Thayne, prophesied that the touch of the sun on Sebestyen's face would be the sign that his life and his rule were over. It's been months since Sophie brought sunshine into the palace, and things are still going well.

Well enough. Sebestyen has me, now, and the rebels are no closer to taking the palace, and with Captain Hern and the Circle on his side, the rebels don't have a chance. Wizards can be wrong."

Isadora knew that to a wizard, who was likely to live an extraordinarily long life, months were no more than the blink of an eye. And she also knew Sebestyen would not have the Circle warriors fighting with his army. She did not think it would be wise to tell Liane either of these things.

The idea of running to Tryfyn with Lucan was a nice one. Isadora could see it in her mind, the two of them—with Franco and Esmun and Elya, of course—making their escape. They would ride fast and hard, and she would finally be free from this terrible place.

But she did not fool herself into thinking she could stay with Lucan forever. Eventually he would learn that she was a witch, and he would hate her. It would be best if she did the leaving herself, before that happened.

She and Lucan could have some time together, if all went well. Isadora wanted that time with him; she even felt that she deserved to have it. Lucan would be the man to get her out of the palace. In spite of his promises, she didn't believe for one minute that Emperor Sebestyen intended to let her go.

WHEN HE FIRST WOKE AND FOUND HIS WIFE GONE, Sebestyen was not overly concerned. Even though Liane had been confined to bed for weeks, she did visit the lavatory often, and she was allowed short walks to stretch her legs.

He rose, bathed, and dressed, and when that was done and his wife had not returned, he became concerned. Since Isadora and Gadhra had ordered her to bed rest, Liane had not been out of this room for more than a few minutes at a time.

Beorn and Serian were stationed in the hallway, guarding the entrance to his bedchamber as they did every morning after dawn and shift change. "Where is the empress?"

They both bowed to him in respect, and then Serian said, "We were informed that Empress Liane and her maid left some time ago, before our shift began. Mahri said the empress was restless and did not wish to disturb you, and that they were going to Level Five."

"Restless," Sebestyen repeated.

Serian nodded, and dipped his head so he would not have to look his emperor in the eye.

Sebestyen loved his wife, oddly enough, and he knew her well. If she were restless, she would not care about disturbing his sleep. She would likely elbow him in the side to make sure that he did not sleep well while she could not.

He headed for the lift, and the two sentinels fell into step behind him. There was little potential for danger to the emperor here in the upper levels of the palace, but at least two sentinels were with him at all times. Only in his personal chambers did he know complete privacy. The three of them made their way to Level Five by way of the lift, and no one said a word. It wasn't as if he carried on idle conversation with his guards. Liane had a habit of getting much too friendly with her servants, but then she had once been a servant herself. She would learn, in time, that those who served were not worthy of the time and effort it took to converse.

Soon, when the baby was sent to the priests for safekeeping and training, Liane would have no one but her husband to lean on. That was as it should be.

Ferghus and Tatsl were stationed outside the empress's quarters, and they snapped to attention when they saw who approached. Even Mahri waited in the hallway, pacing nervously. She, too, assumed a posture of deference.

Ferghus, who stood directly in front of the door, did not move. Sebestyen gestured with his hand, indicating that the sentinel should step aside. He did not.

"My Lady Liane has commanded that she and her midwife not be disturbed until we are informed otherwise," the man said in a lowered but disturbingly strong voice.

"I'm sure she did not include her husband in that order."

At least the man had the grace to pale as he answered, "She did, my lord. Most specifically."

Sebestyen leaned toward the loyal sentinel and lowered his voice. "If you don't move aside, I will have you killed here and now, is that understood?"

"Yes, my lord. Understood. Would it be permissible to send the maid in to see that the women are prepared for your presence?"

Prepared. Good lord, the baby was coming. Sebestyen's heart thumped too hard. He should've realized as soon as he woke and discovered Liane missing from their bed. He nodded curtly in assent.

They both stepped aside to allow Mahri to enter the room. Sebestyen strained to listen, but all was silent in the brief moments the door was opened. Very shortly, Mahri returned. She opened the door, stepped back, and silently invited Sebestyen to enter.

He had never entered the empress's chambers through this main entrance. In fact, he had never visited any of his wives previous to Liane here, and when he had come to her he'd used the secret passageways. Those winding stairways and narrow halls were the only way he could move about the palace alone, without his constant guard.

Beorn and Serian entered the chamber with him, but at his signal they assumed their post in the entryway.

The empress's chambers were laid out very differently from his own. The entrance to his bedroom opened onto one huge space. There were smaller chambers beyond that large bedroom for dressing and bathing, and other rooms on Level One were available for meetings and entertainment and dining.

These rooms were smaller, each chamber with a purpose, each connected to another by a narrow passageway. They were very nicely decorated, but he would suffocate if he were forced to live here. No wonder his four former wives had all come to hate him.

Not that he hadn't given them other reasons to hate him, before he'd dispatched them all to Level Thirteen.

The narrow passageway opened into the bedchamber. He saw Liane before she saw him, and so he was still for a moment in order to watch his wife unobserved. She rested on a soft mound of pillows, and she seemed fine. Maybe he had been wrong, and the baby was not coming just yet. That was a relief. It was too soon, but then Isadora and Gadhra had both said the baby would come early and would be fine.

How sad that he was forced to take the word of witches in such important matters. He caught a glimpse of Isadora out of the corner of his eye. Today she was dressed in a serviceable blue dress unlike those she had been wearing in her charade as Liane's cousin. Another hint that perhaps this was the day they had been waiting for.

He entered the bedroom properly and scowled down at his wife. "What on earth are you doing here?"

Liane looked squarely and bravely at him, in a way no one else dared, and answered, "I'm having a baby."

"Excellent." Sebestyen fetched a chair and pulled it to Liane's bedside, where he sat.

"What do you think you're doing?" Liane snapped.

"You do wish me present for the birth, don't you?"

"No!"

He should not feel hurt that Liane did not want him here, but the pang at his center was a sign of sharp disappointment. "It is my place."

Liane shook her head. "I don't want anyone here but Isadora."

She would choose the witch over her own husband? True, a woman's presence was necessary. Sebestyen certainly didn't wish to deliver the child himself. But Liane *wanted* Isadora to be with her. She did not want him. In what should be a time of joy, he found himself annoyed.

"That's impossible. There must be witnesses to the birth. Father Merryl, with another priest or two in attendance, myself—"

"No!" Liane rose up, slowly but perhaps as quickly as was possible, given her condition. "Look at me, Sebestyen. I am sweating, distended, and laid out upon this bed like a sacrificial cow, where I will shortly and painfully *expel* your very large son from my body. It is not an event I wish to be witnessed by anyone. If I could manage this alone, I wouldn't even allow Isadora in the room!"

"Don't be ridiculous," he said calmly.

Liane's face paled, and her expression changed. She gripped the sheets beneath her hands and closed her eyes. The pain she experienced was so clear on her face, he felt it himself. Her breathing changed, she moaned in agony, and she muttered a few foul words that should never pass an empress's lips.

If he could take the pain from her and bear it himself, he would. Watching her suffer was excruciating in a way he had not expected it to be.

The pain passed like a wave. Starting gently, growing stronger, then fading gradually. When it was done, Liane opened her eyes and looked at him again. "If I were not very sure that neither of us could have a child again, you would not touch me from this day forward. I don't know how it is possible that any woman ever willingly has more than one child." Tears sprang to her eyes. "This is terrible, and I don't want you to see me this way. I should be beautiful for you, always."

He reached out and touched a sweaty, pale cheek. "You are beautiful to me, Liane. Now more than ever."

She actually laughed, though not with exuberance. "You are such a liar."

"No," he said sincerely. "Not about this." He leaned forward and kissed her gently.

When he drew away, she seemed to relax. "Don't tell the priests that I'm in labor," she said. "We can summon them after the child is born and tell them I had an unusually quick delivery."

"They will not be happy."

"The happiness of the priests has never been my concern."

Sebestyen turned his attention to Isadora. "How long?"

"It is too soon to tell. Hours. Perhaps all day."

Liane responded with a succinct curse word.

For a moment, Sebestyen sat in the chair without responding. Even though he wished to be present for the birth of his son, he did not want to sit here and watch Liane suffer for hours on end. Perhaps that made him a coward. But as she did not want him here, it made perfect sense for him to leave the women to their work. He stood slowly. "When the time is near, send for me. I want to be with you when the baby is born."

"No, Sebestyen," Liane argued.

He glared down at her. "I will be here, Liane. If you

wish it there will be no other witnesses, but I will be here, where I belong, when my son is born."

"I will send for you when the time comes," Isadora said. "Don't be impatient. It might be a long while."

Liane seemed to relax when she realized that he indeed planned to leave. Sebestyen went to Isadora and placed his arm around her shoulder. There had been a time when he would not have dared such a dangerous gesture, but she had been here for months, and he had not seen any evidence that she possessed the kinds of witchery her sister had displayed in the grand ballroom. She was, in fact, quite harmless.

He leaned toward her and lowered his voice. "If anything happens to my wife or my son while they are in your hands, you will pray for a quick death before I am finished with you."

"I am doing my best, my lord, and will continue to do so."

Sebestyen wanted to ask Isadora about news from Lucan Hern's bed, but now was not the time. His wife and son were on his mind, and he had no time or energy for any other thoughts.

For today, there was no rebellion, no machinations, no prophesies to fear. For today, there was just Liane and the miraculous birth of their son.

SINCE LUCAN HAD HEARD MAHRI'S CALL AT HIS DOORway early in the morning, he would know why Isadora did not appear for their daily lessons. Still, she wished she could send him a message of some sort. *I miss you; I want you; I can't wait to get out of this place with you . . .*

There was no one in the Level Five hallway—in the entire *palace*—she would trust with such a message. Lucan knew why she was occupied, and so he would not worry. Nothing else mattered at the moment.

Liane grew more contentious and impatient as the day wore on. Her labor pains gradually increased in intensity and very gradually grew closer together. She cursed the soldiers who had brought her to this place nearly seventeen years ago; Sophie, who had wielded the magic that made this child possible; Isadora, who was the only one present to rail against; and her husband, the Emperor Sebestyen, who had done this terrible thing to her and who would pay in a thousand ways before his miserable life was done.

In the moments when pain did not dominate Liane's world, they had talked through their plans for the minutes surrounding and just after the birth of the twins. Juliet had delivered twins in the past, and Isadora remembered that there had been a span of several minutes—a quarter of an hour in that case, she believed Juliet had said—between the births.

If all went well, their plan should work. When the first child was born, they would wrap him in the waiting warm blanket and give him to Ferghus. There would be no time for delivering both babies and choosing which was stronger and which was weaker. Isadora would unseal the secret passageway and send Ferghus out of the bedchamber by that route. She did not know his planned course from there, and did not wish to. He promised safety for the baby, and that was all she needed to know.

When Ferghus was gone, they would send for Sebestyen. With luck, he would arrive in time to see his second child born.

"It's not fair!" Liane screamed as her contraction faded.

"What isn't fair?" Isadora remained calm as she wiped the empress's face with a damp, cool cloth.

"Why don't men have to go through this? Their function

in procreation is all about pleasure, and then they get to sit back and relax while we grow large and ill and irritable, and then suffer for hours before our bodies are stretched in unnatural and painful ways, and a living being is torn from our wombs."

"It is a blessing," Isadora replied.

A single word made clear Liane's opinion on that matter, and Isadora laughed.

"I'm serious. One day, I hope I can have a child." With Lucan? She wasn't sure they would be together long enough for such a miracle to occur. "Did you see Sophie with her daughter Ariana while they were here?"

"Yes," Liane answered, her voice calmer.

"I have never seen such a pure and powerful love as that of a mother and child. We love men, on occasion, and we love our families. But this kind of love is different, and it touches the soul in a unique way. You are very lucky."

Liane breathed deeply. "Yes, I suppose I am." And then another contraction began. Before it became so intense that she could not speak, she caught Isadora's eyes and held them. "The firstborn, the one Ferghus will take away . . . I don't want to see him." Tears filled her eyes. "I don't think I can bear to send him away if I do."

Isadora nodded and grasped Liane's hand, and the woman threw her head back and screamed.

The time was near.

SEBESTYEN HAD SPENT THE DAY IN HIS OFFICE, PIDDLING with papers that meant nothing and snapping at everyone who dared to poke their heads into his domain. How long did it take to birth a child? Had Liane been in pain all this time? A part of him wanted to rush to Level Five and insist on being with her as she went through the ordeal.

Another part of him was perfectly happy to stay here where he did not have to watch her suffer.

When the knock came on his door, he stood up sharply. Finally! But Beorn opened the door to reveal a palace resident who had not set foot in this room for many years.

"Gadhra. What are you doing here?"

The old woman looked as a witch should, in his opinion, with long, straggling gray hair and a dress that looked like it had been made of rags. She had powers of the sort Isadora Fyne never would, and though Sebestyen did not want his fear to show, he was afraid of her.

She took one tentative step into the room. "My dreams are disturbing," she said, her voice hoarse and too low.

"How is that my concern? Surely there is a potion of some sort to cure you of this ailment."

"It is not an ailment but a gift that disturbs my dreams," she said, taking another step toward him.

Sebestyen signaled to Beorn, and the sentinel drew his sword.

Gadhra stopped several feet away and glanced at the threatening weapon. "I must speak to you alone, my lord."

"That is impossible."

"Do you trust these men with all your secrets?"

Sebestyen almost answered, "Yes," but something stopped him.

"If you do not trust me, then hold a blade to me yourself while I say what must be said. This news is for your ears alone, my lord."

At a subtle signal from Sebestyen, Serian handed over his sword, and the two sentinels left the room. They would remain just outside the door, he knew, and with a word they would return.

Sebestyen held the long sword so that the tip barely touched Gadhra's throat. "What brings you here, witch?"

Her old eyes held a hint of sadness, as well as a hint of anger. "The empress means to betray you, my lord. She is plotting at this very moment to send the rightful heir to the throne away from his proper place. Away from his *father*."

"She would never do such a thing," he said, instinctively defending Liane. "I should kill you here and now for even suggesting that she would."

"I have proof," Gadhra said. "Come with me, quickly, and together we will save the rightful heir."

II

Lucan knew that childbirth was not a quick or easy task, so he was not surprised when Isadora did not appear at all that day. He met with Esmun in the afternoon and told him of the plan to escape. He'd expected some sort of argument from his usually hardheaded brother, but Esmun was quite ready to leave the palace and Emperor Sebestyen behind—as long as Elya came with them.

Tonight's meal was eaten in his chambers, as always, but it was Franco who sat across the table from him, not Isadora. As much as he normally enjoyed the company of the warrior who was posing as his valet, the man was a poor substitute as dinner companion.

Like Esmun, Franco was anxious to leave this place. He was not so sure about making their escape with two women in tow. He seemed to think the Hern brothers had been bewitched.

Then again, Franco was young and had never been completely besotted by a female. He would learn, in time.

Franco ate with relish, and dinner conversation was kept at a minimum until both men were finished with their meal. It was then that Franco leaned back in his chair and looked squarely at Lucan. "I'm glad enough that we won't be fighting Columbyana's war, but I don't entirely understand why. You came here specifically to ally with the emperor, did you not?"

"You're anxious to engage in full-out war?" The Circle often fought in clan disputes, and they had taken part in many a bloody battle, but there had not been war with a land beyond Tryfyn's borders since the fall of the Circle, well more than a hundred years ago. If all went well and he retrieved the Star, as he was destined to do, there would not be war within Tryfyn for a long time to come.

"I much prefer sword-to-sword conflict to being your manservant," Franco teased.

"Am I unbearably demanding?"

"Yes, you are," the younger man replied with a crooked smile.

After Franco retired to his own quarters to sharpen his weapons and pack his small bag for travel, Lucan paced his silent rooms. He kept expecting Isadora to come through the hidden entrance, tired but happy to see him. She *would* be happy to see him, wouldn't she?

As he paced, his mind went back to that moment early this morning when Isadora had so plainly told him she did not want to be his wife. He couldn't marry her so he should be glad that she did not desire such ties, but instead he was annoyed. If the choice were his, he would gladly ask her to marry him. She would make a good wife. Did she not think that he would make a good husband?

Lucan lit a number of candles when night fell, so that when she did come to him she would not open the door into darkness. As he waited, he packed his own bag. Isadora would not be able to take many of her things with her, but once they reached Tryfyn he would replace everything she had left behind, and more. He would give her everything any woman could possibly want, and she would be happy. She would not regret leaving the imperial palace for him.

He had not come to this palace looking for a woman, but as he prepared to flee he could not imagine leaving without Isadora.

SEBESTYEN GUIDED THE WAY ALONG THE NARROW, WINDING stair that led to the chamber where Liane was delivering his child. The old woman who trailed along behind him was surely wrong. She was a lunatic who smelled of musty potions and unwashed clothes, who was wild-eyed and unkempt and cryptic. Gadhra represented everything Sebestyen hated and feared about magic and witches.

When they arrived in Liane's room and discovered that the witch was wrong, he'd have Gadhra thrown in Level Thirteen to rot. With the Circle of Bacwyr on his side, he did not need her magic. Other, lesser witches could concoct the few potions they needed. A witch as strong as this one could bring too much trouble to the palace.

Beorn had been sent to the Level Five hallway and the main entrance to the empress's chambers, where Liane's sentinels continued to stand guard. Serian trailed behind Sebestyen and the witch Gadhra, as the three of them took the hidden stairwell he had used on a few occasions to visit Liane.

He had never used the passageway to visit any of the

wives who had preceded Liane. Never, not once in the years he had been married to them, had he desired to see any one of them so desperately that he would sneak out of his bed in the middle of the night and make the short and twisted journey to their bed. Liane was different from all other women; she had always been different. He looked for and even expected betrayal from everyone else—but not from her.

When he reached the hidden entrance to the bedchamber, Sebestyen dropped down and laid his hand upon a cool stone. The door should slide silently and quickly open, but nothing happened.

The witch behind him dropped to her haunches and whispered in his ear, "The witch Isadora has sealed this door."

"Can you unseal it?"

"Of course. Isadora Fyne is not a more powerful witch than I. Any spell she can cast, I can uncast. Any magic she can do, I can undo."

Through the thick wall, he heard Liane scream.

"Do it," he commanded.

The witch muttered words he did not understand, casting her spell in a language that stank of magic, just as she did. A chill crawled up Sebestyen's spine. There was no guarantee that the old woman was doing as he asked; she might be casting a spell on him.

But disgusting as Gadhra was, she had been loyal, thus far.

The witch stopped speaking, then offered to him a vial of Panwyr on her wrinkled palm. "You will need this for the witch Isadora," she whispered. "When she is no longer necessary for the delivery, you must dispose of her. She knows too much; she is a danger to you."

Sebestyen realized that he should've disposed of Isadora Fyne when Bors had first presented her to him. He took the Panwyr and dropped it into the deep pocket of the crimson robe he wore, and once again touched his hand to the low, hidden entrance.

As it had in the past, the small door slid silently open.

AT LAST, THE TIME WAS NEAR. FERGHUS WAITED IN THE entryway and would come at Isadora's call. The last time she'd checked on him, the empress's most devoted sentinel had clearly been nervous. He'd been downright pale and twitchy. Isadora could not tell if it was the birth itself or the intrigue to follow that worried him.

Men who were not afraid to kill and die by the sword could be oddly squeamish where childbirth was concerned.

"It's time to push." Isadora peered over the sheet that had been draped across Liane's knees, to find tired, angry eyes peering at her.

"*You* push, you wicked, tormenting, ungrateful crone!"

It was not the worst Liane had called her during the day. "If I could do this for you, I would," Isadora said calmly. "I can't. You must push. The time is here, Liane. This is the moment we have been waiting for."

Liane nodded, and when the next contraction came she pushed. With a scream and one more curse, the first of the twins was born.

The empress collapsed onto the bed, and Isadora quickly tended to the baby. When the cord was cut and tied, she wrapped the child in a thick, warm blanket, and called to Ferghus.

"Is he all right?" Liane asked, her eyes on the ceiling above, and not on her child.

"He is small but healthy," Isadora said, "as I promised he would be. Are you sure you don't want to—"

"I'm very sure," Liane said in a choked voice.

Ferghus came into the room, casting a quick glance to the empress and then taking the baby from Isadora.

"He's tiny," the big man said in a tentative voice.

"Yes, he is. Get him to his destination quickly. He will need to be fed soon."

"A wet nurse is waiting."

Isadora nodded. A part of her wanted to give her full attention to the child who had just been born, but the night's plan was not yet complete. It was time to send for Sebestyen. With any luck, the second child would wait a good few minutes before he decided to come into the world.

She knelt before the hidden entrance to undo the seal she had put in place earlier, so Ferghus and the baby could escape by this hidden route, but before she could say a word, it slipped open without making a sound. She fell back, as a crouched and crimson-clad Emperor Sebestyen entered the room.

As he stood, the emperor's eyes fell on Ferghus. The empress's sentinel held the newborn babe protectively in his arms. Isadora saw confusion on Sebestyen's face, then a deep and frightening anger.

Gadhra followed the emperor through the low door, whispering in her tinny voice, "I told you, my lord, can you see? This one was trying to take your son from his rightful place."

A green-clad sentinel followed Gadhra, and as soon as he was able to stand he drew his sword with one hand and a short knife with the other, and stood ready to fight.

"Sebestyen," Liane said breathlessly, "I can explain."

The emperor spared her a quick glance. "It would be best if you did not speak to me at this time," he said coldly. He walked to Ferghus, and offered his hands. After a moment's hesitation, the sentinel handed the child to his father.

Sebestyen looked back at the guard who had come with him through the secret passageway. "Kill him," he said without emotion.

Before Ferghus had a chance to respond, the emperor's sentinel moved forward and quickly lashed out. The blow was fast and accurate; the knife went deeply into Ferghus's torso and was then withdrawn.

"No!" Liane screamed as Ferghus laid a hand to his wound and then crumpled to the floor.

Sebestyen looked down at the baby in his arms. "Why is he so small, when the empress grew so large she could barely walk?"

Isadora glanced at the witch Gadhra, who had moved to the foot of the bed. "Because there are two," she said, her old voice filled with wonder. "I did not see that for myself . . . I did not see that there would be *two*."

Sebestyen spared a glance for a motionless Ferghus. "Serian, is he dead?"

"Yes, my lord," the sentinel Serian answered.

"Good." The emperor walked to Liane's bedside, his step slow and precise. She had another contraction, while he watched with emotionless eyes. When she screamed he did not react at all, not even to flinch. After the contraction was done, she collapsed to the mattress once again.

"You're giving birth to two sons; that's why you lied to me," her husband said.

"I knew you would never allow—"

"You would send our eldest son, my rightful heir, away. Where was he going, Liane? Where would you send the rightful heir to the throne of Columbyana?"

"To a place where he would be safe!" she said angrily. "To a place where you could not harm him!" Her eyes filled with tears. "Ferghus was only doing as I asked, and you killed him!"

"I always did think you cared for that one too much. There are other sentinels to fill his position. He will not be missed. Not by me." At Sebestyen's order, his own sentinel covered Ferghus's body with the discarded coverlet from the bed Liane lay upon.

Sebestyen handed his firstborn son to Gadhra, and the old witch took the child with a greediness that alarmed Isadora. The emperor then sat beside his wife and took her hand.

"I loved you," he said without emotion, "and you betrayed me. You lied to me." He squeezed her hand too hard, and she flinched. "I expected lies from everyone else, but not from you. Never from you."

"Sebestyen, I . . ." Liane began breathlessly.

"If you tell me that you love me, I will kill you before you take your next breath. I have my son. I don't need you anymore."

Another contraction came. It was almost time for the second child to be born.

"Move away from her," Isadora ordered. "You can talk about this after we're finished with our work here."

While Liane gripped the sheet with her free hand and pushed, Sebestyen leaned over the bed and spoke to her in a loud, clear voice. "I could kill you, but I won't. You are empress, and you will remain empress, but you're going back to Level Three where you belong. You will make yourself available for any man who desires you, and you will perform any task I order, no matter how demeaning or degrading."

Liane screamed, but Sebestyen continued, raising his voice so she'd be certain to hear.

"Can you imagine what a treat it will be for visiting dignitaries to fuck an empress? Maybe you can entertain an entire delegation while I watch. Maybe you can perform prurient tricks for special occasions." He leaned closer, and as his second son was born into Isadora's hands, Emperor Sebestyen said, "The priests were right about you, Liane, they were right all along. You are not worthy of the place I offered you. I can't love a woman like you. You're not deserving. You're *nothing*."

The second child was a bit larger than the first, and he cried in a louder voice. Liane raised up and offered her arms for her child. "Give him to me," she said hoarsely.

Isadora walked toward Liane, the youngest of the empress's two sons snug in her arms. Sebestyen placed himself between Isadora and the new mother, and he forcibly took the babe from her. "The whore is not to touch either of my children, not ever." He cut his eyes to Gadhra. "This one is stronger, I can see that for myself."

"This one is firstborn," she argued, "and therefore is the rightful heir."

He sighed and looked down at the baby in his arms. "You are right, of course."

"What are you going to do with my babies?" Liane asked as she struggled to sit up.

"There can only be one, Liane, you know that," Sebestyen argued.

She screamed at him, and she cried, but he seemed completely unaffected as he laid the second-born child in a waiting cradle.

Isadora took a deep breath and did her best to reason with the emperor. "My lord, our intentions were noble and in your children's best interests. The empress was very aware that twin sons would confuse the bloodline. She only wanted safety for both of her babies. It is not too late to send one of them away to a place of safety and anonymity. No one need ever know . . ."

He took her hand and lifted it, studying the ring that

adorned her right hand. "I believe I told you once before, this ring is rightfully mine. Is it still stuck? Will I need Serian's sword to retrieve my own property?"

The ring was so unimportant, she did not care to argue. Isadora whispered, *"Avar,"* and the ring slipped off her finger. She handed the piece to the emperor. He placed it on his little finger, then took a moment to admire the fit.

"Please," she begged. "Let us see the youngest child to a place of safety." Their protection was her duty. It was the reason for her presence here, and if Sebestyen had his way, she would fail. She had failed enough in this lifetime and did not wish to taste defeat again.

"You are so bold as to tell me what to do with my own children?"

"I only want—"

She did not get the chance to say more. Sebestyen reached into the pocket of his crimson robe, withdrew a vial of a brown powder that sparkled by candlelight, and before she knew what he intended, he had grabbed her head and shoved the vial up her nose.

Isadora started to fight the emperor, but before she could raise her hands, a tingling sensation filled her nose and her head and then danced through her entire body until she was weak-kneed. The room seemed to swim, and colors swirled around her as if a rainbow had broken apart and was trying to reassemble itself before her very eyes. She could barely lift her hands, and when she did they were limp and weak. She smiled and wiggled her fingers, and they seemed to elongate and flutter in a way they never had before.

She heard Liane screaming again, but the sound was distant and weak and vaguely annoying. The emperor issued orders this way and that, but she wasn't entirely sure what he was saying. It did not matter what he said, not when the world was so attractive and new.

Isadora closed her eyes, and Lucan was there. She could see him as if he stood before her, every line and curve of his face distinct, every nicely honed muscle of his body calling to her. For a moment it actually seemed that she could feel him inside her, and she swayed against the intense sensation.

She opened her eyes and managed to focus on Sebestyen's face. "I must thank you, my lord, for sending me to Lucan."

"I'm so glad you enjoyed your time with him."

In the distance, Liane continued to scream, *"No, no, don't . . ."* Blah, blah, blah. Isadora paid her no mind. "I did," she said with wonder. "I enjoyed my time with him very much. Will you take me to him? I think I need him now."

"I imagine you do."

They did not go into the hallway. Instead, the emperor dragged Isadora to a low opening in the wall. The secret doorway. Maybe he knew the route through these passageways to Lucan's room. Maybe the journey would be quicker this way. The lighting in this passage was better than that between her room and Lucan's. A few of the light sticks which helped to illuminate Level One burned here at odd and distant intervals. The corridor was wider, perhaps even cleaner.

Sebestyen kept a tight grip on her wrist and pulled her along behind him. Isadora tried to keep up, but her feet felt heavy, and her knees wobbled. Still, she did her best to keep pace. They twisted down and down and around until she was dizzy. Shouldn't they be going *up*?

Maybe not. Maybe this was a truly magical passageway, where there was no proper up or down, no left or right.

Emperor Sebestyen muttered to himself frequently as they hurried along, and he held her wrist very tightly—

much more tightly than was necessary. Isadora increased her step, since she was anxious to get to Lucan.

The truth came to her like a wave that washed over and through her entire body. She loved Lucan Hern. It was a wonderful and terrible revelation. There was the curse to consider . . . but at the moment she did not care for curses, not at all. She was happy, she was strong . . . and she wanted Lucan. Her entire body throbbed for him. Maybe it wasn't actually love at all but a powerful and undeniable passion. Lust. She could not deny that her body had been made for his, that he had introduced her to pleasures she had never even imagined.

No, there was that, but love was a part of it, too. She'd tried to deny it, but now it was just too hard to fight what she knew to be true.

They left the hidden stairway behind, and the emperor dragged her along a plain, narrow hallway. This was not Level Four, and it was not a secret passageway. There were oddly shaped, thick doors here, and a rotten odor, and a distant wailing that was more irritating than Liane's screams.

She had been here before, she remembered with an annoying vagueness.

Finally they stopped, and two burly guards lifted the wooden hatch that was set in the floor.

Oh, yes. Father Nelyk had considered this place suitable punishment for his crimes.

"Have you heard of Level Thirteen, witch?" the emperor asked sharply.

"Yes." Isadora peered into the darkness below. In that moment, she was truly afraid. The terror was like the happiness she had felt when she'd thought the emperor was escorting her to Lucan. Deep, intense, dreamlike.

"You should not have betrayed me," the emperor said as he reached out for her.

Isadora knew that she was going to fall into the darkness below, she knew that just before the emperor's hand touched her. As his hand—still adorned with the blue ring Lucan liked so much—touched her, she reached out her own hand and splayed her fingers against his chest.

If she could think clearly, she could curse him in some way, but the words would not come to her. Her mind was so disjointed the language of the wizards was lost to her, and besides . . . Liane was her friend, and Liane loved her husband. As much as Isadora had once loved Will, as much as she loved Lucan. There had to be something good in the emperor somewhere, however small, however lost to the sight of others, for Liane to love him so much. As Isadora looked squarely into the emperor's eyes she saw not hatred, not evil, but pain.

She had sworn not to kill again . . .

All she managed to say was "Don't . . ." and then the emperor shoved, and the darkness swallowed Isadora whole.

12

ISADORA FELL FOR A MOMENT AND THEN LANDED HARD. The impact of her body against the hard ground stole her breath. Again the world swam, and this time it threatened to go dark. She fought her way back from unconsciousness, knowing that to succumb now would be bad. Very, very bad.

High above she saw the emperor's apathetic face for a moment, and then the hatch closed and she was left in complete darkness.

Her heart pounded too fast, and she was confused. Her brain refused to be still, and her thoughts were erratic and rapidly shifting. The emperor had drugged her. How long before the effects of the drug wore off? How long would she have to lie here before her wits returned and she could figure out how to escape from this dark hole in the ground?

She closed her eyes, reaching for a calmness that would

not come. Nothing made sense; nothing was as it should be. Where was Lucan? He would know what to do.

It was a long moment before Isadora realized that she was not alone. She heard the shuffling of movement in the dirt, she heard raspy breathing, and then she felt the tug of a hand against her skirt.

She screamed. She had never screamed in her life, not like this. The shriek of terror was ripped from her very soul. Her scream scared away some of whatever those things approaching might be, but not all of them were frightened. What felt very much like a hand made of leather found her cheek and caressed her clumsily.

"Soft," a hoarse voice whispered near her ear.

Another hand grabbed her ankle and started dragging her away. Her eyes adjusted to the darkness, which was total but for the hint of light that worked its way through the crack in the hatch above. It took her a moment to realize that the things surrounding her were not things at all, but men. Thin, wild-haired, desperate men.

If she could make her mind be still, she could send them away with a spell, but her mind would not be still. She fought against them physically, pushing and slapping, but since she was on her back and being pulled across the ground, it was difficult to fight with any strength.

A face swam above hers, malicious and thin and mostly hidden in a long, untended beard. She knew those eyes. She had seen them before. With a start, she realized who glared at her with such hate.

Father Nelyk was not dead.

"Do you have any food?" a hoarse voice rasped in her ear.

"Panwyr," another voice added from the other side of her head. "We need more Panwyr."

"I don't have anything," Isadora said. "Where's Lucan?" She tried to push the men away, but there were too many of them, and their hands were everywhere, and the drug had addled her mind so that she could not think. She slapped at a hand that wandered near her breast. "He will come for me, and you will be sorry if you hurt me. He won't like it, he won't like it at all." She gathered what senses she could and prepared to strike back. Not to kill—even now she did not wish to kill—but she could stop them. Couldn't she?

She reached out for the closest man, but before she could touch him, someone dragged her swiftly away. The next thing she knew the man was straddling her, and her hands were pinned to the ground. She looked up and did her best to see in the dark.

Nelyk. "She's a witch, the witch who put me here. Don't let her touch you. She is a vile, untrustworthy woman, and she knows heinous spells that will do you grievous harm."

Father Nelyk was stronger than the others, not quite so thin or wild-eyed. Of course, he had not been given the drug which was currently befuddling Isadora's mind. She kept waiting for the effects of the drug to wear off, but looking around her she wondered . . . would it? Ever?

"You!" Nelyk cut his eyes to another man and nodded sharply. "Hold her hands."

The man backed away. "I don't want to touch a witch. You said she has bad magic."

"She needs her hands to cast a spell, if my memory serves me. If you pin her down I can choke the life out of her, and she won't cause us any problems. Filthy witch," he muttered.

Only three men came to do as Nelyk ordered. They held her legs and her arms to the ground so that she could not move at all. Lightheaded and shaking and confused, Isadora waited for the hands at her throat and the end of her life, but they did not come.

Nelyk placed his face close to hers. "I prayed that I would see you once again, witch. When I thought I could not survive another hour in this place, when the darkness and the screams crept beneath my skin, I prayed for revenge. I'm tempted to simply choke the life out of you, but such a rash act would merely release you from your new home. You deserve to experience true suffering for what you did to me." Fingers touched her throat but did not tighten. "I hear that sometimes Panwyr causes an erotic surge, especially among women." His other hand slipped up her leg to her thigh. "Do you feel such a swell, witch? Is your body needful? Would you like me to satisfy your Panwyr-fed urges before I pass you to the next man, and the next, and the next? It's been a long while since they've had a woman with whom they could entertain themselves."

The threat brought a new wave of terror. If she had her wits about her, she could fight . . . and she could win. But her hands were pinned to the dirt floor, useless and weak, and her mind was so befuddled she could not reason, much less plan an attack.

That did not mean she would acquiesce. "I'd rather die quickly than be touched by *you*."

A few of the men around her laughed, but a glare from Nelyk silenced them. "Do you really think you have any choice in the matter, witch?"

Her eyes were playing tricks on her again. A soft glow tinged with purple crept into her line of vision and soon colored the once-black cavern that was Level Thirteen. Such a pretty gleam could not be real, not in this place.

Maybe it wasn't a trick of her mind. The light seemed so real, and it was deeply welcomed, as if she knew it to the depths of her soul. As the purple glow grew brighter, a few of the men scattered quickly, scurrying into the darkness like rats searching for a place to hide. Those who held her

legs released her and ran away, if you could call their awk-
ward half crawl running.

"Let her be," a deep voice commanded, and the man
who held her hands let go and made his escape. With a
curse, Nelyk leaped from her body and ran into the darkness, like the other rats.

Isadora took a deep, calming breath. She was still not
thinking clearly, so when the man with the long white beard
and hair leaned over her and smiled, she considered him to
be a delusion. Maybe she was already dead. He was surrounded by a cool, purplish light that seemed to emanate
from his very body.

But when he offered his hand and she grasped it, he felt
as real as Nelyk and the prisoners who had held her down.
He felt solid and warm.

"Come along, child," he said in a kindly voice that had
no business in this awful place. "I won't let them hurt you."

LUCAN WAITED TWO FULL DAYS BEFORE SENDING FRANCO
to the other servants to make inquiries as to Isadora's
whereabouts. Word had come the day before of the birth of
the emperor's son, a healthy child who had been named
Nechtyn Jahn Calcus Sadwyn Beckyt, and would be called
Jahn.

He gave Isadora time to see to the empress and the baby
and to get some much-needed sleep . . . and still she did
not come.

Franco arrived from his recon mission with a concerned
look on his face.

"Apparently Isadora has left the palace."

"What?" Lucan came up out of his chair with a shout
that shook the walls.

"When the baby arrived her work was done, and so she

went home. No one seems to know where that might be," he added in a puzzled voice.

Lucan reclaimed his chair. Had she been lying to him when she'd said she'd join him in escape? He had not seen any deception around her, but then he had not been *looking* for deception.

"Something is not quite right," Franco said in a lowered voice.

"How so?"

"One of the servants I have become friendly with in my time here was the empress's personal maid, Mahri."

The girl who had come to the door on the morning the empress went into labor. "What does she say about Isadora's departure?"

"Nothing," Franco answered. "I asked about Mahri this afternoon, but apparently no one has seen her since the empress had her child."

"Perhaps she's simply busy with all that's happening on Level One."

"I don't think so. We had taken to meeting for a bite to eat and a bit of conversation in the afternoon, and I believe she likes me."

Lucan lifted his eyebrows and studied the young man before him. "Have you been poking the empress's maid?"

"No!" Franco answered defensively. "Mahri is a sweet girl." He leaned toward Lucan. "I don't believe she's ever been with a man before. It would not be honorable to use her in such a way."

"I suppose not." He sighed. "Do you think she left the palace with Isadora?" His heart lurched as he spoke the words. Would Isadora have run away from him in such a cowardly way?

"If she did, then why didn't she tell someone? She had friends among the servants, and none of them knows where she might be. They believe her to be busy with the duties associated with the new baby. It's too soon for them to be concerned."

"But you're concerned."

"As I said, she's a sweet girl."

Isadora's sudden leaving did not make any sense to Lucan, but then he had allowed her to blind him in many ways.

If she had left with the ring upon her finger, then she had taken his destiny with her.

"Arrange a meeting with the emperor, as soon as possible." Sebestyen would know where Isadora had gone and how he might find her.

Isadora did not want him. That truth hurt more than it should, but he was a man not easily distressed by the vagaries of womankind.

But he needed the ring she wore upon her finger, and he would not allow it to slip away from him. His destiny was a lifetime in the making, and no woman would run away with his heart or his place in the Circle of Bacwyr.

ISADORA SLEPT—FOR HOW LONG, SHE DIDN'T KNOW. BUT the sleep was deep, and she felt safe, and she was always surrounded by that purplish light in an abyss that should be total darkness. In this place, where the white-haired man had taken her, there were no ratlike men clawing at her, no Nelyk, no hands on her body and her clothes. She came to believe, as she slept, that all those things were created by her imagination.

If she believed that to be true she could sleep, and she needed to sleep.

The bed she slept upon was a ragged pallet on a packed dirt floor, in a room of stone walls and rugged stone ceilings.

The food the white-haired man fed her regularly was bland but filling. On occasion she heard voices—women's voices—drifting to her from a short distance away, but she soon relegated them to the same category as the rat-men. They were not real; they were illusions brought on by the drug Emperor Sebestyen had forced up her nose.

On occasion when she woke, to be fed or simply to inspect her surroundings, she saw dark shapes in the corners of the stone room, dark shapes that swirled and shifted but did not come near her. At first she had been afraid of the black shadows that seemed to have a life of their own, but they never came close. In fact, she suspected they were more afraid of her than she was of them.

Nelyk had been right in one respect, though she had not wanted him to know. Lucan had awakened her woman's passion, and the drug that continued to affect her body teased that passion and made her feel as if she had no control. She dreamed of Lucan, and in her dreams he slaked the need. He held her close and made love to her. He made her scream, in her dreams, and the sensations of making love felt almost real. Almost. When she woke and he wasn't there, she felt cheated and empty and alone. Most of all, alone.

At one point, when the man with the white beard and hair was feeding her what seemed to be a warm mushroom soup, she looked into his dark eyes and said in a disturbingly childlike voice, "Emperor Sebestyen is a very bad man."

"Yes, he is, dear," the old man said cordially.

"He's mean."

She received the same answer, "Yes, he is, dear."

"I want to kill him, but I cannot."

"No, dear, you can't."

She liked the way the old man called her *dear*, even

though she did not know him at all, and it was very presumptuous of him to call her by such an endearment.

"You must get word to Lucan that I'm all right," she said, anxious not to think about the emperor any more than she had to. "He'll be worried."

"I'll see what I can do."

"I still don't want to marry him," she said, and then she found herself pouting. "I have been a wife once, and that's enough for any woman, don't you agree?"

"Anything you say, dear."

As she drifted off to sleep again, she heard one of those phantom female voices whisper, "Will you be able to save her?"

The old man answered, "I saved you, and you were in much worse shape than this when I found you. She has strength. She is the one I have been waiting for."

Isadora drifted off toward sleep again. Maybe there was a drug in the mushroom soup that made her sleep, but she didn't care. She didn't care about much of anything.

SEBESTYEN MADE HIS WAY THROUGH THE HIDDEN PASsageways to Liane's room on Level Three. Level Three with the other concubines, where she belonged. He did not dare walk the hallways. Lucan Hern had been insisting on a conference for days, and so far Sebestyen had been able to avoid such a meeting. By the time he told the Tryfynian that Isadora was gone, it would be too late for him to go after her with any expectations of actually finding her.

Sebestyen found his wife, one full week after delivering him two sons, resting in the bed he had provided for her. She was naked and restrained, as he had ordered, and she was not happy to see him when he joined her.

Gadhra stood at a worktable in the far corner of the

room, mixing up some foul-smelling potion. She was the only one he trusted to see to Liane, at least for now. If not for her, he would have been betrayed by his wife and her favorite sentinel and her witch.

"You're still fat," he said as he looked down upon his wife. She was not horribly fat, as she had been when she'd been pregnant, but she had more curves than was normal for her, and she was fleshier. She was beautiful, though he would not tell her so.

"You're still unspeakably vile," she responded.

He reached out and touched one breast, which was swollen and tender. No matter what she had done, he'd missed her. He still needed her. Liane tensed, but she could not move away from him. The silken bonds kept her immobile.

"It is too soon," Gadhra said, without even turning to look at him.

Sebestyen slowly withdrew his hand, and then he leaned down and kissed Liane's bare belly, letting his lips linger on the familiar flesh he could no longer trust.

"I want my babies," she said, tears springing to her eyes.

"You don't have babies," he said softly as he lifted his head. "You gave up the right to have babies when you lied to me."

She licked her lips. "I only wanted them both to be safe, that's all. I simply took the decision of how to handle the problem of twins away from you."

"So, you lied for my sake."

"Yes!" She yanked against the silk scarves that bound her to the headboard.

He had been given to moments of unnecessary sentimentality lately, and he suffered one now, as Liane stared at him with tear-filled eyes. He had loved her more than anyone else; heaven help him, he still did.

"I want to hold my babies, and care for them, and feed them," she whispered. "Don't take that from me, Sebestyen. I will never have another chance. The potion I took for so many years to prevent conception ruined my womb. These babies we made are miracles, and I want them with me. Please, Sebestyen."

"Our son, the rightful heir to the throne, is in the care of the priests. A nursemaid is feeding and caring for him and will continue to do so. Those are not proper duties for an empress, Liane."

"What did you do with the other one?" she whispered. "Where is my second-born?"

He tried to harden his heart against her. Betrayal from within had always been his greatest fear, and she had been the one to bring that fear to life. He could not feel sympathy or love or loyalty to her. "I have taken care of the matter, Liane." Before she could say more, he turned his attention to Gadhra. "Send for me when she is well enough to be of some use."

"Of course, my lord," Gadhra said pleasantly. "Her milk is almost completely dried, and she is healing nicely. Two to three more weeks, perhaps, and then she will be as she once was."

Sebestyen glanced at Liane again, but this time she did not look back. Instead, her eyes were focused on something only she could see. He turned from her and stalked away, wondering at his unwise decision to call upon her today.

After he left Liane, Sebestyen went directly to Level Two to visit with his firstborn son. The child was rather amazing; even the priests agreed that he was clever for a babe only one week old. Jahn had intelligent eyes and a healthy cry and was already growing stronger.

He adored the child more than he had imagined possible. How odd.

* * *

LUCAN WAS SURROUNDED BY SENTINELS WHO HAD DISarmed him. At least, they believed they had disarmed him. Two short but sharp blades were housed in sheaths against his body. They had tried to tell him that the emperor was not receiving visitors, but he refused to back down. If the information he had been given was correct, Isadora had been gone more than a week. Nine days, in fact.

She had the Star of Bacwyr, and so he was obliged to go after her. Only Sebestyen or his empress, who he heard had been confined to her bed, would know where to look for Isadora.

After pacing the hallway of Level One for well more than an hour, Lucan was summoned to the emperor. His patience was at an end, so he stormed into the imperial office with a ferocity that had the sentinels who guarded their emperor on alert.

Lucan dismissed them from his mind and strode to the desk the emperor sat behind. He placed his hands on the desk and leaned forward.

The sound of metal on metal singing as the sentinels drew their swords echoed through the room, but Lucan did not so much as flinch, much less turn his head to give them his attention.

"Where is she?"

Emperor Sebestyen looked completely innocent as he answered the question, though Lucan was quite sure he had not been innocent for a very long time. "Isadora? Did she not say good-bye before she left for home?"

"No, she did not," Lucan said in a lowered voice.

The emperor leaned back in his chair. "I'm sorry to hear that. Apparently things did not progress as you had hoped, in that respect. It's just as well. Isadora can be very difficult when it suits her."

"Where did she go?" Lucan asked again.

"Home."

"And where is her home?" he asked through clenched teeth.

"I imagine if she wanted you to know that detail, she would have—"

Lucan slammed his fist against the desk. *"Where?"*

The tip of a sword touched his neck; another was poised to strike at his back. And still he did not move.

Sebestyen ordered his sentinels back with a wave of his hand, and that's when Lucan saw the ring.

The emperor wore the Star of Bacwyr on the little finger of his right hand. It did not sparkle wildly with magic, as it had when Isadora had worn it, but instead lay almost dormant on the powerful hand. The magic he sensed there was weak. Did the power Lucan sought sleep in the emperor's possession?

Lucan did not stare at the ring, even though its significance was not lost on him. Isadora had not left the palace; and if she had, it had not been of her own free will. The emperor had done something with her . . . something *to* her. A realization struck his heart with an unexpected force. What if she was dead?

"I would very much like one last chance to see Isadora."

"She's been gone more than a week," the emperor argued. "It's unlikely that you can catch up with her. There are other women available—"

"I don't care for your other women. I wish to speak with Isadora."

The emperor's eyes hardened, and he leaned forward. "That is the second time today that you have interrupted me," he said in a soft but strong voice. "Do not do it again."

He would have to play the game with this man, at least until he found Isadora. Dead or alive, he would find her.

And if she was dead, he'd make the emperor and all his sentinels pay dearly.

"I have not yet signed our accord," Lucan said calmly. "I will not sign until I speak with Isadora."

Sebestyen's lips thinned, and his jaw twitched. "I will see what I can do in that regard," he said coldly.

"Thank you."

"I expect you will sign, however," the emperor said with confidence. "Isadora informed me that you are a man of your word, that you would not promise your allegiance in battle unless you were prepared to fight. She also said you are a fine warrior, and that if your men fight like you, you'll win this war for me."

"I did not know I was a subject of discussion between you and your wife's cousin," Lucan said tightly.

"Now that she's gone, I don't suppose it matters that you know the true nature of her part in your relationship," the emperor said coldly, again with a casual wave of his right hand. "While you were sleeping with her, Isadora filed a report with me, *personally,* every day. You look disappointed, Captain. Did you truly believe my wife's cousin cared for you? If I had known she'd make such a good spy, I would have called upon her talents in the past."

"Isadora was not spying on me."

"Actually, she was, and I don't mind telling you so now. You passed the test magnificently, so there's no reason to be irked by my caution. Isadora reported that you are noble, loyal, and trustworthy, a man of your word who fulfills his bargains. You should be pleased."

Lucan studied the emperor with eyes that had been taught to see. The man before him was unnatural in so

many ways, it was difficult to discern truth from lie, goodness from evil. But at the moment Lucan saw what he did
not wish to see: truth.

"Isadora had a friend who was maid to your wife.
Mahri, I believe. Would it be possible for me to speak to
her?"

"They did become good friends," the emperor answered.
"That's why Mahri went with Isadora when she left for
home."

This time the lie was evident, easier to see.

Lucan left the emperor's offices and Level One for his
own quarters. Inside the safety of the chamber, he began
to gather and prepare his weapons. What had the emperor
done with Isadora and Mahri? He had done something,
but why?

When his weapons were sharp and close at hand, Lucan
sat on the floor surrounded on all sides by candles and began a deep meditation. This meditation was the way in
which he prepared for the *hroryk elde*, but it was also the
way to reach deep inside himself for what he had learned at
Zebulyn's side.

Lucan did not have the power of a wizard, but Zebulyn
and the wizards who had followed had taught him to use
some small measure of magic, when necessary. It was necessary now. Where was Isadora? Was she alive? His heart
thudded hard, and his mind spun wildly, and he had a difficult time reaching the place inside himself where truth
could be found.

Zebulyn had taught him that the truth lived inside all beings, but that humans had forgotten how to access that
truth. Lucan fought for it now, as he fought for guidance.
He reached for a fragment of knowing that would ease his
worry . . . or else take away all hope. He shut off the rest of
the world and thought only of Isadora.

He thought of the way she had called to him from the first moment he'd seen her, the way she'd fought their feelings for one another, the way she laughed in his arms, the sensation of her body wrapped around his in all ways. He did not care that she had reported to the emperor. Maybe she had spoken of him to her cousin's husband, but if that was so, then she'd had no choice. Even though she had spied upon him, he trusted her. They had shared bodies and spirit, laughter and immeasurable pleasure in this room, and together they had grown stronger in all ways. In a soul-deep way they remained linked.

And the knowing came.

Isadora was alive. Scared, hurt, and confused . . . but alive. She was close, but not close enough, and wherever she was being kept all was dark. Completely, totally dark . . . until a tinge of purple crept into his vision. He knew that shade of purple and the strangeness of the illumination.

Wizards' light.

Isadora had asked him not to fight for either side, but this afternoon's confrontation with the emperor had decided the matter for Lucan. Sebestyen was an evil man, and he should not be allowed to rule.

As soon as he found Isadora and then confronted the emperor one last time to retrieve the Star of Bacwyr, he would join the rebels and see Sebestyen dethroned.

13

ISADORA OPENED HER EYES SLOWLY, TO FIND THE OLD
man she had been dreaming about hovering over her. His
eyes were dark, his hair white and silky, his face deeply
wrinkled. And there was that purple glow . . .

Apparently he was not a dream at all.

She sat up slowly. Her head pounded, and every muscle
in her body ached. The fall, of course. Emperor Sebestyen.

Nelyk.

A deep shudder worked through her body, and she
grasped her arms to her chest as if to warm herself.

"You are awake at last," the old man said. "That is
good."

She looked at him as bravely as she dared, given that
her body continued to shake. "Who are you?"

"My name is Thayne."

Thayne. She had heard of him. He was the wizard who
had foretold Sebestyen's fall. Isadora had no love for

wizards; none of the Fyne women did. But it seemed she was indebted to this one, like it or not.

"What are you doing down here?"

"This is my home, and has been for a very long time. Approximately eighteen years, I believe."

Isadora looked around the cell-like cave. How could anyone live here for such a long time? How did the old man call this cave home? "You saved me," she said.

"Yes, I did. That's why I'm here, you see. I protect the innocent from the injustice of the emperor."

Isadora cut her eyes away from Thayne's cutting glare.

"There's no need to worry," he said softly, "I have seen that you are not entirely innocent. I smell the aroma of death on you. That aroma gave me a moment's pause, when you were first delivered to me." He took her chin in his hand and made her look at him once again. "But the light of goodness is much stronger on and in you than the touch of death. I did not make a mistake in saving you. What is your name, child?"

"Isadora."

"You have magic, Isadora."

"Yes." She studied the purple light around him. "So do you."

Thayne smiled.

"But not enough to get you out of this place," she added.

He shrugged, as if it didn't matter. "I am here because I was meant to be here. If not for me, many who are innocent would have perished in a most horrible way. I could not save everyone who came to me," he said, sadness in his voice. "But I saved those who were strong enough to fight their way past the Panwyr and the loss of hope." He leaned close to her. "That is the worst," he whispered, "the loss of hope."

"I know," she whispered. She'd lost hope such a long

time ago. After her mother's death, after Will's passing, after the soldiers had burned her home.

Did she really have even a grain of hope that Lucan would find her?

"How long have I been here?" she asked.

"Ten days," Thayne said. "You are healing well. It often takes those under the influence of Panwyr more than twice that time to become as lucid as you are now. You have a strength about you, Isadora. Still, you must fight the need for the drug that will come to you. A second dose would be much more harmful to you than the first."

She didn't pay attention to what the old man was saying, past a certain point. "Ten days," she repeated, and with those words the last of her hope died once again. Sebestyen had surely spun a believable tale for Lucan to cover her disappearance. He would be angry that she'd left him without saying good-bye. So angry he was probably in Tryfyn by now, comforting himself with another woman, or two.

It didn't matter, she told herself as she struggled to her feet. It wasn't as if they had a future of any kind awaiting them beyond these palace walls, no matter what he said about the days to come.

"You said there were others," she said, dismissing Lucan from her mind.

"Yes." Thayne offered his hand, but she declined to take it. She wasn't yet sure that she trusted him entirely. "Come along, and I will introduce you."

Thayne led the way beyond the cave opening and into a hallway of sorts. The stone halls were narrow but sturdy, and they snaked down and down and up again. It wasn't long before Isadora saw a new light. It was warmer than the light that surrounded Thayne, more natural.

He turned a corner, and Isadora followed. She stopped when she found herself in a large underground cavern. There was natural and magical flame to light the place, a spring of fresh water, a garden of funguslike plants . . . and at quick count, twelve people besides herself and the wizard.

There were three women among the crowd, all of them dressed in gowns that had once been fine and which were now filthy and torn. Among the men there were varying styles of clothing, and a few wore what had once been imperial uniforms. She also noticed the blue kilt of a Level Three Master.

They all looked at her with a kind of awe, and some of them even seemed to hold their breath.

"Three empresses," Thayne said with a wave of his old hand. The women he indicated each gave a quick but regal curtsy. "Four empresses were sent here, but only these three were innocent."

Isadora glanced at the seemingly harmless man. "You left the other one to . . . to those . . . those monsters?"

"She had evil in her heart, and she had done many wicked things," he said without remorse. "She survived among the other monsters for a good long while. They were more her kind than we could ever be."

Isadora shuddered at the thought of surviving in the pit where those men had clawed at her dress.

Thayne introduced the others. They were, as she had judged by their dress, former ministers, soldiers, and servants, as well as the Level Three Master. All of them had offended Emperor Sebestyen in some way.

"You all live here?"

"Yes. We live here, and we wait."

"What are you waiting for?"

Thayne smiled, creating a mass of deep wrinkles on his face. "We have been waiting for you, Isadora."

* * *

FRANCO SWEPT INTO THE ROOM, STILL DRESSED AS A SER-vant . . . perhaps for the last time. "Mahri has been seen," he said, sounding relieved.

"Where?"

"Level Three," Franco said, the evident happiness of his relief fading quickly. "Mahri is not a concubine; she has no business on Level Three."

"Her presence there proves that Sebestyen lied to me. He said she left with Isadora." He wondered if Isadora was there, on Level Three, forced to participate in yet another form of servitude.

His worries did not last very long. Isadora would not make a compliant concubine. In fact, she was anything but compliant. It was one of the traits he most liked about her, oddly enough.

Lucan closed his eyes and concentrated on Isadora, as he had two days ago when he'd determined to his own sat-isfaction that she was alive and still in the palace. Level Three was above his head; Isadora was below. He knew that without fail; he felt it in a tug of energy as if she called to him.

Mahri might be kept quiet and obedient on Level Three, but Isadora was a different sort of woman. In order to keep her restrained, she would have to be physically confined.

"Where does the emperor keep his prisoners?"

"Level Twelve, I hear," Franco said. "Two Levels beneath the ground floor. Surely the emperor would not imprison a woman."

"I wouldn't put anything past Emperor Sebestyen," Lu-can said. He strapped on two swords and three knives, and checked to make sure they were well-seated in their sheaths. They were a part of him, and in his time here he had hidden the weapons or abandoned them altogether. No more. Any sentinel who tried to stop him as he made his way to Isadora would die. He laid his eyes on Franco. "Get ready. It's time."

ISADORA SAT WITH THE YOUNGEST OF THE THREE EM- presses. Rikka was a pretty girl who was only a little worse for wear for her time in Level Thirteen. Like the other em- presses, she was dressed in a once-fine crimson gown that designated her former station. She was not as worn down as the others, but then she had only been here a few months.

Everyone was anxious for news of what was going on above, but only Rikka had been outraged by the news that Emperor Sebestyen had married his concubine Liane. The fact that they'd produced twins together—news the others found fascinating—was apparently unimportant to Rikka.

"He actually married *her*?" The petite woman shouted as she scrambled to her feet to glare down at Isadora. Her hands formed small, tight fists at her sides, and when she stood it was evident that she'd lost many pounds since that frock had been fitted. "He threw me in this awful place, and then he married that . . . that whore?"

"Yes," Isadora said gently. "Because she was carrying his child, of course," she added. She had come to like Liane well enough, but she could imagine well why Rikka did not. After all, Liane had been Rikka's husband's mis- tress for the entire time she'd been married to Sebestyen.

"I thought he must be unable to father children," she said petulantly.

"He was. A witch's spell made conception possible."

Rikka sat again, yet still she pouted. "If I had called upon a witch's spell, I would be mother to the heir and still living above, in a fine room with lots of good food and clothes and—"

"Stop it!" The eldest and tallest of the empresses laughed lightly as she ordered Rikka to be quiet. Ghita was perhaps a few years older than Sebestyen—mid-thirties, Isadora would guess. The dust and dirt of Level Thirteen enhanced every small wrinkle on her handsome face. As his first wife, was she the true empress, still? That fact might matter to some of the more proper ministers and priests, but if the emperor had declared her dead . . . then she might as well be dead.

When Sebestyen had married Ghita, they'd both been little more than children. His first empress had fared very well, considering how long she'd lived in this cavelike home. "I do not wish to speak of food other than fungus until I can actually smell and taste it." She had managed to maintain an air of dignity the others did not possess—and perhaps never had.

"I want a bath," Avryl said longingly. "And I want tea, with sugar and cream." She sighed and rested her chin in delicate hands. Avryl was the only one of the empresses who was not fair-haired. Her hair was as dark as Isadora's, and she behaved very much like a spoiled child. It was hard to imagine maintaining that pampered manner in this place. Somehow, Avryl had managed to do just that. Still, there was a surprising strength to her; otherwise, she would not have survived.

Bannan, the Level Three Master, dropped to his haunches beside Ghita. "You females speak of all the things you want when we get out of here. Does not one of you wish to kill the emperor before we leave the palace?"

"Of course we do," Avryl answered. "But killing is man's work."

"Not necessarily," Isadora said beneath her breath. Still, they all heard her. Perhaps some of them even agreed with her.

While she sat there, an unexpected and tantalizing aroma teased her nose. It was not the mushroom soup Thayne prepared daily to keep the prisoners alive. This was sweeter. She closed her eyes. It was *very* sweet, *very* tempting, and she wanted it. Even though the room was cool, a sweat broke out on her forehead, and she felt perspiration gathering and growing on her chest and her thighs. Yes, she was suddenly hot.

A gnawing began in the pit of her stomach, and moving very slowly she rose to her feet and turned away from the group. By the moon and the stars, she was hungry in a way she had not imagined she could be. She was drawn away from the others, pulled toward the hallway that Thayne had led her through yesterday.

Had it been just yesterday?

"Isadora. Isadora!" Rikka tapped her on the shoulder, then took her arm. "Where are you going?"

"Can't you smell that? I want some of whatever that is."

Bannan and Laren hurried her way, and she instinctively moved away from them. The former soldier and the Master wished to stop her; they wished to take away from her whatever was sending her the scent that she needed and keep it for themselves.

"It's Panwyr you smell," Rikka said. "The sentinels have just thrown several doses of the drug, as well as some food, into the area where they threw you not so long ago. You not only smell it, you feel it, don't you? It's in your blood, still. I know too well what you're thinking right now." She sighed. "You must be strong. If you put Panwyr into your body again, it will only be harder to fight off the addiction. It might even be impossible."

Isadora let Laren take her arm and turn her away from the stone corridor. A faint noise reached her ears, and she had to strain to hear. A shout, a scream . . . laughter.

"They kill one another in order to get their hands on a tiny portion of the drug they need," Rikka said in a soft voice. "Thayne told me the first few times the sensations the drug generate are wonderful, but soon those feelings begin to fade, and an addict needs the drug simply to function. One dose can be addictive, or even fatal."

"And once the Panwyr has you, there is no escape," Laren said in a husky voice. "Have you seen the Isen Demon?"

Isadora flinched and took her arm from Laren's. "Demon?"

"Not a proper demon," Rikka explained. "Trapped souls linked together, huddling in dark corners and craving what they will never have: Panwyr."

"The bits of shadow I saw shifting in the corners?" Not here, where there was life and light, but in the cell-like room where she had recovered.

"Yes," Rikka said softly.

"You were all given the drug before you were thrown down here?"

"We were," Bannan said. "Thanks to the wizard and his magic, we all survived. There have been a few who were thrown down here without the Panwyr, but not many."

Isadora turned to Thayne, who looked to be totally engrossed in his preparation of the mushroom soup. "The girls Nelyk threw down here, Ryona, and the others like her, they were not drugged."

"You know of Ryona," he said in a lowered voice.

"Yes."

"She and the baby are well?" He tried to sound disinterested, but she could tell he was not.

"Empress Liane sent them home. When they left here, they were both doing very well."

"Good. She was the only one I could save. The others . . ." Thayne shrugged thin shoulders. "Surviving Level

Thirteen is difficult enough without throwing childbirth into the mix."

Isadora was unable to imagine what their time down here had been like. Ryona was very lucky to have survived. "The man who did this, Nelyk . . . he's out there." She nodded toward the corridor.

"I know," Thayne replied.

Isadora kept her focus on the corridor entrance. It was impossible to see around the corner. What if the ratlike men were there, just waiting to attack? The scent of the drug still called to her, and she wanted it. One more taste; just a small one.

But she did not rise and make her way toward the corridor. The worst of the addiction had passed while she'd slept under Thayne's care. She could fight the battle from here on out. She had suffered before. This new suffering was minimal in comparison.

Besides, she was accustomed to *not* getting what she wanted, what she craved. Like Will, or peace, or her sisters, or true happiness. Even Lucan had never truly been hers.

"Why do they not attack?" she asked, anxious to turn her mind from all she did not have.

"This area of Level Thirteen is sealed," Thayne said matter-of-factly.

"Sealed? How?"

"By me," he said. "By magic. None that I do not allow can pass beyond a certain point."

"Those men out there live in the dark, with only the food the guards throw to them, while you have light and tasteless but nourishing soup. Are you not compelled to help them all?"

Thayne walked to her, his step slow as if each move pained him. He leaned down and looked her in the eye. In a low but strong voice he said, "My gift is protection, but not everyone deserves my care. If I allowed those prisoners here, how long do you think the empresses would survive? How long before someone like Nelyk killed the men who are here not for a crime but for an *insult*?" His expression softened. "Your gift is protection also, but you have not yet learned that not all beings deserve your favor."

Isadora's heart leaped. "How do you know—"

"I know many things," he interrupted. "Destruction is easier than protection, as you well understand. Destruction does not require care and consideration and time and heart. It is easier to strike out in blind anger than it is to shield those who need our care." A gentle hand caressed her cheek. "Not everyone deserves to benefit from your gift, Isadora. You are not beholden to the entire of Columbyana, only to those you love."

"And if I don't love anyone?" she snapped.

Thayne just smiled. "Your heart is filled with love; you just choose to share that love sparingly, for now."

"For always," she responded.

"That is yet to be seen."

She had never met anyone who understood her dilemma, but Thayne seemed familiar with the ways of both aspects of Isadora's gifts. "How do I put destruction aside, once and for all?"

He started slightly, and his old fingers trembled. "You should never abandon any of your powers, Isadora. Destruction is frightening, and often misused, but when you are sworn to protect, it is also inevitable."

"I was told I would need to *choose*," she argued.

Thayne smiled. How had the old man managed to keep so many teeth in this place? "You chose long ago, dear, and you chose well." His smile did not last. "In the practice of protection there is always a time for destruction. For us, that time is coming. Soon."

* * *

THE SENTINELS ON LEVEL FOUR WERE SO ACCUSTOMED to seeing Lucan outfitted for his daily exercises in the courtyard, they paid him little mind as he took the stairway downward. If he had been going up they would have interfered, as he was well-armed. But as he was headed down, away from the emperor, they did not try to stop him. They barely gave Franco a glance, and some smiled at the very idea of the valet serving as sparring partner on this day. They did not know that Franco was a well-trained warrior who could best any three of them.

They reached Level Ten, the ground level where the entrance to the courtyard awaited, and continued downward. Level Eleven was so noisy Lucan's ears were pained. This was the place where the lift and the unnatural lighting devices were powered, Isadora had explained. He did not stop to examine the contraption that made so much noise. Another day, perhaps.

At Level Twelve, the final Level, he encountered a heavy wooden door. It was not even locked, so he opened it and walked boldly into the austere, cold hallway of the emperor's prison.

Three sentinels lifted their heads as he entered. Their faces were familiar; he had seen them about the palace in his time here, which meant they had seen him and would not be alarmed.

"Captain," one guard said as he took a step forward. "I believe you must be lost . . ."

"I am not lost." Lucan drew his long sword, and behind him Franco did the same. "The empress's cousin, Isadora. Where is she?"

All three sentinels drew their weapons; short-bladed swords they handled like men who had used them before.

"Is she in one of these rooms?" The cells would be cool and dark, he imagined, as he had seen in his vision.

"Sir," the sentinel in the lead said as he assumed a fighting stance, "I will only warn you once—"

"I need no warning from the likes of you."

The skirmish that ensued was quick. The clang of blades meeting in air rang loudly in the small stone corridor, but three sentinels were no match for two Circle warriors. The fight that followed the initial meeting of steel did not take more than the span of a few heartbeats. A slash, a turn, a sidestep, and a thrust, and all three sentinels were unarmed and lying on the floor. Two were dead; one was severely wounded.

Lucan knelt beside the wounded man and drew his dagger. He held the tip against the man's throat. "The empress's cousin, Isadora, where is she?"

The sentinel shook his head, and Lucan pressed the tip of the blade into a quivering throat.

"Wait!" the man shouted hoarsely. "Don't kill me. I know who you're looking for. One of the other sentinels talked of it, days ago. The emperor himself brought her here."

"Where is she?" Lucan asked with strained patience.

The sentinel reached behind him and laid one hand on the wooden hatch that was set in the floor. "It's too late," he said. "She's been down there for many days, and no one survives in that place for very long."

"What's down there?"

"Level Thirteen. It's just a hole in the ground beneath the palace. A pit."

"The emperor put his wife's cousin into a *pit*? Why?"

"Isadora Fyne is not the empress's cousin," the sentinel said, a new fear in his eyes.

"Then who is she?"

"She is the empress's witch."

Lucan was tempted to drive the blade into the man's throat and be done with it, but he could see that the truth had just been spoken. This man truly believed that Isadora was a witch. Perhaps that's what the emperor had told his men in order to justify imprisoning her.

In the back of his mind a voice whispered, *Beware the witch.*

Lucan stood and nodded to the wounded sentinel. "Watch him," he ordered. "I'll be right back."

"You're not going after her," Franco said, surprised. "You heard what he said."

"I *am* going after her. Isadora is alive, and I won't leave her down there." Witch or not, she did not deserve to be left behind.

"We could kill him, and then I could come with you," Franco said. The man on the floor shuddered, in preparation for death. "You can't go down there alone, Captain."

"No, we might yet need him." Together he and Franco lifted the hatch in the floor. The odors and the noises turned his usually staunch stomach. The pit in the ground, Emperor Sebestyen's Level Thirteen, was a hellish place, and there were men down there. Filthy, bone-thin, desperate men who spoke and screamed and flitted in and out of the dim light that spilled below.

"Don't," the sentinel rasped. "Lots of men go down there, but none ever come back up again."

"I will," Lucan promised, and then, with a short blade in each hand, he dropped into the hole.

14

THE BOWLS THAT WERE SHARED BY ALL THE RESIDENTS OF the wizard's secured section of Level Thirteen were made of stone. Most were marked with a natural well that would hold a serving of tasteless mushroom soup, while others looked as if they had been purposely shaped with a tool of some sort. Another stone, perhaps. The spoons were fashioned from metal that had once adorned a soldier's uniform or a woman's fancy girdle.

Nothing went to waste in this place.

Isadora had been relieved to learn—through long conversations with the empresses—that a wizard's spell had helped Ghita and Avryl sleep through much of their time here. She could not imagine living in a sunless cave for so many years and surviving with mind and body intact. Rikka had refused his offers of a magical sleep, but if she was here for years instead of months, would she eventually relent? Would anyone? Since Isadora's coming they had all been awake more than asleep, as they waited. She wasn't sure exactly what they were waiting for, but now and then they looked at her with an expectation she did not understand.

With no illumination but the wizard's light, Isadora was unable to tell whether it was night or day aboveground. Not that it mattered. The days moved in a regular enough symmetry, the only event providing any sort of regularity the delivery of food and Panwyr to the prisoners who lived in the darkest section of Level Thirteen.

Isadora had no sympathy for murderers and traitors, and she certainly had none for Nelyk. But to live in that filth and darkness for such a long time . . . it was unnaturally cruel.

Today's delivery had already been made, so when the prisoners once again began to howl, everyone turned their heads toward the stone corridor that led to the center of the pit. Then all eyes turned to Thayne. The wizard's eyes went dark, and his purple light increased, then dimmed.

"It is time," he said in a lowered voice.

When he headed for the corridor, everyone followed. Isadora jumped off the dirt floor and followed Rikka. "Time for what?" she whispered as the walls closed in around her. In many parts of the corridor, there was only room for one person at a time to pass, so she had to lean forward to ask her question.

"Thayne said that after you came, the one who would rescue us would follow."

"Rescue?"

"A true warrior, he said," Rikka whispered. "A champion surrounded by blades and truth and nobility."

Isadora's heart leaped. *Lucan.* "Why didn't someone tell me?" Her time might have been easier, if she had known with certainty that Lucan would come for her.

"Thayne didn't know when the rescue would come. Days, weeks, months. He did not want to raise your hopes, not while the Panwyr was still at work in your system and you were not entirely yourself."

When the corridor widened, she slipped past Rikka and Ghita, and then past two of the more quiet male prisoners who had been here so long their skin was chalky and their clothes were all but falling off their thin bodies. Soon she was right behind Thayne. From her position close behind the wizard she could hear the prisoners screaming.

"I know who that is," she said softly.

Thayne did not turn around to look at her. "Of course you do, dear."

LUCAN HELD HIS SWORDS READY, BUT NO ONE AP-proached. The area where he stood was lit from above, since the hatch in the floor had been left open, and Franco held a torch close to the opening. Beyond the circle of illumination all was dark.

Dark, but not silent. The screams and the rustlings from the darkness were more terrifying than any battle, more bone-chilling than any opponent he had ever faced. He had seen a few of the prisoners when he'd first dropped into the pit. They were thin and stooped and filthy, and the one pair of eyes that had caught his, before running away, had been undeniably crazed.

The stench was almost overpowering. Rot and un-washed bodies and dampness combined to create an odor that turned his stomach. And Isadora had been down here for well more than a week? He could not imagine a woman like her enduring in this place. He could not imagine any-one surviving here for any length of time.

"Isadora," Lucan called in a strong voice. He did not

feel her here as he should, and he did not see the wizard's light he had found in his meditation. He had no idea how deep the darkness went, or if there was another entrance to this hellish place. She could be anywhere.

He should be able to call upon his gift to find her, but he needed a calmness of mind to reach that part of himself, and at the moment his mind knew no calm. "I don't want to hurt anyone," he added. "I am here for Isadora."

"Pretty girl," a voice whispered from the darkness.

"Pretty *witch*," another voice called.

Again, someone accused Isadora of witchcraft. Perhaps the prisoners had heard the sentinels above, or the emperor himself, use that as an excuse for throwing her into this place.

"Tell me where she is, and I'll get you all out of here."

The screaming turned into mutterings, and eventually a few of the prisoners stepped forward. They all pointed in the same direction, into the deepest black shadows beyond the darkness that was Level Thirteen.

His eyes had adjusted somewhat, but he could still see nothing beyond the darkness. Lucan sheathed one sword and glanced up. "Franco, toss me a torch."

A moment later, the young warrior did as his captain asked. A flaming torch dropped into the darkness, and Lucan caught it with his free hand.

Darkness in this place was best. The death and despair he saw in the torchlight was sickening. Still, he saw no sign of Isadora. "Find a rope," he called, not even glancing up at Franco. "A rope ladder, if possible. Kill the sentinel if he doesn't tell you where to find what you need." A few of the prisoners cackled at that command. "We're going to get these men out of here, as soon as I find Isadora."

"You don't see her?"

Lucan glanced in the direction the prisoners had indicated. Beyond the light of the torch, all remained dark. "No. Not yet." He took a step, and then another. Before him, the body of a man lying on the floor was illuminated. Eyes wide open, skin sagging over bones, he appeared to be dead.

And then the body twitched, and the eyes cut toward Lucan. The man squinted against the light, and scurried into the shadows.

Emperor Sebestyen would die for putting Isadora in this place, Lucan vowed as he continued to move deeper into the gloom of Level Thirteen. He turned a corner, entered a narrowing passageway of sorts, and left the small bit of light from the open hatch behind.

IT TOOK LONGER THAN ISADORA THOUGHT IT SHOULD to reach the unprotected section of Level Thirteen. She did not remember making this long trip after Thayne had rescued her from Nelyk, but then she did not remember much after the emperor had shoved the Panwyr up her nose. Had Thayne carried her all this way? He was old, and living down here had sapped his strength. Maybe he had dragged her to safety.

Along the way she spotted more than one Isen Demon swirling along the lower edge of the cavern wall. Or was it the same one, following their path? Sad souls, trapped here the way the emperor had planned to trap her, preferred the darkness, so they did not linger long in the wizard's light. Rikka had whispered once that the demon fed on the souls of the dead, and that with each feeding it grew larger and stronger. And yet it did no more than hide in corners and peek at the living, as it awaited its next meal.

Isadora did her best to put the sad Isen Demon out of her mind. She was bursting to see Lucan. She needed and wanted to see him almost as much as she wanted out of this cursed place. Nothing else was in her mind, nothing but looking at his face and throwing her arms around him and holding on. She'd been alone for so long, with no one but her sisters for companionship and affection. Having Lucan in her life in such a way was unexpected, but it was also a gift, as important as her powers and her calling for protection and her very life.

Just beyond a curve in the natural stone corridor, she saw a new light. Not Thayne's purple light, but the warm illumination of a fire. She grasped the back of the wizard's tattered robe, in barely contained excitement.

"He came here for me?" she whispered.

"Yes, he did, dear," Thayne answered.

To willingly come into such a place . . . he must care for her, at least a little. There had to be something more than the lust they shared to compel him into Level Thirteen. If he knew she was a witch, would he still bother to rescue her? Or would he walk away and leave her here?

They reached the opening, and she could see the magical seal that Thayne had put in place to keep the rat-men at bay. It shimmered, purple like his light. And beyond the shimmering seal, she saw Lucan approaching. He held a sword in one hand and a torch in the other, and he moved forward cautiously. For the first time in many days, Isadora smiled.

"Lucan!" she shouted.

"He cannot see or hear beyond the—" Thayne began, and then Lucan's eyes snapped directly at her and he moved quickly forward. "Interesting," the wizard whispered, as he lifted his hand and said the words that broke the seal.

Once the seal fell, Isadora ran past Thayne and all but threw herself at Lucan. "You're here."

The hand that held a short-bladed sword circled around her, and Lucan lifted her slightly off the ground. "Of course I am here," he said. "Did you think I would leave you?"

She backed away from Lucan and looked up into his face, which was illuminated by firelight from the torch he carried. In all her life, she had never seen anyone or anything that was so beautiful; she had never known a man existed who could touch her heart and her soul so deeply. She would gladly give up all she held dear—her magic, her place on Fyne Mountain, even the simple life she had enjoyed with her sisters—to be with this man, even for a short while. He had known the truth long before she had. Hadn't he asked her to leave Arthes with him? Hadn't she seen the power she felt in her heart in his eyes?

"I can't wait to see Tryfyn in the spring," she said softly.

Lucan smiled at her, and the two of them assisted the other protected prisoners along the way to the main part of Level Thirteen. They turned a corner and saw the light from the hatch above. A rope ladder had been dropped, and prisoners were scrambling up the escape route and disappearing.

Isadora's heart leaped. "Nelyk," she whispered. "Oh, no. Has he already escaped?"

Lucan looked down at her. "Who's Nelyk?"

"A priest," she answered. "He's . . ." *He knows who I am, he means to kill me, he is an evil man . . .* "He's one of the prisoners I would not like to see go free."

"No one deserves this," Lucan said.

"No, but . . ."

Maybe he heard the concern in her voice, because he asked in a sharp voice. "What does he look like?"

"He's . . ." She realized, as the words froze in her throat, that at the moment Nelyk looked like all the others. Bearded, thin, desperate. A few of the prisoners in Level Thirteen had once been in positions of power, so Nelyk was not even the only one who wore a crimson robe.

"I don't imagine any of the prisoners will remain in the palace a moment longer than they have to," Lucan said in a comforting voice. "Don't be afraid, Isadora. I will stay at your side, today and always."

"Always is a long time." And if he found out she was a witch, always would end in a heartbeat.

Thayne and Lucan held the remaining prisoners at bay while the empresses climbed the rope ladder to safety. They tried to get Isadora to follow the other women, but she refused. She remained beside Lucan, determined to see the others out of the pit before she herself climbed from Level Thirteen.

The men Thayne had saved climbed, many of them struggling since their strength was not as it should be, and now and then another filthy rat-man would run to the ladder and shove someone else aside so he could make his way up. They even scurried like rats, darting from the darkness. No one tried to stop them. Isadora watched for Nelyk, but she did not see him. Given his selfish nature, he had likely escaped up that ladder first, shoving all others aside.

Would Nelyk run from the palace like the others, or would he run straight for the emperor?

Finally, there were only three of them left: Thayne, Lucan, and Isadora. Thayne looked at Isadora and nodded.

"You first," she said. The old man was weaker than she, and besides, she was not ready to leave Lucan. She wanted to know that he was right behind her.

Thayne only protested minimally and then he began to

climb. He moved slowly, and his grip on the rope was tenuous. When he reached the top, there were others—Franco and some of the prisoners he had protected—to assist him.

When that was done, Lucan sheathed his sword. "Your turn," he said, smiling down at Isadora. For the first time since she'd seen this place, all was quiet. There was no labored breathing, no mutters or cackles or whispers from the darkness.

"Thank you," she whispered.

She went up on her tiptoes to give him a kiss, but before her lips touched his, a shadow rushed out of the darkness, and a bony hand gripping a sharp rock swung into the light of the torch and bashed against Lucan's temple. He crumpled to the ground, dropping the torch as he fell. The flame illuminated the face of the attacker as it dropped.

Nelyk grabbed Isadora by the throat. From above, many voices shouted, and she heard the rattle of a sword as Franco started down the rope ladder.

Was Lucan dead? She had seen the blood bloom as the blow landed, and he had dropped to the ground with such force.

"You won't get away with this," she whispered.

"I already have." Nelyk grabbed Lucan's sword and held the tip against his chest. That chest still moved, Isadora noted with relief. Lucan was not dead. Nelyk held up a much-too-familiar vial of brown powder before her nose. "Use your magic on me, and I'll drive this blade through his heart."

"What do you want?"

"I've been saving this for you." He waggled the small vial of Panwyr before her nose. "I killed two men to take it for myself, hoping that you and I would have another moment together before this life ended."

She knew that another dose of Panwyr would likely kill

her. According to Thayne and Rikka, she would surely be addicted. And if she died . . . would she become a part of the Isen Demon, the sad entity she had pitied moments earlier?

Franco reached the halfway point on the ladder and then dropped the rest of the way. Nelyk gave the man a swift glance. "This does not concern you, boy."

"You hold a blade on my captain. It very much does concern me," Franco insisted. "Cease now, and I will allow you to escape with the others."

"I will cease when Isadora takes her medicine like a good girl." He handed the Panwyr to her and placed both hands on the hilt of the sword that he held to Lucan. "Take it, and I will let him live. Refuse, and I'll run him through."

"Fine." She uncapped the Panwyr. Her initial addiction had not entirely gone away, and her heart sped up in anticipation. She knew that taking this drug into her body would be the end of her, and at the same time . . . a part of her craved it. A part of her remembered the colors and the euphoria that came with the Panwyr that would tingle as it traveled up her nose.

A deep and dark part of her, the Level Thirteen of her soul, *wanted* the Panwyr.

"Isadora, don't," Franco said softly. "I can take care of him."

"Not before he kills Lucan." She looked squarely at the young warrior. "Once I take this drug I won't be of much use for a while. If this man so much as scratches Lucan, I want you to kill him."

Franco nodded.

Isadora closed her eyes and lifted the vial to her nose.

SOPHIE SAT BACK AGAINST THE LOG NEAR LAST NIGHT'S cold campfire, studied her stomach, and frowned. It was not time for this baby to be born, not yet, and still, something within her was changing. She'd had no labor pains, thank goodness, but unless she was mistaken, the baby had turned.

It was too soon. She knew the baby was well and healthy, but it was much too soon. Not only would the child be small and weak if she came this early, her birth would sap Sophie's powers.

Sophie's magic was always much greater when she had a baby growing inside her, and she needed all her magic in order to break the curse.

She had tried to break the curse. For months, she had tried everything. And yet, the knowledge that it still threatened Kane weighed heavily on her heart. She needed Isadora to end this curse. Juliet, too, if that was possible. But time was running out. Even if this daughter came late rather than early, there was no guarantee that she would find her sisters by then.

She heard men coming long before the rebels around her became alert and readied themselves with their swords, just in case those arriving were not who they should be. As expected, it was Myls and Kane who approached.

Not as expected, they were not alone.

A fair-haired man dressed as an emperor's sentinel walked between Kane and Myls, moving slowly and favoring one side. Sophie rose clumsily to her feet; a nearby rebel moved quickly to assist her with a steady hand.

"Who is this?" she asked, moving forward before any of the rebels dared to do so.

"My spy," Myls said with a grimace. "Former spy," he added sourly. "Apparently Ferghus is no longer welcomed in the palace."

* * *

HIS HEAD HURT. FIRST THERE WAS THE KNOWLEDGE OF pain. Then voices came to Lucan, then light through barely opened eyelids. Shadows danced above and around him, and in an instant he cleared his fogged mind and evaluated the situation.

"Hurry up," the ragged prisoner commanded.

Isadora stood above him, eyes closed and an object held to her nose. A drug, he could tell, and she was about to put it into her body because this ragged man held Lucan's own blade to his chest.

Lucan's arms snapped up and he caught the flat of the blade between his palms. The prisoner, who had been watching Isadora closely, was surprised by the move, and his astonishment caused a deadly hesitation. Lucan whipped the sword from the prisoner's grasp, burst to his feet, flipped the sword in the air and caught it by the handle, and thrust the blade into the heart of the man who had dared to hold Lucan's own sword on him. The prisoner looked almost surprised as he dropped to the ground, crumpling to the dirt floor.

What happened next caused Lucan to start in surprise. A dark shadow that hovered low to the ground darted from the stone wall and enveloped the prisoner's body. In an instant, the body was pulled into the darkness by the dark cloud.

Isadora had not moved. She still stood there with the vial poised at one nostril. One sniff, and the powder in that vial would travel up her nose and into her system. Even when the prisoner was well and truly dead, gone from their sight and no longer a threat to anyone, she did not drop her hand.

Lucan laid his hand over hers and drew it down, away from her nose. "Did you ingest any of the drug?"

She shook her head, very slowly.

"Good." He took the vial from her and threw it into the darkness, where it belonged.

Isadora slipped an arm around his waist. "That was Nelyk, the man I asked about. He was a priest." Dazed wonder made her voice sound almost childlike.

"Something took him," Lucan said softly. He knew much of magic; he had seen it at work many times. And yet, whatever had taken Nelyk's body away was a truly bad magic—he felt it to his very core.

"Isen Demon," Isadora said as she glanced into the darkness. She quickly cut her eyes to him. "You're bleeding."

"Yes, I know." He scowled and touched a hand to his temple.

She laid her hand over his and rested it there.

"Excuse me?" Franco said in a testy tone of voice. "Can we please get out of this awful pit? Women and wounded men first," he added, gesturing to the rope ladder in a gentlemanly fashion.

Isadora gladly climbed the ladder, and Lucan was right behind her. He could not wait to get her out of this place.

In the hallway of Level Twelve, only the prisoners who had been with the wizard remained. The others had run. The sentinel Lucan had wounded lay on the floor, eyes closed, his chest barely moving. Isadora glanced down at the soldier.

The wizard apparently saw the direction of her eyes. "The guard was wounded before we arrived, and many of the prisoners felt compelled to deliver a kick or a punch before they made their escape. He did not fare their attentions well."

The soldier was in much worse shape than he had been when Lucan had left him—perhaps near death.

"You could have protected him," Isadora accused.

"He was not innocent," the wizard answered without emotion.

Franco climbed out of the hole in the floor, and Isadora once again slipped her arm around Lucan's waist. It felt good to have her close again, to know she was safe.

With Isadora caught up against his side, Lucan turned to the wizard. "We have not met, yet I believe I owe you a debt of gratitude that will not be easy to repay. I am Lucan Hern, First Captain of the Circle of Bacwyr."

Bedraggled and dirty, wrinkled and weakened, the hair on his head and his face growing wildly in all directions, the wizard gave a shaky bow that might've once been courtly. "Sinnoch Fiers Camalan Thayne, former wizard to the Emperor of Columbyana."

Isadora tightened her hold on his waist, and then she wobbled and leaned toward the old man. "Sinnoch?" she all but shouted. "Are you . . ." And then she backed away, her hold on his waist remaining firm. "No. It's just a coincidence," she said in a softer voice.

The wizard's old eyes sparkled, but the set of his mouth remained firm. "Isadora, my dear, nothing in life is a coincidence. All that happens is carefully planned in a way that makes sense only to the powers of the universe that we do not dare to understand. To answer the question you are afraid to ask . . . Yes, I am your father."

15

WHEN THE RAGGED PRISONERS OF LEVEL THIRTEEN HAD
made their way to Level Ten, they'd met the resistance of
the sentinels. Many of the escapees had been killed, but
quite a few had slipped past the guards and into Arthes, just
as darkness of night fell. The sentinels had divided their
ranks; some headed up to protect the emperor, as well as
the ministers and the priests, while other soldiers chased
the escapees beyond the palace walls.

For this reason Lucan and Franco, who led the way for
Thayne's group, met little resistance as they escorted their
party out of the palace, into Arthes, and beyond the city
limits. Many times, Isadora wanted to stop Lucan and tell
him that she had to go back. What had happened to Liane
and the babies? What of Mahri? She could not run away
and leave them all behind.

But she continued on with the party, hurrying away
from the city and into a countryside of gentle hills and

thick stands of trees, with a softly shining moon to light their way.

Since she could not yet return to save Liane and the babies—or baby, if only the firstborn had survived—she allowed her mind to wander to other important and startling matters. Thayne was her father. After all these years of wondering and ultimately dismissing the man who had sired her, he had been dropped into her life. Well, she had been dropped into his, more literally. She looked at the old wizard who walked with a slight limp to mark his age, and tried to see the man he had been more than thirty years ago, when her mother had chosen him to be her first daughter's father. Perhaps he had been handsome then, more sturdily built and more apt to smile. His years in Level Thirteen had aged him, and even though wizards lived unusually long lives, his had been shortened by his time beneath the palace.

While Franco set up camp for the night and Lucan went into the wooded area nearby to hunt for the evening meal, Isadora sought out the wizard and drew him aside, so no one else could hear their conversation. Bannon and Laren had built a small fire, and Thayne had already cast a protection spell that would keep the soldiers away—at least for tonight. The other men, the prisoners who had been in Level Thirteen for such a long time, were no stronger than the empresses, and were no help at all in securing the camp.

Tonight they could all sleep in peace, under the stars and in relative safety. The air was cool and wonderfully fresh, and the night was not too cold.

"What do you wish to know?" Thayne asked pragmatically.

"Did you love my mother?" It was not the question she had intended to ask, but it was the one that sprang from her mouth.

"I cared for Lucinda very much, and she liked me well enough. Even if we had been so inclined, love was impossible, due to the curse."

"You know of the curse?"

"Of course. Lucinda told me all about it. Have you broken it yet?"

Her heart thudded. He asked the question so casually. "No. Can it be broken?"

Thayne waved his hand dismissively. "Curses are low magic, easily broken. I told your mother as much, but she shook her pretty head and rejected my advice. She wasn't ready." He turned dark eyes to hers. "I suspect you are, daughter."

"How can the curse be broken?"

The old man shrugged. "The question isn't so much how can it be broken, but why has it been kept alive for so long."

"What do you mean, *kept alive*?"

He took her arm and led her to an outcropping of rocks, where he sat tiredly on an oddly shaped boulder. When he indicated that she was to sit beside him on the cold rock, she impatiently did so.

"When a curse is first cast, it has little power. It's an annoyance. A flea. A bit of bad luck and ill wishes that take form and buzz about like a pesky fly."

Isadora felt her ire rise swiftly to the surface. "Many Fyne witches have buried men they loved, or watched them run away in horror. I buried my husband, whom I loved very much." And she was beginning to accept that she loved Lucan, in a different way but just as strongly as she had loved Will. He would walk away when he found a woman he liked better, or worse, when he learned she was a witch. "You dare to compare that suffering to a pesky fly?"

Thayne shook a bony finger at her. "I said a curse *begins* in that fashion. They can grow much stronger, and often do."

"How?"

"Fed by the fear of those who are cursed."

Her anger grew, and with it her worst fears. "Are you trying to tell me that my own fear is what keeps the curse alive?"

Thayne shrugged. "Yours. Your sisters'. Your ancestors'." His brow wrinkled as he puzzled over the situation. "There's more in this case; I can feel it. Was the curse penned? Did past Fyne witches write of their heartache and the power of the curse?"

"Yes."

"Where are those papers?"

"Burned," she said softly. Would they need those letters to break the curse? If so, then all was lost. "When the emperor's soldiers set fire to the cabin, the letters were inside, stored in a box."

Thayne tsked loudly. "In a special box, I imagine, feeding the curse the power of grief with every passing year." He waved a hand. "It is good that they are burned. That is helpful."

Isadora breathed a sigh of relief. "Does that mean the curse is ended?"

"Oh, no," Thayne said. "You and your sisters still keep it alive. No three ordinary women would be able to feed the curse such power, but you and your sisters are extraordinary in the power you supply. The three of you will have to release the curse once and for all, together."

Her anger and fear did not disappear, but they were now mitigated with something new: hope. Did she dare? "I don't even know where my sisters are," she said.

Thayne looked at her squarely and took her chin in his hand. "I suggest you find them."

It seemed so simple. *Too* simple. Isadora shifted her head so that it was free of the wizard's grasp. Hope alone would not end the curse. She needed specific answers. "Once I find Sophie and Juliet, how do we go about ending the curse once and for all?"

Thayne looked up into the night sky, studying the stars that sparkled above. He seemed lost in the sight for a moment, and then he answered, "Before the curse is broken, what you believe to be impossible will become possible before your very eyes. One, two, three. Nothing stays the same forever, and sometimes a miracle is just the first sign of a coming change, but it seems like a miracle at the time because it is so rare and unexpected. One, two, three," he said again.

"We all must see these miracles, is that what you're saying?"

"You and your sisters will each experience something you once thought impossible. When that is done you will clasp your sisters' hands and together the three of you will cast the curse into a faraway place of insignificance, where it belongs. To do this you will need fire, starlight, and the possession of those things which you believed to be impossible." He looked at her and smiled. "And hope. I see the beginnings of hope inside you, but it isn't enough. You must each have a steadfast belief that the end of the curse is not only feasible, but in your hands."

It sounded simple, and yet . . . not so simple. "You are a seer as well as a wizard."

"Yes," he said harshly, "for all the good it has done me."

"You told of the Emperor Sebestyen's fall after the sun touched his face. How long after?"

"Within hours, perhaps even minutes."

She wanted to believe the old man who told her that the curse could be ended, but how could she, when he was obviously flawed in his predictions? "You're wrong," she said gently. "Sophie brought sunlight into the palace months ago, and Sebestyen is still alive and well."

The old man, her father, smiled. "I have never felt the need to explain my prophesies, especially not to a man as ungrateful and selfish and cruel as that *paivanti* emperor."

"What could there be to explain?"

"Sebestyen never needed to fear sunlight, Isadora." Thayne lifted a wrinkled hand to his own cheek and let the fingers barely lay upon the skin. "His fall will follow the touch of his *son*."

IMPOSSIBLE. NO ONE HAD EVER ESCAPED FROM LEVEL Thirteen, and now the sentinels were telling him that the place had been *emptied*.

Sebestyen considered personally killing the guard who delivered the news, but he couldn't afford to lose a single man. Not now.

"Were there women among the dead prisoners?"

"No, my lord," the gray-faced sentinel answered.

It was always possible that Isadora had died in the pit. He could certainly hope that was the case, but she had never struck him as the sort of woman who would die easily and quickly.

"How did they get past the armed guards on Level Ten?" Sebestyen snapped.

The sentinel's gray face went white. "There were too many of them, my lord, and they took us by surprise." The man swallowed hard. "And they were not all unarmed."

Sebestyen took a step toward the young soldier. "Stop

dancing around the facts of the matter and tell me what happened!"

"It was the Tryfynian captain," the sentinel said. "And his manservant. They had swords and wielded them quite well as they led some of the prisoners out of the palace. There were women among that group of escapees, my lord."

Women? As in . . . more than one? Impossible. Someone had mistaken a long-haired, weakened prisoner for a woman, perhaps. And if she'd survived, Isadora was certainly one of those Hern had rescued.

So much for his alliance with the Circle of Bacwyr. It was Isadora's fault that Hern had turned. If Hern and his men joined with the rebels . . . if Isadora survived and told the world that there were two heirs to the throne . . .

"I want a doubled guard on the empress and on the baby who is being cared for on Level Two. Preserve them with your lives. Nothing else matters."

"Your guard will be doubled as well, my lord," the sentinel said with a curt and respectful bow. Some small hint of color had returned to his face. Apparently he was grateful to find himself still alive.

"That's not necessary." Sebestyen touched the knife that was sheathed at his waist, and the sentinel's eyes flitted there with a touch of fear.

But he did not draw the knife, and the sentinel left to do as he had been instructed.

Sebestyen chased his personal guards from the room, slamming the doors behind them. He bolted the door and crossed the room at a run, tearing a tapestry from the wall to reveal the hidden doorway beneath. It swung open, and he ran down two flights of dimly lit stairs. The door he found his way to opened on a small interior room that was not easy to find from the hallways of Level Three.

Mahri lifted her head as the door swung open. Skittish girl, she had not been happy with her new confinement. She'd actually found her way out of this room once, and had wandered the halls looking for someone to help her. But of course, no one had dared to offer assistance.

He had planned to do away with her, too, as he had done away with Isadora. The nosy girl had found her way into the chamber where the twins had been born, and she knew too much. But apparently he'd lost his heart for handling such matters. Isadora was different. She was a witch, and she was dangerous, and she had killed. She deserved Level Thirteen.

Mahri did not.

The other woman sat in the corner, rocking and knitting. As usual, she did not even lift her head.

Sebestyen crossed the room to the cradle that had been placed against one wall.

"He is sleeping," Mahri said in a soft voice.

"He's well?" Sebestyen asked as he glanced into the cradle. His second-born was healthy, and he was quite sure the baby looked much as he had as a child. Alixandyr had a healthy smattering of dark hair and remarkable blue eyes. Sebestyen reached down into the cradle to touch the baby's head.

"Very well, my lord," Mahri answered.

He should have killed the baby, and if the priests knew there were two, that's what they would do. But Sebestyen had not been able even to conceive of doing such a thing or allowing it to be done. This child was his and Liane's. Alixandyr was a miracle, and miracles should not be lightly undone.

"There are those who would harm him just for being who he is," Sebestyen said, reluctantly withdrawing his hand from the cradle. "I know you do not want to be here."

Mahri swallowed hard. "I do not like being a prisoner, my lord."

"No one does." The nursemaid who continued to knit did not so much as lift her eyes or fumble in her stitching, though she was as much a prisoner as Mahri. Sebestyen needed the wet nurse, but he did not trust her. She had dead eyes, and he had never heard her speak a word of protest or submission. She just existed, and fed his child, and knitted. Did she have a hidden allegiance with someone in the palace? Someone who would do Alix harm? Even though she was his servant, anything was possible.

Sebestyen did not trust the dead-eyed, meek wet nurse. Mahri, at least, had been loyal to Liane. Mahri, a servant who had been invisible to his eyes until that night when all had changed, had the courage to protest her imprisonment.

He flipped the knife from his waist, and a startled Mahri jumped back and gasped.

"I'm not going to harm you," Sebestyen said, flipping the knife and catching it by the blade to offer it to the girl. "Take it."

Mahri was reluctant. How foolish was it to offer a sharp blade to a prisoner? Very. Still, what choice did he have? After a moment of studying the bejeweled handle, she took the weapon.

"Guard my son," Sebestyen said. "Can you do that?"

Mahri studied the blade. "I don't know if I can stab . . ."

"If someone means harm to an innocent child, would you not do whatever you could to protect him?"

The girl studied the blade a while longer, turning it this way and that. Eventually, her grip grew steadier. Sebestyen wondered for a moment if she was about to stab *him*.

But she did not. "I will, my lord," Mahri said, a touch of vigor in her normally weak voice.

* * *

WHEN EVERYONE HAD BEEN FED, AND ALL BUT A HAND-ful of the camping party were asleep, Lucan took Isadora's hand and led her away from the campfire and into the wood. The former empresses and the wizard—Isadora's father—slept, as did most of the others. Franco and Bannon would keep watch for now.

He had come very close to losing Isadora. How odd that the very thought of losing a woman he had known for such a short time had the power to cut him to the core. He had never been in love; in fact, he had often claimed that love was for women and old men. But surely *this* was love.

If he returned to Tryfyn without the Star of Bacwyr, he would not be Prince of Swords. If he were not Prince, he would be free to choose his own wife.

And the strife in Tryfyn would continue until another was called to be Prince. How long? A few years, a hundred, more . . . He could not put his own happiness above the needs of an entire country. But when it came to Isadora's happiness . . .

When they were deep into the woods, he stopped walking, turned, and took Isadora in his arms. She fell against him and rested there, fitting well as she always did, burrowing into him as if only he could protect her.

"I should have known that you would find me," she whispered against his chest. He felt her warm breath there, and her steady heartbeat in the chest he held so close, and the desperation of the small, warm hands at his back.

"Yes, you should have," he said.

"For a while, I thought . . ." She choked on the words.

"You thought that I would leave you there," he finished in a low voice.

"Yes," she whispered.

He smoothed a strand of dark hair away from her cheek. "For a few terrible days, I thought you had truly left me. I mourned, and I was angry, and I was hurt. And then I saw the ring you always wore on Emperor Sebestyen's finger, and I knew he had taken it from you." He did not tell her that he had reached for her and found her. He did not tell her that they were connected in a way that went beyond the needs of their bodies. "What happened?"

At first she was reluctant to speak, but soon the story was pouring out of her. Twins. A sentinel's death. The witch Gadhra. A newborn baby disposed of because it was inconvenient to have two heirs. He'd wondered if he had the right to break his word of allegiance to Sebestyen, but the story Isadora told made it clear that he had no choice.

"Sebestyen locked you away because you knew what he'd done."

"Yes."

The Circle wizards had said Lucan would have a son during his thirty-eighth year. He wanted Isadora to be that child's mother, and he wanted to save his country from the war that had torn it asunder for so very long. Why could he not have both?

"Marry me," he said, the words pouring out of him.

She kept her head down so he could not see even a glimpse of the expression on her face. "You said you could not marry me," she said softly.

"And you said that you did not want to be my wife," he countered. "All things can change. If the path of our lives is not to our liking, we can make the path we desire by the decisions that we make." If he were wed to Isadora when he returned to the Circle wizards, they could not undo what had already been done. And if he returned as the rightful Prince of Swords, no one but those most highly placed in the Circle would dare to say a word. The wizards would complain, and they would try to convince him to undo the marriage, but they could not command him to follow their edicts. "Marry me," he said again.

"I don't know that I can," she whispered so softly he could barely make out her words.

"Of course you can. What can stop you?"

Her hands slipped beneath his vest and settled on bare skin. "Can we talk about this in the morning? My head is spinning. I'm tired. Right now all I want is for you to make love to me."

"Here?" he searched the ground for a soft spot, but saw nothing suitable for a bed for the woman he loved to lie upon.

"Here, Lucan. I don't need a soft mattress and fine sheets and scented candles. I never have. What I need is you. Your arms around me, your mouth on mine, your body and mine linked . . . that is what I need." She laid her hand over his erection and stroked, and pressed her mouth to his throat. "Please don't ask me to think beyond tonight," she whispered against his skin.

He would not lay the woman he loved in the cold dirt, so he raised her skirt and lifted her off the ground, and in the broken shafts of moonlight that slanted through the trees, he gave her what she needed. They had been apart too long, and they reached fulfillment quickly, and with a power that brought tears to Isadora's eyes. As she quaked around him, Lucan muttered the words he had never thought to speak.

"I love you."

It would be right and proper for her to answer in kind, and he wanted to hear those words more than he should want anything in this life. But with their bodies still joined and broken moonlight shining down upon them, she remained silent.

* * *

JULIET STOOD ON THE GENTLE RISE OF THE HILL, ONE hand resting over her swollen stomach, the other caught in Ryn's. The body heat that came with being Anwyn caused her to dress much as her husband did: in little or nothing, depending on who else was present. Tonight she wore a sleeveless and thin gold frock that was generously cut to allow for her pregnancy. The hem—torn by her own hands on a particularly warm day—did not quite touch her knees. Such a garment would be considered scandalous in Shandley, but she was nowhere near that small village, and she no longer cared what anyone in Shandley thought of her.

"They are so close," she said, excitement creeping into her heart. "Sophie is to the south, just a few days' march away. Isadora is west, just a day or two beyond Sophie. They do not realize that they are so near to one another."

Ryn squeezed her hand. "So, we will go south to collect Sophie, and then west to Isadora?"

Juliet shook her head. "No. We will travel to Isadora first, and then we'll all head south to find Sophie. I know it isn't the most logical course, but . . ." Her head pounded with knowledge. She would soon need to put an end to this vision, or it would bring on a headache and pounding heart that might not be good for the baby.

Sophie was distressed, but safe. She was surrounded by men who would die for her, if need be. No danger was near the youngest Fyne sister, at the moment. The eldest was another matter entirely.

"For the first time I can recall, Isadora needs me more than Sophie does. Much more." Juliet looked up at her husband. His face was strong and beautiful in the moonlight, and having him beside her gave her strength. "My goodness, she's about to do something incredibly foolish."

16

ALL NIGHT AND INTO THE COOL, CRISP MORNING, Isadora tried to convince herself that Lucan had said something other than those horrible words. Unfortunately, he'd spoken much too clearly for her to make such a mistake.

The camp came alive slowly. Thayne and Lucan were already plotting the safest route to Tryfyn, and the empresses were anxious enough to be on their way. They wanted to get as far from Arthes, the palace, and Emperor Sebestyen as possible.

Isadora remained silent. She ate the tasteless tubers Franco collected and distributed. She combed her hair with her fingers and braided it snugly. She did her best not to look at Lucan as he made plans for travel.

She didn't know how to tell Lucan that she wasn't going with him.

It was a nice fantasy, to think that she could walk away from all her troubles for the easy life as Lucan Hern's wife.

But that's all it was: fantasy. For a moment or two, when she'd first seen him in Level Thirteen, she'd actually believed that they could have some time together. Not a lifetime; maybe not even a year. But even that one imagined year of happiness was no more than fantasy.

The curse her father assured her could be ended was still powerful. It had taken one love from her; she would not allow it to take another.

As the group began their travels, hiking into the woods where they would be sheltered from view for much of the journey, Isadora hung back. She watched them walk away, all of them gladly headed for safety. The empresses would contact their families—families who believed them to be dead—after they were safely housed in Tryfyn. Thayne would make contact with the wizards of the Circle and perhaps join them. Franco and Lucan were ready to go home, and none of the former prisoners had anything left in Columbyana to keep them here.

Isadora took a few steps, acting as if she intended to follow, and then she stopped. She had never in her life felt as alone as she did as she watched one refugee after another disappear into the forest where last night Lucan had made love to her for the last time. Where he had said that he loved her.

It would not be so easy to separate herself from them, of course. Lucan looked back at her, frowned, and stopped. He lifted his hand and motioned for her to join him, and after a moment Isadora shook her head. He hurried back toward her, as the last of the travelers melted into the forest.

"Come," Lucan said as he approached. "We don't want to fall too far behind."

"You go on," she said.

He frowned. "Not without you."

Isadora lifted her chin haughtily. "I'm not going to Try-fyn. If you will search your memory, you will realize that I never agreed to your proposal. Neither of them." Wife or mistress . . . she had never promised him anything beyond the next encounter.

"What are you planning to do?" he snapped. "Go back into the palace?"

"Yes."

His shocked expression was enough to tell her what he thought of her plan. "I won't allow you to do such an imprudent thing."

She had been accused of much in her life, but never imprudence. "I promised to protect Liane and her babies, and if I don't go back to them, then I have failed miserably."

"Liane and one baby are likely beyond saving," Lucan said gently. "You know that."

"Perhaps that's true. Perhaps not." No one knew, as she did, how much the emperor loved his wife. She'd been deeply affected by the Panwyr when he'd pushed her into Level Thirteen, but she remembered what she had seen on his face as he'd given her that final shove. Not anger . . . well, not entirely anger. She had seen the pain of betrayal in his eyes, not blind rage. It was possible . . . *possible* . . . that Liane and both babies were alive and well.

She expected Lucan to argue with her a while longer. She did not expect him to lift her off her feet and carry her toward the forest. "We shouldn't fall too far behind."

"Put me down!" she ordered.

"Not until you come to your senses," he said in a logical tone of voice.

"I'm not the one who has lost my senses," she grumbled.

"Apparently, you are. Going back into the palace," he muttered beneath his breath.

She knew what would happen, sooner or later. Like it or

not, she did love Lucan. Not as she had loved Will, with a girl's idealistic romanticism, but as a woman loves a man. This love for Lucan was more real than what she'd felt for Will, in a way she was just beginning to understand. Given a chance, it could survive bad times and good, arguments and war and prophesies and stubbornness—his and hers.

It could not survive the curse, however, and she knew how this would end. Lucan would love her, she would love him, and eventually she would begin to believe that they could make what they had last. She could let loose the love she protected, giving him her heart and her soul. And then he would discover that she was a witch, and he'd despise her.

She would lose one love to death and the other to hate.

The longer she waited, the more she loved Lucan, the harder it would be. Were there varying degrees of heartbreak? Could she weather what was sure to come more easily now, when she had not yet fooled herself into thinking that the curse could be beaten? Her father assured her the curse could be broken, and though she did have hope, she did not yet believe.

"Stop," she said calmly. "I have something to tell you."

Lucan did as she asked. He stopped stalking after the others and swung her onto her feet so they were face-to-face. They had just entered the edge of the wood, and his face was partially lost in shadow. She could see clearly one half of a grim mouth, one steely eye, one half of a firmly set jaw.

Would this be easier for him if she confessed that she loved him? Or would it be best if he never knew?

"I cannot go with you because I am a witch."

His expression did not change. "Yes," he said softly. "I know."

Isadora had expected many things to follow her confession. Horror. Denial. Laughter. Hatred. She had never expected such a calm response. "How do you know? You know nothing. You're . . . you're . . ." The explanation came to her, and it was as horrifying as the idea of watching him flee from her in horror. "You're *humoring* me."

"Unfortunately, I am not."

"Last night—"

"I already knew."

"When you said—"

"I already knew." He sighed and touched her face with a gentle hand. "I did not want to believe it was true, but deep inside I recognized the truth when I heard it. I wished once or twice that I might be wrong, but I realized it was a hollow wish. This is an obstacle I never thought to encounter, but when the choice is you as you are or nothing at all . . . I choose you." His eyes narrowed. "Have you ever cast a spell on me?" he asked with only a trace of suspicion.

"No."

The relief was evident on his face. "Good. Promise me that you won't, not for good nor for harm, and I will set aside my fears to have you by my side, always."

"I would never cast a spell to do you harm," she said.

"Not for harm nor for good," he insisted. "That is all I ask, Isadora."

She struggled with the answer. "What if you are in trouble, and I can help you with a—"

"No," he interrupted. "Not even for that. What we have must remain free of magic, love. If you need to practice your craft on others to be happy, then do so. But I want what is between us to be natural and untainted. I want it to be real, always."

He called her *love*, as he had on occasion, and she liked it very much. She had to get past that startling and heart-stopping moment to answer. "If that is what you want, then I give you my word you will have it."

A half smile crossed his face. "I never expected to find myself in love with a witch. It will complicate matters at home, I suspect."

"You should allow me to leave you now," she whispered.

"Perhaps I should, but I won't."

Tears filled her eyes. She hated to cry, to cave to emotion, but Lucan knew what she was, and still he loved her. Could such a love alone not break even the Fyne Curse?

"I have to go back," she said. "I have to save Liane and the babies. They are my responsibility, and I can't put my own well-being above theirs."

He nodded once, and Isadora sighed. He might say he did not care that she was a witch, he might say he still loved her. But he would allow her to walk away from him, after all.

And then he leaned forward and kissed her lightly, his lips barely brushing hers. "You will not go alone."

THE WARNING THAT HAD FRIGHTENED HIM OF WITCHES in the palace concerned the emperor's witch Gadhra, Lucan decided. Isadora might practice the craft, but that did not make her the witch Zebulyn had warned him of. Besides, he had been nine years old when the old man had first whispered the words *beware the witch*, and the deep hatred that had grown from that warning was illogical and unnecessary.

Then again, perhaps it was not his life he had to protect from the witch, but his heart. Isadora had not yet said that she loved him, though he believed it to be true.

She was not happy that he refused to escort her immediately into the palace. If Liane and both babies still lived, then they would be safe for a while longer. If the emperor had killed them soon after tossing Isadora into Level

Thirteen, then no amount of her protection would help them now.

He swung his sword up and knocked the one Isadora wielded out of her hand. It spun away and landed in the brush, and a small brown bird was frightened by the resulting crash and flew up into a blue, cloudless sky.

"You cheated!" Isadora shouted indignantly.

He remained calm. "You left yourself wide open with that last thrust. If I were one of the emperor's sentinels, I could have taken your heart."

She pursed her lips but did not argue, since she recognized that he was right. "I will not learn to be a master swordsman in a matter of days," she argued. "We are wasting valuable time."

"You *will* be prepared before we go back into the emperor's palace, love."

"I am as prepared as I need to be," she argued.

"In my opinion, you are not."

"I can cast a spell, if necessary," she continued. "I do not need a sword to find my way to Liane and the babies."

"It is my wish that you are able to fight in both ways. With your magic, and with my sword." He collected the sword in question from the brush and offered it to Isadora. "Indulge me."

She took the sword and resumed her fighting stance. "I do not see why I should indulge you." She swung, and he easily sidestepped her clumsy move.

"Perhaps because I indulge you in even your most dangerous obsessions." He easily shifted her blade to the side with the tip of his own.

"It is not necessary that you accompany me. You are large and clumsy and will be difficult to conceal, since you insist that my magic not touch you."

He easily defended the thrust she practiced. "I am not clumsy."

"You will distract me, and there is no good reason for you to go back into the palace." She was quickly getting breathless. While the sword he had given her was not heavy, working with it was arduous for someone unaccustomed to sword work. Their lessons to this point helped matters to some degree, but it was clear Isadora was not a swordsman.

He disarmed her again, whipping the sword from her grasp with a twist of his blade. "I was going back anyway, once I saw you to safety."

This time she did not accuse him of cheating or go after the sword. She placed hands on slim hips and glared at him. "What are you talking about? You said Esmun and Elya escaped before you rescued me. Why on earth would you go back?"

Lucan sheathed his sword in the scabbard he wore at his side, and then he smoothed a strand of wayward hair from Isadora's sweaty face. "The emperor possesses something I need."

"What?"

"The ring you once wore upon your finger. Returning it to the Circle of Bacwyr assures my place as Prince of Swords."

Her dark eyes went wide. "That is why you asked for me," she said indignantly. "That is why you insisted that I—" She squealed when he lifted her in his arms. "You sneaky, despicable, lying—"

"I never lied," he said as he held her close. She struggled, but not very much. "And while I began my pursuit in a quest for the Star of Bacwyr, I soon lost my heart and my good sense to you."

She stopped struggling and smiled at him. "Whatever makes you think you ever possessed good sense?"

"Before I met you, love, I possessed an abundance." He touched his lips to her throat, kissed there, made her shudder as he whispered against her skin. "Love causes surprising changes in a man. In a woman, too, I suppose, though of course I have no way of knowing such things."

"You want me to tell you that I love you."

He drew away so he could see her face; she was no longer smiling. "Yes."

"What if I can't?"

He would be hurt, if he did not see the depth of pain in her eyes. Lucan put Isadora on her feet, then guided her to a slope that overlooked a small, almost clear pond. It was a soothing view, one that belied the danger that lay ahead. Sitting there, he draped one arm around Isadora. When they were well settled, he asked, "What is stopping you?"

She hesitated, and he waited patiently. Waiting patiently had never been his strong suit, but he did his best and sat quietly until Isadora began to speak. "You don't know everything about me."

"I imagine not. There are many things you do not know about me. When there is time, we will discuss all these revelations, good and bad."

"This one can't wait. There's a curse. It's more than three hundred years old, it's very powerful, and it killed my first husband."

He turned his head to look down at her. She certainly didn't look as if she were teasing him. Isadora's face was stonelike, as if she'd put on a mask to conceal her emotions. "I don't believe any curse can be more powerful than what I feel for you."

She looked up and met his stare with one of her own. "The curse dooms any man who is unfortunate enough to be loved by a Fyne witch. Those hapless men who are younger than thirty do not live to see that year. Those who are older and perhaps wiser come to see the hideousness of the women who love them, and they flee as if the devil himself were on their tails. It is selfish of me, but I swear I would rather see you dead than watch you run away because you despise me." She pursed her lips. "I thought that desertion would come when you found out that I was a witch, but it did not, so now I'm wondering when it will happen, and how, and I'm wondering if it will hurt as much as death, or more."

He smiled down at her, and one hand crept into her mussed braid.

"I tell you my most dreaded secret, and you *smile* at me?"

"You love me," he answered, his smile unwavering.

"I did not say such a thing."

"No, but you said this curse befalls those men who are loved by Fyne witches, and then you professed your concern for me. It is a rather unromantic way of sharing your feelings, but I will accept it, nonetheless."

She did not argue but leaned against him and turned her gaze toward the pond. "There is more," she whispered.

"Tell me." Nothing could dent his resolve where Isadora was concerned. Nothing.

"Your prophets say your first son will be born in your thirty-eighth year."

"Yes."

"Fyne women produce daughters. If the prophets are correct, another woman will bear your son."

"I will not allow it."

"Since your participation will be necessary, I imagine you will allow it, when the time comes." She burrowed into his side more snugly. "Perhaps you will make another life, after you come to hate me." She shrugged her thin shoulders. "Perhaps this time I will be the one to die."

"I will not allow you to die," he said gruffly.

"You are very insistent today about what you will and will not allow," she answered without heat. "But what is to be will be, no matter what we do to change the course of time and fate."

He laid Isadora in the grass and made her look at him once again. "I will not allow you to talk of death or parting or babies born of other women. I have seen who you are, Isadora. You are a witch, you are often disagreeable, you are a miserable swordsman, and a cantankerous woman determined to argue with me at every turn. You snore when you are very tired."

"I do not snore!"

He ignored her argument. "And you are determined to risk your own life to rescue a woman who would not suffer the smallest inconvenience in order to save you. I know all that, and yet I love you deeply. There is nothing your curse can do to change my mind. You and I, we are stronger than any curse. We will defeat it together. Perhaps we already have. I will never leave you, Isadora, and I will not allow you to die." He laid his body against hers, length to length, so she could feel that he wanted her. "You will be the mother of my son. I will accept no other."

Isadora's arms crept around his neck. Her fingers played in the hair at the nape of his neck. "I love you, too," she whispered, the words very soft and uncertain. When the sky did not fall upon them, she said the words again, more strongly. "I love you."

WRAPPED IN A THICK BLANKET AND SETTLED IN A NOOK of boulders that protected her from the wind, Sophie watched the sun set. Ariana, well and warmly bundled, napped nearby. Poor thing, she was growing up away from the only home she'd ever known, with soldiers all around her and a mother and father who were distracted by what was to come. Maybe she should've left her daughter in another's care, for this time, but when the opportunity had presented itself, she had been unable to part from her child. They were well protected here, more well protected than they could possibly be anywhere else. Still, it was no life for a child who was just barely one year old.

Sophie smiled for Kane, when he turned from the soldiers who claimed his attention and looked her way, but she did not feel the smile in her heart.

In matters of war, all was going very well. More of the emperor's soldiers had deserted and joined Arik and his rebels. The latest word was that days ago the First Captain of the Circle of Bacwyr had left the palace under less than amicable circumstances. Perhaps he would not join with the rebels, but at least Arik and his men would not have to fight against the captain and his warriors.

With the desertion of so many of the emperor's troops, and the healing aspect of time, Sophie's father, who had once been the Columbyanan Minister of Defense, was now trusted and even revered by the rebels. Even by Kane, who had been among the last to offer his trust.

The problem was with the baby Sophie carried. She continued to feel the trouble in a way she could not describe. She did not have Juliet's gift of sight, but instinctively she recognized that all was not well. The baby was shifting, dropping, becoming less active. If she was not very careful, the child would come too soon.

She passed the time trying to picture what her daughter would look like. Would the new baby be like Ariana, perfectly beautiful, pink and round and fat? Or would she have the wrinkled and reddened look so many of the babies Sophie had seen so often possessed for their first few days and weeks? If the baby did indeed arrive early, would she be too small? Would she survive?

Sophie was worried about more than the health and well-being of her daughter. Her own powers were increased substantially when she was carrying a baby. If the child came too soon, if this little girl was born before Sophie was reunited with Juliet and Isadora, would it mean there was no chance to end the curse before it took Kane's life? She rubbed one hand against her belly. "Hold tight, baby girl," she whispered. She still had not decided upon a name for this child. She was considering Lucinda, for her mother, but Kane was less sure, and she wanted him to have a say in naming this child, since he had not been present to assist in naming Ariana.

Ferghus, Myl's former spy, sauntered over to her very casually. Sophie sat up straighter and put on a smile for the ex-sentinel who had become one of Arik's most trusted rebels. The handsome man hunkered down before Sophie. He did not return her smile.

"How is your wound?" she asked.

"Healing nicely, thanks to your assistance."

"It was a clean wound and would have healed very well without my help, I'm sure." She had seen much worse in her time with Arik. Men had died before her eyes, and she'd buried friends. Her friends. Kane's friends. Heaven above, she wanted this war to be over. She wanted a roof over her daughters' heads at night, and a soft bed to share with her husband. She wanted a home.

"I was very lucky that the emperor ordered a friend to kill me. Serian could not refuse the command, but he aimed carefully and made the wound a clean one, and then told the emperor I was dead."

Sophie wrinkled her nose. "I cannot imagine running a sword through a friend."

"Serian saved my life, and I will be forever grateful."

"I do not understand all the soldiers' way of thinking," Sophie said. "And I suppose I never will." The man's face was so taut, she could not believe he had joined her for casual conversation. "How can I be of assistance, Ferghus?"

"I have come to you because I believe you will be honest with me in a way no soldier here will."

"I am always honest."

He nodded, as if he understood that very well. "We move closer to Arthes every day. Arik and his men are talking of taking the palace soon, and I believe they will be successful. I have many comrades there, still, but they are soldiers who can take care of themselves, when the time for fighting comes. But I worry about Empress Liane and her babies. Will they be harmed?"

A flash of something unexpected in the hard man's eyes touched Sophie. "You care for her."

"I do." It was a reluctant but heartfelt confession.

She had no choice but to give the man an honest answer, since that was why he had come to her. "There are those here who would harm Liane simply for being empress. Not all, not most . . . but a few."

"How can I protect her?"

"I don't know, but I will think about the problem. Perhaps if we direct those who would punish Liane for her station to another part of the palace, when the time comes."

"They all respect you. Perhaps if you tell them—"

"Not all the men here respect me. There are those who resent the fact that a woman has Arik's ear." And those were the most likely to harm Liane, she realized.

Ferghus nodded, understanding too well. "If you go into the palace with us, and if you and I can get to Liane first . . ."

Sophie shook her head, as deep inside an unexpected

gentle clenching took her breath away. She would not have the baby tonight, but the delivery would be soon. This child would come too early, here in the wilderness, with Sophie's sisters far away and her husband closer to death than she dared to face. "I will not be going into the palace with you," she said softly.

Ferghus studied her face closely and saw the pain. "My lady, what do you require?"

Sophie nodded. "My husband, please," she said as she settled back against the cold rock. "I require my husband."

The former sentinel rushed to collect Kane, and Sophie smiled weakly at her rounded tummy. "Ferghus called me *my lady*, can you imagine?" Sophie realized that she would be going no farther than this until the child was born. With the proper preparations, she could wait a while before delivering. A number of days, perhaps. Even a week or more. She could rest and meditate and say a simple spell to delay the coming of the child. But nothing could stop the inevitable.

With the birth of this child, her magic would be so weakened that the end to the Fyne Curse at her hand would be all but impossible.

17

Isadora allowed him to train her for three days, and though she complained often, she did pay attention, and she did improve. He could still disarm her with a flick of his blade, but she now made the task more difficult. Improved as she was, she was still far from ready to face Sebestyen's sentinels.

For the first time, Lucan was surprisingly glad that the woman he loved had been born to magic. If swordplay did not help her survive her return to the palace, perhaps her witchcraft would.

The camp where they had fought and trained and made love for three days was in a narrow valley, hidden from the road above by newly leafed trees and protected on one side with a rock wall and a shallow cave. The land had been touched by spring, with wildflowers and butterflies and the small critters that scurried about while keeping their distance. It was a beautiful place, and if he did not know what was to come, he would actually enjoy being here.

If they survived, he would take Isadora to a similar place near his home, and they would camp there for many days, without worry, without pressures of the days to come. This place was not the refuge of the Circle, but was near the home where he had been born. There was a brook in a clearing much like this one where he had often played, during his yearly trips home. He and his brothers had gone there often to play. They had sometimes pretended to be that which they were meant to be—soldiers—but they had also played at other things. On some mornings they had been dragons, and on that same afternoon they might have played at being seafaring marauders. In that place, on those rare occasions, he had been allowed to be a child. He wanted Isadora and the son she would give him to enjoy its peace and beauty as much as he had.

She insisted that she would only bear daughters, but he wanted the son the seers had promised him, and he would allow no other woman to be that boy's mother. As Prince of Swords he could command sons . . . and daughters, too, if they would be like their mother. Lucan smiled as he parried with Isadora and allowed his mind to wander. He had been treated as a Prince for most of his life and was accustomed to getting all that he desired—as the woman he loved was so quick to remind him. Even he could not command the miracle of life.

Isadora was tiring, so Lucan disarmed her. As her short sword landed in the brush a few feet away, he put his own sword aside. "That is enough for now."

Her breath coming with too much difficulty, she put her hands on her hips and glared at him. "Can you not call the lesson to an end without flinging my weapon away? Must you continue to demonstrate that my skills are woefully inadequate?"

"I wish you to remember that your skills are not those of a soldier when you return to the palace."

"I am unlikely to forget," she said sharply.

He scooped Isadora into his arms and held her close, and the expression on her face softened. "I would happily fetch Liane and her children for you when I retrieve the Star of Bacwyr."

"As you have so often offered to do in the past three days," she said gently. "Again, I insist that I will not stay behind and allow you to do that which I have sworn to do myself, at no small risk to yourself. Getting out of the palace with a ring is a much simpler and safer task than escaping with the empress and two babies."

"And Mahri," he added, since Isadora had mentioned the servant often in the past couple of days

"And Mahri," she said.

"I suppose we will also have to rescue anyone else who crosses your path."

"Only those who need rescuing."

He kissed her. It was the only way he could end an argument without giving in to her demands. In truth, Isadora's need to take care of others was one of the traits he loved about her. Perhaps she was a witch, but she had shown him that not all women with witchcraft in their blood were evil. Isadora was anything but evil. She was good, and dedicated, and noble, as any proper warrior should be.

He did not think of Isadora as a warrior as he laid her in the grass and unbuttoned the first few buttons of her dress to expose her neck and her chest and her breasts. She laid back and closed her eyes, and with the warm spring sun on her face she smiled gently.

"This is not the body of a fighter," he said as he lowered his head to take one nipple and then another into his mouth. The tips of those nipples peaked, and Isadora undulated gently to bring herself closer to him. "This is the body of a woman, a lover and a mother. It should be treasured and protected at all costs, not callously thrown into the midst of war."

"I have always been a fighter, Lucan," Isadora said without opening her eyes.

"But not always a lover." He opened her gown to her waist. His shadow fell across her midsection.

"No," she whispered.

The blue gown she had been wearing since before she'd been thrown into Level Thirteen was dirty and torn. She'd done her best to wash it, days ago, but the garment was beyond being saved by a simple laundering. It was certainly not a gown befitting the wife of the Prince of Swords. "When we get to Tryfyn, I will burn this rag of a gown and dress you in something more appropriate."

"I can only imagine what you consider *appropriate*," she said in a lighthearted voice.

"Fine fabrics, rich colors. Light and airy frocks for summer, the warmest furs and daintiest boots for winter." He unfastened more buttons and kissed her pale belly. "And when we are alone, nothing at all."

"Of course."

"Of course." He undressed Isadora slowly, even though it was not necessary to do more than toss up her skirt. He wanted to see her naked in the sunlight. He wanted to witness every trembling of her flesh, every flush of color that rose to the surface of her sensitive skin. She was a woman of strength and angles, not rounded and soft all over as many females were. Her breasts were small but swelled nicely beneath his hands. Her hips were narrow but welcoming and slightly rounded from a tiny waist. Her legs were long and strong, enticingly shaped with a hint of muscle, but they trembled when he parted them and touched her intimately.

"You have said you love me," he whispered as he ran his hand up her thigh.

"Many times," she answered, her voice as soft as his own. "Do you wish to hear the words again? I love you. I love you."

"Those are not the words I wish to hear at this moment."

At that, her eyes opened slowly. "What is it you wish to hear?"

He leaned over her, bringing his face close to hers so he could read her eyes more clearly. As he looked into those dark eyes, he touched her damp folds in a way that made her arch and moan. "I have asked you to be my wife, Isadora. You have not yet said yes."

"Now is not the time, Lucan," she said impatiently. "When we have done what must be done, then, perhaps—"

"Perhaps?"

"If you still want me, we will discuss—" He slipped one finger into her, and she arched against his hand.

"No discussion is necessary. Say yes. That is all that is required of you at this time."

She reached out and pushed his vest off one shoulder, allowing her fine fingers to lightly trace his arm. "Why are you still dressed? The sun feels warm against my skin. You should share in that warmth. We should make love under the sun and forget all else."

"You're changing the subject, love."

"Yes, I am," she answered with impatience.

He removed the vest and tossed it aside, and Isadora reached for his trousers. Before she could touch him, he moved down and away, his lips marking a trail from her breasts to her belly. "I am First Captain of the Circle of

Bacwyr," he grumbled, his lips against her soft flesh. "I am destined to be Prince of Swords. Since the age of nine, I have not had to ask more than *once* for what I desire. And yet you make me ask again and again for what we both know is meant to be."

"There is much to be done before I can even consider what you require, or what I require. Can't we simply enjoy one another in the time we have, without looking so far into the future?"

"I want a yes from you," he said. "That is all."

"Then ask another question."

"This is the only question I have for you, love. Marry me."

SHE NEEDED ONLY THIS, FOR NOW. LOVE WAS UNDENI-able, but everything else was yet to be decided. Liane and the babies, the curse, her sisters. Why could Lucan not be like every other man in the world and be content with the sex they shared so often and so well?

He kissed her inner thigh, and she felt that caress all through her body. "I have decided what I want, love," Lucan whispered, "and I always get what I want."

"I have always maintained that you are incredibly spoiled and badly in need of the lesson that what you wish for won't always be given to you on command."

"I was never particularly good at lessons."

Before she could argue, he laid his mouth on her and flicked his tongue in a way that made her cry out and shift against him. "Can we finish this discussion later?"

Lucan flicked his tongue again, and she waited for his agreement. "No," he said gently. "I wish to finish it now."

Her body trembled for his. She had lived without sex for so long; how was it that she needed Lucan so badly? Love was a part of it, yes, but there was more. This was a primal heat that she had not expected to find within herself. It was crude and powerful and beautiful, with a magic all its own.

But she was not alone in relishing the power. Lucan needed her, just as she needed him. She ran her hands across his broad shoulders and sat up to run her palms down his bare, muscled back. He was built like no other man she had ever seen, so perfectly shaped and strong. And he was hers in a way she had not imagined possible.

"You have not finished undressing," she said as her fingertips teased his hard flesh. "I cannot continue this discussion if you refuse to remove those trousers."

He rose up slightly. "Cannot or will not?"

"Will not," she confessed.

"Fine." He removed his boots and trousers so that he was as naked as she. She watched him undress, a satisfied smile on her face. He moved with masculine grace, even when he rushed through such a simple chore, and she found herself admiring not only the beauty of him, but the beauty of the way he moved.

"See?" Lucan said as he rejoined her. "I am quite compliant when you voice *your* commands."

"Only when those commands suit you," she answered as she slipped her leg between his and pressed her lips to his neck.

Naked, lying entangled in the sunlight, they touched and kissed and argued. There was little heat in their debate, but much heat in the way they came together physically. Her entire body throbbed with need, and had since the moment Lucan had laid her in the grass, but she was not anxious to bring this encounter to an end.

She loved the way he held her, caressed her, aroused her. She loved the fluttering deep in her body, and the answering call of his. She loved the way he responded to her touch.

She loved him.

Eventually, Lucan quit asking her to marry him. He quit talking and put his mouth to better use. Tomorrow, perhaps the next day, they would move back toward Arthes and the emperor's palace, and after that, nothing in her life or his was certain. The only thing in her life that was certain was this moment.

Lucan hovered above her and blocked the sun, but passion kept her warm. He guided himself into her, and in that instant she forgot everything that kept what they had from perfection. Her body and his were perfectly mated, and nothing else mattered.

He pushed hard and fast, and she began to soar. Together their bodies reached a new height, and completion washed over them with such force Isadora's breath was literally stolen away as her body lurched. Ribbons of fulfillment, most pleasurable, fluttered and snapped at the core of her being, and a new heat spread throughout her with an amazing quickness. Lucan growled low in his throat, and she felt his seed bursting forth deep into her body where it would be cradled and nurtured.

The world slowed, and cooled, and Lucan drifted down to rest his head on her shoulder. Their hearts beat together, fast and hard, and each breath was a struggle. "By all that is holy, Isadora Fyne, marry me!"

She threaded her fingers through the hair at the nape of his neck. How could she be expected to be logical at a moment like this? "If we make it out of the palace alive, and you still want me . . . ask again and I will give you the answer you wish to hear."

Lucan lifted his head slowly and looked her in the eye. "Do you mean it?"

"Yes." It was not exactly the yes he was looking for, but it was all she could give at the moment.

* * *

SEBESTYEN PACED IN THE BALLROOM, HIS FOOTSTEPS sounding hollow against the stone floor. He was alone in the massive room, as he had been for days. He no longer trusted anyone to counsel him.

Arik and the damned rebels were getting closer. He felt their coming in a way he could not explain. With the coming of the rebels came his downfall. After all these months, the prophesy was coming true.

He had not seen Liane in days. She was overly sentimental, and her tears distressed him. Perhaps he should tell her that both her children were alive and well, but the witch Gadhra was always nearby, and he did not trust the crone. If the old hag heard his confession she would know about Alix, and she would know too much about what was in her emperor's heart. He did not trust anyone, most especially with such things as his sons and his small, hard heart.

Sebestyen laid a hand over his chest. Perhaps he was ill. Perhaps his heart would give out before Arik and his rebels ever reached Arthes. There was a dull, throbbing ache in his chest, and that ache grew greater with every passing day. When he thought of Liane, the pain grew to a burning intensity.

And so it was best that he did not visit her in her Level Three prison.

When the door to the ballroom opened, Sebestyen laid his hand over the hilt of his sword. A sleep-deprived sentinel warily stuck his head into the room. "The witch Gadhra insists upon seeing you, my lord."

He should order her killed for insisting upon anything . . . but it was possible she had news of Liane, so he tossed his hand in indication that she should be admitted.

The old woman slunk through the partially opened

doorway. The sentinel tried to follow, but Sebestyen ordered him from the room. He did not know what Gadhra wanted to say, but it was possible the news of Liane was for his ears alone. The pain in his heart increased at the very thought.

"You have not been eating," the witch said in a soft, grating voice.

"I have not been hungry. What do you want?"

The witch cocked her head and studied him insolently. Like the others, she knew too much. Eventually, he'd have to get rid of her, but at the moment he needed her assistance. "You have not visited your wife in many days, my lord."

"No, I have not."

"Like you, she does not eat."

"Force food down her throat if you must. I won't allow her to starve herself to get even with me."

"She grieves for her children."

He glared at the old woman. "Is that what you came here to tell me? Have you come to ask me to forgive her?"

"No. The girl lied to you; she betrayed you. She would have sent away the rightful heir."

"Then why are you here?"

The old woman shrugged rounded shoulders. "She is well-healed from the birth, and her milk has dried. If you wish to make use of her as she was intended to be used, or if you wish to offer her to another, she is able." Her eyebrows danced. "I would suggest, however, that you leave her constrained. She is angry and would do you harm if you allowed her hands or her teeth to come too close."

"You make her sound like an animal."

"She is very much an animal, my lord. One who has been forcibly separated from her children. There is no more dangerous beast than a grieving mother." She cocked her head. "Shall I have her prepared for you?"

"No."

"Shall I have her prepared for another? I can slip a bit of stimulating potion into the food I cram down her throat, if you'd prefer her to be willing for whatever man makes use of her."

He suppressed a shudder. In his anger he had sworn to make Liane return to her old station, as concubine available for any man who wanted her. But the idea of putting such a plan into action sickened him. She was empress, mother to his sons, and though he would not say so aloud, she deserved better. "No."

Gadhra took one step back, toward the closed door. "You did not tell me how you disposed of the second-born child."

"No, I did not."

"It is difficult, I know, to do what must be done for the good of the country."

"Many aspects of my position are difficult," Sebestyen said in a biting voice. "Ridding myself of an overly curious old witch who does not know her place would not be one of them."

Gadhra bowed her head, nodded gently, and turned to exit the ballroom and leave Sebestyen alone once again.

And in the vast and cold and solitary room, the emperor placed a thin hand over his oddly aching heart.

18

IT MUST BE A TRICK OF THE MOON. ISADORA SAT UP slowly, so as not to disturb a sleeping Lucan who lay so close. At the top of the hill, at the edge of the line of trees that hid the road from them—and them from the road—a figure stood in shadow. Two figures. She blinked. Was what she saw real? And if so, were the figures animal or human? It was impossible to tell.

And then one of the shapes moved. Not much, but enough for her to be sure the watchers were human.

She reached out and laid a hand on Lucan's arm. Immediately he awoke, though he did not jump up in alarm. His hand crept toward the hilt of the sword that lay at his side. His entire body tensed as long fingers closed over the grip.

They had been found, apparently. Luckily, it would be impossible for those at the top of the hill to descend safely. The hillside was too steep and rocky. They would have to go the long way around, and by then, with any luck, Isadora and Lucan would be long gone.

Lucan would likely prefer to fight, but Isadora was certain they needed to save their fighting for another day. If there was no other choice, she would use the sword as Lucan had taught her, but if they could make a quiet escape . . .

Impossibly, the two figures at the top of the hill began to move downward, their footwork more sure than it should have been on the steep slope covered in loose rock. Away from the shadows of the trees the moonlight illuminated two wild-haired creatures, both barely dressed. As they came closer, she recognized the one in the lead as the beast who had kidnapped Juliet.

Isadora rolled away from Lucan and gripped her own sword. She had seen the strength and speed of this creature once before, and she would not be taken by surprise this time. She would use what Lucan had taught her to bring the beast down without killing him, so he could tell her where Juliet was. Her heart thudded. She wanted to believe that Juliet was alive, but she had not seen her sister in so long, believing became more and more difficult with every passing day.

She and Lucan both rolled smoothly to their feet, swords in hand, and faced the intruders. Isadora's eyes were on the face of the beast who had taken Juliet. In moonlight all was not clear, but the long blond hair and the massive size and the near-nakedness of the creature were much the same as before. She struck a fighting stance as the beast moved closer, and then the second figure reached out a stilling hand that fell gently on a massive arm.

"Isadora, wait. Put down the sword. It's just us. It's me. I have been searching for you."

That voice. Isadora let her sword drop slightly, but Lucan did not. The smaller creature, who had been mostly hidden behind the larger of the intruders, stepped around him, and there was just enough moonlight for her to see a mass of red, curling hair, a familiar face with oddly lightened eyes, and a belly much too rounded with child, considering how long it had been since she'd last seen her sister.

"Juliet?" She was not yet positive this was her sister. Magic might've transformed the creature before her into the one person she most wanted to see, but in this case the magic was flawed. Those were not Juliet's eyes, and her sister could not possibly be so massively pregnant, and prim Juliet would never dare to dress in such a scanty garment.

And yet she so wanted this to be her sister.

The larger creature spoke. "Please put down your weapons. I cannot stop the soldiers from defending their Queen, and at the moment it appears that she very much needs defending."

Queen? A rustle to her right drew Isadora's eyes from the couple who had scurried down the hill. Men as large as the one who had spoken, many of them, had surrounded the camp. They carried long, sharp spears and looked ready to make use of those weapons.

"You should have allowed me to cast a protection spell over the camp," Isadora muttered as she set her sword on the ground.

Lucan did not discard his sword, but he did lower it slightly. "Even for protection, I wish for no magic, love."

"Yes, yes, I know." Stubborn man.

When the woman who looked so much like Juliet—the Queen, apparently—smiled, the last of Isadora's uncertainties vanished. No shapeshifter could duplicate that smile.

"This man who calls you *love* is not your captor, I assume."

"No." Isadora took a step toward Juliet. How could so many changes have taken place in such a short period of time? Just a few months had passed since she'd seen Juliet carried into the cold mountains by the barbarian who now called her his Queen. She wished for sunlight to see more clearly.

"When we first came upon the camp it was impossible to tell, and though my powers have grown, I still cannot discern everything where you are concerned. I do see more now, much more, but still not all."

Isadora could not bear to remain in the dark, not when there was so much to be seen, so she lifted her hand and whispered a few powerful words. Light appeared as a rosy orb, and after the light took form it grew, spreading around her and Juliet. She made sure the unnatural light did not touch Lucan.

The illumination she created was similar to the wizard's light, but it was pink rather than purple, and it was not strong enough to last as the wizard's had. It was a soft glow that confirmed everything she had seen to this point. This woman before her was Juliet. Much changed, but still her sister. The odd eyes were gold, rather than the brown she remembered. The red hair was not neatly and tightly constrained, but hung wild and free. She was also very, very pregnant.

The light died as Isadora threw her arms around Juliet's neck. The large belly impeded her progress, and still she was able to hang on. "Bors said you were dead, but I didn't believe it. I never believed it. But I did not know how I would find you."

A gentle hand settled in Isadora's hair. "I found you," Juliet said sweetly. "Just in time, I believe."

There was a censuring tone to Juliet's voice, and a confidence in that censure that was as new as the eyes. Isadora pulled back to look into those eyes. "Why *just in time*?"

"You cannot go back into the palace."

"I have to—"

Juliet lifted a silencing finger. "Not yet. And not alone."

"She was not going into that place alone," Lucan said sharply.

There had been a time when Juliet would have cowered at such a firm tone of voice from a man, but no longer. Juliet looked Lucan in the eye. "You will need an army to take what you need from the emperor." She smiled and lifted a hand to indicate the spear-toting soldiers who continued to stand guard. "You now have such an army."

LUCAN WAS ACCUSTOMED TO LEADING SWORD-BEARING, uniformed warriors into battle, not half-dressed, spear-toting wild men, many of whom stood a head or more taller than he. Still, when it came to taking on Emperor Sebestyen, he'd take what he could get.

There would be no more sleep on this night. He'd built a fire to illuminate the camp, though Isadora's sister and the man who was her new husband did not come too close. They should be cool, dressed as they were, but apparently they did not want or need the heat of the flame. The explanation came soon enough, at Isadora's insistence.

Anwyn. He had believed the shape-shifters to be legend, not fact. In all the prophesies the wizards had spoken, he had never been told that he would one day lead an Anwyn army. And yet here he was, surrounded by them. Even Juliet was Anwyn, which accounted for the speed of the progression of her pregnancy.

As he listened to Isadora and Juliet exchange tales of

their past eventful months, he realized that Juliet was not only a witch, a Queen, and Anwyn, she was a seer. A powerful one, from what he heard. As dawn approached, and the sisters' tales were done, Lucan leaned toward the red-haired, gold-eyed seer.

"Perhaps if you inform your sister that she is meant to be my wife, she will believe you. She needs a bit of a push."

Juliet answered with a smile. "Over the years I have learned to *push* Isadora as infrequently and gently as possible."

"But if you see what's meant to be, isn't it only right to share that which is inescapable?"

The Anwyn Queen was a beautiful woman, but her eyes were so odd they spooked him a little. The gold was an unnatural color, and those eyes were powerful and enthralling. They were ancient eyes that saw much, that shared much. There was humor and love and intelligence and strength in those gold eyes. Lucan made himself remember the long-ago warning about the witch. Juliet was many things, and a witch was one of them.

"I do not often see clearly that which is meant for those I love. Since becoming Queen I see much more than I ever thought possible, and still, there are some things that are not shown to me." She shrugged her shoulders. "I used to worry about what I did not know, but I have learned to accept what I am given and dismiss the rest. If I am meant to see, the knowing will come."

It was a roundabout, insufficient response that helped him not at all. "Then inform Isadora that she will be the mother of my son."

Juliet just smiled.

"You are as stubborn as your sister," he said, before standing sharply and taking his leave of the gathering by the dying fire in order to wash his face and gather his composure by the pond.

Lucan Hern had always embraced the control his situation offered him. His control, his command. All he had planned, all he wanted, was spinning out of control. He would take back his authority, he decided as he wiped his wet face.

When he returned to the camp, he felt somewhat better. Isadora *would* say yes to his marriage proposal, once they accomplished what they had to do. She *would* be the mother of his son. He was First Captain of the Circle of Bacwyr, soon to be Prince of Swords, and he would not be agitated by the ramblings of a woman. A *witch*.

As he approached the fire he said in his most commanding voice, "We will march toward the palace today, and attack tomorrow morning at dawn."

Juliet lifted her head and once again cast him that serene, condescending smile. Her golden eyes caught and held his. "No. It is too soon."

"I will not be directed in battle by a *woman*," he insisted.

Juliet's husband, the oft-silent Ryn, seemed to growl. A few of the soldiers stepped closer. Already Lucan was calculating his battle plan. That one first . . . he looked fiercest. That one next, and then—

"Lucan!" Isadora stood and touched his arm almost protectively. "You must listen to Juliet. She can tell us when the chance of success is greatest."

He looked down at Isadora, and the truth of his animosity came to him. "I do not wish to be guided in battle by magic."

"The Circle makes use of wizards," she argued.

"Yes, but in warfare it is warriors who formulate the battle plans, not wizards or witches." Besides, how accurate could Juliet be? She did not even see that Isadora would be his wife.

"You would risk your own life to discard my advice," Juliet said in a gentle, unconcerned voice. "Would you also risk my sister's life? Have you considered that perhaps the reason I do not see what you wish me to see is that you must first get past this test . . . and survive?"

He looked down at Juliet and tried to set aside his emotions to see what he could see of her. The wizards had taught him well, though he had not always been the best student. He shut out everything but Juliet, and he stared into her eyes.

Juliet was incredibly powerful, and deeply kind, and unflinchingly devoted to those she loved. And she was right.

"Fine," he snapped, not entirely happy at the revelation. "We will wait."

FESTIVALS MADE THE PEOPLE BELOW HAPPY, AND SO HE indulged them. The priests had insisted that residents of the city needed to see the child who would be their next emperor, and the Spring Festival was the perfect opportunity to present the babe Jahn to the subjects who would one day be his.

They made a pretty picture standing on the Level Six balcony, Sebestyen imagined. Liane's hair had been styled, and she wore a plain crimson gown with long sleeves, which disguised the fact that her hands were tightly bound. Her face was pale, but a touch of rouge disguised that fact as well.

He himself held his firstborn child, Jahn, and when he lifted the baby high, the crowd below cheered. The crowd was smaller than it had been at the Winter Festival, which had been smaller still than the Autumn Festival. The city was shrinking. Sebestyen suspected throngs were deserting the city to join the rebels, and one day they would all turn on him, as he had always known they would.

No one below could see that armed sentinels and a number of priests stood just inside the doors that opened from the Level Six meeting room to the balcony. If Liane tried anything, anything at all, she would not get far. She had been instructed to remain still and quiet, to look and behave as a proper empress should, at least for a few minutes.

Sebestyen gave a curt bow and stepped back into the room. He held the baby snugly with one arm and drew Liane with him with the other. The cheering died, and the crowd below continued with their celebrating, which included drinking to excess and dancing like clumsy fools.

One of the priests who had been entrusted with the care of the heir reached for the baby. Liane came to life as he did so, her head snapping to the child and then to Sebestyen. "Let me hold him," she asked breathlessly.

"I'm sure that's not wise," Sebestyen answered, and yet he did not release the child to the impatient priest. In the corner of the room Gadhra waited. She would be among the escort that would see Liane back to her prison. The witch shook her head, indicating that she did not approve.

"I'll willingly do anything you ask of me," Liane whispered. "*Anything.* Just let me hold him for a few minutes."

He should not allow it, after what she'd done, but the pain he'd been suffering increased as he watched her face. She was desperate. He had never known Liane to be desperate until this moment.

Ignoring the protests of the priest and the obvious disapproval of the witch, Sebestyen cut the bonds at her wrists and handed the baby to Liane. She took her son with tender, anxious arms, and she actually smiled. "He has grown so much."

"Yes, he has."

"My goodness, he looks very much like Duran," she said, her fingers barely ruffling the pale strands of his fine hair.

He had always been jealous of Liane, and as she mentioned another man's name, he felt a surge of anger. "Who is Duran?" he asked sharply, shooing the pesky priest away.

"My brother," she snapped.

The anger faded as quickly as it had come upon him. "I did not know you had a brother."

"I once had four of them. Duran was the baby. He's dead, beheaded by one of your soldiers last year."

"He was a rebel, then?"

Liane nodded and did not take her eyes from the baby. "Yes, as were the other three. Valdis and Stepan are also dead. I killed the man who murdered Duran. I cut his throat and watched him die on the floor of one of your prison cells. Only Kane lives." She lifted her gaze briefly to look at him. "Do you remember him? I suppose you knew Kane only as Ryn, which was a false name. He's the rebel who took Sophie Fyne out of this palace. He is your son's uncle." She seemed to take some perverse pleasure in the fact that his child had rebels among his blood relations.

Liane dismissed him and looked at the baby again. In spite of her apparent refusal to eat, she had not lost all the weight she'd gained during her pregnancy. The slight roundness to her face and her bosom suited her very well, and as he watched her, he was assaulted with unexpected sensations he could not push away: love, regret, hopelessness, ruination.

It was ruination that he felt most deeply. Ruination not at the hand of traitors or rebels, but by his own.

He leaned forward to speak to Liane in a low voice no one else could hear. Gadhra and the priests and the sentinels could see, but they could not hear his words. "I wish I had made different choices, Liane. I wish when Arik had professed a desire for the throne I had given it to him. I wish I had offered my bastard brother this palace and all that goes with it, and taken nothing from this place but you. Maybe we would have been happy, then. Maybe we would both know peace."

She lifted her head and looked him in the eye. "Do you think I could ever know peace with the man who disposed of my second-born son because he was *inconvenient*? What did you do to him, Sebestyen? Did he suffer?" Tears filled Liane's eyes. "Did you do what had to be done yourself, or did you pass the unpleasant task to another so your hands would not be soiled?"

He wanted to tell her that the child he'd named Alixandyr was alive and healthy, that he had never intended to murder his own flesh and blood. This is what she thought of him. She thought him a monster who would coldly murder his own babe . . . and that hurt more than anything he had imagined possible.

She returned her attention to the baby in her arms and even bent down to kiss his soft forehead. "I, too, wish that I had made different decisions."

Perhaps she wished, as he did, that they could go back and undo all that had gone wrong. "Do you?"

"Yes." She lifted her head and looked him squarely and bravely in the eye, and she whispered, as he had, so no one else could hear. "I wish with all of my being that when I finally had the opportunity to stand before you with a knife in my hand, I'd found the strength and the courage to drive the blade through your heart."

19

"WE'RE MOVING *AWAY* FROM THE PALACE!" LUCAN COMplained. It was not the first complaint he'd voiced in the past two days, since they had been joined by the Anwyn party.

"That's correct," Juliet answered calmly.

"Exactly how long do you expect me to wait?"

Juliet cast a gentle smile at him. "I expect you to wait until the time is right, as any shrewd soldier would."

He continued to grumble. "I don't need an army to do what needs to be done. I could turn back and go into the palace on my own."

"You could," Juliet countered. "But you won't."

Her confidence told Isadora that while Lucan did not like waiting, he would.

Juliet looked at Isadora and smiled. "This man of yours is very impatient."

"He can be." *But there are times when he has an abundance of patience.*

Juliet smiled as if she knew her sister's thoughts. Maybe she did.

Isadora took Lucan's hand as they continued on, moving deeper into the forest, following a trail that just barely lived up to its name. They were moving toward Sophie, Juliet said. Within a matter of hours, she would finally be reunited with both her sisters.

There would be hugs and kisses and apologies. There would be a depth of gratitude she had never before known.

And then they would address the issue of the curse. With Juliet's enhanced powers and what Isadora had learned from Thayne, perhaps they could make what had always seemed hopeless—breaking the Fyne Curse—a reality.

Thayne had said that before that happened, they would each hold that which they'd believed to be impossible in their hands. *One, two, three.* What could those impossible things be? If she could easily conceive them, they wouldn't be so impossible, now would they?

One step at a time. First, the reunion. Then saving Liane and her baby. Only then would she have time to ponder the details involved in breaking the curse.

"I do not like this," Lucan said in a lowered voice.

"I can see that."

"Your sister has taken complete charge of my battle plan."

"She knows what is best."

He scoffed but did not offer an argument. "The red-headed, surly soldier, he eyes me as if he would like to rip off my head."

"If you persist in yelling at his daughter, he might try."

Isadora would have thought it a great coincidence that she and Juliet had both found their fathers in recent past, but if she had learned nothing else, she knew that there was no coincidence in life. All that happened was meant to be.

Juliet said she'd seen that Sophie had found her father, too. What did the three men Lucinda Fyne had taken as lovers have to do with what was happening here and now? Was it possible that they would play a part in ending the curse that had kept Lucinda from daring to love any one of them?

Maybe it was just a gift, of sorts, that these men had reappeared in their lives, one after another. As women she and her sisters had rarely spoken of the men who'd sired them, but as children there had been moments when they'd wondered, aloud to one another and in quieter moments to themselves, about their fathers. Their das. Their papas. Maybe, just maybe, that long ago wondering was being rewarded now, years later. Could they have drawn the men to them . . . or rather, drawn themselves to the men?

It was only supposition, and still . . . she wondered.

"Juliet has become a bit demanding since being made Queen," Isadora observed. "I suppose that's only natural,"

"I suppose," he grumbled.

She squeezed his hand. "Don't worry. You'll like Sophie. She's so gentle and sweet-tempered she wouldn't harm a fly."

"GET YOUR HANDS OFF OF ME, YOU FILTHY, WRETCHED, good-for-nothing *man*!" Sophie screamed.

Kane looked quite taken aback at her outburst. Then again, he had missed labor with Ariana, and had no idea what to expect.

Sophie's anger turned to tears. "I'm sorry, but it hurts, and it's too early, and I tried to make the baby wait a while longer, but she won't wait, she insists on coming now, and the timing couldn't be worse." She gasped for breath. "I don't like pain. I know another beautiful daughter is worth any sacrifice, and I should be stoic and mature and I should suffer in silence, but why does it have to hurt so much? Pain is not good, Kane, and I don't like it at all. It just isn't right that something so beautiful should be marred by misery." Her apology turned to blubbering, but when a hapless soldier opened the tent flap, she screamed at him, "Get out!"

Well beyond the tent, the flame of the campfire grew with a burst of power, flooding the campsite with light for a moment. What little bit of sense she had left understood how dangerous directing her anger there could be, so Sophie turned her roiling passions up, away from the rebels and friends who camped near the tent where she lay. In the distance, a crack of thunder rumbled in the night.

"I'm sorry," she said again. "I do not handle my emotions well when I'm in labor."

Kane nodded. "I can see that. Should I clear the campsite? Are the soldiers here in any danger?"

"No," Sophie answered, only slightly offended. "Odd things may happen, I'll grant you that, but I promise not to hurt anyone." Ariana was in another tent placed far away from this one, in the keeping of Maddox Sulyen—Sophie's father, Ariana's and this child's grandfather.

"How long before the baby comes?" Kane asked, a touch of hope in his voice.

"By morning, if we're very lucky," Sophie answered.

His eyes went wide, and in the glow of the lantern it seemed he paled. "By morning?" he asked, as if he might have misheard.

"If we're lucky."

Kane nodded and began to prepare. He had never delivered a baby, but then neither had anyone else among the rebels. This was not Sophie's first child, however, and she would be able to direct him as the hours passed. He helped her to remove her clothes, and then he laid her on a thick bed of blankets and the finest sheets available to such a poor band of soldiers. He wrapped her warmly, and then he sat beside her and held her hand.

Ariana had been born in a soft bed in the family cabin on Fyne Mountain. This little girl would come into the world in a small tent, padded ground as her bed. For now.

Sophie squeezed Kane's hand. "Just remember, no matter what I say in the hours to come—I do love you."

"I love you, too." She could tell he was more scared than she was about what was to come and about the fact that the baby was arriving early.

She could feel a new pain coming, and she tried to ignore the gentle warning signs. "The next child will be born in a bed. With a midwife to care to the delivery while you wait in another room, as is right and proper for an anxious new father."

"Maybe in a little house on a farm," Kane said.

"A farm?" she said, her voice rising in hope. "You've never said much about what you want when this war is done. I thought maybe you'd like to be a soldier, still."

"Arik offered me a post in the palace."

Sophie's heart lurched. "He did?"

"I declined."

She squeezed Kane's hand very tightly as the pain grew to a height she could not ignore. As disturbing as the physical pain was the realization that ending the curse would now be all but impossible. Without Kane's baby inside her, without the added power, she would be weak again. Just a few months ago, a year together had seemed like such a long time. A year to share love, and try to find a way to end the curse, and simply be together.

Eight months later, that year seemed very short.

Sophie swore, using words she had heard in her months with the rebels. Above her head, another rumble of thunder sounded in protest.

The pain faded. She took a deep breath. And Kane leaned down to kiss her sweating forehead.

"I like the idea of a farm," she said, as if their conversation had not been interrupted.

"Me, too."

"I think you have seen enough soldiering in your lifetime."

"That I have."

Kane was months from thirty. Mere months! If she did not break the curse, he would not live to see that birthday—or his farm.

THE WIND CAME IN UNEXPECTEDLY, PUSHING AGAINST the travelers and all but forcing them back. Overhead, thunder and lightning crashed and crackled on occasion, coming and going, coming and going. No rain had begun to fall as of yet, but Juliet had assured them rain would soon fall.

They had walked through the night, at Juliet's insistence. Even though she was very pregnant and considerably smaller than any of the soldiers she commanded, she led the way with assurance and without a hint of tiredness.

Dawn was coming, graying the sky, but true light was not yet upon them as Isadora ran past a handful of soldiers to reach her sister. She did not have to look back to know that Lucan was with her.

"This is not a natural storm," she shouted, to be heard above the wind.

"No, it is not," Juliet said, without slowing her step.

"Sophie?"

"She's in labor."

The soldiers fought against the wind, and the trees in the forest danced dangerously, limbs bending almost to the breaking point. The lightning flashes and rumbles of thunder came closer together than they had when the storm had begun. "She's *causing* this?"

"Yes."

"This didn't happen last time," Isadora argued.

"If you will remember, it did rain a bit, there toward the end. We didn't think anything about it, at the time. Sophie is much stronger than she was when Ariana was born. Frighteningly so. She cannot always control what happens around her." The wind whipped tangled red curls, but Juliet did not seem to be affected by the gusts she fought to move forward. "We must hurry."

Behind her, Lucan mumbled, "I could not have fallen in love with an only child. No, that would be much too simple and ordinary and easy."

"If you love me, then you must love my sisters, too."

"I did not say I would not love them," Lucan said in a louder voice. "I only made the observation that they are not simple or ordinary or easy."

"Neither am I."

"No." He took her hand, as he had often through the night. "You are none of those things."

She threaded her fingers through Lucan's. Her small hand felt at home enveloped by his larger, more muscled hand. With him behind and beside her, she felt safer than she ever had before. Nothing but danger and uncertainty awaited them in the days to come, and yet she was not afraid. "What if we never have easy?" she asked as she lifted her face to the wind and dancing fingers of lightning whipped across the sky.

"Then we will make our happiness surrounded by all that is difficult. If we can do that, then when easy comes, we will have no worries."

No worries. It was a nice idea, but at the moment she could see nothing but worries.

* * *

THERE WAS A MOMENT OF TENSION WHEN JULIET'S SOL-
diers and Arik's rebels met, but Juliet quickly commanded
truce, and there was truce. Isadora still had a difficult time
understanding how and why her sister had changed—and
then there were those moments when she looked at Juliet
and realized that in many ways the middle Fyne sister had
not changed at all.

Sophie was easy to find. Dawn lit the camp, which had
been ravaged by wind. The lightning storm continued, and
at last the rain began, falling slowly but in fat drops that
plopped on the ground and the soldiers and the sisters.
"There." Juliet pointed—a gesture that was unnecessary—
to a large tent in the middle of the campsite. A ray of unnatural light rose from the tent, and it was from that ray of
light that the storm originated.

Like the rebels, the Anwyn soldiers and Lucan hung
back, keeping their distance. Juliet and Isadora fought the
wind and rain to run to the tent.

Inside the tent, Sophie was screaming vile words to her
beloved husband, and Kane looked as if he were about to
pass out on his feet. Apparently it had been a long night for
both of them.

Kane's head whipped around as he heard them enter.
Isadora had not thought the man would ever be relieved to
see his wife's sisters, but at the moment that's what she saw
on his face: relief. "I don't know why or how you're here,"
he said, "but thank the heavens." He studied Juliet carefully, noting the changes in her appearance, and his forehead wrinkled with a frown. There was no time for
explanations. Not now. "I thought I could do this on my
own, but I need your help."

The contraction ended, and Sophie lifted her head

wearily. She even smiled, though it was certainly not her best effort. "You're here! Both of you!" The raindrops that had been pelting the tent gentled, and the wind died down substantially. Kane seemed to breathe more normally.

Isadora gave the weary man a glare. "You may wait outside with the other men."

Kane backed away from Sophie, but he did not leave the tent. "I'm not going anywhere. I need your help, and I'm grateful that you've come, but I'm not running away now." He moved to give the women room to hover around Sophie, but he did not leave, and Isadora did not try to force him from the tent. If he'd survived Sophie's labor so far, he deserved to stay.

The delivery of the new baby was near. Poor Sophie; she had never been one to endure suffering with grace, and she had experienced a rough night.

"I thought I would never see either of you again," she said, tears making her eyes glow. She studied Isadora's ragged gown and Juliet's gold eyes, and shook her head. "We have much to discuss, once we see this little girl into the world."

"Yes, we do," Juliet said. Her eyes and even her manner might have changed, but her amiable voice had not.

"I'm going to name her Lucinda," Sophie said with a touch of anger in her voice. "Kane doesn't like the name, but she was our mother, and if I'm the one who has to go through this ordeal, I should be able to name the baby whatever I want, right?"

"Of course, dear," Kane answered.

During the next contraction, Sophie screamed. In answer, thunder cracked close by and lightning added illumination to the tent. Kane shuddered, and Isadora knew that he had suffered each pain along with Sophie during the long night.

"If I could have taken the pain for her, I would have," he said when the scream stopped.

"Don't be silly," Sophie said breathlessly.

"I love you," Kane answered.

"I love you, too, but at the moment I cannot imagine that I will ever allow you to touch me again."

Since Kane appeared to be distressed, Isadora turned to him and mouthed, "She doesn't mean it."

"I do mean it!" Sophie responded, even though she had not been able to see Isadora's mouth. That said, she relaxed. "But I will probably change my mind in the very near future." She looked Juliet in the eye. "It's time," she said. "The baby is coming now."

As if the child had been waiting for her aunts to arrive, the delivery progressed quickly. Kane held Sophie's hand and offered words of encouragement, while Juliet and Isadora tended to the delivery of the child.

"Head," Juliet said, as the baby crowned. "Oh, what a pretty baby. Lucinda has a little tuft of dark hair."

"Dark?" Sophie said as she caught her breath.

"My mother had dark hair." Kane squeezed Sophie's hand as the next contraction began.

"Push," Juliet ordered, and Sophie obeyed. "Head," she said as the child was born. "Shoulders, arms . . ." And then Juliet held the new baby in her arms.

"Penis," Isadora added in wonder. "Lucinda has a penis."

Sophie and Kane both reacted sharply, heads popping up.

"A son?" Kane asked.

"Fyne women do not have sons," Sophie said. "There must be a mistake."

Juliet held the baby high so both parents could see. The naked child squalled, cold in his new environment, so Juliet wrapped the baby snugly in a blanket and handed him to his mother.

With the birth of Sophie and Kane's child the rain stopped with amazing suddenness. The howling wind died abruptly. There was no more thunder or lightning. As Sophie held her son, a bright and warm sun shone down upon the tent, and their world.

The new parents studied their baby with wonder, peeking at his little face beyond the blanket and smiling at one another widely. For the moment, at least, revolutions and emperors and curses were forgotten.

"We certainly cannot name him Lucinda," Sophie said. "I have no idea what to name a boy! I never even considered names for a son, since I thought it was impossible."

A chill walked up and down Isadora's back. *Impossible.*

"Do you mind if we name him Duran?" Kane asked. "For my brother."

Sophie nodded. "I like that name very well." She looked down at the baby. "Duran. The name suits him, I think."

Soon Sophie put the baby Duran to her breast, and instinctively he knew to latch on. "I wonder if we will have more sons or if all our other children will be girls?" Sophie asked, completely disregarding curses and war for this moment.

"I thought you weren't going to let me touch you ever again."

"Don't be silly. I didn't mean it, and you know that very well." Sophie glanced to Juliet. "I suspect Juliet could tell me. She's much stronger than she was when last we saw her."

Kane shook his head. "I don't want to know everything the future holds. We will be surprised next time, like all other parents."

There would not be a next time if the curse wasn't broken, but Isadora felt a ray of warm hope in her heart.

One.

20

SEBESTYEN LEANED OVER THE CRADLE WHERE HIS FIRST-
born son, Jahn, the next emperor of Columbyana, slept. He
was growing so fast! The other one was growing, too. They
had both been very small in the beginning, but he saw
changes in them every day. It was a miracle either of them
had survived, let alone both.

It struck him that all the miracles in his life concerned
Liane and these babies. There were certainly no miracles
to be had in the ruling of this country. Those closest to the
emperor tried to protect him from unpleasantness, but he
saw the truth. Sentinels deserted every day. The guard at
the palace was always on alert, but was not what it had
once been.

Arik had not yet marched on the palace, and already he
was winning.

The baby woke, and the nurse in the corner stirred as if
to see to him. Sebestyen shooed the woman away, and she

retreated into the corner where she had been standing and watching, and waiting for him to depart. He reached into the cradle and lifted the child. Jahn was so light, and yet he was sturdy. His eyes were bright and seemed to see everything, though the women and the priests all said babies of this age could see little or nothing with any clarity. Still, when his son looked at him, he felt as if the child saw.

The baby cooed as Sebestyen cradled him to his chest, and one little hand reached for him.

In an instant before the small hand made contact, Sebestyen had a flash of understanding. All those years he had hidden from the sun, he'd been a fool. This was the touch that would signal the end. The touch of his son. *The* son, the firstborn who was destined to be emperor.

There was time to move away, to catch that little arm and push it aside before the damage was done, but Sebestyen just stood there and let the small, soft hand fall on his cheek. It was a gentle, loving, innocent touch, and for all the world he would not rob himself of this moment. Was there any touch more pure and soft than that of a child? Surely not. And when that touch came from one's own child, a miracle of life, it was surely a sign that at least in some small way, all was right with the world.

The door to the room burst open, and Father Merryl ran inside. Sebestyen had not seen the old man move so briskly in more than a decade.

"They are coming," the old man said. "Dear Lord above, from all sides they come."

"Who?" Sebestyen asked, but his sinking heart knew.

"Rebels from the east, Tryfyn warriors from the west. A band of half-clad warriors I cannot identify from the north, and a rebellious contingent of our own soldiers from the south."

He did not even feign surprise. "Then it is over."

Father Merryl shook his head. "No. We have time to get out, if we hurry." He looked at the nursemaid who had been seeing to the basic needs of the baby in Sebestyen's arms. "Pack what the child will need for at least three days." He dismissed the woman as she quickly went about her chore. "We will disguise you as a servant, my lord, and together we'll make our escape through the hidden stairs. But we must leave quickly."

"How long before the rebels arrive?"

"Soon. We have just enough time to get you and the heir to safety."

"No." With the baby in his arms, Sebestyen rushed from the room.

"Where are you going!" Father Merryl shouted. "You and the child must be saved if there is to be an answer to the revolt! We don't have the troop strength and the support now, but with time—"

"There will be no revolt," Sebestyen shouted. "Arik can have the palace and all that comes with it."

Father Merryl chased Sebestyen into the hallway. "You don't know what you're saying. I can't allow you to give up everything!" The old man grabbed at Sebestyen's crimson robe and held fast.

Sebestyen turned and pushed the old man away. Father Merryl lost his balance and his grip and fell to the floor. "Align yourself with Arik, old man. Maybe he'll allow you to get your parasitic hands on him. Then again, maybe he will see through you, as I did not. I should have thrown you in Level Thirteen years ago." With that he ran . . . down the hallway, to the storeroom where the entrance to the hidden stairways was located, and down to the third floor. The child in his arms squirmed and mewled as Sebestyen hastened down the narrow, spiraling staircase. "Don't worry, Jahn. Don't cry. You're going to see your mother."

If the prophesy was right, there would be no saving himself, but he would get his family to safety before the palace was invaded.

JULIET'S SOLDIERS PROVIDED A DISTRACTION SO THAT Isadora and Lucan could slip into the palace unnoticed. The guards near the entrance were so completely surprised by the large men who wore so little and carried large, sharp spears, they allowed themselves to be blinded.

Once she and Lucan were safely inside the palace, the Anwyn would retreat; that was the plan.

Thank heavens Juliet had found her before she and Lucan had returned to the palace! Not only did her soldiers provide a safe way in, she'd also provided much-needed information. Not everything, *never* everything. But enough to make the task easier.

Both babies lived. They and their mother all resided in the palace, still, and they were all physically well. Liane was on Level Three. Juliet had not known of the Levels, but she had seen the empress surrounded by many women in blue, and she said the scent of sensuality was always in the air in this decadent place. Definitely Level Three.

As soon as they were well into the open area of Level Ten, Isadora realized that something was wrong. It took her a moment to realize what had caught her attention. In the past the low hum from Level Eleven had always been present at the ground entrance, but today all was silent. Whoever had the keeping of Level Eleven had deserted their machines, which meant neither the lift nor the light sticks would be operational.

Even if the lift had been working, she would not have used it because Lucan would not make use of it. They rushed for the stairs. There was not much time before the palace was overrun, and before that happened she had to get Liane and the babies out. Once they were safe, she didn't care what happened. She didn't care who sat on the throne, as long as the war was done and those she had sworn to protect were safe.

If sheer numbers were the answer, Sebestyen would not be emperor much longer.

She and Lucan hurried upward. Isadora's heart thudded in her chest, and the hand that gripped the small sword he had given her was sweating.

The plan was simple. She and Lucan would rescue Liane together, and then the three of them would collect the babies. While she and Liane got the children and themselves out of the palace, Lucan would retrieve the Star of Bacwyr. That stupid ring! It was the reason he had courted her in the first place, it was the power that had drawn him to her. If not for that piece of jewelry he would not have looked at her twice.

Not such a stupid ring after all, perhaps.

They ran into three sentinels at the landing for Level Six, and Lucan dispatched them quickly and with ease. The encounter did nothing to still the pounding of Isadora's heart. Steel on steel was loud in the enclosed stairwell, and to see the sentinels die . . .

She had killed two sentinels herself, this past winter. One in her home, the other in the forest as she searched for Juliet. They had deserved death, she still believed that, but those killings had also opened the door to a dark side of herself. She had put that darkness away for good, but she could never go back and undo what had been done. Thayne said that destruction was not always separate from and opposed to protection, but was a part of her gift. She did not see it as true. More, she did not *feel* it.

There was turmoil on Level Three. Many of the girls

had already left, but a few remained. Many were very pregnant . . . a month or less from delivery. They were afraid, and they cried. Those who had a place to go had gone there days ago. Apparently everyone had realized that the end was coming.

As she and Lucan made their way down the hallway, Isadora issued orders. She commanded even the pregnant girls who swore they had no place to go to leave the palace *now*. A few complained, but they soon saw that she was serious in her directions, and they went. One man, a master-in-training named Brus, had remained, and Isadora placed him in charge of the fleeing women. Surely the guards at the palace gate would not detain the women. Besides, they were trying to keep people out of the palace, not hold them in.

No one remembered seeing Liane, and the Level Three rooms they searched were empty. Isadora was beginning to believe that she was too late. She never should have waited as Juliet had instructed. She should have come back here immediately and found Liane and the babies.

Babies. It was such a relief to know that the emperor had not killed one of his own children. Liane had believed him capable of such an act, even as she'd loved him. And yet the pain in his eyes as he'd pushed Isadora into Level Thirteen had given her hope.

A man who had no heart did not feel that kind of pain.

It was a faint cry for help that caught Isadora's ear, and Lucan's. They stopped in the hallway and listened, and the cry came once again, as faint as before. It was a woman's voice, coarse and desperate.

"Here." Lucan opened a door to a room they had already searched once. It remained undisturbed, but when the cry came again, it was clearer than before. They crossed the room, tore down a faded tapestry of a lewd nature, and revealed a hidden door.

Lucan made Isadora stand back as he opened the door on a seemingly empty chamber.

A bed dominated the room. It was mussed. Long scarves tied to the headboard and the footboard had been left dangling. The cry for help came again, and Lucan rounded the bed.

"It's the witch," he said.

Isadora joined him. Gadhra lay on the floor, bleeding from a wound in her side. She was half sitting up, and wiry, loose gray and white hair fell in disarray around her disheveled body.

"Who did this to you?" Lucan asked.

"The boy," she said hoarsely. "The emperor. After all that whore did, he came here to save her. I tried to stop him, and he stabbed me." She looked at her bloody hand in wonder, and then returned it to the wound.

"Where are they?" Isadora asked.

"I don't know."

Lucan assisted the witch up and onto the bed, where she sat on the edge and examined her wound. "Did he wear the ring?"

"Ring?" Gadhra asked, seemingly dazed. "What ring?"

"The Star of Bacwyr," Lucan snapped. "It's blue, and about so big . . ."

"You are blind," the old woman said.

"Did he wear such a ring?"

"Perhaps," she snapped, and then she looked at Isadora. "You survived."

"No thanks to you."

"How did you find Thayne?" The old woman smiled, as if she knew the wizard was Isadora's father. As if she had known they would find one another in that cursed pit.

"Very well," Isadora said without emotion. She looked up at Lucan. "Let's go. Maybe we can catch them."

"You're going to leave me here?" Gadhra asked. "Patch my wound and take me with you. I'll make myself useful."

"The wound is not so bad," Lucan observed. "You'll survive."

Gadhra coughed and fell back onto the bed, gasping for air. Lucan leaned over her, appearing more annoyed than concerned.

Beware the witch. The words popped into Isadora's mind, and then they sprang from her mouth.

Lucan reacted to her warning just as Gadhra swung the knife she'd had hidden in her ragged attire up and toward his midsection. He shifted to one side, caught the arm in one strong hand, and snagged the dagger from the witch. The tip of the blade came within a hairsbreadth of his flesh.

"Why would you try to kill me?" he asked as he made use of the scarves that had apparently once been used to restrain Liane.

"Because the two of you are going to ruin everything!" the old witch spat.

"How?"

Gadhra pursed her wrinkled lips, but as Lucan and Isadora left the room, she shouted, "The boy is meant to be emperor!"

They did not ask, as they left her behind, which *boy* she spoke of.

RESCUING AN ANGRY WOMAN AND REUNITING HER WITH her baby was not a quick and easy task. It didn't help matters that Liane refused to listen to a word he said. Her attention was reserved for Jahn, and she did not want to let him go. He explained to his wife that she needed to dress in a gown that was warm and appropriate for travel, but it was all but impossible to draw her attention away from the child in her arms. He helped her dress, he all but led her through every step as if *she* were the child. He even slipped boots onto her feet and tied them securely.

As he led Liane along narrow hidden hallways, Sebestyen explained to her that she must get out of the palace, but she seemed not to hear him. Still her attentions were all for Jahn, and he wondered if she heard him at all.

Outside the doorway to the room where Alixandyr and Mahri waited, Sebestyen stopped and turned to his wife. "I am not as heartless as you believe me to be, Liane."

"You are," she said, not taking her eyes from her child. "You are heartless and soulless and cruel."

He did not have time for this conversation. Her own eyes would show her the truth soon enough. He opened the door, only to find Mahri standing in the middle of the room, poised to do battle with the knife he had given her. When she recognized him, she let the knife fall. "It's you, my lord. I thought perhaps it was the invaders."

"We're getting out," he said curtly.

He would prefer to leave the nursemaid behind, since he did not trust her, but he needed the woman and her prodigious boobs to feed the babies. The woman stood slowly, looked at him and then at Liane, as the empress entered the room behind him.

It took Liane a moment to realize that her second-born child rested in this very room. Still holding Jahn in her arms, she ran to the cradle and scooped little Alix into her arms. She held them both as she spun to face Sebestyen, an expression of wonder on her beautiful face. "You didn't—"

"Of course not."

He studied the occupants of the room with a weary eye. How would he manage to get three women and two babies out of the palace unnoticed? The prophesy was coming true around him, so he did not expect to see himself to safety, but his family . . . Liane and the babies would survive, and she would need Mahri and the nursemaid, at least for now.

"The rebels are coming," he said solemnly. "Liane is empress, and she will be endangered if she falls into the wrong hands. The children are the next rightful heirs to the throne, and so they are in danger, also."

"My lord, surely no one would harm the *babies*," Mahri said.

He glared at the naive maid. "You do not know what horrors men in pursuit of power are capable of. I do."

Mahri paled, but Liane did not. She had never been naive or fearful, and he knew he would be leaving his children in good hands.

"We can get to Level Seven by way of the hidden stairwells. After that we'll have to use the main stairway to Level Ten. There's a secret exit through the courtyard. If we can reach that exit before the rebels arrive, we can make our way to safety."

"And then what?" Liane snapped. "Where will we go?"

He looked his wife in the eye. "I don't know. I don't care." He didn't expect to survive, but if he did, by some miracle . . . he would not look back. "Arik can have the palace, and the country." She did not look at all forgiving. "If you still feel the need to kill me, can it at least wait until we get out of here?"

LEVEL ONE, WHICH WAS USUALLY BUSTLING WITH SENtinels and ministers and priests, as well as the daily goingson of the emperor, was eerily silent. Those sentinels who had not deserted had moved down to the perimeter of the palace in order to protect it from the invaders. Did they realize that they were badly outnumbered? If not, they would realize that fact quite soon.

Lucan searched the bedchamber, and the office, and the ballroom, rifling through boxes and drawers in search of the Star. He found jewelry and coins and proclamations, but he did not find the ring he was searching for.

Isadora was anxious to move downward, even though to Lucan's mind the witch's confession proved that Liane was not in danger. Sebestyen was seeing to her safety. Still, she was not satisfied, and would not be until she saw the empress and the babies for herself.

"It isn't here," he said angrily. "And if it is, then it's well hidden."

"I could try a location spell, if you'd like," Isadora said.

He glared at her. "I must find the Star on my own. And I have told you—"

"No magic. I have not forgotten, I was just trying to help."

If he did not find the ring, then it was not meant to be. He had done his best, and he would continue to do so. But if it was not meant for the Prince of Swords and the new King of Tryfyn to come now, then it was not time. Not all things were in his hands.

"We will find the Empress Liane," he said, dismissing his earlier distress. "If the Star presents itself, then I will know it's time to retrieve it. If not . . ." He shrugged. "I still have you, so I can't very well call the trip a failure."

Isadora had not yet agreed to marry him, but as soon as Liane and the babies were safe, she would. She had all but promised him as much. Lucan rifled through a pile of precious stones and gold, just in case he had missed the ring he sought.

The silence of Level One had lulled them into a false

sense of security, and when the green-clad sentinel burst into the room and found Lucan with a handful of gems in one hand, he and Isadora were both startled. The sentinel shouted, "Thief!" and then he raised his sword and turned on Isadora.

21

WHEN THEY REACHED THE MAIN STAIRWAY ON LEVEL Eight, Sebestyen heard the roar of the armies that approached. Time was running out—no—*time* had already gone. He should have been faster. He should have forced Liane to move more quickly, when she dawdled over her baby instead of listening to his commands.

As they descended the stairway, he realized that the sounds of fighting came from outside the palace. The rebels had not reached the interior of the palace—not yet. There was still time . . .

The sentinels who remained under his command, who had not deserted out of fear or disloyalty, held the invaders at bay, at least for now. There might be some resistance to the rear of the palace, beyond the courtyard, but no aggressor would see the three women and two babies as a danger. Liane was not dressed in crimson, he had seen to that, and none of the opposing soldiers knew what the empress looked like. Surely none of them would be on the lookout for twins.

For a moment, Sebestyen thought that perhaps he would be able to escape with Liane and the babies and their retinue of two servants. For one fleeting moment he imagined the life he might have had, if he'd stepped aside years ago. He imagined a life outside the palace, far from the city of Arthes, where there were no duties beyond a man's duty to his family.

They were very near the doorway to the courtyard, escape so close he could almost taste it, when the ragged old witch ran from the shadows, knife raised and obviously intended for Liane's back.

Sebestyen· rushed forward with a shout of warning and knocked Liane aside. She stumbled but did not fall. The knife that had been aimed at Liane's back sliced into his arm, and an inordinate amount of blood spurted forth. He grabbed the witch with his uninjured arm and yanked her away from Liane. The old hag had one of the scarves that had been used to bind Liane to the bed cinched around her midsection, there where he had stabbed her.

He should have made certain she was dead, but how could he have known that she'd have the·strength to stage an ambush?

He turned to Liane. "Go. Now." Liane cast him a quick, questioning glance, and then she and the others ran into the courtyard. She knew the hidden doorway, and if he could hold off the witch and the soldiers and the priests, maybe she and the babies would be safe. Nothing else mattered, not the fate of his country or his life.

"Don't let them escape!" Gadhra shouted as she tried to pull away from his grasp. "I need the boy. I must have the boy. Don't you see? He is meant to be emperor, and with me at his side he will be the most powerful emperor Columbyana has ever seen."

"Why would my son want you at his side?" He felt oddly dizzy, and blood poured down his arm.

"To take the place of his deceased mother, of course. To advise and coddle, and teach him the power of dark magic, so that sleeping but potent energy can return to Columbyana, as is right. I have seen the possibilities in my dreams," she whispered hoarsely. "I have waited patiently for this time to arrive, and I will not allow you to ruin it. All of Columbyana and all the worlds beyond will tremble at the feet of your son, and he will be under my command. All will fear and respect him, and his influence will spread like a wildfire until the very earth shakes with fear of his power. No, I will not be imprisoned in Level Seven when Jahn is emperor, as I was beneath you and your father. No one will dare to challenge me. I will teach Jahn, I will coddle and nurture him. I will be the only family he can call his own, once you and the whore and the other babe are dead. He will have no one else to turn to; he will listen only to me."

"You will not touch Liane or Alix. Jahn will not be emperor," Sebestyen said. "And there will be no dark magic in this palace." The arm that had been wounded did not work properly, so he released his hold on the witch to draw the knife at his waist. He swung with all his strength, aiming for her heart. For all the years of training, for all the lessons on swordplay and knife work—he missed, catching bone.

Gadhra aimed for his gut and her blade sank deep. "You are no longer necessary," she said as she withdrew the blade.

Sebestyen sank to the floor, feeling boneless and woozy and . . . dying. He was dying at last, as Thayne had said he would.

At least Liane had escaped. She would be safe now. She and the babies. He wanted to close his eyes and be done with this life, but he wasn't finished. Liane and the babies were not safe, not yet. The witch planned to kill all but Jahn and then . . . he did not want to imagine what plans she had for his eldest son.

If Gadhra got her hands on Jahn, she would find a way to control him. Through magic and through grief, she would wield her influence. She would bring dark magic to power, and his son, his innocent son who might one day be the good man his father was not, would be at the helm of it all. The ragged, evil hag would ruin Jahn's only chance at a happy life.

He whispered hoarsely, nonsense passing his lips, and the witch leaned down. "What did you say? Perhaps I will one day tell Jahn of his father's last pathetic words, and we will laugh together," she taunted him. "Do you beg for your life or for your soul? Both are lost, and always have been. Jahn will not be weak like you," she said. "I will not allow it."

He muttered again, nonsense even he did not understand.

"If you're trying to delay my pursuit, you can save your precious breath. I can find those I seek with the magic I embrace, no matter how far ahead of me they are, no matter how long they have been out of my sight."

Sebestyen shook his head, and he reached weakly for the old woman, the old witch. "You must tell . . . it's important . . ." What would make her come closer? "The gold," he finished in a breath.

The hag, intrigued at last, leaned down a bit farther, and with his last bit of strength Sebestyen grabbed at her ragged garment and pulled her down. This time, when he aimed for her heart, he did not miss. "You will not touch my family," he whispered. "You will not have my son."

He did not have the strength to push the dead witch off his body, but it wasn't long before someone else moved the body for him. A soft voice twittered at him, scolding and angry and perhaps sad. When the weight of the witch was gone, Sebestyen opened his eyes.

Liane dropped down to her knees beside him. "Foolish man," she said. "What have you done?"

"You should not have come back," he answered. "Take the babies and go."

"Mahri and the nursemaid have the babies, and we have arranged a meeting place," Liane said sensibly.

"Why didn't you run? Why did you come back?" She could be well away from the palace by now, perhaps past the worst of the fighting.

"I came back for you." She tore back his ripped robe and looked at his wound, and then she went very still. "Gadhra did this."

Sebestyen nodded, or at least he tried to.

"And you killed her."

"The old hag wanted Jahn," he explained. "She was going to kill you and Alix and . . . and take Jahn. She wanted to do to him what the priests did to me, only what she planned for him was much worse. I couldn't let her have him." His fingers gripped Liane's skirt and held on tight. "Take the babies away and hide them. Don't let anyone know who they are. Until Arik has children, they are the first and second in line for emperor. The witch is dead, but there are others who would use them, others who will want to kill them, and you. Don't let that happen, Liane. Don't."

A few tears ran down her face, even though she rightly hated him. "I'll bind your belly, and you can come with me."

He shook his head. It was too late. He was dying, and while he feared what would come after his death, since he hadn't exactly lived a life of virtue and honor, he was ready to go. It was time. "I'm sorry." Sorry for more than he had time to say. Maybe she knew . . . maybe she understood him in a way no one else ever had.

"You can apologize for all you have done to me later."

"There is no later, Liane. *Go.*"

"Not yet."

"Go, before someone sees you."

She leaned down and kissed him, not as she had in the years when she'd been his concubine, not as she had in the months she'd been his wife, but sweetly. Gently. It was a good way to go, he imagined.

"After everything you've done, I still love you," she said.

"I have loved you for as long as I can remember," he confessed. "I love the babies, too, in a very deep and unexpected way. I'm glad I got to see them. I'm sorry I . . . I'm sorry."

He lay there for a moment and thought about the babies. One fair in coloring, one dark. Away from the palace, what would they grow to be? Strong men, he imagined. Strong, decent men who would take care of their mother. Without Gadhra's influence or the interference of the priests, each would have a chance to become what he had not: a good and honorable man.

Liane still hadn't left his side. Soon the palace would be overrun with invaders, and she could not be here. Sebestyen knew the best thing he could do for the woman he loved was to die quickly.

So that's what he did.

LUCAN DIDN'T HAVE TIME TO REACH ISADORA BEFORE the blade fell, but the lessons he had given her had instilled her with an instinctive talent. She turned, stepped smoothly aside, and deflected the attacker's blade with her own. By the time the sentinel had gathered his wits to try again, Lucan was there.

"I am no thief," Lucan said as he disarmed the sentinel.

The soldier glanced at the handful of jewels, which Lucan tossed aside. "I am searching for something that belongs to me, but I suspect it is not here. Where is the emperor?"

"I don't know, Captain." The sentinel waited bravely to die.

"The empress?" Isadora asked, her voice low and quick.

"I have not seen Empress Liane since she and the infant prince made an appearance at the Spring Festival." He swallowed hard. "She did not seem well."

"You have not seen her *today*," Isadora pressed.

"No. I believe they have made their escape and left a handful of us to fight for the throne. The battle has begun, and we are badly outnumbered." He glanced at his sword, which lay on the floor several feet away. "I suppose you'll kill me now."

Normally, he would do just that. The man had tried to strike Isadora with his blade! But Isadora had been very insistent about not killing unless he found it necessary. This sad little boy would live to make foolhardy decisions another day. "I can kill you, or I can take you prisoner."

"I would rather be dead than tortured on Level Twelve, or worse, dumped into Level Thirteen and forgotten."

"Arik doesn't strike me as the kind of man who will torture his prisoners, and I suspect Level Thirteen will be forgotten. I will have to bind your hands, however."

The sentinel gratefully offered his hands, and Lucan bound them tightly with a length of cord that had once been used to pull back a heavy drape. He then bound the man's ankles, and lashed him to the bedpost.

"You're going to leave me here!" the sentinel shouted as Lucan and Isadora headed for the door.

"Don't worry," Lucan called back. "You won't be alone for long, I imagine."

The palace was eerily silent without the hum of the unnatural lights and the Level One fans and the occasional screech of the lift. Strange that he should have become accustomed to those sounds in this short time here. Still, as he and Isadora descended the stairway to Level Ten, Lucan felt an unexpected relief. Maybe the Star of Bacwyr was gone forever, and he would not be Prince of Swords. His country needed a King, and a lasting peace would be welcomed by all the clans, but perhaps it was not yet meant to be.

As First Captain, he held great influence over the Circle. Even if he were not Prince, he could do his best to bring peace to the clans until the coming of the rightful Prince and the new King was upon them. And he could do it with Isadora at his side.

For now, his only objective was getting Isadora safely out of the palace. There was intense fighting beyond the palace walls, in the streets of the city surrounding the massive edifice, but Sebestyen's soldiers were so badly outnumbered they did not stand a chance. What kind of a man would willingly die for a ruler like Emperor Sebestyen?

As they approached Level Ten, Lucan saw the witch's motionless form, and his heart skipped a beat. He had bound the old woman's hands tightly before leaving her alone in the room where the empress had been held captive. Some unnatural magic had freed her, he supposed. Had she succumbed to her wound? Or had someone finished her off as she'd attempted escape?

Before he took two more steps, he saw the other body and realized what had happened. Emperor Sebestyen was half sitting against one wall, his body as lifeless as the witch's, his eyes open and glazed. Lucan glanced down at the man's bloody right hand with a short-lived burst of hope, but there was no ring on his little finger.

Isadora placed her short sword aside and placed three fingers at the witch's throat, searching for a sign of life and finding none. She then turned to the emperor, and even though it was quite clear that he was dead, she touched her fingers to his throat as well.

"It appears they killed one another," she said.

"I can't say I'm sorry to see either of them dead," Lucan said without emotion, as he collected the sword Isadora had carried on this long day. She would have no more need of it, so he sheathed the weapon in the scabbard at his side.

Isadora glanced up at him in obvious annoyance. "Yes, but who will tell us where Liane and the babies are? Are they safe? Did he secret them somewhere before Gadhra killed him? How will I prove to myself that my job here is done if I can't find Liane?"

Lucan offered his hand, and Isadora took it. He helped her to her feet. "I suggest we start by asking your sister."

"You have always insisted that you didn't care for magic," Isadora said sullenly.

"I don't want magic to touch me, that's true. But if making use of your sister's talents is what it takes to satisfy you, then that is what we will do." He did not release her hand. "I have always taken the counsel of wizards, love. Asking Juliet for guidance will be no different. Now, come. We can put an end to this battle with the news that Emperor Sebestyen is dead."

"Good." Isadora threaded her fingers through his.

"And once we learn of the empress's whereabouts from your sister, I will ask you to marry me once again. I never thought I'd have to all but beg a woman to marry me."

"Yes, your ego is quite healthy in those respects."

They moved toward the exit hand in hand, and before they walked outside, where the din of battle reached their ears much more clearly, Isadora said, "I do not wish to return to this place, ever."

"Done," he said, happy to grant her this one simple desire.

"And I hope I never have to wield a sword again."

"I will protect you with my sword, and you will have need of no other."

He climbed up onto a stone wall that surrounded and protected the palace entrance and surveyed the scene before him. In all directions, soldiers fought. Juliet's Anwyn and their spears, Arik's rebels, sentinels who had turned against their leader. Circle warriors and representatives from three clans of Tryfyn had already moved from the west to the center of the battle, and they were very swiftly making their way forward. Soldiers had fallen in all directions . . . Sebestyen's soldiers and Arik's.

Lucan lifted his hands to his mouth and shouted, "Emperor Sebestyen is dead!" At first, there was no reaction to his announcement, so he shouted again, more loudly this time. A few heads turned, but not enough. What was he to do? Running into the fray, he could reach some of the soldiers, but it would take much too long to get word to all the combatants in that fashion.

"Darling," Isadora called, and he realized this was not the first time she had tried to catch his attention.

Lucan glanced down at her. With her head tipped back to look at him, and her hair and gown mussed from the excitement of the day, she was more beautiful than he had ever imagined any woman could be.

"I can help, if you will allow it," she said, raising her hand slowly.

After a moment's hesitation, he sat on the wall, leaned

over, and reached down to her. When she laid her hand in his, he clasped it tightly and drew her up. When she was well balanced, she stood, and after standing there for a moment she cast an uncertain glance his way. "It will not touch you," she said softly. "But it will help you."

He nodded, and she turned to the battle scene spreading across the streets of Arthes and lifted her hands. She said, *"Laleh antaga."* And then she looked at him and translated, in a softer voice, "Hear well."

Again, Lucan shouted the news that Sebestyen was dead. This time, many heads turned his way. Swords fell. Weary men stopped fighting and faced Lucan as if they awaited more words. A few soldiers continued to fight, either because they had not heard or because they did not care. Lucan shouted the news once more, and a few more of those who continued to do battle stopped. Gradually, with the assistance of other soldiers in the bloody streets, the fighting ceased.

With the heat of battle fading, the soldiers began to see to the wounded among their friends and comrades, and they began to mourn the dead.

Lucan leaped down from the wall, landing gracefully on his feet. He reached for Isadora and assisted in her descent. He had never cared much for witchcraft, but today she had used hers in a powerful and simple way, and she had honored his wish that magic not touch him.

"You are a good woman, Isadora Fyne," he said. "You are as noble and brave as any Circle warrior."

In her dark eyes he saw a momentary flash of uncertainty. "We must go to Juliet."

When all was settled with the empress and the children, there would be no more uncertainty. There would be nothing but love in her eyes and in her heart, as soon as their obligations were done.

He led Isadora through the streets of the city, protecting her at all times not only from the men who had, moments earlier, been fighting here, but from the scenes of death that surrounded her. She was a gentle woman with no tolerance for such ugliness. He had never known a witch could be kindhearted, but then his opinions of such magical women had been influenced by a long ago prediction he had never understood.

Zebulyn should have been more specific.

They were a little more than halfway through the city when Isadora gasped, jerking her hand from his. She turned her back on him and ran frantically, and he followed, calling her name. She did not go far before dropping to her knees beside a fallen soldier. All he could see of the man was a tattered cape, a motionless hand, and a long twist of oddly streaked and bloody hair.

"No, no, no," Isadora said softly as she rolled the man onto his back.

Kane Varden wasn't dead, but neither was he far from departing this earth.

22

ISADORA LED THE WAY INTO CAMP. LUCAN—ALONG WITH two rebels they had grabbed off the streets of Arthes— carried a quickly fashioned litter directly behind her. Kane had suffered a head injury, and while there were no life-threatening wounds that she could see, he had not stirred since she'd discovered him. Not a moan, not so much as a twitch.

There had been a time, not so long ago, when she'd hated this man. For touching Sophie, for leaving her, for coming back—for making the youngest Fyne sister love him. She couldn't hate him anymore. A soldier who made room in his heart for love, for family, and for babies had redeeming qualities that should be preserved.

Besides, it would break Sophie's heart to lose him. Maybe Sophie had reasoned all along that the curse would make the time she had with her husband short, but it wouldn't make losing the man she loved any easier.

Just as watching Lucan walk away from her would not be easy. If they could not break the curse quickly, then that's what would happen. Kane would die, and Lucan would leave. What of Juliet's Ryn? He was young, and had a few years before thirty—and to be completely honest, the man was not entirely human. Would that fact save him from the curse? Maybe, maybe not. If not, those years would go by quickly, and too soon Juliet would also be forced to bury the man she loved.

The youngest Fyne sister had held her impossibility in her hands, as Thayne had predicted, but that left two miracles to take place before the curse could be broken. Isadora suspected that might be two too many to hope for.

Sophie saw Isadora as the party entered the camp. She smiled widely, and stood with the new baby Duran caught in her arms. "Finally!" she said as she walked forward with long, anxious strides. "It's so good to see you well. Did you find Liane and the babies? Did you see Kane? Myls said Sebestyen is dead. I know it's wrong to wish anyone harm, but I can't say I'm—" Sophie stopped dead in her tracks when she saw the litter and the man upon it. "No," she said softly.

"He hasn't lost much blood," Isadora said calmly. "He took a blow to the head, but that's all."

"It isn't the blow that will kill him. It's the curse. Kane is just a few months from thirty, you know." Sophie walked beside the litter, as it was carried toward her tent. She did not cry, and she did not scream. Instead, she was determined and rigid, and she remained dry-eyed. "We must end the curse. With all that has happened, with the new powers we've discovered, surely we can accomplish what seemed impossible in the past."

"It will take all three of us," Isadora said. She might as well tell Sophie and Juliet together what Thayne said was required, so there would be no need to repeat herself. "Where's Juliet?"

Sophie snorted in disgust, as she held back the tent flap for the men who carried the litter. "She and that husband of hers went into the woods shortly after you left this morning. Two of her soldiers, the ones who stayed behind to act as her bodyguards, went with them."

"Did they go to the battlefield?" Isadora experienced a moment of fear, as she imagined the gentle Juliet caught in the midst of battle.

Sophie shook her head. "I don't think so. They were headed in the opposite direction."

"And Juliet didn't say where she was going?"

"No."

The men carefully moved Kane to a pallet on the tent floor, and Sophie knelt beside her husband. "I will require warm water and clean rags," she commanded without tears or panic. One of the soldiers nodded curtly, as if he were accustomed to taking orders from Sophie. Lucan nodded at Isadora as he left the tent, and she knew, without even a hint of doubt, that he would be waiting for her when she was done here.

Isadora helped Sophie as the new mother cleaned and bandaged her husband. She held Duran when Sophie needed both hands free, and then Sophie took the baby while Isadora performed a simple protection spell that might—or might not—keep Kane alive until the curse could be broken.

And then they waited. Kane still did not stir, and Juliet did not return. Soldiers returned to the camp, one at a time and in small groups. They were rightfully glad of victory, but they had all lost comrades on this long day, and many of them were worried about Kane and the others who had been wounded. One rebel or another checked on the wounded man often, and Sophie spoke to each of them in a calm, unwavering voice. Liane had been right when she'd told Isadora that her youngest sister possessed a new strength.

It was well after dark when Arik opened the tent flap, ducked down, and walked inside. He looked very much like his brother, just enough to give Isadora a start. But Arik was bigger, a tad taller, and larger of build. His skin was deeply tanned, and a small scar on his left cheek marked him as a fighting man. The day of battle had left him tired, but not exhausted in the way some of his soldiers were. In his own way, Arik was much harder than Sebestyen had ever been.

"We are moving to the palace," Arik said, after taking a long, pained look at the wounded man. "I'm sure Varden will be more comfortable there."

"No," Sophie said sternly. "I will not ever again set foot in that terrible place, and neither will Kane."

"Sophie," the new emperor said in a gentle voice. "The palace is not a terrible place any longer."

She looked up at him, and in that instant Isadora realized exactly *how* strong her sister had become. "Hatred and cruelty and pain linger long after the reasons for them are gone. They live in the fabric, and in the stone, and in the very air. Dark energies remain in that palace. Kane will not be taken there. I forbid it."

Isadora wondered if her little sister realized that she was putting her foot down to the new emperor, and then she realized that Sophie had earned the right to speak her mind to any man. Even this one.

"Whatever you wish, my lady." Arik nodded his head once, and backed out of the tent.

The camp did not break and disband at once. Emperor Arik and a few rebels left, while others remained. They took down tents that were no longer needed, and drank to excess in celebration or sorrow, and packed their belong-ings for their own journeys. Some would be joining Arik in the palace. Others would be going home. Quite a few had been ordered to remain in the camp as long as Sophie and Kane remained, bodyguards as dedicated to the Varden family as Juliet's half-dressed, immense soldiers were to their Queen. No one would disturb them while they waited for Kane to heal—or to die.

Hours after Arik had left, they heard a familiar voice. A female voice. Isadora left the tent quickly, searching for Juliet among the returning soldiers. The Queen, red-haired and barely dressed and surrounded by men who stood a head taller than the tallest of the others, was not difficult to spot.

Sophie told an incredible tale of being kidnapped by Ryn on her journey to Arthes. Apparently, the Anwyn had been confused by Juliet's scent on Sophie, but his confusion had not lasted long and he'd soon released her. Sophie obviously had a soft spot in her heart for the very large man—but she had not completely forgiven him.

"Where have you been?" Isadora cut around a knot of rebels to approach her sister. When she did, she had a much better view of the Anwyn party, and she came to a halt.

Juliet carried a bundle in her arms, and she was no longer pregnant. Gathering her senses, Isadora rushed to her sister. "You should not be walking around like this. Are you well? Is the baby well?"

"I am fine, and the baby is more than well. She is beyond amazing." Isadora peeled back a section of the animal skin the baby was wrapped in to reveal a perfectly beautiful face and a tuft of red hair. The baby's eyes were a striking gold, like those of her parents, and she seemed very aware for a newborn.

The Anwyn guards, who until this moment had been extremely attentive to Juliet, both watched the baby with undisguised awe. You would think they had never seen a baby before, the way they gawked. There was a stoic reverence in the way they watched the newborn.

The child reached up a small, perfectly shaped arm, and by the light of the half-moon the arm, from fingertips to elbow, transformed. Tiny fingernails turned into sharp claws, a little hand shifted until it was shaped like a paw, and red hair sprang thick and long from the hand and forearm. A moment later, like the receding of a wave, the limb became a normal baby's arm once again.

"This should not be possible," Juliet said in a lowered voice. "She should not be able to do that."

"I should think not," Isadora agreed. She glanced back toward the tent where Sophie and Kane waited, and saw Lucan standing nearby. He, too, waited, with a patience she had not thought him to possess.

"I knew Keelia would be special," Juliet continued, "but I had no idea how special." The new mother looked at Ryn with a loving censure. "You promised me I would not have to deal with unruly children who turned into wolves at the appearance of every full moon."

Ryn looked up. The big man was in awe himself. "In case you have not noticed, *vidara*, not only are we too far away from the mountains to be affected by the cycles of the moon, there is no full moon on this night. Our daughter is powerful in a new and unexpected way, as you said she would be."

Across the camp, Isadora caught Lucan's eye. Sophie and Juliet held miracles in their arms, just as Thayne had said they would. All that was left was for Isadora to hold her own. She knew very well that nothing in this world was impossible, that miracles happened every day. But what could compare to a Fyne son after all these years, and a baby girl who apparently had the power to shift into a wolf cub at will? Whatever her miracle might be, it needed to come quickly in order to be of any help to Kane.

Isadora shivered. If the miracle did not come soon, Sophie wasn't the only one who would lose a loved one. At any moment, Lucan might look at her and see something that repulsed him. If he walked away from her in horror, he would not come back, and she would live the rest of her life alone. Her sisters had their families, they had bright futures ahead of them, as long as the curse could be ended.

But what of her own future? She had been given a glorious second chance at love. If this failed, she did not expect there would ever be a third chance.

The baby cooed and burrowed into her mother's chest, and purred deep in her throat.

Two.

LUCAN HERN, FIRST CAPTAIN OF THE CIRCLE OF BACWYR, the man destined to be Prince of Swords, had little patience. Once again Isadora was testing his, as she had done so often. She and her sisters and the new babies and a wounded Kane Varden had been huddled together in one of the few remaining tents in this camp all night. There was work to be done before he could ask her, *again*, to marry him. Isadora would not rest easy until she knew what had become of Empress Liane and the babies. She would not plan for her own future until she knew theirs was secure.

Sunrise approached once again, and he had not slept all night. If he had known that Isadora would be occupied with her wounded brother-in-law and her sisters through the night, he would have slept for a few hours. Instead, he had watched the tent and waited.

Myls, one of Arik's most trusted soldiers and a sour man Lucan himself did not like, had arrived hours earlier with bound and beaten prisoners in tow. Since Sebestyen was dead, most of Arik's men saw no reason to take prisoners.

The sentinels who had been loyal to Sebestyen had laid down their weapons, after all. They were going home, or swearing allegiance to the new emperor.

But Myls swore these prisoners continued to present a danger. Lucan almost felt sorry for the men, whose only crime had been loyalty to their emperor. Perhaps that loyalty had been misplaced, but still . . . they were not criminals, and Myls had been treating them as such.

The prisoners were not his concern, however. The tasks he had immediately set before him were simple: find the empress and her children, ask Isadora to be his wife, and go home. Before he could do any of these things, she had to leave the blasted tent!

She did, finally, not long after sunrise. Like him, she had taken no time for sleep during the night, and she was obviously exhausted. There were dark circles under her eyes, and if it was possible she seemed to be thinner. He wanted nothing more than to carry her to a large, soft, warm bed, where he would make love to her and feed her and cherish her.

Soon.

She walked toward him, and before he could make a move to meet her, one of the prisoners gasped. "Dear lord, the dark witch. Don't let her touch me, please. Don't let the dark witch touch me. I'll do anything you want, just please . . . don't let her touch me."

Lucan turned his head and glanced down at the babbling prisoner. "What are you talking about, fool?"

"That one," the man whispered in an obviously frightened voice. "The dark Fyne witch, she killed a man in our company with a single touch and a few evil words. I saw it happen. Weeks later she killed another with a knife, when he caught her stealing bread from the camp. I was not there when that murder happened, but that is what I heard."

Lucan shook his head. "Your brain has been addled,

soldier. Isadora Fyne is a gentle woman who would not harm any man, even if she had cause."

"You don't know her," the man rasped. "You didn't see what I saw." He shuddered. "Don't let her touch me."

"I'm sorry," Isadora said as she approached, unaware that the conversation Lucan had been carrying on concerned her. "Juliet and Sophie and I have plans to make, and I've been relaying to them what Thayne told me before he left for Tryfyn. Juliet has much to share, too, so . . ."

Lucan turned away from the soldier and faced the woman he planned to make his wife. She was beautiful, he knew that to be true, and yet when he looked at her in the morning light it was not beauty that he saw.

The prisoner was telling the truth. There was death and ruin in and around Isadora Fyne, and that devastation showed on her face in a way he had never before known possible. The circles beneath her eyes were large and dark, her mouth was thin and twisted, and he could see the beginning signs of decay on her once-fine body. Her hands, hands that had caressed him many times, were more like claws than the delicate hands he remembered.

"This prisoner tells me you killed two men," Lucan said. "Tell me it isn't true."

Isadora stopped, and her face went pale. Beyond pale, it was almost white as snow. No, her face was white as *death.* "And what if it is true?" she asked.

He knew that beneath the ugliness he now saw, the woman he loved remained. But what if the woman he loved was the lie, and this monstrosity was the real Isadora? "You made such a fuss about *not* killing. Was that all a lie for my benefit?"

"No," she whispered, "but I don't expect you to believe that."

"I believe the truth. I *see* the truth, as I was taught to see."

Her hands twisted and formed small, knotty fists. "The truth is not always as simple as you would like to believe, Lucan. It's complicated, and . . . and sometimes people do things they regret, but we can't go back and undo the wrongs we've done. We can only try to do better."

"I see the truth of who you are, and it is as if I've never seen you before."

"What you see is the curse, not the truth."

Lucan wanted to run, but he held his ground. "You are not the woman I believed you to be."

Anger showed on Isadora, like fire flaming to the surface. "I killed one of the men who invaded and burned my home," she shouted. Heads in the almost-deserted camp began to turn. "I killed a man who threatened to cut my throat when he caught me stealing food so I could survive. Should I have let him kill me instead of fighting back?" She took a step away from him. "I suppose I should have. It would be easier than *this*.

"Do you know what the worst of my crimes are?" she asked in a calming voice. "I ran." She pointed to the prisoner who sat on the ground behind Lucan. "And when I ran, soldiers like *this* one took their rage out on a village of innocents. I carry the pain of those deaths in my heart and always will, but do not ask me to apologize for defending myself and my home, as you or any other man would have done in my place."

Lucan blinked hard, trying to wipe away the images before him. He could not possibly love the figure of ruination that stood before him. Isadora was everything he had always feared about witches and their magic; she was exactly what Zebulyn had warned him about, all those years ago. *Beware the witch.*

"You want to run from me, don't you?" Isadora asked in a surprisingly gentle voice.

"Yes," he answered truthfully.

"Run then," she said as she backed away from him. "It was meant to be, and we were wrong to think that anything else could come of us." She turned, so he could no longer see the ugliness of her face. When she was halfway to the tent where her sisters waited, she said, in a lowered voice he was likely not supposed to hear, "Have a good life, love."

"HE'S NOT REALLY GONE!" SOPHIE SAID, RUNNING TO THE tent flap to look out on what remained of the camp.

"I was not quick enough to stop the curse," Isadora said sensibly. "There's still time to save Kane, however, and that is what we must see to." There was no time to nurse her broken heart. Later, when she was alone, she would cry for what might have been if she'd been faster—or the curse had been slower.

Sophie held her son and looked out over the camp with a frown on her face. "I can't believe he would leave when we're so close. She turned to Juliet. "We are close, aren't we?"

"Yes," Juliet said in an almost confident voice. "Very close, I think. Tonight, if all goes well."

Tonight. If only Lucan had been able to withstand the curse for another day . . . but he hadn't, and there was no use pondering what might have been.

Sophie and the new baby in her arms returned to her wounded husband and her sisters. "What do you mean, *if all goes well*?"

"The wizard said we would each see an impossibility become possible, before the curse was ended. Isadora's miracle has not yet arrived. Without it, the spell we've crafted won't end the curse."

"What is her miracle?"

"I don't know."

Juliet was so powerful, but she still did not see all. No one was meant to see everything; Isadora understood that. But why hadn't she seen that Lucan would leave this morning? Maybe if she'd been prepared for the revolted expression on his face, it wouldn't have hurt as much.

Then again, perhaps nothing could ever mitigate that sort of pain.

Liane could be anywhere by now. When the curse was ended—if that was indeed possible—and Sophie and Juliet went their separate ways, Isadora would dedicate herself to finding the empress and her children and making sure they were safe. It was the least she could do, and it would give her purpose.

Right now she desperately needed purpose. She needed something meaningful and important to keep her from becoming a bitter old hag like Gadhra. It would be so easy to lock herself away from the world and live only for her magic. Like Isadora, Gadhra had touched both protection and destruction. In the end, destruction had killed her.

Lucan had gone, and her sisters had their own lives to lead, but she did not want to become such a sad figure of a woman as Gadhra had been.

Isadora wanted more, but at the moment everything in this life worth having seemed so very far away—so impossibly out of reach.

It would be nice to think that she could make her way to Tryfyn and find Lucan once the curse was ended, but it was too late. He had seen the ugliness in her, and he had been repulsed. Nothing would take that memory, that disgust, that *truth* away.

23

LUCAN KNEW HE COULD WALK STRAIGHT TO THE PALACE and demand a horse from the new emperor, if he did not find his own men still in the city. But instead of following the path in that direction, he headed south through the thick woods. He was not ready to face anyone, not even his own warriors.

He was tired, and heartsick, and confused, in part from lack of sleep. So when he ran across a sheltered cave he sat to rest for a few minutes. Perhaps here he could gather his wits and his resolve to move forward.

Isadora Fyne was a witch, and it was possible he had never been in love with her at all but had been under a spell of some sort. She'd promised not to use her magic on him, but how was he to know she'd kept that promise?

He did not deal with failure well. First he had lost the Star of Bacwyr, and then . . . and then he had lost what he'd believed to be love. Two failures, both momentous, and they emptied him. Heart and soul, he felt *empty*.

Lucan closed his eyes, only for a moment, and when he opened them, he saw the last person he expected to find before him.

"Zebulyn. But . . . you're dead." The old man looked much as Lucan remembered, but he seemed spryer. Happier, even.

"Yes," the old wizard answered in a gruff voice. "I am dead. Could be worse. At least I haven't ravaged my entire life in a matter of minutes."

"This is a dream." Lucan stood, and when he did, he knew he was dreaming. The cave he'd crawled into was not large enough for standing. Unlike the many meetings he remembered from his younger years, he was taller than the old wizard.

"It is a dream and not a dream," Zebulyn said with a wave of his hand. "We are meeting in the world in-between, a world where the living and the dead and the lost can come face-to-face for a while, when the powers of the universe so decree."

"Why now?" Lucan asked. How many times had he wished for the old man's advice in years past?

"Because you are in need of a swift kick in the pants, that's why!"

"I did not retrieve the Star," Lucan admitted.

"No, you did not."

"I failed."

"Miserably."

"You came back from the dead to *scold* me?"

"Yes!" The old man banged his cane on the hard earth, and the entire cave shook.

Not only had he lost the Star and what he'd believed to

be love, the powers of the universe had come together to slap his hand, as if he were once again a powerless boy. "Perhaps it is possible that I might still recover the Star of Bacwyr," Lucan said.

"It is possible," Zebulyn grumbled. "Not likely, but possible."

"I searched the palace as well as I could with the time I was allowed, but now that Arik is in power, perhaps he will allow me greater access. All I need is more time—"

"The Star is no longer in the palace."

"Where is it?"

"If I told you where to find the Star, what kind of a challenge would this be?" Zebulyn shouted. And then he calmed considerably. "We're wasting time. No one can stay for very long in the land in-between. I have only come to remind you that I taught you to see with your heart and your soul. It took years of instruction, and you were not always my best student, but you did learn. Still, there are times when you see with your untrained eyes, and you forget to tap into the power I gave you. Don't waste what you have learned."

The old wizard began to fade, and the cave began to shrink. "Wait!" Lucan shouted. "I have questions!"

Zebulyn smiled. "Of course you do." And then he disappeared.

TONIGHT THEY WOULD TRY, FOR THE FIRST—AND HOPE-fully the last—time to break the curse. Kane's condition had not changed. Perhaps if they were successful, he would awaken and all would be well. There was no guarantee that the curse would loose its hold on the wounded rebel, no matter what happened tonight.

Isadora did not hold out much hope for the spell or for

Kane. The requirements for the breaking of the curse were incomplete, and she felt as if she'd run out of miracles.

She was surprised when Myls called out at the tent's entrance. The boorish rebel likely would have stormed in without asking, if Ryn and Juliet's guards weren't diligently guarding their Queen and the new Princess.

The sour soldier stuck his head into the tent and spared a passionless glance for Kane before turning his attention to Sophie. "There's a woman here, and she's asking for you. She gives her name as Mahri, and Ferghus has confirmed her identity."

Isadora could not stop the leaping of her heart. If Mahri was all right, then maybe Liane and the babies were safe, as well. "Send her in."

A moment later, a drably clad woman with a large brown kerchief covering her hair stooped down to enter the crowded shelter. Isadora knew, as soon as she saw the woman's hands and the blue ring on the middle finger of the right, that this was not Mahri.

Liane lifted her head, and her eyes met Isadora's. A light of surprise and relief lit her eyes, and a touch of a smile turned her lips. "Please don't give me away," she whispered as she drew nearer.

"I was so worried about you," Isadora said softly. "What of the babies?"

"Jahn and Alixandyr are well, for now. Mahri is watching them." Liane dropped to her knees beside Kane and laid a hand on his forehead. "Is he going to be all right?"

"We don't know yet," Sophie said. "I think so. Juliet says maybe yes, *probably* yes, but I won't be satisfied until he comes around. Is that why you're here? You heard that Kane was injured?"

Liane shook her head. "I did not know my little brother was wounded until I heard that oaf who calls himself Myls mention the injury in an offhand manner." She looked at Sophie as she ran a comforting hand through Kane's hair. "I came here searching for you."

Sophie's eyes went wide. "Why?"

"Because you're the only one who might be able to help me. I don't know if anyone can but . . . I have seen you do miraculous things, Sophie, and I need a miracle today."

Isadora's heart leaped again, at the mention of miracles.

"The nursemaid who was with us ran away this morning. I suspect she was little more than a slave, and with Sebestyen dead . . ." She averted her eyes and trembled visibly. "The reasons for her leaving are not important. Gadhra, that evil old bat, gave me some foul-smelling potion to dry up my milk, and the nursemaid is gone, so how am I to feed my babies? If anyone can . . . can fix me, it's you."

"I've never tried such a spell," Sophie admitted. "I don't know that it would work."

"Will you try?" Liane asked.

Sophie nodded, and then she closed her eyes and began to breathe deeply and strangely, as if she took the air into another place. It was a meditation not so much different from that which Lucan practiced.

There had been a time when the youngest Fyne sister had possessed very little power, but that had changed—as evidenced by the way she'd influenced the weather during her long labor with Duran. Even now, as she searched inside herself for what Liane needed, she seemed to glow. She'd always had a sort of attractiveness that men craved and women envied, but this glow took her beyond earthly beauty.

When it was time, she called Liane to her and laid her hands on the former empress's breasts. Liane closed her eyes and took deep breaths, as if willing Sophie's machinations to work. Sophie did not speak. There were no words of magic to assist the power she fed to Liane. And then, without warning, the spell was done, and Sophie dropped her hands.

"When will we know if it worked?" Liane asked.

"Soon," Sophie answered.

While they waited, Liane was introduced to her nephew. She shed a few tears upon learning that the baby had been named Duran. Still holding the baby, she hugged Isadora with a touch of passion and emotion and deep relief, and told her simply that it was good to see her well. There was no mention of the night Liane's husband had thrown Isadora into a pit in the ground to die.

When Liane had returned Duran to his mother, Isadora asked about Ferghus—who had lied to Myls about the visitor being Mahri. Liane just shrugged her shoulders. "He was always loyal to me," she said.

If she did not realize that the sentinel was in love with her, then she was blind. That blindness was possible, considering the way Liane had lived most of her life. She still loved Sebestyen, after all that he had done to her. She would likely always love him. Her life in the palace as a concubine and even as an assassin had twisted her emotions to the point where it was possible the only love she would ever recognize was that of a man who had imprisoned her and debased her, and in the end done his best to take her children away.

Sebestyen had loved Liane, of that Isadora did not have a doubt. But his love had been as twisted and incomplete as hers for him. Was her own love for Lucan twisted by her time in the palace? Was it as true as it seemed to be?

After a short while, Liane twitched as if she'd been startled. She laid one hand over a breast, and then she smiled. "I can feel it," she whispered. "The milk is coming in."

"That is good."

"I can feed my babies."

"Abundantly," Sophie answered with a smile. "When do I get to meet my nephews?"

Liane stood and shook her head. "Never, I'm afraid." She twisted the ring on her hand. "Those who still believe that Sebestyen was the rightful ruler will insist that Jahn is the new emperor, and there will be more war. More death. Worse, the priests will lock Jahn away and use him for their own purposes, their own quest for power. And if they know that Alix lives, there is no end to what they might do. I promised Sebestyen I would take the boys far, far away from the palace and those who would use them. That's what I'm going to do." She held her hand aloft. "This is all Jahn and Alix will have of their father; an ordinary ring with his blood caught in the setting."

Lucan wanted that ring very much, but he was gone, and even if Isadora was willing to take the only valuable possession Liane had left, Lucan would likely not accept it from her. He not only did not love her anymore, he despised her and everything she touched.

Juliet offered her palm, upturned, and asked if she could see the ring more closely. Liane reached out, and Juliet touched the blue stone. "There is magic here," she said with a smile.

Liane sighed. "Would I be well rid of it, then?"

"No, not at all," Juliet said as she allowed her hand to fall away. "It isn't a forceful magic and shouldn't alarm you in any way. At one point, long ago, this ring was blessed to rid it of the negative energies of the past wearer. It now carries with it a touch of good luck. Not a lot," she said, "but a trace. Just enough to make it glimmer, when I study it just so. It's drawn to power." With that, she glanced at Isadora. "It was drawn to *you*," she added softly.

"Perhaps it will bring me and my boys luck in the days to come."

"Perhaps," Juliet responded.

"I have to go. Do me a favor," Liane asked as she backed toward the tent's entrance. "Tell everyone that we're dead. Make up a sad tale about the way I and the babies perished, so no one will ever come looking for us."

"Where are you going?" Isadora asked.

The former empress shook her head. "I don't know. Far away. As far as I can get from Arthes, that's where I'm going." She nodded to Sophie. "Thank you, for my babies and for the return of my ability to feed them." Liane dipped her head to Juliet. "I thank you, too, for the information about Sebestyen's ring. It's good to know." Then she looked at Isadora, and her eyes misted. "I cannot thank you enough for being my friend. I'm so glad Sebestyen didn't kill you."

"You really shouldn't—" Isadora began, but Liane spun and ran before she could finish.

Chasing after Liane would alert Myls, and others, that something was amiss, so Isadora did not leave the tent. She looked to Juliet, who had been silent through most of the long visit. "Will she be all right?"

Juliet nodded. "It won't be easy, but she and the boys will be fine." She cocked her head and smiled. "The one who is so devoted to her, the one who lied . . ."

"Ferghus," Isadora supplied.

"Ferghus is going to follow her. He's going to protect her."

Isadora felt better, knowing Liane and the babies and Mahri would not be out there all alone.

"Oh, no, what am I going to do?" Sophie asked in obvious distress.

"What's wrong?" Isadora asked.

"I can't tell Arik that Liane and the babies are dead."

"Why not?" Isadora asked. "You know very well it's the only chance they have for a safe life."

"Yes, I know, but . . . I can't lie to Arik. He's my *friend*."

"I can lie to Arik," Isadora said pragmatically. "I barely know the man."

"So can I," Juliet said. "Sophie, all you have to do is look sad and keep quiet."

Sophie shrugged her shoulders. "In the name of a good cause, I suppose I can do that."

Isadora looked toward the tent opening. There was a small slit she could see beyond. "I wonder if Ferghus is following Liane already?"

Juliet nodded and smiled. "He's right behind her."

AS THAYNE HAD SAID, THERE WAS A BLAZING FIRE, AND stars above. Two impossibilities had presented themselves, and Sophie had suggested that Liane's recovery and the safety of her babies was a third miracle, and while it was not technically Isadora's miracle, it did touch the eldest Fyne sister in an undeniable way. Isadora had sworn to protect Liane and the babies, and she had done so against all odds.

The Anwyn guards and a handful of rebels who had been instructed by Arik to keep the camp safe remained. Most of the men stayed well away from the women. The rebels knew Sophie to be a witch, and they knew what she could do, but to see three powerful women with their heads together was frightening for them. They knew something was about to happen; they just didn't know what.

Myls was gone, and so was Ferghus. Isadora tried to imagine where her friends from the palace might go. Liane and the babies, Mahri, and Ferghus. She wished them a good life, and when the curse was settled she would cast a spell to make it so—if she could. Spells cast over a distance were not always effective, but if nothing else, it would make her feel better to know they had an extra bit of luck to carry with them.

It was well after dark when they began the ritual. Thayne said they had to believe the curse was powerless before it would be so, and Isadora recognized the seed of uncertainty in her heart. It was too late for her, in any case, but she was still waiting for her miracle. She tried to force out that kernel of doubt, for Kane's sake, for Sophie and Juliet and Ryn.

She knew the language of the wizards more deeply than her sisters, so it was she who began to chant the spell they had devised last night and today. They stripped the power from the curse, they dismissed it as unimportant and weak. They embraced the futures they and their daughters would have, free of the powerless curse.

Isadora tilted her head back, and her gaze swept the heavens. A shooting star streaked across the clear sky. An omen, perhaps? A sign from above that they would be successful?

Juliet had a few words to chant. While the middle sister—so changed and yet still the same Juliet Isadora loved so dearly—did her part, Isadora looked beyond the fire to Ryn, who was such a devoted husband. Juliet swore that because Ryn was not entirely human he would not be affected by the curse no matter what happened, but Isadora was not so sure. Maybe he wasn't human, but he *was* a man, and Juliet did love him.

When it was Sophie's turn to speak her portion of the spell, her voice trembled. Isadora tried to give her sister strength, courage, and hope. Hope most of all. They could not waver, they could not doubt.

Movement nearby Ryn, who held his own daughter and Sophie's Duran in his massive arms, caught Isadora's eye as Sophie finished her part. For a moment Isadora held her breath. She blinked twice. It couldn't be. Lucan would not have come back, not after he'd seen the ugliness of destruction in her with his own eyes.

But he moved slightly forward so that the firelight fell upon his face, and she knew it was not her imagination playing tricks on her. Lucan had returned. He looked tired and a little disheveled, but she saw no hint of the disgust she had witnessed earlier in the day. He stopped a few feet away from the fire, and mouthed the words *I love you*.

Three.

Isadora broke from the circle and ran to Lucan. Without saying a word she threw herself at him, and he caught her. He caught her very well.

"You came back," she whispered.

His arms encircled her, and she held her very own impossibility tight for a moment. Lucan placed her on her feet and kissed her, telling her more with that kiss than he ever could with words. He had seen the worst of her, and he loved her still. Their love was strong enough to withstand the curse and all that came with it. He had fallen victim to the curse and walked away, but he had come back.

The flame she and her sisters had danced around flamed high. Juliet and Sophie both lifted their heads, and so Isadora did the same. Three shooting stars dashed across the sky together, and as they faded away, Isadora felt the curse lift, as if a weight had been taken from her heart.

"Is it done?" Sophie asked breathlessly.

"Yes," Isadora said confidently. "It is done."

Sophie ran for the tent, but before she reached it, her husband stepped into the night. Kane held an uncertain hand to his bandaged head; he was pale and none too steady on his feet. But he was alive.

Sophie squealed in happiness and ran to her husband.

Juliet walked toward Ryn and their remarkable daughter with a contented smile on her face.

Lucan leaned down and whispered, "I'm sorry. I knew it was the curse that caused me to see . . . and still . . ."

"Don't explain or apologize; it isn't necessary. You did what had to be done." She smiled widely. "You came back."

"Of course I came back. I was disturbed by what I saw, I was even frightened. But I always loved you, Isadora. Good and bad, dark and light, I always loved you."

"I love you, too."

He kissed her again, more deeply this time, and ignited a depth of wanting she had never known existed. And when the long kiss was done, he took her hands in his.

"Isadora, love, will you be my wife?"

"Yes," she answered without hesitation.

He grinned at her. "Yes, finally."

And so it was done.

WHEN ALL WAS FINISHED AND THE CURSE WAS TRULY gone, Juliet admitted to her sisters that she had seen more of the future than she'd revealed to them. She had known that the curse would be lifted, but she had been afraid that telling her sisters all she knew would rob them of the passion and power they needed to do what had to be done. She was afraid that her interference would change the future she'd seen.

The Anwyn Queen and her King had left for their home, The City, the next morning. Keeping in touch would be difficult, but far from impossible. Nothing was impossible.

Kane and Sophie were headed, with Ariana and Duran in tow, back to the Southern Province. The would build another house on the land where the Fyne cabin had stood for so long, and there they would farm the land and make more babies and live without war. It would make for a good life.

Lucan and Isadora had returned to Arthes, and even though Isadora had sworn she would never again enter the palace, she and Lucan found themselves on Level One once again, standing before the new emperor in the ballroom. As Lucan had been so helpful in seeing to Sebestyen's downfall and then bringing the fighting to an end, Arik had gladly given the Circle Captain two of his finest horses. He had offered the words of a palace priest, when he learned that Lucan and Isadora were to be married, but they declined. They would be married soon . . . but not in Sebestyen's palace.

Isadora told Arik that Liane and the babies were dead, murdered by some unknown assailant as they'd tried to make their escape. Arik had been disturbed to know that someone under his command had murdered women and children, so Isadora twisted the story to clear his conscience and made the murderer a thief who'd stolen the few imperial jewels the empress had on her person.

Telling that tale, convincingly so, was the reason she'd consented to visit Level One again. Liane and her sons would be safe from any who considered them a threat and from those who would use them to gain power.

And then they were gone, leaving the rebuilding of a palace—and a country—to the new emperor.

Franco had been very glad to locate his Captain, but once his fears about Lucan's safety were assuaged, he traveled well ahead with the other Tryfynians who had fought for Arik. They were in no mood to dawdle, and Lucan and Isadora very much enjoyed dawdling.

They were married in a small church near the Tryfyn-Columbyana border, with no witness other than the parson's chubby, pretty wife. Simple gold rings were exchanged, slipped with love onto the middle fingers of their left hands, and then they rented a room in a small inn near the edge of town.

Even though the bed was soft and they had been resting upon the hard ground lately, they did not get much sleep.

Isadora had told Lucan that Liane possessed the ring he wanted so desperately, but he seemed not to care. He said perhaps the time for retrieving the Star would come again. Perhaps not. She'd offered to try to cast a spell to locate Liane and her traveling companions, if he desired. She did not want to take the only possession of the emperor's the woman had left, and Juliet had said there was badly needed good luck attached to that ring. But Liane would need money in the years to come, and Lucan could pay her handsomely for the simple piece. Perhaps that was the good luck Juliet spoke of.

But again, Lucan did not want her magic to assist him. He loved her as a woman, and he had no desire to use her powers for himself.

Naked and entangled, they watched the sun rise beyond the rough window frame of their rented room. The sunshine illuminated the land they were leaving behind; Isadora did not know what to expect of what awaited them to the west.

Well, they knew to expect love, and laughter, and a son sometime in Lucan's thirty-eighth year.

"It is amazing that your pursuit of a ring brought you to me, and ultimately brought us to this place. If you knew where it was located, why did you not retrieve it long ago?"

Lucan wrapped long arms around her. "I did not know it was a ring I sought until I saw it upon your finger and glimpsed the magic. Long ago, the wizards of the Circle told me when the time would be right, and they told me I would know the Star when I saw it. They told me the Star had power I would recognize, and I did."

She rolled over to face her husband and ran a finger across his beard-roughened cheek. "A star of power."

"Yes."

"And you did not know it would be a ring."

"No. They only said I would retrieve the Star and deliver it to the Circle, and when that was accomplished, I would become Prince of Swords." He kissed her throat. "I do not wish to speak of my failure, love. I want to make love to you here, one more time, before we renew our journey."

"But—" Isadora began as Lucan rolled her onto her back and fit himself above her.

"No more talking," he said as he lowered his rough cheek to her neck and nuzzled.

"But Lucan, it's important."

"So is this." He touched her intimately, aroused her quickly, then pushed inside her and held himself there where he fit so well.

Lucan made love to her, and she dismissed what she had been about to say to savor each sensation, each kiss and stroke, every flutter of her body.

Soon enough her husband would learn that when spoken in the language of the wizards, her middle name, Sinnoch, meant *Star*.

Since the publication of her first book in 1994, **Linda Winstead Jones** has published more than forty novels and novellas. She's a three-time finalist for the Romance Writers of America's RITA Award and a winner of the 2004 RITA Award for Best Paranormal Romance. She's also a two-time winner of the Colorado Romance Writers Award of Excellence. A compulsive taker of classes, she has studied Asian cooking, belly dancing, cake decorating, yoga, real estate, candy making, and creative writing. She was a full-time wife and mother for several years, and spent a few months here and there as a Realtor and candy maker. Linda and her husband owned a picture frame shop for several years before she left retail to pursue writing full-time. An active member of the Romance Writers of America, she lives in northern Alabama with her husband of more than thirty years. Visit her website at www.lindawinsteadjones.com.

Three sisters are about to change
destiny, and bring a terrible
family curse to an end.

Don't miss the rest of the

Sisters of the Sun
trilogy by
Linda Winstead Jones

Sophie's story
The Sun Witch
0-425-19940-1

Juliet's story
The Moon Witch
0-425-20129-5

Available wherever books are sold or at penguin.com